THE BATTLE OF WOOD GREEN

ANDY MELLETT BROWN

ANDY MELLETT BROWN

Copyright © 2014 Andy Mellett-Brown
All rights reserved.
ISBN: 150040487X
ISBN-13: 978-1500404871

THE BATTLE OF WOOD GREEN

This book is dedicated to:
My beautiful wife Patricia, for sharing my world.
And to Tony Mellett who passed away on Thursday 1st May 2014, while I was type setting the final script.

ANDY MELLETT BROWN

Prologue

Saturday 16th April 2005

Harry Stammers wiped the sweat from his forehead with his free hand and began the ascent. Ahead of him, by no more than a few feet, his companion was making slow progress. That he was able to walk at all, given the injuries he had sustained less than a year before, was remarkable. That he was climbing stairs, unaided, seemed little short of miraculous. And yet, watching him, Harry's prevailing emotion wasn't joy or admiration, or even sadness. It was guilt.

Guilt, because no matter how often his friends had tried to convince him that it had been their choice to involve themselves in the search for Martha Watts, the missing log reader from Bletchley Park, and in Ellen's attempted rescue, Harry knew that the decisions had been his. Guilt because there had been consequences. Not just for him, but for all of them.

For the man on the stairs above him, the consequences would certainly have been fatal, had he not found the strength to haul himself from the depths of the Hertfordshire woods, where his assailant had left him for dead, to the side of the B656, where he'd been found, unconscious, by a passing motorist. How he had managed it, when one foot had been reduced almost to pulp inside his boot and with a hole blown clean through his shoulder, was a mystery that neither Harry nor the police had been able to explain. Whatever his reasons, the Norwegian had offered them little by way of any explanation and Harry had decided not to press him. Some memories, Harry reflected, were best examined in your own good time.

Ahead of him, his friend missed a step and might have fallen had he not been holding on to the handrail. Harry covered the distance between them in two hurried strides. 'Are you all right?' he said, placing an arm, protectively, around the Norwegian's shoulder.

'Sure,' said Mikkel Eglund, grinning. 'Just making sure you were paying attention.'

The likelihood of finding Martha Watts alive had been negligible from the start. The log reader had been missing from Bletchley Park since November 1944. Harry had always assumed that she was dead, whether through accident or deed. And yet, he had been so utterly determined to find her that he'd allowed both his own safety and that of his friends to be compromised.

They'd tried to make him feel better about involving them. Mike had insisted that once Ellen had been taken, he'd had little choice but to accept their help - that to have refused it would have condemned Ellen to an unknown fate. Mike had been right. Abandoning Ellen had never been an option. But did it justify the risks that he'd taken, or his friends' appalling injuries?

Mikkel Eglund had not been the only casualty. Marcus Dawson, on whose skills - and ropes - they had depended, to get them down into the underground shelter at Belsize Park, had suffered such terrible injuries that he would probably never walk again.

But even that was not the worst of it. There had been two fatalities. While he knew this to be the case, Harry was still struggling to find a way to square it in his mind. That men had lost their lives as a consequence of his decisions was a surreal thought. The stuff of nightmares. The kind of thought that might bring you suddenly awake at night, covered in sweat. And not just at night. Harry had found himself sweating suddenly, even in broad daylight. Often without warning or any obvious trigger. First, his chest would begin to constrict and then he'd find himself unable to breathe. As though a polythene bag has been placed over his head. Once, he had blacked out entirely. And seen the shattered face of one of the dead men. Eyes wide and unblinking, staring at him. Tomasz Dobrowski's eyes... Harry shuddered and tried to banish the vision from his mind. 'Do you need this?' he said, holding out the aluminium crutch that, nowadays, rarely left his friend's side.

Tomasz Dobrowski. Why he had betrayed them had not been established and would not, Harry reckoned, until the man called "Stephens" was found. That Stephens had been behind the young Pole's actions seemed beyond doubt. But how he had persuaded him - what lever he had used, sufficient to coerce him to such extremes - was another question to which Harry had no answer.

Whatever Stephens had promised Dobrowski in return for his collusion, one thing was certain. It had not saved him. One morning, shortly before Christmas, Harry had woken to the news that Dobrowski's decomposing body had been found, with half its face missing, caught in the sluice gates at Aldenham Reservoir.

'What? So I'm going to pole vault my way to the top?' Mikkel Eglund said, grinning.

Harry forced a smile. 'You're such a bloody marvel, Mike, I wouldn't put it past you.'

The Norwegian shrugged. 'If it's all right with you, bud, I'll do it the regular way. Unless, of course, you want to go up top and throw me down a rope.'

Had anyone else made the remark, Harry might have been affronted. It had been his willingness to accept, without question, the plan proffered by Dobrowski, to access the tunnels at Belsize Park by abseiling down the lift shaft and to climb back the same way, that had resulted in such dire consequences. But Harry knew Mike better than that. While the Norwegian had mastered the subtleties of the English language well enough, he had failed, utterly, to learn the art of tact. It was a failure that had lost him several friends. Which was their loss, as far as Harry was concerned. Mikkel Eglund was a good man and the most loyal of friends. It was just unfortunate that narrowly avoiding the loss of one of his feet didn't seem to have dulled his propensity for putting both of them in it, often at the most inopportune of moments. 'I don't do ropes,' Harry said, pointedly.

If he noticed the *faux pas*, the Norwegian didn't so much as flinch. 'Sure,' he said, still grinning.

The two men made it to the summit. They crossed the still crowded foyer without further incident and, pushing their way through the glass doors, stepped out onto a wind swept Oxford Street.

'Cool venue,' said Mike, glancing back at the illuminated sign beside the awning over the doorway.

'One of my favourites,' Harry agreed. 'What did you think of the band?'

Mike hesitated. 'Better than I thought they'd be.'

Harry looked at him questioningly. 'And you thought they'd be?'

'Awful. Reunion tours normally are. Tired old has-beens, trying to re-live their former glories.'

'You didn't have to come, you know,' Harry said, semi-seriously.

Mike shrugged. 'I could hardly have let you come on your own. I'd never have heard the end of it.'

Harry was well aware that Jane had applied a three-line whip in order to secure Mike's attendance. Although, whether he knew it or not, the truth was that it had been more for Mike's benefit than for Harry's.

'Hey,' Mikkel Eglund grinned 'I've got no problem with you oldies trying to re-live your former glories, if that's what floats your boat. Just so long as you don't turn into one of those fat guys with Steve Marriott hair do's. Do that, bud, and you can hang with somebody else.'

'What, like I'd be cramping your style,' Harry said, clapping his friend on the back. 'Fancy something to eat?' he added, changing the subject.

Mike looked at his watch. 'Do you know what, I think I'd better get home?' he replied, apologetically.

Harry looked at him with concern. 'You OK?'

'Oh, sure. I just promised Jane that...' he hesitated. 'Well, you know.'

Harry did know and he had no intention of incurring the wrath, come Monday morning, of Jane Mears, with whom he shared a common employer. 'Say no more,' he said, turning to hail a taxi.

Oxford Street had been busy but Tottenham Court Road was busier still. Maybe the theatres had just turned out, Harry reasoned, watching the line of people queuing at the entrance to the Underground station. Or perhaps it was like this every evening. It had been a while since he had spent time in London's West End. Even late at night, the pavements were as packed with people as the streets were with cars - possibly more so.

'I meant to say,' Mikkel Eglund announced, settling back into the taxi's wide rear seat. 'The girls were chatting the other evening. You know, the night they had supper?'

'Were they? About what?' Harry had chosen the little fold down seat behind the driver. He was already regretting it.

'About that interview you did for Radio 4.'

'Oh, that. You'd have thought that they'd have lost interest by now, wouldn't you? It was eight months ago,' Harry said dismissively, as they passed *The Jack Horner* public house on the corner of Bayley Street.

Mike shook his head. 'Listen, bud. They are never going to lose interest in the man who brought down Max Banks. So you might as well get used to it.'

He was probably right. The revelations concerning the MP had led to the biggest media frenzy since the death of the Princess of Wales and had put Harry's face on the front page of every national newspaper for a month. Eight months on and the media circus was still rolling. 'Did you know that Safe House, the company that have the lease at Belsize Park, are actually considering doing guided tours?' Harry said, incredulously. 'After all the aggro they gave me for just asking to be given access. Can you believe that?'

'Oh sure, I can believe it,' Mike replied. 'Money. Has a way of opening doors. Always has. Always will.'

Harry nodded in agreement. 'No argument there.'

'Talking of Belsize Park...' Mike said, nodding in the direction of a small, squat, red brick building, set back from the road on their left.

It took him no more than a few seconds to recognise the entrance to the underground shelter. 'Goodge Street DLS,' Harry replied, watching the stream of pedestrians passing the building, without so much as a glance. It was odd that, as different as the shelter entrance was to the buildings on either side, still it seemed to be anonymous. There but not there. A building from another time, painted into the landscape of modern London. Now without purpose or reason. And all but invisible to the many thousands of pedestrians who must surely pass along Tottenham Court Road every day. 'I wonder whether any of them have the slightest idea what's down there,' Harry said, 'lurking beneath their feet?'

'I doubt it. Wouldn't mind a look myself, though. If the lift is working,' Mike said, bending down to rub his calf muscle. He looked up. 'You don't suppose...'

'No. I don't,' Harry interrupted him.

Mike grinned.

'So what were the girls saying about the interview, exactly?' Harry asked, after a short silence.

Mike hesitated. 'They were discussing your reaction to the question about your mother.'

Harry's face fell.

'Well, it was a bit extreme. And that was just the stuff they broadcast. They must have cut shit loads out?' said Mike.

'I made it perfectly clear, before we started, that the subject was off limits,' Harry replied, defensively.

'Sure but…'

'But what?' Harry interrupted. 'So, I gave her a hard time. She deserved it.'

Mike said nothing.

The truth was that he hadn't just given the presenter a hard time. He had lost it. Thank God, Harry reflected, they had cut most of his tirade from the final programme, or he'd have made the front pages all over again. And this time, for all the wrong reasons. As it was, the programme had made him sound like a troubled man with a guilty secret. 'Look, they manipulated the whole bloody thing, Mike. They'd already decided what they wanted me to say. They just manoeuvred me into filling in the blanks. I mean, all that bollocks about the search for Martha Watts, really being about…' Harry hesitated and then fell silent.

'About your search for your mother?' Mike offered.

Harry said nothing.

Mike was thoughtful. 'So what if it was? What's the big deal?'

'It wasn't,' Harry said with finality.

Mike turned his head and stared, vacantly, from the taxi window.

Harry followed his eyes. The lights were still on in Euston Tower. A building which he would forever associate with London's Capital Radio. He wondered where the radio station had gone.

'Jane was saying that the thing about your mother had been troubling you,' Mike said suddenly. 'I mean, long before you started looking for Martha Watts.'

'It has always troubled me,' Harry said, honestly. His mother had disappeared, without trace, when he was eight years old. But what had made it worse - far worse - was that his father had, since the day of her disappearance, refused to have him, or his sister Kate, so much as mention her name. It was as though he had tried to erase her from their lives. Like she had never existed. 'But how, exactly, is that anybody else's business?'

The comment had not been aimed at Mike, but that was how it had sounded. 'Look, I'm sorry,' Harry said after an uncomfortable silence. 'That wasn't aimed at you. I meant that if I wanted my life story splashed all over the media I'd have written about it myself.'

The Norwegian held up his hand. 'No need to apologise, bud. You're right. I mean, sure it's your private business. But we're talking here about the press. Can you honestly see your average hack worrying about your privacy, if he thinks there's a story in it?'

Harry said nothing.

'Besides, it's not all bad. Celebrity does have its benefits.'

Harry couldn't argue with that. Everybody loved a David versus Goliath story. And, for a while, Harry had enjoyed his portrayal as the little man who taken on the giant that was Max Banks. The trouble was that, as easily as the media could build him up, so it could just as easily knock him down again. When a reporter from one of the tabloids had run a piece about his mother's disappearance - and Harry had his suspicions about the source - it had seemed to turn the tide. Suddenly, there were reporters and paparazzi poking their noses into every aspect of his life. And, just as suddenly, stardom had become an intrusion.

If that wasn't bad enough, Harry's new housemate had been pushing him to investigate the truth about what had happened to his mother on the basis that if he didn't, sooner or later, some reporter undoubtedly would. His apparent reticence, so far as she was concerned, and the continued media attention had led to tension between them where none had previously existed. Probably not on a scale sufficient to threaten their relationship, but he could certainly have done without it.

'Which one of them put you up to this?' Harry said, irritably. 'Jane?'

Mike shook his head.

Which surprised him. Maybe even scared him a little. It was one thing to be talking to them about it - Jane and Mike were their closest friends - but to be asking Mike to talk to him about it, as though she could no longer raise the matter with him, herself? That was not good. Not good at all.

'Harry, she's worried. About you. About what this is doing to you both,' Mike said, as if reading his thoughts.

It wasn't reticence. That was the thing. He wasn't trying to avoid it. He didn't have his head in the sand. Or any of the other things that she had thrown at him. It was that the issue had become more complicated than either she realised or Harry had hitherto been willing to admit. He wanted to think it through. He needed time - the one thing that they seemed determined to deny him.

'So what else did she have to say?'

Mike shrugged, awkwardly.

'Well, its good to know that my personal life is keeping the three of you entertained, Mike, along with half of bloody Fleet Street.'

'It's not like that,' Mike replied, sounding genuinely hurt.

Harry took a breath. For as long as he could remember, he'd been telling himself that his mother had simply vanished. That one moment she'd been there and the next she'd been gone. Her clothes in the wardrobe. Her shoes under the stairs. And for most of that time he had been blaming his father. For blotting her out of their lives. He'd held onto the story for so long that, in his mind, it had taken on a reality of its own. But scratch below the surface - and that is what the media had been doing - and Harry knew that it was not the whole story. That the truth wasn't as simple. He just needed time to work out what the truth was... 'So come on. What else did she have to say?' Harry pressed.

'She said that that whenever the subject comes up, you...' Mike stalled, as though he had already said too much.

'I what?'

'You get up tight about it. OK? Just like you did during that interview. Just like you're doing now.'

Harry snorted.

'That you damn near bite her head off.'

'Those were her actual words, were they?' Harry said, indignantly. He didn't know why he was giving his friend such a hard time. Mike looked about as uncomfortable as it was possible to look.

'Look,' Mike said after a few moment's awkward silence. 'She's worried about it. That's all. We all are. You've not been yourself at all, these last couple of weeks. I've known you for, what, fifteen years?'

Harry shrugged.

'Well, in all that time, I've never known you lose your rag like this. Do you know that? Not seriously. Not once.'

'That's bollocks,' replied Harry

'No, it isn't.'

'Yes, it is. What about that time we were chased from that old receiving station on the Leighton Buzzard Road. By that farmer. What was his name?'

'Pickles,' replied Mike, straight faced.

'That's right. Pickles. Bloody stupid name.'

'That was different.'

'Was it?' Harry turned and gazed from the taxi's window at the lights of London's West End, as they flashed by. Of course it was different. He just needed time. Time to sort out what he remembered - genuinely - from the story he'd been telling himself for best part of the last thirty years. Time to piece together the fragmentary memories of an eight year old child. Time.

'Look, bud. Forget about the girls. I just wanted you to know,' Mike said, 'that if you ever need to talk about it...'

They'd been a tension. Between his mother and father. Harry couldn't remember them actually arguing. Not ever. But something had changed between them. Something which Harry had *felt*. It had given him butterflies in his stomach. Kept him awake at night. Harry remembered the feeling. A feeling that something was going to happen. Something bad.

'I mean, man to man,' Mike added, awkwardly.

She'd taken them to the seaside. Suddenly. Without their father. They'd played on the beach. Paddled in the sea. Harry remembered the mud between his toes and staring back up the breach towards her. His mind had taken a snapshot of her and had stored the picture away with all of his other memories. He had examined every detail of it a thousand times. For the presence of some clue. An answer. She'd looked up, as he called out. 'Mummy, look! A crab!' Harry could see her face, now, in his mind's eye. Distant. Lost. As though her thoughts were elsewhere.

And then there'd been the big, tall tower block, where they'd stayed. And a black lady who had looked after them until their father had come to collect them. It was after that - Harry was certain of it - that the police had come to the house. His father had taken them into the living room and closed the door, leaving Harry outside holding Kate's hand. He was sure that he remembered it…

Harry sighed. 'You know that my father hasn't spoken since his stroke last year,' he said, suddenly. 'Not so that anyone has been able to understand him, anyway,' he added, turning back toward the Norwegian.

'Sure,' Mike replied.

'Well, actually, that's not quite true.'

'What do you mean? You're saying that he has spoken?'

Harry nodded. 'Two weeks ago.'

'Well, that's great,' Mike said, leaning across the taxi awkwardly and clasping Harry's shoulder.

'Yes and no.'

Mike stared at him. 'Sorry bud, you've lost me.'

'This is between you and me, right?'

Mike hesitated.

'I'll talk to her, when I'm ready. But I want to be certain. I need to piece it all together first. OK?'

Mikkel Eglund stared at him and then nodded.

'He told me that he thinks that she may still be alive,' Harry said, quietly. 'My mother, that is. He isn't certain. But he thinks so.'

Mike's mouth made an "Oh" shape.

'But that's not all.'

Mike said nothing. Harry's next sentence left him gaping.

'No shit,' Mike said, when he'd recovered from the shock of Harry's words.

Chapter One

Saturday, 23rd April 1977

Alright. So maybe it wasn't the cleverest thing he could have done. Hurling a traffic cone at Freeman Hardy and Willis with a mounted policeman no more than a few yards away. Within striking distance in fact and as he shortly found out. But it had just happened. Like everything had seemed to happen that afternoon. In a blur of excitement and righteous indignation.

Neither had he actually intended to smash the window. In truth, there hadn't been any conscious intent to his actions, at all. One moment, he'd been pushing through the crowd with Sonia holding onto his arm like her life depended on it. The next, they'd reached a gap and he'd stopped abruptly and taken hold of the red and white striped cone. Holding Sonia back with one hand, with the other he'd swung the cone in a wide arc.

It was an odd sensation. In the instant that the cone had left his hand, he'd found himself wondering what he was doing. As though he were merely a bystander. Watching himself. Watching the cone soar through the air. Seeing the kids who had been gathering shoes from the racks outside the shop, to hurl at the passing demonstrators and policemen, step back, their heads turning in unison like the crowd at a tennis match. Except that it wasn't a tennis ball that held their attention, but a bright red and white striped traffic cone. He had watched it in silence as it advanced towards the window.

He'd become aware, vaguely, that someone was pulling at his arm but time had slowed, almost to a halt. People always said that it did at times like this and they were right. His vision had narrowed and the sound of the crowd had dulled. The chanting. The shouting. The whistles and car horns. All receding, as though somebody had cupped their hands over his ears.

Then the cone had found its target and time didn't so much re-start as explode in a cacophony of light and sound. It was so spectacular that, for an instant, he was dazzled.

The first thing that had happened was that the window had blown inwards with an almighty crash. Then the crowd had cheered and surged forward around him while he stood panting. The third thing that had happened was that Sonia, who still had hold of his arm, had whirled him around like a spinning top.

He had looked at her blankly. Mouth open. Wondering who she was. Who he was.

'What the fuck is wrong with you, Karl?'

These things had taken no more than a few seconds to happen and it only took a few more for the mounted policeman to turn his horse and to nudge it toward them. Karl saw them coming over Sonia's shoulder. That was all the warning he got before they were both knocked sideways by the advancing horse and pain tore through Karl's shoulder as the policeman's baton found its target. But that wasn't the worst of it. As he went down, he felt a sudden weight on his leg and a tearing sensation. It bought tears to his eyes.

He lay on the ground, clasping his left leg. When he let go, his hand was covered in blood. 'Babylon…'

'Karl?' Sonia reappeared out of the melee. 'Karl!' She was screeching like a woman possessed.

All around them was chaos. He looked from her to what was left of the shoe shop. The mounted policeman had succeeded in driving a small portion of the crowd into the broken shop front, where they were rapidly setting up a barricade behind a fallen shelving unit. Chanting *"Ban-the-filth"*, they began to hurl shoes and other items at the police horse. Unable to advance any further, the rider was trying to back away but was struggling to maintain control. He looked like he was about to fall. Karl hoped fervently that he would.

'Come on!'

He stared at her blankly.

'Come on!' Sonia yelled above the noise.

As he lurched to his feet, a face appeared out of the crowd. A face that he recognised. 'Johno?'

'Jeez, was that you?' Johno said, with a broad grin.

'What?'

'It was you, wasn't it? What was it? A fucking traffic cone?'

Karl nodded.

'Wicked,' Johno said, still grinning. 'I wish I'd got a picture. I'd have got you on the front page of tomorrow's Star, no sweat.' He held out his hand.

Karl took hold of it.

'You're hurt,' Sonia said, seeing the blood for the first time.

'It's nuttin',' he said looking down at his leg. 'The fucking horse, man.'

'Come on, let's get you two back to the Common. There's a first aid station,' Johno said.

Karl looked at him doubtfully.

'Behind the stage. In case they smoke too much of the old wacky backy and need to lie down for a bit.'

Karl attempted to put some weight on his injured leg and flinched.

'Come on man,' said Johno, looking towards the policeman. 'Unless you want to spend the night in Wood Green nick.' He put Karl's arm around his shoulder, took hold of Sonia's hand and together, they hurried away.

The crowd was thinner outside the Underground station. Karl could feel the booming of the sound systems in his stomach from the lorries parked at the far end of the Common. Most of the crowd had moved northwards, pushing the demonstrators back up the high road. He could just about make out the Union Jacks fluttering in the distance. They had been determined not to let the fascists pass and it looked like they were going to succeed. Today, at any rate. The Battle of Wood Green was won, if not the war. Karl knew that much.

When they had reached the Common, Karl asked Johno to stop. 'I got to rest, man.'

'Alright, stay here. Don't move. Either of you. I'll be back,' Johno said, looking at Sonia, who nodded eagerly and waved him away.

Karl lowered himself onto the grass and sat with his leg out in front of him.

Sonia examined it carefully. 'I think you're going to need stitches.'

Karl looked at his leg. 'Maybe.'

'Why did you do it?'

'Why did I do what?'

'Don't give me that.' Sonia gave him one of her looks. 'The window.'

Karl considered the question. 'Jah know. Me don't know,' he said with the best Rasta accent he could muster and then he grinned.

'I don't believe you. Mum and Dad are going to go ape shit if they find out. You do know that, don't you?' she said, leaning towards him and kissing him.

'Well, I'm not going to tell them and Johno didn't get a picture,' he said still smiling.

'Karl Dixon. My dad drives a taxi for a living. He won't need a copy of the Morning Star to find out. Fuck, he probably knows already.'

In the event, he didn't need stitches. There had been an ambulance crew at the first aid station, tending to the mounting injured from the demonstration. Johno had returned after five minutes with an ambulance woman.

'You're lucky,' she said, examining Karl's leg. 'It's little more than a scratch.'

'It's bleeding a lot for a scratch,' said Sonia, peering at the wound doubtfully.

The ambulance woman pulled up Karl's trouser leg and held his calf with one gloved hand, while cleaning the wound with the other. 'It could have bled a lot more, believe me.'

Karl was enjoying her attention. She was skinny and blond.

'Closure strips should do it,' she said, producing a pack from her bag. 'Just go easy and make an appointment with your GP in a couple of days. If it bursts, get yourself to Casualty.'

Karl nodded. He could see Sonia from the corner of his eye. He knew what she was thinking.

The blond applied the last of the strips. 'Stay out of trouble.' She flashed him a grin.

She was pretty. Especially in uniform. 'The harder the battle, the sweet of Jah victory,' Karl said cooly.

'Oh please,' interrupted Sonia, shaking her head. 'Don't worry, he isn't going within a hundred miles of another battle,' she said, turning to the ambulance woman. The two women laughed.

After that, they sat for a while on the grass, enjoying the sunshine, listening to the sounds and watching people return from the high road. There were men and woman of every colour - black, white and asian - along with an uneasy coalition of Greek and Turkish Cypriots from Green Lanes, punks with pink spiky hair, hippies and Rastas, groups of kids who looked like they'd never been to a rally before, as well as seasoned rally goers in yellow, anti-Nazi tee-shirts, standing in huddles, smoking ganja with one eye out for the law.

'Do you want to stay and see the band?' said Sonia, between mouthfuls of rice. She had insisted on getting them some food from one of the stalls at the edge of the Common.

'Might as well.'

They finished their food and made their way across to the stage, where a large crowd was beginning to gather.

As the sun slowly sank toward the trees, and then disappeared behind *The Curzon*, the old cinema at the southern end of the Common, Sonia danced and Karl danced, gingerly, but mostly he sat on the grass and watched her. Which wasn't so bad.

Karl loved the smell of her hair when he held her close. He remembered the first time he had kissed her. Standing here, on her porch. She'd been fourteen then and he had been sixteen. He'd floated home on a cloud, with his hands behind his head.

He had been in the year above her at school. He'd hated the school and had wished, a thousand times, that his parents had chosen to send him to the comprehensive in Tottenham but they had insisted on a church school and a boys' one at that. "Karl Dixon, the Lord blessed us when he gave you to us," his mother had said. "The least we can do is let him finish the job." More than once. Fortunately, the Lord had blessed him too, by convincing the school's governors to amalgamate the boys' school with a local girls' school and within a few months he and Sonia had become an item.

It had caused something of a stir, her being a white girl and younger than him. Especially among some of the white boys. They'd taken it way too personally. That was Karl's opinion, anyway. So Sonia had liked him more than she had liked any of them. Who could blame her? Karl grinned.

'What?' Sonia whispered looking up at him.

'Nuttin'.' He paused. 'I was just remembering how much I liked kissing you the first time.'

'What, so you don't like kissing me now?'

He bought a hand up and held the back of her head, her long brown hair flowing between his fingers. She closed her eyes as their lips met and they kissed again.

'It's not so bad,' he said when their lips had parted.

She pushed him away, playfully. 'Watch it, Dixon. There are plenty more fish in the sea you know,' she said, dropping her voice to a whisper 'and I bet they don't throw traffic cones through shoe shop windows.'

'Sonia?' called a voice from inside. 'Come on now. Say goodnight to Karl and come inside. It's getting late.'

'Shit,' Sonia whispered. 'Alright Mum, I'll be there in a minute,' she called out.

'Goodnight, Karl,' called the voice from inside.

'Goodnight, Mrs Smithson,' he called back.

'Are you going to be alright, walking back?' Sonia said, stroking the side of his face.

'Why wouldn't I be?'

'You're leg. I could ask Dad to drop you home in the taxi. He's off tonight. I'm sure he wouldn't mind.'

'I'll be fine. Seriously.'

'Well alright, but steer clear of the Westbury Arms. They're scum in there at the best of times and tonight...' Her voice drifted away.

Karl sucked his teeth.

'So go around the other way.' She said it like she meant it.

'No sweat. I can handle myself.'

'What, like you handled that horse?' She had her hands on her hips. Karl liked it when she played the school teacher.

'Sonia. Come on now,' said the voice from inside.

'Go on,' Sonia said, kissing him quickly. 'I love you.'

'Sweet.' He turned, stepped out of the porch and walked away. He didn't have his hands behind his head. They were in his pockets. But she always made him feel like he was floating on a cloud.

For all his bravado, Karl Dixon wasn't stupid. He had no intention of going anywhere near *The Westbury*. Sonia had been right about the pub's reputation. And tonight was not the night to discover whether it was justified.

The back streets were empty but still, he made slow progress. His leg was hurting more than he had let on. Sonia fussed so much. Which was kind of nice, sometimes. But, had he told her just how much it was hurting, she'd have insisted on her dad taking him home in his taxi.

It wasn't that he didn't like Mr Smithson. To be fair, a lot of white blokes would have had a fit at the thought of their daughter going out with a black boy. Mr Smithson had done his best to accept it but Karl just got a feeling about him. He couldn't blame him. He didn't blame him. It was always going to be an issue. But it made things kind of awkward between them. The last time he'd given Karl a lift they had both sat in silence all the way back to Tottenham. Both wanting to say something to break the ice but neither able to manage it. By the time they'd pulled up outside Karl's place, there'd been icicles on the inside of the windscreen.

Karl headed north, crossing side streets one by one. He didn't see anyone. Not one face. Maybe after the trouble in the high street, the locals were staying indoors. *Holding their breath,* Karl thought. With the atmosphere as charged as it had been, only hours before, it wouldn't take much for it boil over again.

At the final junction, he hesitated. He could either finish his journey on Westbury Avenue or he could take the footpath. It would be quicker. He looked at his watch. The Westbury was behind him but it was closing time and, if they hadn't already, people would soon be spilling out of the pub onto the street. The footpath was poorly illuminated. The fence that had been erected to keep intruders out of the adjoining gardens, also acted to block any view from the houses that bordered the footpath on one side. Still, it would get him to where he wanted to go and, so long as it was empty, it would be a safer bet.

So long as it was empty. Which it wasn't. As he turned the first bend he heard voices. He stopped and listened.

Drunken voices. White voices. There were three of them. He could see them in the shadows ahead of him. Three men.

One of them looked like he was relieving himself against the alleyway fence.

Karl's first thought was to turn around and walk back the way he had come. He took two cautious steps backwards, at which point his heel caught a beer can. It clattered away, spraying lager up the back of his trouser leg as it went.

One of the men looked his way and started to walk towards him. 'Oi, you.'

Karl stood still. Running was out of the question. The police horse had made certain of that.

The man approached him. He was wearing jeans and boots. He turned and called over his shoulder. Even in the half light, Karl could see the Cross of St George tattooed on the side of his neck.

Shit. Karl had come across his kind before.

'Jimmy. Put your knob back in your trousers and get over here. It's a nig-nog.'

Karl stared at him.

He was a big man, with long, greased back hair and a gut that spilled out of his shirt and flopped down the front of his trousers. When he grinned, Karl saw that he had a tooth missing.

'What're you looking at, boy?'

By now, the other two had joined them. The second man was shorter and thinner and looked like he was off his face. He could barely stand still. Hopping from one foot to the other like he was standing on hot coals. The third man stood back from the others. Karl couldn't see his face but he could see enough to know that he was another big man.

'I said, what are you looking at?'

Karl took another step backwards. He knew, with a sinking feeling in his gut, that his options were fast running out. 'Nuttin'. I'm looking at nuttin'.' Karl tried to sound defiant but he wasn't feeling it.

'He was looking at your knob, Jimmy,' the first man called over his shoulder again. 'I reckon he's a bloody shirt-lifter as well as a nig-nog.' The man turned back towards him. 'You a fucking bender too, black boy?'

Karl shook his head.

The man pushed him in the chest. 'I asked you a question.'

Karl lost his footing and slumped backwards against the fence.

'Fucking niggers. Come over here and behave like you own the fucking place.'

Karl regained his balance. 'I did not come over here,' he said, brushing himself off. It was pretty stupid to argue. He knew that, but his pride would not allow him to remain silent.

'What?' The man had his face pressed up against Karl's so that their noses were almost touching. He smelt of cigarettes and beer. And something else. Karl found himself wondering what it was. He returned the man's stare. 'I said, I didn't come over here. I was born here. Just like you.' If he was going to take a kicking, he might as well show some balls. And then he recognised the smell. Brylcreem.

Karl saw the third man approach out of the side of his vision. Just as the first man head butted him, hard in the face. He felt the bones in his nose crunch and a taste of iron in his mouth. He slumped back against the fence, bringing his hands up to guard himself from a second blow. But there was no second blow. Instead the third man pushed the first aside and Karl saw a flash of something hard in the man's right hand. Their eyes met as Karl felt a searing pain in his groin. The man's eyes were black. Unblinking. He held the knife there for a moment, as Karl gasped. Then slowly, Karl felt the knife twist.

The pain was like nothing he'd ever experienced. It was as though he was on fire. He could not breath with it. As he began to lose his footing, he felt the pressure in his groin release as the man withdrew the knife. His vision began to blur. Then there was another blow, this time to his chest. It felt like a punch but as the man stepped away, Karl looked down and saw the handle of the knife sticking out from his shirt.

Oh.

He sank to his knees.

Oh.

His thoughts beginning to wander.

Is this what it feels like to be stabbed?

Oddly, he could hear music in the distance. What was it? Marley or Black Slate? He couldn't quite make it out. He put his hand to his chest. His blood was hot. Sticky. It was funny really. Blood didn't feel that hot while it was inside you but, soaking your shirt-front, it felt like hot raspberry jam. He could see Sonia, dancing in the sunshine to the music. Their eyes met and she smiled. Such a beautiful smile. Suddenly, her perfume was all around him and she was speaking. He could see her lips moving, but he couldn't hear what she was saying. The music had been replaced by a buzzing that seemed to be coming from inside his head. Behind his ears. He opened his eyes wide and looked up, long enough to see the boot as it came towards him.

Doc' Martens he thought. *Eighteen holes.*

It was the last thought that Karl Dixon had before he died.

Chapter Two

Wednesday, 27*th* April 1977

I was vaguely aware of a voice. I'd been a million miles away.
'Liz?'
'Hmm?' I looked up.
'I said, you look knackered. Are you sure you're up for it tonight?'
I yawned. 'You'd look knackered if you had just taken Four C for double human biology. There's only one branch of human biology that lot are interested in and they don't need any lessons in it from me.'
Simone sank into the seat next to mine. She leant back and rested her head against the wall behind her. I could smell the coconut oil in her hair. She let out a long sigh. We both stared silently into our coffee cups.
'I saw Sonia Smithson this morning,' Simone said, breaking the silence. 'She came in with her mother.'
I looked up. 'Did she?'
Simone nodded.

'Such a lovely girl,' I said, a picture forming in my mind of the pretty teenager.

'She looked utterly wasted. I don't think I've ever seen someone look so... blank.'

She would be, I thought. They had been so in love, like only teenagers can be. When you are young, love is exciting and beautiful. It all seems so simple. Until life, which has a nasty habit of intervening, comes along and screws it for you. If you've got any sense, you learn not to make the same mistake twice. And if you haven't, you do it all over again. I knew all about that. 'It's only been a few days. I don't think it's really sunk in with anyone yet,' I said. I couldn't think of what else to say.

We were both silent again.

'Did they say anything more about what happened?' I ventured after a few moments.

Simone took a gulp of her coffee and shook her head. 'I don't think they know.'

I tried to picture Mrs Smithson. I'd met her once, at a parents' evening but could summon only a vague impression of a faceless, friendly woman in her mid-forties. I hoped they had a good relationship, Sonia and her mother. Sonia was going to need her. 'Are they going? To the meeting, I mean?' I asked.

'They haven't decided. That's why they came in. I think Dora Smithson is worried about the publicity. The last thing they need is Sonia's face all over tomorrow's *Daily Mirror*.'

'Bloody journalists,' I said. 'They've been outside all day, you know. I caught one of them talking to Judson through the fence at lunchtime. Can you believe that?'

'Believe it? I'd be surprised if she wasn't on tonight's Parkinson. Wendy Judson and drama go together like bluebottles and shit.'

I turned to Simone with my mouth agape. She had a habit of speaking her mind. It was one of the things that I liked about her. But, even for Simone, the comment was insensitive.

Simone held up her hand. 'Alright, I'm sorry but I just can't stand that girl. Did you see her at assembly this morning? From the state she was in you'd have thought that she and Karl were related. Weeping all over the place. Did she even know him? I mean, at all?'

I shook my head. 'I doubt it.'

Simone sucked her teeth.

It had been three days. I'd been making the children their breakfast, with the radio on in the background. Just like I did every morning. Except that it wasn't going to be like any other morning.

I'd almost missed it. The news presenter hadn't mentioned Karl by name but a knot had formed in my stomach nevertheless. When the telephone had rung the knot had tightened. Call it intuition if you like. I don't know. Whatever it was, I knew it was not going to be good news.

'Ted?' I called out. 'Can you get it? I'm doing Kate's hair.'

I'd heard him come down the stairs and, moments later, Ted had come into the kitchen, looking worried. 'It's Greg Philpot.'

'Philpot? What does he want? He never calls me at home.'

'I don't know but he wants to talk to you. He says that it's important.'

I had listened to Philpot's voice in silence. When he was finished, I returned the phone to the receiver and sat down heavily on the bottom stair.

Karl had been such a bright lad. Outgoing and confident. Sometimes a bit full of himself but who isn't at that age? Student romances were usually nothing but trouble, but theirs had been a joy to behold. Truly. She had rounded his rough edges. Given him a focus. He'd been a real pleasure to teach, during his final year at school.

'It is just so sad. Karl was such a nice lad and they were… well, so sweet together. What a waste. What a terrible bloody waste,' I said.

Simone looked at me and reached for my hand. 'I know, honey. I know. Let's just hope that they catch the bastards. And soon.'

I frowned.

'Otherwise, there's going to be more trouble.'

If Simone was worried about trouble then trouble was imminent. She lived on the Broadwater Farm Estate, where she and her brother Leroy had grown up with their mother. Built in the sixties, *'The Farm'* was a collection of concrete tower blocks linked by a system of interconnected walkways at first floor level, with car parks below. The walkways were supposed to promote community cohesion, but offered an easy escape route for criminals of every kind and pretty much every kind of criminal occupied them.

It was a tough place to be, let alone to live. I had often wondered why Simone had stayed. I'd gone as far as asking her once. She had answered that, as bad a place as it could be, it was her place and the residents were her people. 'What, so you think I could just walk away and leave them to it?' she had said. 'Get myself a nice little place in Muswell Hill and pretend to be somebody I'm not?' I had thought *'Well why the hell not? I did.'* But I had kept my thoughts to myself. I was good at that.

'Trouble?'

Simone nodded. 'There's talk of a march on Tottenham Police Station.'

Shit. 'You don't think that it's going to blow at the meeting tonight, do you? If it's going to turn into a bloody riot, I'm staying at home, whatever Piss-pot says.'

Greg Philpot was the school's head teacher. I wouldn't say that I disliked him, exactly. You couldn't really dislike the man. He was supportive to his staff, a skilled leader and an inspirational teacher. I just found him too good to be true. Sickly-sweet. Like he should have had a halo. It grated with me.

'There'll be trouble if they don't handle it right. There's a lot of very angry people in Tottenham right now.'

I must have looked like I was going to back out.

'You are still coming aren't you.'

She asked it like it wasn't a question, but I answered it nevertheless. 'I don't know.'

'Oh, come on Liz. The school should be represented. Philpot is right.'

'Yes I know. He's always bloody right.'

'So?'

'Where am I going to park the car, for one thing? I'm not leaving it outside the town hall for somebody to torch if it all goes off.'

It was an excuse and it didn't get me anywhere.

'So get the Tube. I'll pick you up at Seven Sisters,' Simone announced, suddenly getting to her feet. 'Seven-thirty.'

It was obvious that she was going to escape before I could refuse. 'Wait a minute. I didn't say…'

Simone was on her way to the door. 'Don't be late. It's a shit hole, Seven Sisters. You don't want to be standing about, waiting for a bus.'

She was right about that.

Chapter Three

'Take your feet off the seat, please.'

Harry pulled a face at me. Kate giggled.

I watched them both in the rear view mirror. How had I ever deserved two such gorgeous children? Broad set and with a shock of thick, unruly, light brown hair, Harry looked like a character from the *Famous Five*. Especially in his school shorts. And Kate was my little elf. She was a skinny little thing. She always had been, no matter how much we fed her. Where had Kate inherited her features? Thin faced, and a nose and ears that were ever-so-slightly pointed. Just like an elf, in fact. She certainly didn't get them from her father.

'Harry Stammers, I saw that. Do it again and I will box your ears when we get home. Do you hear me?'

'Sorry Mum.'

Kate giggled again.

'And I'm watching you, young lady.'

Kate looked at me in the mirror on the windscreen and wrinkled her nose.

I poked out my tongue and then put my hand to my mouth in mock horror. 'See. You've got me at it now. Prepare your ears for a boxing, both of you.'

'No!' they both screeched as the car pulled up outside the house. I undid my seat belt. 'I'm coming...'

Ted disliked it when I got the children excited in the car. He grumbled that it wasn't safe and that one of these days, they'd dash from the car and under a bus. I suppose that he was right but I did it nonetheless. I just loved to see them happy.

The children squealed again.

I got out and opened the rear door. 'It's alright, I'm not really going to box your ears.'

Harry got out, still giggling.

Then Kate, looking very serious. 'Mummy, are you sure you're not going to box our ears?' she said, in a tiny voice.

'No, I am not sure!' I made my voice as big and as loud as I could.

They ran, screeching, to the side gate. Harry lifted the latch and they disappeared into the alley to the back garden, still making a racket.

I stood still. Watching them disappear. Enjoying the moment. *If I ever forget how lucky I am, slap me,* I thought. I don't know who I was talking to, but at that moment I meant it. With all of my heart.

I collected my shopping bags from the boot and went around the side of the house. 'Come out, come out, wherever you are,' I called out as I stepped into the back garden. I could see Kate's feet, poking out from beneath the forsythia that Ted had planted beside the garden shed.

I put my key in the lock and opened the back door. 'Oh well,' I said out loud, casually. 'In that case, I suppose I'll just have to eat your chocolate myself.'

That did the trick as I knew it would. Both children leapt out from their hiding place and hurtled into the house.

'Shoes off and straight upstairs. Then, perhaps, I'll share the chocolate.'

The children kicked off their shoes.

'After tea.'

They charged past, into the hallway.

'And don't just throw your uniforms in a heap,' I called out, as their feet pounded up the stairs.

I glanced at my watch. Twenty past five. I had an hour, maybe an hour and a quarter before I would have to leave. If I was going to make it to Seven Sisters by seven-thirty. And I better had, or I was never going to hear the end of it. Simone would make sure of that.

I spotted him as soon as we entered the hall. He was standing at the back, against the wall. It had been more than seven years since our last meeting but I recognised him immediately. It looked as though he was wearing the same, grey suit.

It was odd that nobody else seemed to be taking the slightest notice of him. His was one of very few white faces in a sea of black. He caught my eye. I looked away. *Shit.*

'Liz?'

'What?'

'Come on, Leroy said he'd hold a couple of seats for us.'

'Leroy?'

'Hello? Planet Muir, come in please,' Simone said, looking at me oddly.

What the hell is he doing here? I was working hard not to glance towards him again. Perhaps his presence had nothing to do with me. Perhaps, if I didn't look at him, he wouldn't be there.

'Sorry.'

'Are you alright?'

'Yes, I'm fine.'

I realised that I hadn't moved. It was as though a lightning bolt had struck me on the top of my head, passed through my body, down my legs and out of the bottom of my shoes, welding my feet to the wooden floor.

I glanced nervously around the hall. In all directions but one. It was filling rapidly. There was Philpot and a couple of the others from school. He waved at me and I nodded back. He mouthed 'thanks for coming.' I gave him a withering look. I just couldn't help myself. *What an arse.*

It was a big hall. I reckoned, big enough for three or four hundred people. Maybe more, without the seating, which was arranged in rows with a wide isle down the middle. There was a small stage at the front with a long table, behind which were the chairs for the speakers.

Simone took hold of my hand and led me toward the front, where Leroy was sitting with two men who I didn't recognise. All three had dreadlocks. 'Liz, you know Leroy.'

Leroy and his companions stood up. I leant forwards and kissed Leroy on the cheek. 'Hi, Leroy.'

'This is Maurice,' Simone said, 'and Isiah.'

I shook each man's hand in turn.

'Mum decided not to come then,' Simone said to her brother.

'Did you really think that she would?' he replied.

I had met Leroy maybe half a dozen times before but his voice always took me by surprise. Perfect English. Hardly London at all and not a trace of Afro-Caribbean. Somehow BBC English just didn't sound right coming from a man with dreadlocks. A case of stereotypes, I suppose. As liberal as I considered myself to be, I was not immune to them.

The noise in the hall was beginning to build, along with the tension. I could feel it buzzing in the air around me. Evidently Simone could feel it too.

'She was right to stay at home,' Simone said, looking around the hall with a worried expression. 'Look,' she said, nodding to my right.

I turned. Sonia Smithson was making her way down the central isle. Her mother had hold of her hand. Her father followed behind. It was touching to see the reception they were receiving and I felt my throat and chest constricting with the emotion of it. Those older men who were wearing hats, removed them as the Smithsons passed by. The older women bowed their heads. I'd had no idea that the community were so aware of their relationship. That they were willing to show the family - a white family - such respect was a surprise. I wondered whether the white community would have been so accepting and respectful, had the tables been turned. It was an uncomfortable thought but I couldn't help thinking it.

I watched the Smithsons as they advanced towards the front of the hall. Sonia and her mother looked terrified. Mr Smithson looked liked this was the last place on Earth he wanted to be at that moment, which it very probably was.

As they neared the front, the local pastor stepped out and touched Sonia on the shoulder. I recognised him from an assembly he had taken at the school. I couldn't hear what he said but I saw Sonia bow her head and her mother hug her.

I felt an overwhelming sense of sadness sweep over me. A week ago, Karl and Sonia had been among these people. Two families. Two happy young people, full of optimism for the future. Their future. Ripped away. *And for what? Seventeen years old, for God's sake.* I could feel my own anger rising in my throat and I could see anger too, in many of the faces around me. And who could blame them?

The pastor shook Mr and Mrs Smithson by the hand and showed them to their seats.

I looked over my shoulder, my eyes involuntarily darting to the back of the hall, but the view was blocked by the mass of people. They had started to take their seats. A sea of solemn faces.

I turned back towards the front in time to see a line of people file out from the side of the stage. They slowly took their seats behind the table. Two police officers, one in dress uniform, the Mayor, his chain of office around his neck, two suited men who I didn't recognise, and, taking their positions in the middle two seats, Mr and Mrs Dixon, both dressed in black.

Mr Dixon was a large man with greying hair and a big, round face. Mrs Dixon looked tiny beside him. She was, in any case, a small woman but tonight she looked smaller still, as though she had shrunk under the weight of her grief.

The hall fell completely silent. Everyone in the place seemed to be holding their breath.

One of the men on the stage leant forward and tapped his microphone with his pen. The tapping sound, from the PA system, echoed around the hall. He turned to the policeman beside him and whispered in his ear. The policeman nodded and pressed a button on his microphone. 'Ladies and Gentlemen, if I can have your attention, please?'

I thought it a crass thing to say since, from the silence, it was self evident that he already had the attention of everyone in the hall.

'Thank you. I am Metropolitan Police, Deputy Commissioner Gordon Hayle. To my left are Mr and Mrs Dixon, who many of you will know. Fred Steele, Mayor of Haringey'.

The Mayor held up his hand, as if expecting a round of applause. He didn't get one.

'To his left are David Collins and Greg Hughton from Tottenham First.'

The man on the far right activated his microphone and interrupted. 'Houghton. It's Greg Houghton.'

A ripple of resentful voices ran around the hall.

'My apologies, Greg,' the Deputy Commissioner said smoothly and without a flicker.

'Slick,' Simone whispered in my ear.

'And to my right is Chief Superintendent Simon Broadbent.'

The Chief Superintendent nodded. He looked like he hadn't slept for a week.

'Firstly, on behalf of the Metropolitan Police, I want to offer Mr and Mrs Dixon, Karl's family and friends, as well as all of those of you who knew Karl, my sincere condolences. I am sure that I speak for everyone here tonight when I say that our thoughts are with you,' he said turning towards Mr and Mrs Dixon.

The hall was completely silent now.

'Last Saturday evening, the twenty-third of April, shortly after eleven o'clock, Karl Andrew Dixon was murdered. We believe that he'd been walking northwards, along Sirdar Road in Wood Green, that he turned right at Mannock Road and then left into the alley between Mannock Road and Frome Road, with the intention of walking to Turnpike Lane to catch a bus home. There he was accosted by a person or persons unknown. He was found some hours later, with two knife wounds. One to the stomach and the other to his chest. Tragically, Karl was pronounced dead at the scene.'

From behind me, I could hear a woman weeping.

'It was a callous and vicious assault. Karl Dixon was, by all accounts, a wonderful young man, with a bright future ahead of him. His murder has appalled every right thinking person in this community.'

I could not take my eyes from Karl's mother. She had lowered her head at the Deputy Commissioner's words.

'Before I ask Greg to read a statement for Mr and Mrs Dixon, I want to ask you all to think carefully about whether you saw Karl and Sonia that day,' he nodded towards the Smithsons, 'and, if you did, to speak to me or to one of my officers. It is very important that anyone who saw them comes forward. Did you see them leaving Ducketts Common at approximately ten o'clock? Did you see them crossing Green Lanes and walking away from the Common, along Westbury Avenue? Were you in the Westbury Arms Public House, at any time that evening?'

At that point, there was a voice from the back of the hall. 'Why are you talking to us about the Westbury, man. You know who was in there and they weren't black.'

A ripple of agreement ran around the hall.

The Deputy Commissioner held up his hand. 'I would ask you all, please, not to jump to any conclusions at this time. We do not know the identity of the assailant or assailants, nor do we yet know their motive. That is why we need to hear from anyone who was there.'

'Do you know that whoever did it was in the Westbury?' called out another voice.

'No, not with any certainty. But a group of men were seen leaving the pub shortly before eleven o'clock. They crossed Westbury Avenue and turned left into Hawk Park Road. We would like to know who they were and where, exactly, they went.'

'Well, dem surely weren't black men. Why d'ya ask us, man,' called out another voice, followed by a rumble of agreement.

'I can assure you all that we are talking to everyone who was in The Westbury on Saturday evening, whatever their background.'

'Maybe we done talking,' called out a voice from the back of the hall. 'Maybe, it's time to fight fire with fire.'

I don't know why, but I turned and looked over my shoulder and scanned the back of the hall. The man in the suit had gone. I took a long, deep breath.

Smith. I'd only ever know him as Smith. The name had always seemed absurd. It had been obvious, from the start, that it wasn't his real name.

It was odd, but for the first time, sitting there beside Simone Jackson in Tottenham Town Hall, I found myself wondering about his real name. About the man behind the suit. Who was he? Did he have a wife, a family? I'd never really thought about it before.

My mind drifted back to our first meeting. I'd joined the Met, aged twenty in 1958 and been a probationer constable for two years. But, at the end of it, I'd decided to leave and to re-train as a teacher. It had been a difficult decision. I'd applied to join the force because I had wanted to make a difference. It had been naive. Two years in and I had realised just how naive.

I'd been a good probationer. So good, in fact, that when I was called in for what I'd assumed to be an exit interview, I'd been sure that they were going to ask me to reconsider.

I was shown into a small room. It was empty, save for a table and two chairs. I mean completely empty. Not so much as a telephone on the desk or clock on the wall. I sat down on one of the two seats and waited. I was on the verge of getting up and leaving when the door opened.

He introduced himself as "Smith". Not "Sergeant Smith" or "Inspector Smith". Just "Smith". I'd assumed that he was from Personnel. Somehow, he just didn't carry himself like a police officer.

He seated himself, looking at me from across the desk in silence, as though trying to weigh me up.

I tried to hold his eyes but there was something unnerving about him and I failed. 'Look, how long is this going to take?' I said, uneasily.

'Not long.'

I remember being struck by how softly spoken he was. It was menacing, somehow. It wrong-footed me. Put me on guard. 'I'm not sure what the point of this is.'

'The point?' He said it evenly, with just the trace of a smile.

'Yes. I mean, if you're going to try to talk me into changing my mind, you're wasting your time.'

His smile broadened. 'No, Miss Muir, we are not going to try to change your mind.'

'So what then?' I had begun to lose patience.

He appeared to consider the question. 'Very well,' he said after a few moments, leaning back in his chair. 'The point, Miss Muir, is that we wish to make you an offer.'

'An offer?'

He nodded.

I was thinking *'What the hell is this?'* I tried to read his face, but it was entirely neutral. It was as though he was toying with me. 'What kind of an offer?'

'One that I am sure you will find interesting.'

I decided to play him at his own game. 'Why?'

He smiled. 'Because…' he chose his words carefully. 'Let us just say, that we have been watching your progress and we think we can make good use of your not inconsiderable skills.'

'Which are? And you keep saying "we". Who are you?'

He chose not to answer either question. 'You begin your teacher training, in two week's time, I believe.'

It wasn't a question and so I didn't answer it.

'We are confident that you will find Ealing an excellent college,' he said.

I began a retort, but he stopped me. 'Very well. Let us get to the point.'

I closed my mouth and waited.

'You have been an extraordinarily able probationer, Miss Muir. Indeed, one of the brightest probationers our friends here at the Met have seen in some years.' He paused, waiting for me to reply, but I chose to remain silent.

'When you announced your decision to leave,' he continued, 'let us just say that telephones rang and that one of those telephones was mine.'

'Alright stop right there. You either tell me who you are, or I leave. Right now.'

'Very well. I work for the Security Service. Once you have signed on the dotted line, I will happily tell you which one, if you so wish.'

The Security Service. 'Hang on. Hang on. You're telling me that you're a spook. That you are, what, an MI5 agent?'

Smith said nothing.

'This just gets better and better. What in God's name does the Security Service want with me?'

'We wish to offer you a job, Miss Muir.'

'I've got a job. Or I will have. I'm going to become a teacher.'

'Indeed and while you are training, we wish you to work for us.' He held up his hand. 'We ensured your place at Ealing because we need someone on the inside there.'

What? 'What the hell do you mean you ensured my place at Ealing?' I was furious now. I had earned that place. I'd prepared for the interview. I'd compiled a portfolio. I'd turned up and been grilled for an hour and a half.

'And you did extremely well,' he said, as if reading my thoughts. 'They would certainly have offered you a place, without our intervention. As indeed, would the other colleges to which you applied. All of them, in point of fact. Let us just say that we discouraged the others.'

'You did what?' I pushed the chair out behind me and stood up. I was bloody furious and had every intention of leaving.

'Miss Muir, please sit down.'

I hesitated.

'We needed you at Ealing. That is all.'

'Why?'

'Because, while the students at other colleges across the country seem determined to ban the bomb - a matter which we have in hand - a rather more unpleasant group appears to have established itself at Ealing which is of increasing concern to us. We would like you to join it.'

I sat down. 'What group?'

'You have heard of Mosley's Union Movement.'

'Oswald Mosley? You're not serious,' I laughed.

Smith said nothing.

'Mosley and his Blackshirts are a spent force. Everybody knows that.'

'The Right is a fractured force, Miss Muir. Fractured but not spent. Mosley should not be underestimated. He has friends in some surprisingly high places, here and in Europe. While we have had our eyes to the left, he has been building his right wing Union Movement. He may even stand for Parliament again and, if he selects his constituency wisely and with a fair wind, he may well be elected, but what is of most concern to us is that he has begun to establish a foothold at a number of universities, most particularly at Ealing.'

'Let me get this straight. You want me to spy on a group of fascist students, for MI5.' It sounded all the crazier for saying it out loud.

'It is the Ealing group that we wish you to infiltrate. Exactly so.'

I thought about it. 'Why me?'

'Because your training here has identified that you have exactly the right skills and qualities we are looking for.'

I looked at him doubtfully. 'You think I'd be good at spying on my fellow students? You think that I have the skills to lie to them? To gain their trust and to betray them? You see that as a quality, do you?'

Smith hesitated and, for a moment, there was the tiniest flicker of irritation in his face. I noticed how well he masked it.

'You are an intelligent young woman. Your background and upbringing have given you a balanced view of the world. You said in your application to join the police that you wanted to make a difference. To contribute to society.'

'The Force is a dinosaur. It was naive of me to think that I could make a difference here. That is why I am going to be a teacher.'

'Indeed and, all-in-all, very probably a wise decision. You are, perhaps, a little before your time here.'

I didn't reply.

'The Right is a threat. Not just to the immigrants and others in Britain that it so willingly persecutes, but to the very fabric of our society. Make no mistake, Miss Muir, these people would destabilise our society, through a campaign of lies and intimidation, with the aim of overthrowing our democratically elected government and, in its place, establish a fascist state in Britain. We wish to stop them gaining a foothold among the young people of our country. We are offering you an opportunity to truly make a difference.'

He was serious.

'For Queen and Country,' I said, a little more scornfully than I intended.

He smiled. 'You will be working for Her Majesty's Government, yes.'

I laughed.

He looked at me. As straight as a cricket bat. 'Is it so inconceivable to you that you would ally yourself to the government of your country, and declare yourself against fascism?'

'I do declare myself against fascism, Mr Smith. Every day. I always have. You are not asking me to declare it. You are asking me to conceal it.'

'Oh come now, Miss Muir, I thought that you had done with naivety. You can declare it all you like, for all the good it will do you and anyone else. The question is whether you are willing to do something to stop it.'

He had said it with force and open irritation. In all my future dealings with him, there was only one other occasion when I saw his mask truly slip.

Our eyes locked and this time, I didn't look away. He had me hooked and he knew it.

'Were I to accept your offer...'

I was interrupted by his smile.

'That is an "if", Mr Smith, not a "when".'

'I'm sorry,' he replied. 'Please continue.'

But I had lost my direction. 'What if I am discovered? I cannot afford to jeopardise my new career. You must see that.'

'If you are discovered, then you... and your career... will be taken care of. We do not abandon our men and women in the field. If you offer us your loyalty, then be in no doubt that it will be returned.'

We sat in silence then.

I cannot say, even now, that I wish I had walked away though it is certainly true that, had I done so, a very great deal of suffering might have been avoided. But I did not walk away. I said 'Let me get one thing straight, Mr Smith. If I decide to accept your offer, and it is still only an "if", then I do not wear shirts and I look terrible in black.'

'I believe that is two things, Miss Muir,' Smith said, without the trace of a smile.

That was how it started.

The meeting concluded noisily. It was Mr Dixon's intervention, in the end, that prevented it collapsing altogether into chaos. Following a bitter exchange between the Deputy Commissioner and several young men in the audience, Mr Dixon had slammed his hand down on the table in front of him. The hall fell instantly silent.

'You want more trouble?' he began, glaring out into the audience. 'You think we want more of the youth cut down in their prime? Our houses burned? The streets ablaze? Fire with fire? Cha!'

A whisper ran around the hall.

'I came to this country from Jamaica, to make a better future for myself and for my family.' He bowed his head.

There was complete silence, save for the sound of someone weeping.

'A better future for my boy. Lord! You think, we gonna get that by shoutin' and hollerin'? By burnin' and fightin'? No, man! Those devils that took my Karl.' He spat, quite deliberately, on the floor behind him. 'They want fire on the streets. They want nuttin' but ruination. I say no, man.' He hit the table again with his hand. 'You want to show my Karl some respec'? So then. Help the police to bring us justice. Not fire and more suffering. Justice! You hear me?'

Several of the older men and women in the hall called out 'We hear you!' but many of the younger ones remained silent.

The tube train doors opened and I stepped onto the southbound Victoria Line train. The carriage was empty, except for a young couple at the far end of the carriage. One of them had bright yellow spiky hair and the other, a purple mohican. Both of them were wearing boots. It wasn't obvious which one of them was female or, indeed, if either were, until the girl turned towards me. Despite her black lipstick and eyeliner, she was strikingly beautiful. I decided to err on the side of caution and sat down on the seat nearest the door. I looked at my watch. It was ten-thirty. I'd told Ted that I would be back around eleven. Knowing Ted, he wouldn't be waiting up. His job meant an early start and he was often in bed before me.

Just as the doors began to close, a man in a grey suit stepped onto the train and sat down next to me. I could see his reflection in the window opposite. He was watching me.

Smith. So he had been there for me. I had all but convinced myself that his presence at the meeting had been a coincidence.

'What do you want?' I said, looking back at his reflection.

After a moment's pause he leant sideways and spoke quietly into my ear. 'You look well, Liz. Very well. How is the teaching going?'

I turned and looked at him. 'I said, what do you want?'

'And motherhood. How are Harry and little...' he hesitated. 'Kate, isn't it?'

I said nothing.

'Just a brief conversation. That is all.'

'We have nothing to discuss.'

Smith smiled. I could see his face in the reflection.

I started to get up. Which was pointless, since the train was already moving. I had nowhere to go. But at that moment, a few feet away from the bastard was preferable to sitting next to him.

Smith put his hand on my leg. I pushed it away and stood up. 'What the hell do you think you're doing?'

He had no right. I had ceased working for him a long time ago and I was not about to start again anytime soon.

The two punks at the far end of the carriage stared at us but said nothing.

'Sit down.' He said it quietly, but loud enough for me to be in no doubt that he meant to speak with me.

'We agreed, when I left, that I'd never hear from you again.'

He smiled wryly. 'Needs must, I'm afraid.'

'Whose needs? Certainly not mine.'

'If you will sit down for a moment, I will explain.'

'I don't think so.' I walked past him and stood at the door. He had no right. No right to be there. No right to be talking to me. No right at all.

He got up and stood next to me. 'A few minutes. That is all. I have a car waiting at Turnpike Lane,' he said.

I turned and faced him.

'You what?'

'I'll drop you home.'

'No. You won't. You will sit back down. Right now. Or I am going to start screaming.'

'Liz.' He put his hand on my arm.

I turned and shoved him hard in the middle of his chest.

He hadn't been expecting it and staggered backwards, thrown off balance by the push and the motion of the train.

'Get off me,' I said turning toward the two punks. 'Help!' I shouted and started to walk towards them, holding onto the ceiling handrail as I went. Both of them watched my approach, but neither reacted. Smith had regained his balance. I turned to face him, with my back to the door into the next carriage. I glanced down at the two punks. 'He tried to touch my arse.'

'Nothin' to do with us, lady,' said the male punk.

Smith had moved towards me but hesitated when the female punk put her leg out, her boot blocking his way.

'I don't think she's interested,' said the girl with the purple mohican, without looking up. 'Although I might be. If you play your cards right.'

God, I wish I'd been that self confident at her age.

Smith stopped and I caught his eye. Any anger was already masked. He smiled and stepped backwards.

The train, which had already begun to decelerate came to a halt with a jerk. The door hissed and opened.

'Thanks,' I said to the girl with the mohican.

'No problem,' she said.

I stepped off the train and walked away quickly. I did not look back.

Chapter Four

Tuesday, 31st January 1961

'Whose idea was this?'

Peter Owen smiled. 'Watch and learn, John. Watch and learn.'

'But he doesn't have a hope in hell,' observed the Scotsman.

'Of course he doesn't have a hope in hell. You have only to look at the haircuts, or the lack of them, to realise that. Layabouts and communists, the lot of them.' Owen's eyes swept the University hall. 'God help us all, if this rabble are our future.'

'Aye,' John nodded in agreement.

There had been uproar when the motion had been put that "The Opposer be not heard". Even the communists had exchanged glances. All the motion had done was to allow Mosley to demand freedom of speech, winning the sympathy, if not the allegiance, of the majority of those in the hall. It could not have worked better for him had the great man scripted the motion himself. Owen would not have put it past him.

'Who was the proposer. Neeman was it?' Owen said it into John's ear, so as not to be overheard. It was not difficult, given the hubbub around them.

John glanced towards the stage. 'Never seen him before. A Jew, no doubt.'

Owen smiled. So far as John was concerned, every conspirator in the world was a Jew. Although with a name like Neeman, on this occasion he was probably right.

'All those in favour of the motion,' the Speaker had announced, when the noise had finally abated. No more than two dozen young men and women had raised their hands. The hall had erupted again, with many of the students waving their papers in the air.

'Order! We must have order!' the Speaker had shouted above the tumult.

It had taken several minutes for order to be re-established.

'All those against.'

A sea of hands were thrust into the air.

Owen had his eyes on Mosley.

'Abstentions?'

One hand.

'The motion is defeated.'

There were deafening roars of 'Here! Here!' and 'I should bloody well say so!'. And there it was. A smile. Not in the line of his mouth, but in his eyes.

Owen had seen Mosley speak many times and at times to the most hostile of audiences, but he had never seen the man truly lose his composure. There had been passion and fire. Always. Sometimes it had seemed to boil within him as though he were a great, capped volcano. At other times it would appear to break free, in sizzling gusts of pure oratory. Owen had recognised in Mosley, from the very first, a rare ability to appear as a man both possessed by such a force of conviction as to be on the very edge of incoherency, while at the same time in complete and total control of himself and his words. It gave his speeches tremendous force. An edge that left audiences breathless with the power of the man. Owen had seen women pass out in Mosley's wake. Although on this occasion, Owen had to concede, John was right. He had not a hope in hell of winning but then, on this occasion, winning probably wasn't Mosley's game.

Owen listened to the prospective Liberal candidate's opening speech with disinterest and disdain in equal measure. Britain was not at the centre of an inter-racial commonwealth, it was at the head of an empire and rightly so. When the Liberal cited the Universal Declaration of Human Rights, a young woman in the audience shouted out 'What about our rights? Our jobs?'

Owen's eyes flicked from the young woman to Mosley. He was staring at her with some intensity. When Mosley nodded, even from a distance, Owen saw her blush.

Finally, after much heckling, the Liberal took his seat and Mosley slowly rose to face this audience.

He began quietly, outlining the problems caused by coloured immigrants and arguing that the influx of cheap labour could only lead to economic disaster. John had applauded, loudly, when Mosley had said that the recent race disturbances in Nottingham had been caused by "coloured wide boys armed with knives".

'My brother has a pen knife,' a young man shouted out, to a ripple of laughter.

'I expect that it was made in Sheffield,' said Mosley, rising to the challenge. 'As much of our steel is. If your brother is lucky, he may even find a job there one day, as generations of our young men have. If, that is, the jobs have not been taken by the Asians who are flooding into Sheffield from that far continent. You may laugh,' he said, wagging his finger and turning to address the wider audience, 'but I wonder whether the young men of Sheffield will be so amused when they find themselves without work, unable to support their wives and children?'

'All the Asians have brought to this country is T.B.,' called out another voice, this time from the back of the hall.

'So have cows,' called out another voice, 'and there are plenty of them here.'

And so it went on. At times the Speaker struggled to maintain order. The more raucous the heckling, the more strident Mosley became. Not once, did he show the slightest sign of hesitation. He had an answer for everything and turned every counter-point shouted at him from the floor, effortlessly, to his advantage.

'He's a master,' John said in Owen's ear.

'No. Not *a* master. *The* master. The greatest Prime Minister this country never had.'

Owen was interrupted by a roar from the audience. Mosley had sat down, to thunderous applause. Owen scanned the hall and noted, once again, the young woman who had flushed at Mosley's nod of approval. 'Who is the girl? Red top, dark hair?'

John followed his line of sight. 'That's Muir,' he said after a moment's hesitation.

'I've not seen her before.'

'No, she's new.'

'Introduce me sometime, would you?'

John raised an eyebrow.

'I like women with a bit of a spark,' Owen said. 'Unless they're communists or dykes and let's face it, most of the women around here are both.'

Mosley did, as they had predicted he would, lose the vote. He had, in his summing up, lost the sympathy of his audience by arguing the merits of European integration, even arguing for a single European state. At the vote, the Liberal had turned the debate on its head, arguing that Mosley's brand of European nationalism would take away the freedom of the British people.

'Rubbish!' the woman in the red top had shouted again. 'Tell that to the men of Sheffield!'

But Mosley had lost by one hundred and eighty votes to thirty nine, with forty abstentions.

Chapter Five

Thursday, 28th April 1977

I opened the refrigerator door. 'Bugger it,' I said out loud. I turned and walked into the hall. I undid the latch and opened the front door, peering out into the street with bleary eyes. I had half expected to see one of the Rovers from Barnard Road, parked outside. I'd been there once to collect a car. It had been a nice car too. A dark brown Rover 2000TC, with leather seats. I'd had it for a trip to Durham University and told everyone that it was my father's car, which they had all seemed to accept. I suppose it was a typical dad's car.

It had been wired, of course. That is what they did at Barnard Road. I never did find the microphones but the transmitter had been in a black box, tucked away behind the rear seats. A bit obvious, but nobody had noticed.

I studied each of the cars parked along either side of the street, checking them off in my head, one by one. I recognised them all as belonging to neighbours. Except for a bright red Wolseley Hornet. I looked at the car for a moment and, after a moment's further thought, dismissed the idea. Smith would never stoop as low as a clapped out old Wolseley.

I picked up the milk bottles and closed the door. 'Ted?' I called up the stairs. 'It's half six.' It was unusual for Ted not to be up before me, but the job he was doing was local.

I went back into the kitchen, put the kettle on the stove and turned on the gas. Last night was unlikely to be the end of it. Smith would undoubtedly try again and, if I rebuffed him again, there might be others. In the years that had passed since our last contact, I had gradually dismissed any thought that they might still have had any interest in me. But last night Smith had said that he had a car waiting at Turnpike Lane which meant that he knew my route home. And he had asked about the children. So they had been watching me.

Damn it. I'd played my part. Smith had agreed that I would not hear from them again. *So what the hell do they want with me after...* I counted the years off in my head... *seven, no nearly eight years?*

It had been Ted who had provided me with the reason to end it. He was such a good man. I'd known it from the beginning. And I had come to love him in a way. He had offered me a new start and a different life and I'd grabbed it with both hands. Well why not? Didn't I deserve a break? I was not going to repay him now with yet more deception. I owed him more than that.

I heard footsteps on the stairs. Shortly, Ted put his head round the kitchen door. 'Tea?'

'Kettle's on,' I replied.

'Thanks, love.' He yawned, putting his hands behind his head and stretching his arms.

'God, you're a handsome bugger,' I said and I meant it. He was.

We'd been married for seven years and he was thirty-five, with two small children. This was the point when many men would have relaxed, put on weight and headed happily for middle age and who would have blamed him? Certainly not me. But not Ted. It wasn't just his job at the Post Office either, climbing telegraph poles and hauling heavy cables, that had kept him in such good shape. It was a sense of self-discipline that he had picked up in the army and a determination to build the marriage and family that had been missing so markedly from his own childhood.

He smiled and stretched again. His biceps were bigger than my calf muscles.

'Mind you,' I said, wrinkling my nose, 'you smell like a pig.'

Ted leapt into the kitchen, grabbed me round the waist and lifted me off my feet. 'You like it. Now come here and give me a kiss.'

'I do not,' I said trying to wriggle out of his grasp, but I knew that resistance was going to be futile.

'I said, give me a kiss,'

'Not until you've had a wash.' I wriggled some more.

He squeezed me.

'Ouch! You're hurting me.' I grinned and our eyes locked for a moment. I kissed him. 'Yuk. You taste like a pig too,' I said as he released me.

'Alright, alright. Harry was in the bathroom,' he said, sitting down at the kitchen table.

I poured him some tea.

'How was the meeting last night? You seemed a bit flustered when you got in.'

'It was alright. A bit heavy, I suppose.' And there it was. My first half-lie. Secrets and lies were all that had ever come from my contact with Smith.

'Well, what did you expect?' he said, between gulps. 'I told you not to get involved.'

I ignored the comment. He had told me nothing of the sort. Why was it that men always had to be right? 'Had it not been for Mr Dixon, there might have been real trouble.'

'Dixon?' Ted asked.

'Karl's father.'

'Oh, yes, of course.'

'It was all getting out of hand until he told them that if they really wanted to show his son some respect, they'd help the police find his killers.'

'All well and good,' Ted said doubtfully. 'But they're going to want results and you can hardly blame them for that.'

I heard feet on the stairs. Harry appeared in the doorway. Miraculously, he was already dressed.

'You're up early,' I said.

'There's a trip today. We've got to be there early. Remember?' he said, trying unsuccessfully to tuck the shirt into his shorts.

'Oh yes, I'd completely forgotten about that. Bruce Castle, isn't it?'

Harry nodded.

'Come here,' I said, grabbing him by the waist band. 'What time have you got to be there?'

'Eight o'clock.'

'So we had better get a move on then.'

Harry nodded again.

'Is your sister up?'

Harry shrugged.

I walked out into the hall and called up the stairs. 'Kate? Kate, are you awake? Come on. It's time to get up.'

'Don't worry. I'll get her up,' said Ted. 'After I've had a wash. I wouldn't want to go to work smelling like a pig.' He pinched me as he brushed past.

Friday 29th April 1977

Peter Owen entered his office on the third floor of Excalibur House and removed his coat, shaking off the rain, before carefully arranging it on a coat hanger which he hung on the hook on the back of the door. He walked across to his desk and removed a pipe, a tin of tobacco and a box of matches from the desk's top drawer. He turned and looked out of the arched window, down onto Great Eastern Street, slowly filling the pipe with tobacco and then lighting it with a match. He took several puffs, sending a cloud of tobacco smoke billowing up toward the ceiling.

There was a knock at the door.

'Enter.'

He listened to the sound of the door opening and the shuffling sound of the man who had entered. 'What is it, Justin?' he said, without turning.

Justin Hughes hesitated.

Owen turned. 'Oh for God's sake, man.'

Hughes was over fifty, over-weight and balding. He'd been the Union's chief administrator for five years and in the whole of that time, Owen had never once seen him look presentable. He usually looked and smelt like he hadn't been to bed or washed for a week. This morning it looked as though he'd been to bed alright, but evidently he had forgotten to take off his suit.

Hughes was panting and sweating profusely. 'When are we going to get that bloody lift fixed? I don't know how much more of that staircase I can take.'

'Tuck your shirt in, man and the lift is your job. So sort it.'

Hughes reached for his shirt but struggled to insert the hem into his waist band, which was several sizes too small for his waist, such as Hughes had one.

Owen sighed. 'Do you actually possess an iron, Justin?'

Hughes thought for a moment. 'I don't know. I leave that sort of thing to Judy.'

'Judy,' Owen said doubtfully, taking another puff on his pipe.

'You know my...'

'Yes,' Owen said, taking his pipe out of his mouth. 'I do know who Judy is. I was just wondering...' he tailed off. 'Oh just sit down, Justin. You're making the place look untidy.'

Hughes found the chair in front of Owen's desk and sat down, glancing up at the portrait of the Queen on the wall as he did so. After a few moments Owen pulled out his leather seat and also sat down, resting his pipe in an ashtray on the desk and picking up a pile of papers. 'So. To what do I owe this small pleasure?' he said absently, scanning the papers one at a time.

'You asked me to have a word with the Chief Superintendent.'

Owen looked up. 'So I did.'

Hughes said nothing.

'And?'

'And he wasn't very helpful.'

'What did he say?'

'He said that his hands are tied. They were seen leaving the Westbury Arms on Saturday evening.'

'So what? It was last orders. The whole pub must have emptied at the same time.' Owen interrupted.

'Yes, but another witness says that he saw somebody matching Jimmy's description in the alley.'

'He saw somebody who looked like Jimmy. Did he see Jimmy or didn't he?'

'Broadbent says that the witness saw a face, illuminated by the street lamp. He's agreed to do an identity parade.'

'When?'

'This afternoon. Three o'clock. Hackney nick.'

'Why Hackney?'

'Tottenham's too hot. One spark and the whole bloody place will go up.'

Owen looked at Hughes steadily. 'Where's Jimmy, now?'

'Down at the station. They picked him up at eight o'clock this morning.'

'Damn it,' Owen cursed, banging his fist hard on the desk. 'What the hell does Broadbent think he's doing? If it comes out that Jimmy's one of ours, we'll have every lefty do-gooder this side of the Iron Curtain camped outside.'

Hughes held up his hand. 'Don't shoot the messenger.'

Shooting him was, unfortunately, out of the question. Punching him from across the table was a possibility that held certain attractions. 'Where's John?' Owen said irritably.

'Not back from Scotland until tomorrow.'

'And when am I getting that replacement for Sheila?'

'Closing date's next week. I'll run through the applications with you on Tuesday or Wednesday afternoon, if you're around. Interviews will be as soon as we can arrange them. I could always get a you a temp.'

'I've told you, no temps and make sure you run the proper checks on everyone you shortlist. We cannot be too careful.'

'Already in hand.'

Justin Hughes might look a mess, but he could do his job, Owen had to concede that. It was the one reason that his services had been retained. 'Is anyone with Jimmy?' Owen said.

'Neil Hardman. I sent him down there as soon as I heard.'

'Get a message to him. Tell him to stall them for as long as he can.'

Hughes smiled.

'Good. Now get out. I've got a phone call to make.'

Hughes dragged himself up, out of the chair.

'Wait,' said Owen. 'The others. Where are they?'

'Laying low, I would imagine,' said Hughes, already perspiring at the thought of facing the stairs again.

'Well raise them. My office in one hour.'

'What the hell do you want them here for? Fletcher is a good for nothing and we'd all be better off if Kevin stayed low, permanently. The man's a psychopath.'

Owen sighed and re-lit his pipe. 'My office,' he said between puffs. 'Both of them. One hour. And tell them to come in via the back door. There's a reporter sitting outside in a brown Rover.'

Hughes looked at Owen doubtfully. He walked across to the window. 'How do you know she's a reporter?' he said, peering down at the car.

'Well she's hardly here to photograph the bloody wildlife, is she?' Owen said, tersely. 'Now, get out.'

Hughes, shrugged and trudged from the office.

Owen waited for him to close the door, lifted the phone and dialled a number. 'Get me Chief Superintendent Broadbent.'

The day had started badly for Chief Superintendent Simon Broadbent. Tottenham was on the brink and the press were on his back. To cap it all, Jimmy Dobson was locked in a Hackney cell, suspected of murder, which in any other situation might have cheered him. Broadbent had good reason to want Dobson locked up. But Dobson's incarceration presented him with a problem. Or several of them, in point of fact. And one of them, he suspected, was about to present itself.

Broadbent opened the bottom drawer of his office desk, removed a bottle and a glass and poured himself a Scotch. It was early, but the way things were going he had a feeling he was going to need it.

As if on cue, the telephone on his desk began to ring. He let it.

Broadbent's rise through the ranks of the Metropolitan Police Force had been rapid, by anyone's standard, aided in no small part by an ability to spot a winner and a willingness to back it, no matter how bad the stench as it galloped by. And one man had looked like a sure fire winner from the start.

He counted to ten, reached for the receiver and waited for the inevitable.

'Sir, I have a Mr Owen for you.'

Peter Owen. It wasn't so much that backing him had been a mistake. Owen had impressive connections in some particularly high places and Broadbent had used them to his not inconsiderable advantage. And, if he was right about Owen, then his continued rise through the ranks was going to be a lot more likely with Owen's patronage, than it would be without it.

Nor was it that Owen's patronage had come at a cost. Patronage always did, although in Owen's case, the costs were certainly mounting. The expected payback had been a get-out-of-jail-free whenever the Union's activities put them on the wrong side of law. All well and good while Union members confined themselves to the occasional bout of Paki-bashing on a Saturday night, or breaking into some Chinese chip shop and pissing in their deep fat fryer. But over the last twelve months, the Union's activities had been on an altogether different scale.

The mistake had been trusting the man. The truth, no matter how unpalatable, was that he'd allowed his personal impressions of Owen to cloud his judgement. Because while Broadbent had been busy climbing the career ladder, Owen had made it his business to discover his weakness. And discover it, he had.

Broadbent took a breath. 'Put him through.'

The line clicked.

'Peter. How are you?'

'I'd be a damn sight better if Jimmy Dobson wasn't sitting in one of your cells,' said the voice on the other end of the line.

'I'm sorry about that Peter,' Broadbent lied. He wasn't sorry about it at all. 'It is beyond my control, I'm afraid.'

'Nothing is beyond your control, Simon. Your are the Chief Super. I should know. I put you there.'

Broadbent hesitated. 'Look, I'm in a difficult position, Peter. We're not unsympathetic to your position, you know that. Half the lads at Hackney would be paid up Union members if they could be and you surely can't be in any doubt about where I stand personally.'

'I know exactly where you stand personally, Simon. Need I remind you of that?'

Broadbent didn't need reminding. He'd had plenty of time to think about it. 'As I told Justin earlier this morning,' he persisted, 'there's a witness. He's already made a statement and he's adamant that he saw a man matching Jimmy's description at the scene. We had no choice but to bring him in.'

There was a pause, during which Broadbent reached for the Scotch bottle with his free hand and poured himself another.

'Where's this witness now?'

'Sitting in the canteen.'

'Good. Send him home.' Owen hesitated. 'No, better still, take him home in one of those nice new police cars you've just had delivered.'

Broadbent put his glass down. 'Now, just a minute…'

Owen interrupted him. 'And I want his name and address.'

Broadbent hesitated. 'You can't be serious.'

'Oh, I'm serious. What's his bloody name and address?'

'I'm sorry but I can't have the Union leaning on witnesses. This is getting out of hand. Tottenham's about to blow. One whiff of…'

'Enough.' Owen's tone had hardened.

Broadbent knew what was coming next. He picked up his whiskey glass and sank the remainder in one. 'And what would you like us to tell him, exactly? The man's expecting a bloody identity parade.'

'I'm sure you'll think of something. Tell him that you couldn't find enough people to take part in the parade. Be creative, Chief Superintendent.'

Broadbent could feel his anger rising.

'His name, Simon.'

Broadbent said nothing.

'I take it that Mrs Broadbent is as yet unaware of, how shall we put it, your particular pen-chance on those long Friday evenings, when duty keeps you at work half the night, serving the people of London?'

He had been expecting it.

'And that boy of yours. Mark isn't it? He must be, what, sixteen now?'

He lowered his whiskey glass. 'You go too far,' he said slowly.

'Then let's get something straight. The people of this country want change and change is what we are going to give them. And sooner than you might think. You, Chief Superintendent Broadbent, are either with us or you're against us. Should the former be the case, then I have no doubt at all that you are destined for great things. Declaring yourself against us, on the other hand, is likely to have a somewhat detrimental effect, not only on your career but, I suspect, on your marital status. Do I make myself clear?'

The bastard had him. For now. There was only one way that he was going to be able to turn the table on Owen and, for now, that was not within his grasp.

'Yes,' he said icily.

'Excellent Simon. I knew that we would be able to sort this out. Now, the witness's name and address.'

Broadbent reached across his desk and retrieved a sheet of paper from his in-tray. 'Jack Donaldson,' he read out loud. '105, Pelham Road, Wood Green. He'll be home by midday.'

'Thank you Simon. I think you'll find that Mr Donaldson will want to withdraw his statement and, of course, memory is a strange thing. One can be entirely clear about something one minute and riddled with doubt the next.'

Broadbent sighed. 'Go easy on Donaldson. He's an old man, for God's sake. The last thing we need is another…'

'Simon. We're not all thugs you know. Although, come to think of it, Kevin can be a bit excitable, I will admit that.'

Broadbent almost choked. 'You are not sending O'Neil to see him, surely to God.'

'We're getting rather religious aren't we? That's twice you've mentioned the Almighty in the last thirty seconds.'

'O'Neil is a bloody animal and you know it,' Broadbent protested.

Owen was silent for a moment. 'Well I can hardly send Jimmy now can I?' he said, with more than a hint of sarcasm.

Chapter Six

Monday, 2nd May 1977

I stood by the staff room kettle waiting for it to boil. I'd heard nothing further from Smith and it was bothering me. *What's with the silence?* It wasn't like Smith to give up. I'd heard nothing from him, or from the Service, in seven years. *So why now?*

I had been wracking my brain all weekend. Smith could have approached me at any time but he'd chosen to be at meeting at the town hall in Tottenham. Which made it likely that he had an interest in Karl's murder. Given Smith's history, that probably meant that they suspected far-right involvement. Which was hardly surprising. Half of Tottenham suspected it. But what exactly had he wanted with me? What had he said on the tube train? *"Needs must"*. Smith knew perfectly well that I'd never agree to work for him again. Nothing, not even the fact that Karl had been the victim, was going to persuade me to go there and Smith, of all people, knew why.

So what, exactly, did he want with me? And why had his appearance rattled me so badly? Smith had broken our agreement, certainly. And sure, by holding back now, he was toying with me. Pulling my strings. Just like he always had.

But Smith was only half the story. That was the truth of it. What was really getting to me was that I wanted to hear it. I'd spent seven years trying to put it behind me. Trying to forget all about Smith and the rest. But the truth was that like an alcoholic offered a sniff, I wanted more. I longed for it. Even though I knew that one swig and I'd want to sink the whole damned bottle. Still, a part of me wanted to know. 'Damn it,' I said under my breath.

'Damn what?' said a voice from behind me.

My stomach flipped. 'Jesus, Simone,' I said, turning to face her.

Simone grinned.

'You scared the hell out of me,' I said irritably.

Simone gave me one her penetrating stares. 'A penny for them?'

I breathed out and stood blinking at her.

'That bad eh?'

I shrugged. 'I've got a lesson.'

'Not yet you haven't. Sit down. I'll get the coffee and you can tell Auntie Simone all about it.'

I smiled, despite myself. *If only you knew.*

It was the same now as it had always been. Simone was one of very few people who I could genuinely call a friend. But she could never know. Nobody could. The passing of time had made it no better. If anything, it had made it worse.

I turned, walked the short distance to the nearest chair and slumped down into the padded seat.

Secrets and lies. They gnaw away at you and the deeper you bury them, the more they consume. Until there is little left of the person you once were. There had been times when it had felt like I was little more than an empty shell, going through the motions. But somehow, I'd managed to shove it to the background and, having got it there, to lock it away. I'd told myself a thousand times that it was behind me. And I had believed it too. Until now. That was what was getting to me. The realisation that I'd been kidding myself.

'Here,' said Simone, handing me a cup of steaming coffee and seating herself in the next chair to mine. 'So, what's up?'

These were my secrets. Nobody else's. I'd kept them to myself, completely, for so long that they'd become a part of me. Part of the way that I dealt with the world. The internal conversation that I had with myself. The life I could escape to in my head, whenever reality became a bit too much. Or too little.

'It's nothing.' I tried a smile but the look on Simone's face suggested that I had failed.

'Yeah, right,' said Simone, shaking her head.

'I just saw someone at the meeting the other night.' The words had slipped out before I could swallow them back.

Simone looked at me sideways. 'The meeting?'

I tried to think of something harmless to say. 'It was one of those blast-from-the-past moments. You know?'

'You mean an old flame?'

'Kind of,' I lied. 'No, not exactly.' Where was this going? Why was I even having the conversation?

'But kind of?'

'In a way.'

She took another gulp of coffee.

'It just reminded me of a past life' I said and then stopped myself. I had already said too much.

'As in, before you and Ted?'

I nodded. *If only you knew.*

Simone smiled. 'I can't actually imagine you without him. You're like peas in a pod. You always look so right together.'

'I know,' I said, forcing a smile. This time, with a little more success. 'We are. I'm just being morose, that's all.'

Simone frowned. She knew me well enough to know that I was trying my damnedest to close the conversation down.

'I think it's all this business with Karl,' I said.

Which should have shifted us onto safer territory. But it didn't. I could see the cogs turning behind her eyes.

'This blast-from-the past,' she said, after a short silence.

I looked at her.

'I take it that we're talking about the white bloke in the suit.'

So someone else had noticed him. 'What white bloke in a suit?' I said, dismissively.

Simone sucked her teeth. 'Don't give me that.'

I pulled a face.

'The one you stood, staring at.'

I waited.

'Like you'd seen a ghost.'

A ghost was exactly what I had seen. I needed to get out of this conversation. 'It was nothing.'

'Which is why I barely got a word out of you all evening.'

Had I really been so transparent? 'Look, I'd rather not talk about it. It was a long time ago. It just took me by surprise, that's all.'

'Have you seen him again?'

'What?'

'Since Wednesday?'

'No, of course not.'

She looked at me like she didn't believe it.

'It's nothing like that.'

'Liz Muir. How long have we known each other? Six years?'

'Seven,' I said, staring into my coffee.

'Seven then. So I think I know you well enough to tell that you've got something on your mind. Something you're not telling me.'

I remained silent.

'Do you want my advice?'

I shrugged. She was going to give it to me, invited or not.

'Don't go there. You and Ted are good together. I've seen the way he looks at you. He adores you.'

'I know he does,' I said. She was right. He did. 'I told you, its nothing like that.'

'Yeah? Well make sure it stays that way.'

'Sure,' I said. 'Like I said, I'm just being morose. I haven't been feeling right since we found out about Karl.'

If she believed that she'd believe anything.

I stepped out of the staffroom, letting the door swing closed behind me. For once, the corridor was empty. I paused, took a breath and ran my hands through my hair. More lies. It wasn't Karl's death that had been troubling me. It wasn't even Smith. It was what he was capable of bringing back into my life and the fact that a part of me still longed for it.

'Oh, Liz, I am glad I bumped into you.'

It was Teresa. Philpot's secretary. She had emerged from the door opposite. I hadn't even noticed her approach.

Teresa was a slim, mousy woman who rarely smiled, with a narrow mouth and a manner that made her look like she was sucking lemons. She was wearing a trouser suit. She always did. Simone and I used to joke that the trousers were so tight you could hear her arse cheeks squeak when she walked by. She and Philpot were made for each other.

'The Headmaster wishes to see you,' she said.

'Philpot? What does he want?'

Her look was one of undisguised disdain. 'Mr Philpot,' she said with emphasis, 'didn't say why he wants to see you. He simply asked me to tell you that he wishes to see you, at your earliest convenience.'

'Right. I'll drop in to see him at the next break.' I began to walk away.

'I believe that he's free now.'

I stopped and sighed. 'Now?'

'Yes.'

I glanced towards Philpot's office, which was a few yards further down the corridor. Whatever he wanted, I could have done without it at that moment, but Teresa had me cornered and the bloody woman knew it. She looked at me triumphantly and almost smiled. Almost, but not quite.

'He did say at your earliest convenience. Shall I see if he will see you now?'

It was obvious that she was enjoying my discomfort.

I stared at her. *Bitch*. 'Yes, alright. But I'm due in class in,' I looked at my watch, 'ten minutes.'

'I'm sure that will suffice.'

The secretary walked the few paces to the Headmaster's door, knocked and entered without waiting for a reply. After a few moments she re-emerged looking decidedly smug. 'The Headmaster will see you now,' she said, holding the door open.

I brushed past her, without further comment.

It was a modestly sized room with a wide window overlooking the main playground. On the wall was a wooden cabinet with glass doors which housed the school's trophies. The school's students were arranged into five houses and each year, having awarded points for such things as "sporting merit" and "community spirit", the Headmaster took great delight in awarding variously sized trophies to the houses with most points, along with an especially large trophy to the "House of The Year". Last year the winners had been Blue, Karl Dixon's old house.

Philpot was seated behind his desk, looking unusually solemn. It was not a good sign.

'Liz. Thank you for coming to see me,' he said, rather too formally for my liking. 'Please, take a seat.'

I decided to remain silent until I had worked out what was going on. It was usually the best strategy with Philpot. I pulled the seat out and sat down.

He looked at me from across the desk.

I raised my eyebrows, inviting him to say something.

'So,' he said, looking down at some papers.

I waited. I had absolutely no idea why he had asked to see me.

'So,' he said again.

It was not good news. That much was obvious.

'So?' I asked and waited.

'Well, I must say that I was a little hurt, Liz.'

'Hurt?' It was not a word that I had been expecting.

'Yes, I would have expected a little more from you. Especially given how closely we have worked together over the years.'

'Greg, If there's a problem, I'm sure…'

'It is not a problem,' he interrupted. 'It is just that I would have expected you to have spoken to me in advance, although I must say that I am surprised.'

Now I was feeling confused as well as uncomfortable. Whatever it was, Philpot was obviously upset about something. 'Look, I really have no idea what this is about, Greg.'

Philpot stared at me.

I tried to hold his gaze. The man did look hurt. Genuinely so. 'What is it?'

After a moment's further hesitation he passed me a sheet of paper from across the desk.

I read the first few lines. It took a few moments for them to register. 'There must be some mistake,' I said, struggling to make sense of it.

'Mistake?'

'Yes. I have no idea…', I said looking up at him and then back at the document. I read the first few lines again and then stopped. *What the hell is this?*

Philpot waited. I was struggling for words. For breath. At the top of the document, a name in the letterhead stood out. A name that I recognised. A name that made no sense at all.

'Liz, it is perfectly reasonable that you might want to move on. That is not the issue here.'

'I don't want to move on,' I stammered. I looked at the document again. It was a mistake. It had to be. *But the name…* 'I love it here. You know that, Greg.'

Philpot held up his hand. 'The least you could have done was to speak to me first.'

My eyes were still fixed on the name.

'And The NUGB, Liz? You? Seriously?'

The Nationalist Union of Great Britain. I had barely even registered it. 'It's a mistake, Greg.' But as I uttered the words, I knew that it was no mistake.

'A mistake?'

Peter Owen. A name from my past. A name that I had tried to bury. Every day, for the last seven years. *Peter Owen.* A face that, until that moment, I had banished from my thoughts, so completely, that I only saw it when I slept.

'Yes, of course, it's a bloody mistake. Why the hell would I want to work for the Union,' I snapped.

Philpot recoiled as though he'd been slapped.

As quickly as Owen's face had appeared in my mind, it was replaced by another.

'What are you saying Liz?'

Smith. It was no coincidence that he had appeared just days before and now this. I tried to pull my scattered thoughts together. This was his doing. It had to be. 'Look, Greg, I'm sorry. I don't know what the hell is going on here but I'll sort it out.'

Philpot looked completely lost and I can't say that I blamed him.

'What are you saying, Liz?'

I wasn't saying much but I was thinking, fast. Smith was behind this. It had his fingerprints all over it. And if I was right, then unless he was acting on his own, which I very much doubted, then the Service was also behind it. Just like they had been behind my place at Ealing, seventeen years previously. I knew how it worked and I knew, with a sudden stab of fear, that it was not going to be easy to escape.

'I'm saying that I will sort this out. I'm asking you to trust me.'

Philpot sat back in his seat.

I had known that I hadn't heard the last from Smith, but I had not imagined for a moment that he would go this far. I had underestimated him. They wanted me back. For some reason that, as yet, I could not fathom. And they were serious. This was serious. I felt it in the pit of my stomach. What was scaring me, such that I had to sit on my hands to stop them from shaking, was the thought that Smith would not have acted had he not been confident of success. Which meant that he had something more. An ace that he was yet to play. An ace that frightened me more than I had ever been frightened in my life before.

Chapter Seven

Wednesday 18th April 1962

I swung my legs out of the van and stepped down onto the pavement. They were stiff from sitting still for so long. The Commer was hardly the most comfortable of vehicles for a trip of any distance. The seats felt like they'd been stuffed with sawdust. I stood, stamping my feet and stretching my arms.

'Thank God we're here. I've been dying for a wee for the last three quarters of an hour.' Sheila Mulhaven had climbed out of the van behind me. She was the only other female to have made the trip with us, northwards.

I liked Sheila, to a point, but God, could she talk. I had stopped listening to her as we joined the new motorway at Watford, pre-occupied as I was with the day ahead and how I was going to get any new information back to Smith without it becoming obvious to the others.

'Why didn't you say? I'm sure that Martin would have stopped,' I offered.

'Oh, sure. He'd have followed me up the grass verge too, to watch me pee. Bloody pervert.'

She had a point. There was definitely something unsettling about Martin Reynolds. The way he looked at women, for one thing. It had made me feel uncomfortable on more than one occasion and, as a result, I tried never to be alone with the man. I pulled a face. 'You're not wrong there. What is it with him? He gives me the creeps.'

'Mind you, he would have regretted it,' Sheila said, grinning.

I could believe it. Sheila's favourite sport was rugby and she had the build to match. Rumour had it that she would have been selected for the university's first team had women been allowed. Thankfully, for the opposition at least, while she was allowed to train with the men, she was not allowed to play for the first team. The thought of her charging towards you would be enough to send anyone in their right mind - man, woman or beast - running in the opposite direction.

'Can you help us out with the banners, ladies?'

'Oh, sorry John. Yes, of course,' I said, walking toward the back of the van.

'No can do,' said Sheila. 'There's a cafe over there. Call of nature, John.'

'Righto,' he replied, cheerily.

We unloaded the banners.

John Taggart was, on the face of it, a decent enough sort of chap. His broad, Western Isles accent sometimes made him difficult to understand, but once you got used to it, he appeared affable enough. He came from a wealthy family and was extremely intelligent. Possibly one of the most intelligent people I met while I was at Ealing. He wasn't bad looking either. Tall, dark and handsome. Well almost. Until he got around to talking politics. There was nothing handsome or affable about his political views. He was about as anti-semitic as it was possible to be. It seemed incongruous that such an otherwise mild mannered and intelligent man, should hold such extreme views. Where had they come from? Surely not from his upbringing in the Western Isles.

'Any idea when Peter is due to get here?' I asked, as we unloaded the last of the banners and bags.

'Aye. He said he'd meet us in *The Bull*, for a briefing at eleven.'

A briefing. 'Why didn't he travel up in the van with the rest of us?' I knew the answer perfectly well, but I asked it to see whether Taggart would reveal anything further of Peter's plans.

'Och, you know what they're like, him being a lecturer. They get a wee bit twitchy about the company he keeps.'

Nothing I didn't already know, but why the briefing in The Bull? If he knew, John was keeping tight lipped. I decided to risk another question. 'I thought we were going to join the rally outside the Town Hall?'

'That's better,' said Sheila who had reappeared suddenly out of nowhere.

'So we will, but perhaps Peter has something else up his sleeve,' Taggart said cryptically.

'Well, I'm up for that, whatever it is,' said Sheila grinning.

So he did know. But I couldn't risk another question.

'Well, he can't have you. We'll be needing all the muscle we can get,' John said, putting his arm around Sheila's bulging shoulder, 'for the main event.'

The others had gathered themselves together and, with banners and bags in tow, we set off through the back streets in search of *The Bull*. Martin took the lead. It surprised me how well he seemed to know Birmingham. I found it difficult to tell one street from the next. Row upon row of semi-derelict warehouses and shops, or drab terraced houses, interspersed with patches of furious development, throwing featureless blocks of concrete-grey up, angrily, into the heavens.

'He's a Brummie,' said Sheila in answer to my unspoken question.

'Martin?' I said. I replayed his South London accent in my head. 'Are you sure?'

'Sure I'm sure. His family moved to Tooting when he was twelve.'

'Well, you'd never have guessed it.'

'They beat the Brummie out of him at school. He dropped it pretty damn quick.'

I glanced across at Sheila.

'You seem to know rather a lot about Martin,' I said nudging her in the ribs. Which carried with it a certain risk, but I got away with it.

'I got drunk with him once.'

I looked at her with my mouth open.

'And only once.'

'You got drunk with Martin Reynolds? Why would you want to get drunk with Martin Reynolds?'

Sheila grinned. 'Oh, you know me, Liz. I'll get drunk with anyone. As long as they're buying.'

The Bull didn't look particularly inviting but it had been a long, hard slog with the banners and bags and, by the time that we marched into the pub's car park, I was more than ready for a pint. The pub was housed in a modern brick building, with stark metal window frames that were glazed, on the ground floor at least, with wired glass. I wondered whether the wire was to prevent bricks being throne in or bar stalls being thrown out. From the cracks in several of the panes and the noisy presence of an Alsatian, straining against a chain in a pen at the far end of the car park, my guess was that trouble was a not infrequent visitor.

Peter was standing at the bar, talking to the barman who was pulling pints and loading them onto a tray. I glanced around the pub. There was a smattering of others. No more than three or four. Regulars, by the look of them. Men in donkey jackets, coming off the early shift at one of the local factories or coal yards, having a pint before heading home.

We found a group of tables in one corner of the pub and soon Peter came across with a tray full of beers. 'Will you get the others, John? I could only carry six. Here.'

He handed John what looked like a five pound note. A good deal more than John would need to pay for a dozen pints.

Not for the first time, I wondered where Peter Owen's money came from. It was by no means the first time that I'd seen him flash it about. There always seemed to be money to fund the group's activities. Like money to fill up the Commer with petrol. It occurred to me that I'd never heard anyone in the group discussing money. It seemed to be taken for granted that the money was there. Which was very odd indeed for a predominantly student group.

As this thought crossed my mind, Peter caught my eye. He smiled. I blushed. Damn it, I always blushed. What was it about him? Smith had wanted me to get close to him, for obvious reasons. I had anticipated, given Owen's political allegiance, that this would be a challenge and that I might struggle to mask my true feelings about the man. But in fact, from my very first meeting with him, I'd been drawn to him.

It was John who had introduced us. He'd come across to me in the college canteen one lunchtime and said that Peter had been impressed by my comments at the Mosley meeting. Which had, of course, been my intention. When, a few days later, I had met him in the bar at Ealing, I had been completely wrong-footed.

Peter had been charming. Intelligent. Polite. Well spoken. An undeniably good looking man. Impeccably well dressed. All the things I would not have associated with a right wing activist. But there had been something else. Something extraordinary. It had happened in the moment our eyes met. I can only describe it by saying that it was as though, behind our words and gestures, there was another exchange taking place. A silent greeting. A meeting of souls. And in that moment, I knew, without speaking or thinking it, that I had come face to face with the person who was going to change my life forever. It sounds like nonsense to say so now but that is how it was, truly. I had never experienced the like of it before and I don't expect ever to do so again. It had taken me completely by surprise.

It should have terrified me. If I had known then what I know now, it would have terrified me. But if I was afraid, it was not Peter Owen who frightened me. It was the knowledge that, because of his politics and my work for Smith, I was going to have to betray him. As we spoke and as I struggled to control the flush that I could feel rising from my neck across my cheeks, something I had never been able to control since the latter years of my childhood, it was not fear but fascination that already held me in thrall.

We had to pull three tables together so that we could sit in a reasonably tight huddle. Peter was keen that we should not be overheard. There were twelve of us there, including myself, Sheila Mulhaven, Martin Reynolds, John Taggart and, of course, Peter. He lit a cigarette and waited for John to hand around the remainder of the drinks, before calling the group to order. 'Alright. Is everyone clear about the purpose of the day?' he asked quietly.

There were a few nods and several vague faces.

'The rally, on the square behind the town hall, begins at one o'clock.' He looked at his watch. 'That is in a little under two hours time. Gaitskell is due to begin speaking at two-thirty, which is roughly when the Act is expected to be given Royal assent.'

He looked around the group. 'You will meet the others in Holliday Street at twelve, by the old canal wharf. John you know the place?'

John nodded.

'Good. Yesterday, I spoke to Rory from the local group. So far as he is aware, the police have no idea what we're planning.' He looked around the group again.

Nobody said a word. They all had their eyes on him. I kept my face as neutral as I could, even though I knew that the authorities were well aware of what had been planned. They knew it because I had passed the information to Smith myself.

'If all goes to plan, you will get to the Town Hall just as Gaitskell begins to speak. The plan is to take them by surprise, disrupt the rally and, if you can, force Gaitskell from the stage.'

Peter waited. 'Keep your banners down until you get into the square. The local group will take the lead. You will only raise the banners once you have secured a place, as close to the front as you can.'

Martin put his hand up. It seemed such an absurd gesture. Peter nodded at him.

'You said "you". Does that mean you won't be with us?'

'I won't be in the square, no. I have alternative plans for you, Liz and me.'

Martin looked surprised.

'I need your local knowledge,' Peter said, answering the question in Martin's face.

I glanced from Martin to John. His eyes remained steady. He knew exactly what Peter was planning for the three of us. I shifted my gaze to Peter and there it was again. The smile. He was enjoying my uncertainty.

'And what alternative plans would they be?' asked Martin, grinning.

'We will discuss that in a moment, after the rest of you are on your way,' Peter said with finality. There was a limit to what he was going to tell them.

I waited.

'Suffice it to say,' he said, looking around the group, 'that it might help you if, as you are arriving in the square, there is a small distraction elsewhere to draw away the attention of the police.'

Damn it. What was he up to? There was only so much that three of us could do. But it was evidently going to be serious enough to pull the police away from the rally. I was already worrying about whether I was going to be able to get word of it back to Smith.

'If there is any trouble and you lose each other, meet back at the van by five at the latest.'

He looked at John, who nodded silently. 'Liz and Martin will try to find you before you leave, but don't wait for them if they're not there by five.'

'Hang on a minute,' I said, interrupting him. I was not about to be left in the middle of Birmingham, especially if there was going to be trouble.

Peter smiled. 'It's alright Liz, if we can't get you both back to the van, I'll drive you back to London myself.'

I felt immediately foolish.

There was a murmur of voices. Peter waited for it to subside. 'Is everyone clear?'

Sheila looked none too happy. I think she'd been hoping to join Peter's little elite group, but she nodded, along with the others.

'Alright. Finish your beers and lets get on with it,' Peter said, downing his in one and banging the glass down on the table.

We waited while the others filed out of the pub. Martin had got to his feet and was having a hushed conversation with John. Peter offered me a cigarette. 'Are you alright? You look nervous.'

I hesitated. I was nervous but not for the reason he had assumed. Still, it wouldn't hurt if that is what he thought. I declined the cigarette. 'A little,' I said quietly.

He reached across and put his hand on my arm. 'Don't worry. It will be fine.'

It should have been an uncomfortable moment, but it wasn't. His touch was like electricity. It gave me goose pimples and I was certain that my cheeks and neck were blazing. Crazily, I wanted to lean across and kiss him. For the smallest fraction of a moment, my body almost did. Like it was acting on its own. Nothing to do with me. On autopilot. What was I thinking? *Get a bloody grip.* 'I think I'd better visit the bathroom before we go. Do you mind?' I said, a little shakily.

'No, go ahead,' he said, releasing my arm.

I got up and walked across to the bar. I had it in my mind to ask the barman if there was a pay phone in the hall outside, but as I approached him, I spotted the phone on the wall behind the bar. There was no way I was going to be able to call Smith without Peter and Martin seeing me do it.

I had already caught the barman's eye. 'Toilets?' I said, awkwardly.

He pointed to the left. 'Outside, turn right.'

When I returned to the bar, Peter and Martin had evidently discussed Peter's plan and were getting ready to leave. 'Come on, I'll tell you what we're going to do on the way.'

I picked up my jacket and followed Peter and Martin out into the car park. Peter walked over to his car. It was a rather smart looking grey *Humber Super Snipe*, with green leather seats. We got in. Peter wanted Martin in the front to give directions. The Humber's front bench seat looked wide enough for three, but I didn't much fancy being squeezed up against Martin Reynolds. We pulled out of the car park. I waited while Martin gave directions.

'Are you sure we'll be able to park around the back?' Peter asked. 'I'd rather not be noticed.'

'I am and, if we park on the street at the end of the alley, it's only a short walk, so we ought to be able to get in and out without any problems.'

'Excellent.'

I waited and tried to work out where we were. I'd studied a map of Birmingham a few days earlier, but in truth, I had little idea where Peter was taking us.

We drove along a main street full of shoppers, passing what looked like an old, white-bricked cinema on our left. There were blue painted hoardings across the front of the building, announcing that a new *Littlewoods* was being constructed behind the façade. It didn't look to me like much building work was going on. 'Alright. Is someone going to tell me where we are going?' I ventured.

Martin looked at me over his shoulder and grinned. I could smell his breath. God, he was revolting.

'We're going to pay the local socialists a visit,' Peter announced, keeping his eyes on the road ahead. 'I am banking on them being out for the day.'

'I bloody well hope so,' said Martin.

Chapter Eight

The alley behind the row of buildings would have been wide enough for the Humber, but it would also have been impossible to turn the car around and Peter didn't want to have to reverse out, for what turned out to be understandable reasons. The buildings appeared to be mostly shops. Each had a small yard to the rear, bounded by a low brick wall adjoining the alley. The yards were mostly full of bins and rubbish, although occasionally there was a washing line or some other sign that people were living in flats above the shops.

After a few minute's walk, Martin stopped outside a black wooden gate into one of the yards. 'This is it.'

'Are you sure?' Peter asked.

Martin nodded.

'Good.'

Martin tried the gate and it opened at the first attempt. We entered and Martin closed it behind us.

'Hurry. I'd rather not be overseen,' Peter said, over his shoulder.

We walked swiftly across the small yard, into the space between two short extensions that had obviously been added to the buildings at some point. We stopped outside a half glazed back door. Peter had handed us gloves and balaclavas as we pulled up in the car. He now removed his from the bag he had slung over his shoulder, put them on and nodded at us to follow.

My hands were shaking as I did so. Peter grasped my arm. 'Stay calm, Liz,' he said quietly. 'There is nothing to worry about. They are just a precaution.'

I tried to smile, as I slipped the balaclava over my head.

Peter removed a reel of tape from his pocket. He pulled off several strips and stuck them to one of the door's glass panes. Then he pulled out a small, blunt headed hammer from his bag. 'Stand back,' he instructed.

Martin and I both took a short step backwards.

He gave the window a single tap in the middle of the pane. It cracked in a surprisingly neat circular pattern. Peter put the hammer back in his bag and gently pushed just enough glass inwards to make a hole. It tinkled to the floor. I glanced about nervously.

'It's alright. There is nobody at home,' Peter said.

'How can you be sure?' I replied, tensely.

'They'll all be in the square behind the town hall. Bound to be.'

Peter began widening the hole in the window pane by removing small shards of glass. He placed them carefully on the ground. As soon as it was big enough, he put his arm through the hole. I heard the lock click.

'That was good of them,' he said. He pulled his arm back out and opened the door. 'The idiots left the key in the door. And there I was thinking that I was going to force it.'

We entered as silently as we could. Martin closed the door quietly behind us.

We found ourselves in the building's kitchen. To say that it had seen better days would be an understatement. Once, the walls would have been bright yellow, but now they were an unpleasant shade of nicotine brown. An old cupboard which could have done with a lick of paint stood against one wall and there were high shelves full of old pans. An overflowing ash tray was in the centre of the kitchen table. There were empty beer bottles on just about every surface. An old butler sink in the corner was loaded with dirty cups and plates.

'How the other half live,' Martin said. I couldn't tell whether he was grinning behind his balaclava.

I was thankful for mine. It helped to cover my nervousness. I was sure that the police were going to burst in behind us at any moment. 'It reminds me of my Grandmother's kitchen, when I was a kid,' I said, trying to make small talk. 'Except that she would never have allowed it to get into this state. If there is one thing she couldn't stand…'

Peter grasped my arm. 'Alright,' he said calmly, looking at me through the slit in his balaclava.

For a moment, our eyes locked. I took a breath.

He waited.

I exhaled.

'Now, let's do this methodically,' Peter said, removing his hand. 'According to Rory, there are three rooms. The general office is at the front. There's also a smaller office and a store room. We're looking for the membership records. I want names and addresses.'

He looked at Martin as though he was going to say something but appeared to change his mind. 'I want every filing cabinet emptied and searched. Keep anything else you find of any interest. Got it?'

We both nodded.

'Martin, you take the back rooms. Liz and I will take the front.'

Martin disappeared through the kitchen door.

'Ready?' Peter asked.

'Ready.'

We made our way along a corridor which ran from the kitchen at the back of the building to the front office. As we passed a small office door to our left, I could see Martin already emptying the contents of a filing cabinet and scattering papers over the floor.

The front office was a large open space with a counter at one end, a row of cupboards against one wall and a large wooden table in the middle of the room, around which was a scattering of office chairs. Presumably the building had been a shop at some time in its life. The counter now functioned as a reception of sorts. Peter gestured towards the cupboards. I walked across to them and began emptying their contents, checking documents as I went. Peter started to empty the shelves under the counter. I watched him out of the corner of my eye.

The cupboards were full of campaign material. Leaflets, posters and copies of the Birmingham Star, the local socialist newspaper. There was little of interest. 'There's nothing much here,' I said.

Peter had removed a pile of box files and emptied their contents on the table. We sorted through the papers together.

After several minutes, Martin appeared with an arm full of loose leaf files. 'I've got them.'

'Show me,' Peter said.

Martin spread the files out on the table. Peter pulled the papers from each of them. 'Excellent,' he said, gathering papers together and stuffing them in his bag. 'Have you checked the store room?'

'Yup. Nothing much. General correspondence and financial records mostly.'

'Fine. I think we've got what we came for. I want everything else piled on the table.'

Martin disappeared again and returned a few minutes later with another arm full of files. He dumped them on the table.

Peter stood back. 'Ready?'

Martin removed something from his pocket. It was small yellow tin. It took a few moments for me to register what it was. I gasped, my stomach in my mouth. 'What are you doing?'

Martin hesitated.

'Go ahead,' said Peter.

'Wait. You can't be serious.' I was beginning to panic now.

Peter walked across the room towards me.

I backed away.

'Liz, we came here to create a diversion.'

My mind was racing. 'But there's a flat upstairs. There could be people up there,' I stammered.

'There isn't. The flat is empty.'

'Do you know that?' I yelled.

'Yes, I do,' Peter said calmly.

'How?'

'Because Rory told me.'

'And what if he's wrong? What if there is a family up there? Somebody's grandparents. Children.'

'Liz, there isn't anyone up there. I promise you.'

'And even if there is, they'll be coons or paki's. Bound to be,' Martin added.

Peter looked at him. 'Shut up Martin. The flat upstairs is empty. It has been for years.'

This wasn't happening. Working for Smith was one thing, but I couldn't be party to this. People could be killed. Nothing could justify that. Nothing. I pulled off my balaclava. 'You didn't tell me.'

'I know.'

He stood completely still, facing me.

'You said nothing about setting fire to the place.'

'I'm sorry. I should have told you.'

'Yes, you should have told me.'

'And what would you have done?'

I hesitated. I would have warned Smith. I would have stopped them. I would have blown my cover and that would have been an end to it. And then it dawned on me that I was in danger of blowing it now.

'Liz...'

I looked away. If I didn't regain control, I'd would be all over. 'Let me check upstairs,' I said.

'What?'

'Let me check. That there is nobody up there.'

'Liz, come on.'

'No. I can't be party to putting the lives of people at risk. Whoever they are. I believe in the cause, the same as you do. I want the same things that you want. That's why I joined. But murdering innocent people wasn't part of the deal.'

Martin laughed. 'Oh, for God's sake. I told you in the pub that we should have brought somebody else.'

Peter remained silent.

I told you in the pub that we should have brought somebody else. I stared at Martin. *Scumbag.* And then back at Peter. 'Maybe you should have chosen somebody else. I don't have a problem with that. But I am here and I am not going to be party to it. End of.'

Martin started to speak but Peter held up his hand.

There was a tense stand off between the three of us.

'Alright. So we check, but Martin will do it. I don't want any more problems.'

'What?' Martin sounded incredulous. 'Are you serious? And what if there are people up there? What am I going to say? Excuse me, but we're about to set fire to the building?'

Peter turned to him calmly. 'There is nobody up there, but I want us to be absolutely certain.' He walked over to the reception desk and produced a set of keys from underneath the counter.

'Here,' he said, tossing the keys to Martin. 'Try these. There are bound to be stairs up to the flat,' he said, gesturing towards the main door. 'Knock on the door. If there is no reply, break it down and check every room. If you find anyone, tell them that they have two minutes to get out. We'll wait for you.'

Martin looked at him and for a moment I thought that he was going to refuse.

'Now,' Peter said.

Martin walked across to the main door and tried several keys before he found the right one. He undid the lock, opened the door and stepped out into the hall. I heard his foot steps on the stairs.

Peter and I stood staring at each other. He took a step towards me, removing his gloves and balaclava. 'I'm sorry. I should have warned you.'

My heart was pounding. I could not look away from him.

He touched my face. 'Liz, I'm sorry. Truly. It was too much for you. I should have known.'

He pulled me towards him. I did not resist. I couldn't. As I looked into his eyes, every other thought faded. I could see only him. I could feel only him. When I kissed him, I knew that he was all that I wanted.

I could already hear bells ringing in the distance as we got into the Humber.

'Take it easy Martin. We don't want any attention. Just pull away, normally,' Peter said quietly.

I looked over my shoulder. Black smoke was already rising into the air from the row of buildings behind us.

I should have been horrified by what we had done. I should have been thinking of the families living in the flats next to the now blazing Socialist Party office.

'I still say that it was crazy to call the fire brigade,' Martin said irritably, as he pulled the Humber out into the middle of the road. 'The upstairs flat was empty.'

'I know. But Liz was right. We had no way of knowing how quickly the fire would spread. Raising the alarm was a sensible precaution.' Peter said it without turning his head. 'Besides, a few fire engines will add nicely to the chaos.'

'Fine. Let's just hope we're not stopped.'

'Like I said, just take it easy.' Peter looked at his watch. 'Right now the police are going to have enough on their hands. We've just made sure of that. They have no reason to stop us. Just take us to the drop off point, nice and slow.'

I should have been trying to work out what I was going to say to Smith. How I was going to explain my failure to warn him. But I wasn't thinking of any of these things. I was thinking about the man sitting in the passenger seat, next to Martin.

Until that moment, when his lips had finally touched mine, I'd managed, somehow, to keep my feelings for him in check. That there was a bond between us was beyond doubt. We both knew it. I could see it in his eyes and in the crease of his mouth, each time we spoke. But Peter was a married man and my contact with him had another purpose. A purpose, which as Smith kept reminding me, meant that a relationship with him was out of the question.

But in that moment, everything had changed. It had been a crossroads and I had chosen a path. Or perhaps the path had chosen me because it didn't feel as though the decision had really been mine at all.

I'd never, until then, been a believer in fate. The idea that certain key events in your life could be predetermined by some external force. But sitting there, in the back of Peter's Humber, it felt as though a train of events had been set in motion, that neither Peter nor or I would be able to stop. It was an unfamiliar feeling. There had been times in my life up to that point, when I had been impulsive, certainly. But I had always, ultimately, steered my own course. Now, for the first time, life had taken its own turn and I had absolutely no idea where it was going to take me.

You'd have thought that it would have scared me but it didn't. It excited me. Gazing out of the Humber's window, as the streets of Birmingham flashed by anonymously, it felt exhilarating to be on a journey which I needn't try to steer. Perhaps it was a madness of sorts. A dereliction of responsibility. But there, in the back of Peter's car, I closed my eyes and felt myself letting go.

Martin turned the car off the main road, and drove down a ramp, into a car park beneath a large, grey, block of flats. We pulled into a parking space and Martin switched off the engine. The car park was dimly lit and three-quarters empty.

'Liz, pass me the bag, would you?' Peter said, after a pause.

I reached across to the bag which he had thrown onto the seat beside me and handed it to him.

'You have the number?'

'Yes, of course,' Martin said, flatly.

'Good. Remember, give them the files we took and nothing else and make sure you're wearing gloves when you handle them.'

'What are we going to do with the bag?'

'We are going to do nothing with the bag. You, on the other hand, are going to burn it. Find somewhere out of sight on your way back to the others.'

Martin gave Peter a sideways glance.

'Liz and I are going to drive straight back to London. Liz,' he said turning towards me. 'Is that alright with you?'

'Sure,' I said, trying to sound casual.

'Tell the others not to wait for us and, remember, there is to be absolutely no discussion about our activities. I'll wait until you come back down with the empty bag, in case there are any problems. Clear?'

Martin turned and looked at me. I couldn't tell what he was thinking, but I didn't much like the look he gave me. He turned back to Peter. 'Clear.'

Martin got out of the car with the bag, walked across the car park and disappeared up a flight of concrete steps. Peter slid across the bench seat into the driver's position. He turned towards me. 'Come on,' he said, gesturing to me to join him. 'Unless you want to spend the journey back to London in the back?'

I shook my head.

He smiled.

I got out, walked around to the passenger door and got in beside him.

We were silent for a moment.

He turned and looked at me. 'You look… different.'

'Do I?'

He smiled. 'Yes. Scared?'

'No, not scared.'

His smile broadened. 'I hope not. There's no need. We've known each other, how long?'

I shrugged. 'Long enough.'

'It was always going to happen. Sooner or later. Don't you think?'

I nodded. 'I've known it all along. I just didn't know that it was going to happen today.'

'So, now it has.'

I reached for his hand. 'And now, I want more.'

'You live in Hanwell, don't you?'

I nodded. 'How do you know that?'

'Oh, I have my sources.'

'And have your sources told you that I live on my own?'

'Perhaps.'

I thought for a moment and then the penny dropped. 'Sheila bloody Mulhaven,' I said laughing. 'That woman has got a mouth as wide as the Mersey Tunnel.'

He laughed. 'True. So now I suppose that I am just going to have to see you to your front door.'

'I would like that,' I said, just as Martin appeared from the stair well. He looked across at us and nodded.

Peter reached for the ignition and started the car.

Chapter Nine

Monday, 2nd May 1977

I let the door swing closed behind me and walked briskly towards the car park. I had spent the day avoiding Simone. It wasn't that I didn't want to speak to her. I was desperate to speak to someone, but I couldn't. Smith was behind the letter that Philpot had received. I had no doubt about that. But to what end? I'd thought about it endlessly but to no avail. I was not going to find out until I spoke to him and yet he was the last person on the planet I wanted to speak to.

As I climbed the steps to the car park, I glanced behind me. No sign of Simone or of anyone else.

Smith had set up the whole thing. It had to have been him. He knew full well that I would never agree to it. Not willingly. Which could only mean that he had the means to compel me. But he couldn't know. It wasn't possible. Nobody knew. And yet, as I walked across the car park, I knew in my gut that he did. It was the only explanation.

Oddly, the car was unlocked but I hardly noticed it. I suppose my head was somewhere else. I got into the driver's seat and sat for a moment, trying to put my thoughts into some sort of order. Trying to force down the fear that had spread from my stomach, where it had been sitting all day, twisting my guts. I glanced over my shoulder, towards the school and, as I did, Simone came out of the main doors and started to walk towards me.

Flustered, I turned the key in the ignition, reversed quickly out of the space and drove towards the ramp which led from the car park up onto the street beyond. I looked in my rear view mirror, expecting to see Simone in the distance. But it wasn't Simone who I saw. It was Smith, staring back at me. I slammed my foot on the brake. The car screeched to a halt.

'Get out,' I said, panting hard.

'Liz, I'm sorry. I startled you.'

I said nothing.

'We need to talk.'

I was gripping the steering wheel so hard, it was making my knuckles hurt. 'I said, get out.'

'I can't do that.'

'Get out,' I screamed. 'Get out, you bastard. Get the fuck out of my car.'

There was a moment's silence.

'Your friend has already seen us.'

I looked over my shoulder. Simone was walking towards us. Even at a distance, I could see the look of concern on her face.

'Unless, of course, you want to explain to her who I am and why I'm here.'

'I don't know why you're here,' I said between clenched teeth. 'I don't know why you're doing this. I just want you gone. Leave me alone.' I was sobbing now.

'Liz, I'm sorry but that is just not going to happen. You either drive away now, or we are both going to have some explaining to do.'

I looked in my rear view mirror. Simone was less than twenty feet away.

I put my foot down. The car lurched forward and up the ramp toward the street. At the top, I turned hard to the left. The car rolled violently and, for a moment, I thought that it was going to turn over.

'Good. Now turn left again at the bottom of the road.'

I did as he asked. 'Where are we going?'

'Alexandra Palace. The car park by the old television studio. Nice view.'

It took less than ten minutes to get there. He was right about the view. Alexandra Palace sits on the top of hill overlooking Hornsey, Highgate and much of North London. From the top, you can see as far St Paul's and the City.

I pulled into a parking space. Smith got out and walked around to the front passenger door. I had it in mind to drive away while he was out of the car, but it was pointless. I had no choice but to listen to him.

Smith opened the door and got in. We sat for several moments in silence, transfixed by the view, before Smith broke the spell. 'We need your help. The Nationalist Union of Great Britain are planning something. We don't know what it is but intelligence suggests that it's serious.' He waited.

I closed my eyes.

'We have been trying to get someone on the inside for months but they are being careful. Owen is suspicious and they have a new head of security who is vetting everyone, personally.' He waited again.

I said nothing.

'After a great deal of effort, we were able to...' he hesitated, 'create a vacancy.'

'What vacancy?' I said quietly.

'Owen's press and publicity advisor, Sheila Mulhaven. Do you know her?'

I thought for a moment. 'Yes I know... I knew her,' I corrected myself. 'She was part of the Ealing group.'

Smith waited.

'Their Head of Security. Who is he?' I asked.

'His name is Jimmy Dobson. Does the name mean anything to you?'

'No. Should it?'

'No, but it was worth a shot. He appeared on our radar last year. Prior to that, we have nothing. No record of him. No national insurance number. No record of his birth. No history at all.'

'So he's using a false identity.'

Smith looked at me. 'Evidently…'

'But you're worried about him?'

'To a point.'

'So why don't you pull him?'

'We've tried.' Smith hesitated. 'But Mr Dobson is being protected.'

I wanted to ask more, but I needed him to get to the point. 'What has this got to do with me?' I waited.

'Owen will appoint you as Mulhaven's successor.'

I turned to face him. 'Are you mad?' I couldn't believe what I was hearing. He was mad if he thought that Peter Owen was simply going to appoint me, as though nothing had ever happened between us. 'You can't be serious.'

'Oh, we're serious, Liz. In fact we're banking on it. You and Owen were…'

I closed my eyes. 'History. Ancient history.'

Smith was thoughtful. 'Maybe. But he trusted you. Completely. In fact he never doubted you. Not for a moment.'

'I was nothing to him,' I said, with more bitterness than I had intended. 'I was just another of his conquests. He is still married, I take it?'

Smith said nothing.

'Yes, of course he is,' I said, bitterly.

'He's a womaniser. We both know that. You perhaps more than anyone.'

I laughed. 'Oh, I know it. You better believe it.'

There was a moment's silence between us.

'Your application will appeal to him. He'll be intrigued. Besides, you have an excellent CV. He won't find anyone better. He won't want to find anyone better.'

'Forget it. It isn't going to happen.'

Smith was thoughtful. 'Think about it, Liz.'

'No.' I didn't need to think about it. 'I can't. You know I can't. I did my tour of duty and it nearly killed me. You know that.'

'I know that you resigned from the Service because you couldn't cope. Because you wanted a different life. A family. Children. I understood that. But that was seven years ago, Liz. And this is now. We need you.'

'No.' I shook my head. 'No. You're wasting your time.'

'Owen will take you into his confidence. He will have no reason not to. You were as committed to the cause as anyone.'

'I walked away from the fucking cause.'

'As far as he was concerned, you ended your involvement with politics because of your relationship with him. He will assume that you wish to resume your support for the cause and, if he thinks that there might be more to it than that, that perhaps you are still interested in him, then all well and good.'

All well and good. My relationship with Peter Owen had taken me to the brink and now Smith wanted me to go back there. I'd sink. He knew that. He was already tying the bricks to my ankles. 'No. I can't do what you're asking. I've got children. I will not put them at risk.'

'You won't need to put them at risk. Owen need never know. He has no idea that you are married or that you have children. You're Liz Muir. The same Liz Muir he knew seven years ago.'

'You're crazy. I use my maiden name at school, that's all. Everyone knew me as Miss Muir. It was just easier that way. Peter Owen might be lots of things, but he isn't stupid. It will take him five minutes to discover the truth.'

Smith waited for me to finish.

'And what about Ted? He'd never understand me getting a job at the NUGB.'

'He won't need to. You'll give him the same cover story that you will give your colleagues and anybody else who wants to know. You have been offered a secondment to the Polytechnic in Hackney. It's a great opportunity that you can't refuse. So, it will require you to work longer hours, but it will be good for your career. Ted will understand. They all will.'

He had it all worked out. 'Lies. You know what living like that did to me. I couldn't do it then and I can't do it now.'

Smith smiled ruefully. 'You managed it well enough for a time. It gets to us all in the end. But a few months, Liz. That's all it will take.'

'And what about this new head of security? If he's any good at all, he'll spot me a mile off. All he'll have to do is follow me home. I'm not putting Ted and the children at risk.'

'You will use our safe house in Finsbury Park. That is the address we gave on your application form. You will return there after work. Draw the curtains. Put the lights on a timer and thirty minutes later, leave by the back door. In the morning you will return there, enter via the back door and will leave there to go to work. To all intents and purpose, it will be your home.'

I shook my head. 'But Philpot just got a reference request from the NUGB. He thinks I've lost my mind and so will my colleagues. All it will take is one of them to call me at home and speak to Ted and the whole thing will come apart.'

'I am sorry about the reference request. We had hoped to intercept it, but it slipped through. Greg Philpot will be spoken to tomorrow. He will be given the cover story and it will be made very clear to him that it is to be adhered to for reasons of national security. Your colleagues will be told the same. Six months, Liz. Do it right and it won't even take that long. Find out what they're planning and we'll take it from there. You walk away.'

'I can't. It isn't going to happen.'

'Liz, please.'

'And if I say no?'

Smith was silent.

I had to know. He had an ace in his pocket. It was obvious, but I needed to know for sure.

'Don't make me threaten you. There is no need.'

'Oh, there is every need,' I spat back. 'I won't do this voluntarily. Do you understand? I won't go back,' I said, turning towards him. 'So let's hear it.'

Smith looked me straight in the eye. 'Then your husband will discover that you haven't been entirely honest with him.'

My eyes wavered. I had been determined that they wouldn't. But they did. I looked away.

'Because you haven't been honest with him have you?'

I bowed my head. *Bastard.*

'Have you told anyone the truth, Liz. Family? Friends? Anyone at all?'

'What truth?' I said bitterly. I had to know.

'That you've never loved your husband.'

I laughed. 'You know nothing.'

'Oh I know, Liz.'

'Yeah? What do you know?'

'I know that you've used him.'

'No.' I shook my head.

'That you have taken him for a fool.'

'Get out. Get out of my fucking car.'

'Does Ted know that while you were dating him, you were screwing Owen?'

Tears were running down my face and dripping into my lap.

'Does he know that Harry isn't his?'

'Liar,' I shouted. 'Liar.' I turned to hit him but he caught my wrist. I struggled to free myself, but he would not let go. He'd never let me go.

Smith shook his head. 'Liar? I don't think so and neither will Ted.'

Chapter Ten

Saturday, 21st December 1968

I had learned to detest parties and Christmas parties most of all. I was thirty and a primary school teacher working in London's East End. All that School parties did for me was to highlight that, among my colleagues, I was the only one who wasn't married or, at very least, in a relationship. Or a normal relationship.

All I wanted was to be with Peter. It was all that I had ever wanted. A home. Children. A family. The normal things. Yet, it was my feelings for him that had prevented it. That would always prevent it. Six years of begging him, of trying everything I could to convince him to leave his wife. All for nought. How could I have allowed this to happen? Could it really be six years? He was no nearer leaving her now, than he had been at the beginning. That was the truth, whether I chose to acknowledge it or not.

I had tried to end it with him. Over and over again. It wasn't simply that he was married or the affairs with pretty, young students that I had discovered but refused to acknowledge. It was that for some reason, a reason that I would never truly understand, what mattered most to him was maintaining his sham of a marriage. He might promise that he would divorce her. He did promise it. Next year. The year after. Always at some unattainable point in the future. There was always some reason. Emma was ill. Emma depended on him. Their money was tied up in her business. She needed him. The fact that I needed him seemed to count for nothing.

I glanced around for a seat. I was not in the mood for dancing.

The tables were arranged along both sides of the hall. Each one had been decorated by one of the school's seven classes. They had been working at the decorations all week, which seemed a little unfair given that it was a staff party. Still, the children in my class had enjoyed making the decorations and, I had to admit, the tables did look lovely. I found the table decorated by my class and sat down.

Emma knew. She had to. Either that or she was a fool. The weekends away. The late nights. The whispered telephone calls. How could she not know? I had come so close to confronting her. I entertained an almost permanent fantasy in which I would turn up at their house and tell her everything. Tell her that it was I who loved him. I who could make him happy. That he would choose me. That he was mine.

But he wasn't mine. He had not chosen me. On the occasions that I broke it off with him, in the vain hope that it would force his hand, he had not left her. It had been me who had spent night after heartbroken night, in a bottomless pit of depression and despair. Sitting by the telephone, smoking my head off. Longing for the phone to ring.

On those occasions, I would fall asleep and dream of being woken by the door bell. Of leaping to my feet, rushing to the door and flinging it wide open to find him standing there with a suitcase in his hand. But it never happened and it never would happen. I knew it in the pit of my stomach and the despair was overwhelming.

While our on and off relationship had prevented me from finding anyone else and the life for which I yearned, it was as much my work for Smith that had served to alienate me from potential friends. Much of my time outside school was spent at rallies and meetings. In crowded pubs or somebody's back room, worming my way into local groups, discovering their plans and passing on intelligence to Smith, which I did with some success.

It was a mostly secret life too. Membership of some of the groups with which I was involved would not have gone down well at school, especially given that a growing number of the families served by the school were immigrants. There had been some narrow escapes. Times when I'd been recognised and had to make up some excuse or other for being somewhere I should not have been. There had been rumours around the school, from time to time, and while none of my colleagues had ever confronted me, I was not deaf to them. The consensus seemed to be that I was a secretive woman with questionable motives. Someone you didn't want to get involved with. Someone to avoid. Someone with secrets. I was certainly that. My whole life seemed to be a secret and a sham.

I needed a drink. I got up and walked across to the table where all the drinks had been laid out. It was a *bring a bottle* party, as usual, so the table was covered with an array of odd bottles and cans. Mostly cheap rubbish. I tried to find the bottle I had bought with me but gave up after a minute or two of searching and settled for bottle of Blue Nun. It was not one of my favourites but, at that moment, it didn't need to be.

It was a wonder that I had been invited to this particular party, but then I suppose they could hardly have left me out, it being the school's staff Christmas do. I don't know what made me attend. I certainly wasn't enjoying myself. Stood there, pouring myself a drink, listening to 'Lilly The Pink' for the umpteenth time. Pathetically, I guess it was loneliness. I hadn't seen Peter for a week. He was away for Christmas, visiting Emma's family. It made my stomach churn, just thinking about it. Had I not attended, I would have been sat at home, mulling it all over in my head for the thousandth time. On my own. Always on my own.

I sank the glass of wine that I had just poured for myself and reached for another.

There was only one person that I'd ever shared my agonies with. I decided, at that moment, to call her first thing the following morning. I was low. So low that it felt like there were heavy weights tied to my arms and legs. If I didn't talk to someone soon, I was going to sink out of sight.

'Sorry Liz, can I get to the red wine?'

'What?'

It was Evelyn Jones, one of the new reception teachers. 'The red wine?' she said in a tone like I was an idiot.

'Oh sure, sorry,' I said, stepping sideways.

Avoiding my eyes, she reached for the bottle and poured red wine into two glasses. It would be two glasses. Of course it would. I laughed.

She turned to me. 'What?'

'Oh, sorry, no, its nothing.'

She looked at me for a moment longer than was comfortable.

I smiled awkwardly. 'It's just that I think that I must be the only single person here,' I said, gesturing at her two, now full glasses of wine.

'Probably,' she said caustically and walked away.

What a bitch.

Rosemary Sellers. The only person I'd ever spoken to about Peter, Smith and my secret life. Unburdening myself to Rosemary had been a risk because, like Smith, she was an intelligence officer. Had she been like Smith in any other way, then I might have been in trouble. But she was nothing like Smith. I trusted her. From the moment I met her.

I do tend to do that. I think I always have. Make a snap judgement about people. Which isn't always a great way to be. First impression's might count, but pigeon holing people on the basis of them is a little unforgiving.

I was right about Rosemary, though. There had been something about her. An empathy. I don't know. I just trusted her and I'd kept in touch with her, on and off, since our first meeting during the summer of 1966.

Friday, 14th July 1966

I'd been covering Sir Oswald Mosley's General Election campaign for Smith. By then, I'd forged links with a number of groups around London, especially in the East End. When Sir Oswald decided to stand at Shoreditch and Finsbury, I'd been the obvious choice. Shoreditch was on my home patch after all and Peter was a great admirer, so we were able to attend rallies and meetings together.

I'd first seen Sir Oswald speak in 1962 and while, secretly, I did not share his convictions, I must say that, personally, I had warmed to the man. Peter and I met him several times during the sixties and often found ourselves working for him on one of his campaigns or speaking engagements. In many ways, he was an old fashioned politician. Perhaps one of the last of his kind, many would say, thankfully. He was always charming to me. Polite in a way that modern men rarely are. And he had an incredible aura about him. A sense of other-worldliness. Perhaps it was his passion and deep self-belief. Or perhaps it was the man's history. There were not many men who could say that Adolph Hitler had attended their wedding and not many men who would want to.

I'd been helping to pack up after a stormy meeting in Shoreditch. The hall was still full of people. Small groups, talking excitedly or being interviewed by reporters. I'd been gathering papers, discarded by those who had attended, when I noticed a woman watching me. She looked to be in her mid-forties, maybe older. Elegant, blond haired and stick thin. I caught her eye and she smiled. She was moving among those in the hall, greeting people occasionally, but always with her eye on me. Or perhaps it was I who was watching her.

Eventually, I decided to approach her. 'Liz Muir,' I said, holding out a hand.

'Rosemary Sellers,' she said, shaking it warmly.

'What did you think of the speech?'

She tilted her head, very slightly to one side. It was an odd gesture. As though she was trying to appraise me from a different angle. 'The speech was a triumph,' she said in an accent that was archetypically upper class English. She lowered her voice. 'A veritable whirlwind of bluster and rabble rousing, as only Sir Oswald can. The man's a powerhouse, darling,' she said, raising her volume 'an absolute powerhouse.'

I smiled but I couldn't quite decide whether she had just complemented or ridiculed him. I decided to take a risk. 'I know. You'd have thought that would have given up by now and retired to the Algarve.'

'The Algarve?' She seemed appalled. 'Paris, darling. Paris. The man might be a raving fascist, but one has to give him some credit.'

It was a risky statement for her to make but she carried it off with such aplomb that, for a moment, I was speechless.

'Besides, what would *we* do without Sir Oswald?' she said, with definite emphasis on the word. As though she was acknowledging that we had something in common.

'No, well, I…' I stammered.

She reached into her bag and withdrew a small card. 'I believe that you and I share an interest, Liz.' She handed me the card.

I read its contents and looked at her, studying her expression carefully. Her eyes were brilliant blue. Somewhere in her face, was a hint of concern. Whether for me, or for some other reason, I could not tell. But if I was any judge of character at all, she meant me well.

'Call me,' she said.

'I will,' I whispered.

'And if I were you, I would not mention our meeting, either to your handsome college lecturer,' she said looking at me knowingly.

'Oh, he's not mine. Were just..'

'Or,' she interrupted 'to the not so handsome, Mr Smith.'

I gaped. I couldn't help myself.

'So lovely to meet you, darling,' she said at full volume and swept onwards.

I was left standing there like an idiot.

The card she had given me included her name, and the address and telephone number of Claridges Hotel, in Brook Street, Mayfair. The following morning, I called her. She had not wanted to talk on the telephone. Instead, we arranged to meet later that day. For afternoon tea at the famous hotel. I'd never been to Claridges and I'd had no idea what to wear. What I looked like, when I finally walked through the revolving doors, God alone knows, but I suppose that I must have passed the dress code or I would have been denied admission.

The foyer at Claridges, where afternoon tea is served, took my breath away. From the black and white marble floor, to the elegant art deco interior, every inch of the place exuded a sense of glamour. I felt like a character from a 1930's B-movie.

I was shown to our table by a uniformed waiter.

Rosemary Sellers was already seated. 'Liz, darling. How wonderful to see you.' She greeted me like a lifelong friend.

I sat down, ever so slightly lost for words. 'What an amazing place,' I managed. 'I hope I look alright. I didn't know what to wear.'

'You look positively radiant.'

The waiter returned and took my order. I tried not to think about the bill. 'I thought you had to book a table here months in advance?'

'Indeed. So tiresome.'

'Then how comes…'

Rosemary smiled, her eyes twinkling. 'One has an arrangement. It does to have friends in high places.'

'Oh.' It was all I could manage. After a few moments, I added 'Yesterday, you said that we share a common interest.'

'I believe so.'

'May I ask you what you think it is?'

The waiter appeared. Rosemary waited for him to serve my tea.

'You're working for a certain Mr Smith,' she said, once the waiter had departed.

I hesitated. 'Go on.'

'He and I share a common employer.'

This was becoming surreal. 'Hang on. Are you saying that you both work for the same organisation?'

'In theory, at least.'

In theory at least. She could see the confusion in my face.

'Mr Smith has his own agenda which, as yet, is not entirely clear to me. This is something that interests me. I have been watching him for a rather long time which, incidentally, is how I came to notice you.'

'And there I was thinking that I was doing so well.'

'Oh you are, darling. In many ways you have exceeded expectations.'

'Whose expectations?'

'Well, Mr Smith's, certainly. He has made very good use of the intelligence you have provided,'

'But, evidently, I didn't fool you.'

'No, I'm afraid not.'

I was silent for several moments. 'Why did you approach me, Rosemary?'

'Oh, but I did not approach you. If you recall, it was you who approached me.'

She was right, of course. 'Alright, but it was you who suggested that I call you.'

Rosemary thought for a moment. 'I was concerned about you.'

'Concerned? Why?'

'For two reasons. Mr Smith may not be what he appears. I wanted to warn you to be careful.'

'Are you saying that I should stop working for him?'

'Not necessarily. You are doing important work. You have managed to infiltrate a number of groups that have hitherto been difficult to infiltrate. So long as Smith is putting that to good use, then it is worthwhile work and a job well done.'

'But?'

'Smith is ruthless. I have seen just how ruthless he can be. I wanted you to know that, should you find yourself in difficulty, there is someone that you can contact.'

It would indeed be a relief to have someone to confide in. But could I trust her… 'What kind of difficulty?'

'Mr Smith uses people. When he detects a weakness, he exploits it. Rather like your Mr Owen, though for an entirely different reason.'

'Oh, no, Peter and I are..'

'No matter,' she interrupted. 'But, you should understand that Mr Smith has no scruples at all. You must be cautious. Do as you will. Make your choices. Take your own path. But do not allow yourself to be fooled into believing that there is no alternative to the path that Mr Smith will set out for you.'

I thought about Smith's reaction to my relationship with Peter. Far from disapproving, he had positively encouraged it. He had urged me on. With little or no concern for the impact it was having on me. 'You said that there were two reasons. What is the second?'

Rosemary took a sip of tea. 'As well as watching Mr Smith, I have, more latterly, been keeping an eye on you.'

'You have been spying on me?'

It was as though I had mentioned a forbidden word. Her reaction was really quite comical. She put down her tea cup with a chink, as though it were burning her fingers. 'Tush. Tush. We do not spy, darling. This is Great Britain, not the United States of America. We observe. We watch.'

She was wonderful. The mood of the conversation was immediately lifted. 'I'm sorry.'

It was a performance worthy of an Oscar.

'You are forgiven, darling.'

I smiled. 'And?'

'Hmm?' she murmured, returning her tea cup to the saucer.

'While you were watching me, what did you observe?'

'I observed,' she said with emphasis, 'a bright, talented and beautiful young woman, slowly losing her happiness.'

I was stunned. I knew exactly what she was referring to. But how could she possibly know? I felt suddenly exposed.

She reached across the table and took my hand. 'I made a mistake once. It was a stupid, innocent mistake but it had consequences, not least for someone I held dear. To this day, it haunts me. Rather like tossing a stone into the ocean, the ripples of it seem to go wider and wider as time progresses. It has brought me - and others - nothing but anguish.'

'What has that got to do with me?' It was an unnecessarily blunt question and I immediately felt ashamed of it.

She released my hand. 'You're right, dear,' she said sadly. 'It is none of my business, of course.'

'I'm sorry. That was unnecessary.' I held her gaze for a moment. If I was any judge of character, any judge of character at all... And I was certainly in need. Not just of a confident but of a friend. In Rosemary's face, I recognised genuine concern and an offer of the kind of friendship that was otherwise entirely missing from my life.

'I can see a little of myself in you, Liz,' she said. 'A life of secrets comes at no small cost. Alas, mine must continue for a time at least. Perhaps yours, also. But the burden might be lighter if you share it. I asked you to call me because I wanted you to know that you are not alone.'

Saturday, 21st December 1968

The party had dragged on. I didn't know what I was doing there and was thinking about leaving when a man came across to the table where I was sitting. 'Mind if I sit down?' he said. 'My legs are killing me.'

I shook my head. 'No, not at all.'

'Do you teach here?' he asked, after a few moments.

I wasn't keen to make small talk. I wasn't in the mood for it. I nodded.

'I thought so. You look like the teaching type.'

I didn't know how to take that. 'Is there a teaching type?'

He looked at me. He wasn't a bad looking bloke. Long hair, broad set - muscular, not fat - and big lips. A bit like Mick Jagger.

'Sure there is. I bet you drive a 2CV.'

I laughed. 'What, in open toed sandals?'

'Yes.'

'Well, you're wrong on both counts.'

'Really? Let me take another guess.'

I sighed. I still wasn't really in the mood. But being chatted up by a good looking bloke did make a change. 'Alright. But only if you get me another drink.'

'Deal.' He looked at my glass. 'White?'

I nodded. 'Liz Muir,' I said, holding out my hand.

'Ted…'

I missed the surname. The music was too loud. I shook his hand anyway.

He got up and went off in search of a bottle. It was only when he was upright that I noticed how tall he was. I watched him wind his way across the hall, dodging dancers as he went. He was easily the tallest man in the hall.

I saw him talking to Nicky Stammers. She'd been at the school for years, apparently. I hadn't had a great deal to do with her, but then I hadn't had a great deal to do with any of them. Or rather they hadn't had a great deal to do with me.

He was back within a few minutes. He handed me my drink and sat down.

'So?' I said.

He looked at me. 'So what?'

'What's your second guess.'

He scratched his chin. 'Mini… no, no, that's not right. Now, let me think.'

I laughed. He'd obviously been talking to Nicky. I wondered if she had any idea of the car I drove.

'Morris Minor,' he said triumphantly. 'Dark grey with cherry red seats.'

I took a mouthful of wine. It was Blue Nun. He was slick - I had to give him that. 'You cheated.'

'I did not!'

'Yes, you bloody well did. You asked Nicky. I saw you.'

He laughed. 'Guilty, Your Honour. Cigarette?' he said, slipping one out from a packet that he had produced from his pocket.

'No, I'm trying not to…' I hesitated. 'Oh bugger it, what the hell. Yes. Thank you.' I liked him. He lit my cigarette and I inhaled. 'I'm amazed she knew, to be honest,' I said, after I'd finished coughing.

He looked at me as if trying to work out what lay behind the comment. 'Nicky? Oh, very little gets past her.'

'You know her?'

He pulled a face. 'Yes. She is my cousin.'

'Your cousin?' I don't know why it surprised me, but it did.

'Oh dear. How many glasses of wine have you had? Ted Stammers,' he said, pointing to his chest. Then he pointed across the hall. 'Nicky Stammers.' He grinned. 'Me tarzan, you Jane.'

I laughed. 'I'm sorry. I missed your surname. The music,' I said, pulling a face.

'ObLaDi ObLaDa. Where did Lennon and McCartney dig up that little gem?' he said.

'Who knows? Almost as bad as Lilly The Bloody Pink.'

We both laughed. I definitely liked him. 'What else did Nicky tell you about me?'

'Oh nothing much,' he said, ever so slightly evasively.

'Let me guess. She told you to steer well clear.'

'No, of course not,' he said. But he looked uncomfortable saying it.

'It's alright. I'm used to it.'

We sat, watching the dancers.

'What do you do for a living?' Now I was making small talk.

'Post Office. Electrical engineer. Dull as ditch water, but it pays pretty well and hauling cables keeps me fit.'

I had noticed.

There was another pause.

'You're on your own. Tonight, I mean,' he ventured.

'Yup,' I said. 'I usually am.'

He gave me a sideways look. 'You're not a dyke are you? Not that I've got anything against…'

'No,' I said, slapping him on the arm.

He grinned. 'Well, thank God for that.'

'I do,' I said grinning. 'Every day. I'm unpopular enough as it is.'

'Why?' he asked, after a few moments. It was a serious question.

'Oh, I don't know Ted,' I sighed. 'I've given up trying to work it out. Ask Nicky.'

'I'd prefer to find out for myself,' he said, hopefully.

I looked at him. I liked him a lot. Which made me think of Peter. The love of my bloody life. Tucked up in bed beside his adoring wife or, more likely, wedged between her legs, pumping away. The thought of it, made my stomach churn and something else. It made me angry.

I'd been angry before. Angry with her for keeping him from me. Angry with myself for putting up with it. Angry that he wasn't with me. Angry about being on my own. Angry with life. But very rarely angry with him. The truth was, I always made excuses for him. It was never his fault. But at that moment, I was angry with Peter Owen. For accepting everything that I had given him and for giving me nothing in return.

I think, with hindsight, that something clicked within me that first evening with Ted Stammers. Somehow, Ted had helped me to throw a switch. A switch that I'd never been able to reach by myself. I loved Peter. There was no getting away from that. But loving him didn't mean I had to like him or what he had done to me. And it didn't mean that I had to put up with it. Forever.

'Would you, now?' I said, giving him my best school teacher look.

'Sure,' he said, confidently. 'Never judge a book by…'

He hesitated.

'Hmm?' I said, smiling.

'Uh.. Never judge a book by the reviews of its readers,' he said, warming to the task. 'Especially if they've only seen seen the abridged version.'

'Ted Stammers,' I said, shaking my head, 'and you were doing so well.'

Chapter Eleven

Wednesday, 4th May 1977

Peter Owen stepped out into the corridor, turned and locked his office door. He looked at his watch, before walking the short distance to the building's stair well. Noting the sign on the lift, he took the two flights of stairs down to the floor below. He punched a series of numbers into the combination lock and smiled. It was an in-joke.

He found the Union's general office as he had expected. Mainly deserted. But not quite. 'Working late, Justin?'

Hughes looked up from the pile of papers he'd been scrutinising. 'Don't I always?'

To be the fair to the man, he always did.

Owen retrieved a chair from a vacant desk, turned it to face Hughes and sat down.

Hughes reached into his pocket. 'Cigarette?' he said, pulling one from the packet.

Owen, waved it away. 'Has Jimmy gone?'

Hughes nodded. 'At three. He said he had some urgent business to attend to.'

Owen leant back in his chair. 'What about you, Justin? Haven't you got anything more important to be doing tonight?'

Hughes considered the question. 'What could be more important than serving our great cause,' he said sarcastically.

Owen smiled. 'Well evidently, Jimmy doesn't share your devotion.'

Hughes snorted.

'You don't like him, do you?' said Owen.

'Jimmy?'

Owen nodded.

'Does it matter whether I like him or not?'

'Not particularly, no. I'm just interested.'

Hughes shuffled his papers.

'Oh, for God's sake Justin, I'm interested in your opinion. That's all.'

Hughes tapped a pile of papers into order and put them down on his desk. 'He scares the hell out of me.'

'Really? Why?'

'After last week's events, I would have thought that would be fairly obvious,' Hughes replied. 'And it's not exactly the first time, is it?'

Owen tilted his head in agreement. 'But he has always scared you, hasn't he?' he asked.

'Off the record?'

'Yes, off the record.'

Hughes took a draw from his cigarette. 'Yes,' he said, exhaling.

'Why?'

Hughes thought for a moment. 'What do we know about him, Peter? Apart from the fact that he's quite prepared to stick a kid in the guts for no good reason?'

'They were provoked. The kid gave them a load of verbal. He got what he deserved.'

'Are you sure about that?'

'Does it matter? He's our Head of Security, not a bloody Sunday school teacher. So the man has a short fuse.'

Hughes, was thoughtful. 'Alright, but how many times are we going to dig him out of trouble?'

'As many times as it pays us to dig him out of trouble. The day it doesn't, will be the day he goes down.'

'Which is fine, providing he doesn't take the rest of us with him.'

Owen was surprised by the remark. 'Do you think he'd turn?'

'I've no idea. He's got his own agenda. I haven't got the faintest idea what it is. Have you?'

Owen ignored the question. 'Go on.'

Hughes hesitated. 'In all the time he's been here, I've learned nothing about the man. Nothing at all. He's a blank page. What's he doing here, Peter?'

'Scaring the shit out of the opposition, for one thing,' Owen retorted. 'He sorted that trouble down in Park Royal, a couple of weeks ago and he sorted it single handed.'

'With a baseball bat.'

'Exactly. The Union needs people like him, Justin, for now. Until we've got the law on our side.'

Hughes took another draw on his cigarette. He supposed Owen was right.

'Then there'll be no more need for baseball bats. We'll ship the coons back to Bongo Bongo Land and the commies off to the Outer Hebrides or some other backwater. They can set up their little socialist state there.'

'Excuse me, but might I remind you that the Hebrides are part of Great Britain. Ship them off to the Channel Islands. Jersey's nothing but an island of cheese eating surrender monkeys anyway,' said a voice from behind Owen's shoulder.

Owen turned. 'Ah, John. How did you get on?'

John Taggart took off his coat, threw it onto an empty seat and sat on the corner of Hughes's desk.

'I think I have us a venue. Dobson will need to take a look, but that should be a formality. It will be safe enough.'

'Excellent. I knew Hilary wouldn't let us down. She will be in attendance, I hope.'

'That, she will,' Taggart said nodding.

'Good. Well done, John,' Owen replied, getting to his feet. 'We can go over the plans tomorrow,' he said, looking at his watch. 'I've got an evening appointment.'

Taggart looked at him knowingly. 'Blonde or brunette?'

'I will ignore that,' Owen said, slapping Taggart on the back. 'Brunette, as a matter of fact.'

The two men laughed.

'Before you go, Peter,' said Hughes.

Owen turned.

'You wanted the shortlist,' he said, reaching into his desk draw and removing a blue pocket file. He handed it to Owen.

'Oh, yes. I'll run through it tomorrow. I'd better get going. See you both in the morning.'

Owen climbed the stairs to the third floor, scanning the papers from the file that Hughes had handed him, casually as he went. His feet echoed on the stairs. He turned into the corridor that led to his office and was just about to stuff the papers back into the file, when a name caught his eye. He stopped in his tracks. He rearranged the papers and stood, scanning one of the forms from the file. When he'd finished, he walked into his office, dropped the remainder of the papers and the now empty file onto his desk and sat down in his chair. He read the form again, this time from beginning to end. When he'd finished, he put the form down, removed his pipe and a pouch full of tobacco from his top drawer, filled the pipe and lit it with a match from a box that had been lying on his desk.

He stood up and walked across to the window overlooking Great Eastern Street. For several minutes, he stood motionless, puffing on his pipe. Then he returned to his desk, tapped out his pipe into the ashtray on his desk, collected his coat from the back of his door and went out into the corridor. As he turned to lock the door, he was smiling, broadly.

Justin Hughes, removed the keys from the lock of the main door at Excalibur House and dropped them into his coat pocket. He glanced up at the column of arched windows, that fronted the building's stair well. A stair well with which he had become all too familiar over the last few months. He sighed and made a mental note to contact the leasing company in the morning to berate them, once again, about the absence of a working lift. Something had to be done and nobody else had seemed inclined.

He glanced at his watch. It was late, even for him. The temperature outside had dropped as the sun had gone down behind the steel grey clouds that had hung above London all day. The tall office buildings on either side of Great Eastern Street acted as a funnel, sending great gusts of wind, billowing along the high street, to the disadvantage of anyone foolish enough to be heading for home in the dark. Always a risky business in this part of the Capital. Or perhaps, Hughes reflected, they had as little reason as he did to hurry.

He glanced over his shoulders, one after the other, fastened the top button on his coat, picked up his bag from the pavement and set off towards the bus stop.

The bus shelter at Rivington Street was occupied by a solitary figure in a tweed coat. A woman, and elderly by the way that she carried herself. He could barely see her face, due to the poor light and the fact that the woman was wearing horn rimmed spectacles and a blue scarf. She seemed to be having trouble reading a map which was flapping, uncontrollably, in the wind.

He tried to ignore her but, having endured several minutes of muttered curses, he finally relented. 'Do you need some help?' he said, without enthusiasm.

'Oh, thank you, so much' the woman said. 'I'm trying to get to Monument.'

'Monument?'

She looked at him, her eyeballs magnified ridiculously in the lenses of her glasses. 'Yes. It's my eyesight you see. I can see very little in this light.'

The woman looked like an owl, blown down onto the pavement by a passing bus. Not that there were many owls in

Shoreditch. She thrust the map into his hands. 'Would you mind? I can't make head nor tail of it.'

'Yes, alright,' he said. 'Now, let me see.' Hughes folded the map so that only the necessary part of it was showing. 'Here,' he said pointing.

The woman moved to his side and stood, peering at the map.

'We're here. Rivington Street. See?'

She moved closer. 'Yes, I think so.'

She smelt of mothballs and cat pee.

'You need to take a 135 from the other side of the road. Over there,' he pointed back along Great Eastern Street.

'Oh, goodness.'

'Change at Liverpool Street. Most of the busses running from there will take you to Monument. Try a 26,' he said.

'And to think, had I got on a bus here I would have been going in entirely the wrong direction.'

'Yes, you would,' he said, handing the map back to her.

'Over there, you say,' she said, pointing.

'Yes, it's not far.'

'Thank you so much.'

'My pleasure.'

'Goodnight then.'

Hughes was still watching the woman, when his bus arrived.

The woman in the tweed coat stood in a vacant doorway opposite Excalibur House and watched the bus pull away with Justin Hughes on board. She waited a few moments more, before crossing the road.

She tried several keys from the bunch she had taken from Hughes's coat pocket, before the lock turned. Once inside, she closed the door and locked it. Then she removed the scarf and the horn rimmed glasses and put them in her handbag, from which she produced a small, silver torch.

She made her way, cautiously, up the stairs to the building's second floor.

She stood outside the Union's main office and punched several combinations into the panel beside the door, but none of them had the desired effect. She thought for a moment. Then she punched 2-0-0-4-8-9. There was a click. She smiled to herself at the in-joke.

She shone the torch around the empty office and, having located her first target, walked across to a row of five steel filing cabinets. She tried several drawers but they were all locked. She put her hand in her pocket and removed the stolen key bunch. She unlocked and opened the filing cabinets one at a time and riffled through the suspended files in each drawer. It took her several minutes to locate the file she was looking for. She laid its contents out on a vacant desk, removed a small camera from her bag and photographed each of file's documents in turn. As she took each picture, the empty office was briefly illuminated and the silence pierced by the whine of the re-charging camera flash.

When she had completed the task, she returned the file to the pocket in the filing cabinet and locked each of the cabinets in turn. Then she left the main office and made her way up the stairs to the third floor.

Outside Peter Owen's office, she stood trying each of the keys in turn until she found the right one. She opened the door and shone the torch into the Union leader's office. The room smelt of stale tobacco smoke.

She walked across to Owen's desk and sat down in his chair. She tried each of his desk drawers but they were locked. She was about to apply herself to the locks, when she noticed a pile of papers on the desk. She reached across to them and shone her torch at the documents, each in turn.

'No,' she said under her breath, as she read. 'This cannot be.'

When she had finished reading them all, she sat back in the seat and closed her eyes.

Then she said one word out loud.

'Smith.'

Chapter Twelve

Tuesday, 31st December 1968

Peter rang me on New Years Eve. I hadn't seen or heard anything from him since he and Emma had left to visit her in-laws for Christmas. I'd seen Ted three times since the party and he'd taken to ringing me every day. Sometimes twice. I'd had the happiest week that I could remember. Ted had positively showered me with attention and I had loved every minute of it.

'I'm not making a nuisance of myself, am I?' he'd asked during one late night telephone conversation.

'Making a nuisance of yourself? Are you mad?'

After years of yearning for a man who was never there for me, Ted's sudden devotion felt like a miracle. Like someone up there, had parted the clouds and shone a light down into my life. There was no way that Ted was ever going to make a nuisance of himself.

'It's just that last night, you know, when I invited you back to my place?'

'Yes?'

'You seemed a bit reluctant. I thought, maybe, I might be rushing you. I mean, I don't want to scare you off. I have a habit of doing that.'

'No, of course not. I'm just not ready to...' I hesitated.

'No, no that's fine. Look, I'm really sorry. I can back off a bit if you'd prefer.'

He really did mean it. I could hear the anxiety in his voice. Such a sweet man.

'Ted Stammers. If you ever manage to make a nuisance of yourself, I will tell you. I promise.'

'You will?'

'Yes. I will. But listen to me, you idiot. I have had the best week ever. I really can't remember the last time I felt as happy as this.'

'Good.' He sounded so relieved.

'So backing off, is definitely not required. Understood?'

'Understood.'

He was right though. I had been reluctant to go back to his place. It wasn't that I didn't want to spend the night with him. But I had to resolve the situation with Peter, first. One way or the other.

Peter was as full of himself as he ever was. He'd missed me, of course, but they'd had a wonderful Christmas. He actually told me that. He seemed oblivious, entirely, to my feelings.

'I'd like to see you. Tonight. Wear something nice for me will you?'

It was stunning. How could I have gone for so long without seeing it? Or, worse. Perhaps I had seen it all along and chosen to accept it.

'Oh, I'm sorry, I'm out tonight,' I forced myself to say. 'In fact, I'm not going to have much time until next weekend.'

Peter was silent and suddenly I was having doubts. I loved him. Could I really push him away? Did I have the strength?

'Where are you going?' he asked flatly. I couldn't tell what he was thinking.

'A colleague is throwing a New Year's Eve party,' I lied. 'I promised that I'd help with the food, so I can't get out of it.'

'When will you be back?'

'Thursday, probably. Given that it won't finish until the small hours of tomorrow morning, she suggested that I stay over for the bank holiday.'

He was silent again. 'That's great,' he said, after a pause. 'Have a great time and Liz?'

'Yes?'

'Happy New Year.'

'Happy New Year, Peter.'

The line went dead.

I sat staring at the phone, my stomach in knots. It was the first time that I had ever said no to him.

Summer, 1969

I don't know how to describe the first six months of 1969. I continued to see Peter but there was a growing gulf between us and, when we slept together, our love making felt cold, almost mechanical. It was the first time that sex with Peter had been anything but wonderful.

By July, I had begun to feel bereaved. That is the only way I can describe it. As though something inside me was dying, slowly. I wanted rid of it. I knew the damage that holding on to it was doing but, try as I might, I could not face the loss of it. The loss of him.

And then there was Ted. Kind and gentle. Never demanding. Always there when I needed him. It felt, sometimes, like he was leading me by the hand, out of the darkness that I had constructed for myself. Inch by inch. One tiny step at a time.

But still, as the summer wore on, I could not let go of Peter Owen. I would jump whenever he told me to jump, straight back into his arms. I felt powerless to resist him.

I was also still working for Smith at this time, attending meetings, sometimes with Peter and sometimes without him, passing information back to Smith, where I could without blowing my cover. I'd worked out a way of keeping Smith happy, while avoiding passing information to him which related to Peter directly. Or, if Peter was implicated, of omitting small details to protect him. I told myself that in this way, I was not betraying him. Although I didn't believe it. Not truly.

Perhaps it was the self-inflicted agony of it all that prompted me to start erecting barriers. Or maybe it was the fear of losing Ted. Of extinguishing the tiny, flickering candle-flame of hope that he had held out to me. Perhaps it was something deeper in my psyche. Some buried coping strategy from my childhood. I don't know. But that's what I did. First, I began to cordon off my feelings for Peter and then, to lock them away. Piece by piece.

It was, of course, a way of avoiding the truth. If I could lock them away, one hurtful memory or impossible fantasy at a time, I would not have to lose them entirely. If I could bury my feelings for him, just deep enough, perhaps I could get on with my life without ever having to truly let him go. He would be my secret. I knew that sooner or later, having locked them all away, I would have to find a way of getting rid of the key altogether, but as July became August and August became September, I kept telling myself "not yet".

Ted continued to shower me with attention. I wonder, now, whether he knew why I was holding back. I always avoided inviting him to my flat. My bed there was the place where Peter and I made love and, even though the occasions that we did so were less frequent, I still could not bear the thought of Ted occupying the same place as Peter. I managed to all but convince myself that, by keeping them separate, occupying both a different physical space and a different emotional space within me, somehow I was being true to them both.

It was nonsense of course. A kind of mental contortion and, as Rosemary Sellers had warned, my secrets were not without a cost. I was now leading a quadruple life. My life at school, my life with with Peter, my work for Smith and my time with Ted. The strain of maintaining it was becoming unbearable and, as the summer waned, so did my endurance. I realised that it had to stop. My sanity was beginning to waver.

While maintaining a relationship with Ted was part of the problem, conversely, it was because of it that I had survived. Ted Stammers was in love with me. It was obvious. From the way he behaved towards me. From the things that he said. Things that touched me, deeply, so that I could never be truly angry with him, or want to hurt him, or think badly of him. He was the dearest man and he held me up, when without him I am sure that I would have fallen to pieces. What touched me most of all and, in the end, convinced me to act, was the unconditional nature of his feelings for me. In the first seven, almost eight months of our relationship we did not once have sex. Not once. He wanted to. I had no doubt about that. But he never once put pressure on me. Never once questioned me. He simply accepted that, for reasons that I could not share with him, I was not ready. I had never, in my life, been loved like that. Not by anyone.

At the beginning of August, I told Smith that I wanted out. That I couldn't stand the secrets and lies anymore or cope, any longer, with the toll that it was having on me. I told him that I wanted to settle down, to find a new job, have a family and a normal life. In short, to re-start my life over again.

Smith tried to talk me out of it, of course, but I think that even he could see that I was beginning to fall apart. Perhaps he foresaw that, if he didn't release me, I would breakdown altogether. It must have been obvious to him that I was no longer able to cope. In the end, I think it was the risk that I had begun to represent to him. That, if I cracked, I might reveal not only myself to Peter Owen, but that I might also reveal Smith, himself. It was that, I am convinced of it, rather than any concern for me that led Smith to accept my resignation and, ultimately, to promise me that I would not hear from him again.

Later that month, I saw Peter for what proved to be the final time. Had I known then the events that our last meeting would set in motion, I would have chosen a different course, but hindsight is a wonderful thing and life has a habit, even when we take hold of it by the reins, of steering us in an entirely new and unforeseen direction. It was to be the bitterest of all journeys.

Thursday, 21st August 1969

Ted had been away for a week, working on a new installation in Manchester and he was not due back for another fortnight.

Peter arrived at my flat at half past eight. It had been threatening to rain all afternoon and looking out of my window, I could see a bank of angry black clouds. It felt like an omen. As Peter arrived, there was a torrential downpour that sent rivers of water gushing down the gullies at the side of the road outside the flat. When I let Peter in, he was drenched and stood dripping rain water onto my hallway carpet.

'Take your coat off,' I said. 'I'll get you a towel.'

I went into the bathroom. As I turned, to reach for the towel, I saw myself reflected in the mirror above the bathroom sink. I looked gaunt. I had lost so much weight over the last year that the skin on my face looked stretched, almost to the point of tearing. I thought about what I was going to say. I'd been thinking about it for days but, no matter how many times I rehearsed it in my head, I doubted that I was ever going to be able to say the words.

I returned to the hall and handed him the towel. He followed me into my sitting room, drying his hair as he went. It wasn't the largest of rooms. I'd painted the walls white when I moved in to try to make the room seem larger but it didn't seem to me to have made a great deal of difference.

'I'll put the fire on. You can dry off a bit, before dinner.' I reached down and ignited the gas.

'I meant to tell you. There is a meeting in Tooting next week,' he said. 'On Wednesday evening. John and Sheila are coming. I'll pick you up at seven.'

My stomach was immediately in knots. I simply nodded.

My hands were shaking as I served dinner and tried to open the bottle of wine that I'd picked up from the corner shop on my way home from school that afternoon.

'Here,' Peter said from the doorway. 'Give it here.'

I handed him the bottle and cork screw.

'Are you alright, Liz? You seem...'

'I'm fine.' I interrupted.

He looked momentarily confused.

'There is something I want to tell you. But lets have dinner first.' I carried the plates across to the dining table and we seated ourselves.

Peter ate like his life depended on it, but I mostly pushed the food around on the plate with my fork. We hardly spoke but Peter didn't seem to notice. I felt like my insides were full of ashes.

After the meal we seated ourselves on the sofa beside the fire. Peter had a glass of wine in his hand. 'You are coming on Wednesday evening?' he said. 'I should be able to stay over afterwards. Emma is going to be away on business for a few days.'

Something snapped within me. 'Peter, stop it. Please.' I got up, walked across to the window and stood, gazing out but I saw nothing of the rain washed street outside.

Peter stood and walked across to me. He put a hand on my arm.

'Just stop it,' I said, without turning to look at him. 'I can't stand it any more.'

He hesitated.

'I can't do this.'

'Do what?'

'Us. I've had enough, Peter. I've had enough of the secrets and lies. All of it.'

'What are you saying?'

I turned around and looked at him. 'Oh come on. Even you must have noticed that it hasn't been the same between us.'

'Look, if this is about Emma, I've told you before..'

He really had no idea. I almost felt sorry for him. 'Stop it. For God's sake. It has changed between us Peter. I have changed. I look at myself in the mirror and I don't even recognise the person I have become.'

He removed his hand. 'I've told you before. I love you but I can't just walk away from Emma. Not yet. She needs me. You know how fragile she is.'

It was the same stock reply.

'It is not about Emma,' I shouted. 'It is not even about you. It is about me. I can't do it anymore. Our relationship is a joke, Peter. A fucking joke. Loving you has ruined me. I have no friends but you. No interests away from you. No life, but this joke of an existence. Waiting for you. Waiting for the phone to ring or for a knock on the door. Waiting for the next time you can find a space to see me, by lying to your wife.'

He looked shocked. I don't think I'd ever spoken to him like that and, for a moment, his confidence wavered. He took a step backwards.

'I wanted you. So much. I would have done anything. Fuck it, I have done everything to hold onto you. To ignore the voices in my head, telling me that it was no good. That you were no good. That you were never going to deliver. Never going to be the man I needed you to be. I have driven myself half mad with it.'

'You should have said.'

I looked at him open mouthed. 'What?'

'You should have said. If I'd known, then perhaps I could have given you more.'

'You can't be serious. You can't be fucking serious. Have you never stopped to wonder what it was like for me?'

He stood blinking at me.

'You haven't have you?'

'Yes, of course I have. I love you Liz. It breaks my heart to see you like this.'

'Love me? Don't make me laugh. You don't know the meaning of the word.'

'Calm down.'

I had lost it. It was the only way. I had unlocked the door and I was not even going to try to control the tidal wave of emotions that was now pouring forth. 'Do you think loving someone means watching them suffer from afar? Never being there when they need you? Letting them down over and over again? Promising them things that you know you will never deliver?'

'It is not like that.'

'Do you love me when you are fucking Emma?'

He looked horrified.

'Do you love her, when you're fucking me? When you are promising me that one day you will leave her? When you are lying to her about where you're going? Where you've been?'

He started to speak, but I interrupted him again.

'Did you love me when you were fucking the others?'

I was destroying it all. I knew that I was doing it. I was saying things that could never be unsaid. Saying the things that I should have said long ago. Taking it past the point of no return. Driving a knife into my own heart as well as into his. Cutting out the feelings that I had held on to so jealously, for so long.

'What others? What are you talking about?'

I laughed with the bitterness of it. 'You're a cheat, Peter, a cheat and a fucking liar. You lie so much and so often that I don't think you even know that you're doing it. Not just to me but to your poor wife and to all the women you take from. Do you think I'm blind? Stupid?'

'They were nothing to me. I'm sorry. It isn't like that.'

'Yes it is. It has always been like that. Since that day in Birmingham when you kissed me. Since the first time I bought you back here. In all of the months and years since. You have never been there for me, Peter. Not once. Your life is nothing but lies. You have taken it all and given me nothing in return.'

He took a step towards me.

'And do you know the worst thing about it? Loving you has turned me into a liar too. A fraud. I have held onto your lies - our lies - for so long that they have become part of me. My whole life has turned into a sham. No wonder that people avoid me.'

He reached for my hand, but I pulled it away.

'Don't.'

He paid no head, taking hold of both my shoulders and pulling me towards him. 'I love you,' he said.

He kissed me. As his lips touched mine I felt a sudden disconnection. It was as though a fuse had blown in my head. The tidal wave of anger and hurt had waned and, in its wake, there was nothing but emptiness.

He led me by the hand to my bedroom.

He undressed me. Sitting on the bed in front of me, he removed my skirt and underwear. I stepped out of them mechanically. There was no emotion. None at all. I felt nothing when he pulled me towards him. Nothing when he put his fingers and then his tongue between my legs. When he pulled me on to the bed beside him and rolled me over onto my back. Only emptiness. I watched him undress like I was watching a film. As though I was seeing him through a camera lens. When he pushed himself into me, it hurt and I cried. But he did not stop. It was not love making. There was no love in it. He took me, harder and harder until he reached his peak, pouring himself into me. And then it was over.

He lay on his back in silence. We said nothing for several minutes.

'It is over Peter. It is finished between us. I am leaving the group. Leaving you. Leaving it all. I have done with it. I want you to put your clothes on and go. I don't want to see you or to hear from you again.'

'What will you do?' he said quietly.

'I will start again. I will move out of the flat. Leave the school. Start a new life in a new place. Please don't try to find me.'

'I won't. If you are sure.'

'I am. Go. Now. Please.'

He got up and dressed in silence. I closed my eyes. I could not watch. I heard him open the bedroom door and, a few moments later, I heard the front door close behind him. I cried like I had never cried before.

Chapter Thirteen

Wednesday, 4th May 1977

He stood in silence at the window, watching the woman as she stepped out onto Great Eastern Street. He saw her glance furtively over each of her shoulders before she bent to lock the large white doors. Stepping away from the window, to avoid detection, he watched her turn to her left and walk hurriedly away. He moved quickly then. By the time that she had crossed Willow Street he was watching her from the door way of the empty office building, opposite Excalibur House.

   He waited until he was satisfied that she would not observe him, then he walked briskly across an empty Great Eastern Street. He took the keys that she had left in the door and put them in his coat pocket. He could still see her in the distance.

The woman in the headscarf, turned to her right. Phipp Street was deserted and silent, save for the sound of the wind whistling around the iron down pipes that served to funnel rain water from the gutters high above her to the sewers below her feet. Overhead, the stars were obscured by heavy cloud. The single orange street lamp did little to illuminate her way, throwing deep shadows into each of the doorways that, during the day, provided access to the turn-of-the-century office buildings and warehouses that bordered the street on either side. They loomed above her like great brick giants, waiting to take a slow, grinding step forward, to squash anyone who dared to break their brooding silence.

She knew that she was being followed before she had turned into Luke Street. She could feel it, prickling the hairs on the back of her neck. But it was only when she had turned the corner that she stopped, briefly, to listen. Along with the distant creaking of an open window buffeted back and forth by the wind and the faint drone of London's perpetual traffic, she could hear the unmistakeable sound of approaching feet, tip-tapping on the street's cobbles behind her.

She peered into the gloom. Up ahead, the smudge of grey that was her car was barely visible in the darkness. She pulled her car keys from her pocket and began to run, the sound of her feet clattering on the pavement matched by the pace of her pursuer.

She reached her car, gasping for air and fumbling with her keys. As she inserted the key into the lock she felt a hand on her wrist. Before she could react, he had pulled her arm up behind her back. She gasped, as he pushed her forward.

'If you struggle, I will break it.' He pulled her arm up higher.

She cried out.

'Turn around slowly.'

As she did so, she saw the flash of a blade.

He released her right arm and held the blade to her throat. 'I will take those,' he said, removing the car keys from her trembling hand.

'And now,' he said reaching, first for her headscarf and then for her glasses, 'we will see the identity of our burglar.' Removing them, he smiled in recognition. 'Of course.'

'If you use that,' she said, glancing at the knife, 'you will spend the rest of your life in prison. If you are lucky. You do know that don't you?'

He laughed. 'I hardly think that you are in any position to make threats. Now, I will take what you stole and then I would like to have the answer to a question. You will provide it or I will remove your head. Is that understood?'

She hesitated. He was a big man and the knife gave him a certain advantage. But like all big men, while he might have ample force at his disposal, an ability to move quickly was unlikely. And men, whether big or otherwise, always underestimate a female opponent. She nodded.

'Who do you work for? Evidently not the man who told me of your little incursion.'

She did not stop to consider the comment. There would be time for that later. Moving with sudden speed and as much force as she could muster, she put her knee hard into his groin. The space that was available meant that the blow was somewhat less than she had hoped for but, given her options, which were limited and declining, she was reasonably pleased with the result. He crumpled forward, the knife slipping from his hand. It clattered to the ground in front of her.

'Bitch,' he said under his breath.

Her odds had slightly improved but she knew that this was a temporary state of affairs. She needed to follow through quickly. If she bent to retrieve the knife he would be on her. So, as he straightened to face her, she launched a second attack, this time aiming for his eyes. She missed, but felt her nails sink into his cheek. However, on this occasion he was better prepared. He reached for her hand and removed it with ease. He stared at her and slowly applied pressure. She met his gaze without blinking.

'I said, who do you work for?'

'Go to hell,' she said between gritted teeth.

He smiled a bloody grin that made him look like a madman. And then, with a sudden twist, snapped her wrist.

She howled in pain and sank to her knees in front of him.

'Get up, bitch.'

She could not.

He twisted her wrist again and hauled her to her feet. The pain was overwhelming.

The punch to her abdomen ought to have felt like she had been hit by a train, but by the time that the blow landed, rupturing her spleen, she was already losing consciousness. The blow to her face, broke her cheekbone and the rim around her left eye socket.

Had she been conscious, which she was not, she would have seen how he held her by her mangled wrist and shook her like a rag doll. She would have heard him call her 'Miststück' and 'die Hure'. She would have seen the man and woman, who came running towards them from the far end of Luke Street. She would have felt herself collapsing, her head hitting the ground with a hollow thud, and heard the sound of her car start and pull away. But she neither saw nor heard any of these things.

Chapter Fourteen

Friday, 5th September 1969

I'd spent the first day after telling Peter that it was over, shut away in my flat. I'd called in sick and taken the day off, which I hated doing. I always felt so guilty, knowing that my children would have to put up with a supply teacher. But I had no real choice. I had barely been able to speak to anyone, let alone take a class of children. I couldn't even answer the telephone when Ted called.

On the Monday morning I'd woken up feeling horribly ill, so when I called in sick again, it was with justification and, ironically, I felt better about it. I slowly started to clear my head. I was not going to be able to wholly forget about Peter. That was not going to happen - perhaps it never would. Rather than battle with it, I tried to acknowledge the feelings that I could not change and put them away, to make space for the things that I could.

I finally spoke to Ted at Monday lunchtime. He'd been so worried that he was considering driving back to London, putting his job at risk. I told him that I had been terribly ill and had pulled the telephone plug from its socket and gone to bed. He was full of concern, but I had managed to convince him that I was on the mend and that nothing else was wrong.

By the Thursday, however, one week to the day since I had last seen Peter, I knew that something else was wrong. I had woken up feeling sick every morning of that week and thrown up my breakfast whenever I had forced myself to eat it. By the time I visited my Doctor, on the Monday before Ted's return, I knew with a degree of terrible certainty what she was going to tell me.

'Congratulations, Liz. You are almost certainly pregnant. Come in for another test in a week's time, to confirm it.'

I had looked at her like she was talking a foreign language. 'I can't be,' I said, but I knew that I was. I could feel it somehow. In all the time that Peter and I had been seeing each other we had always taken precautions. I had been so careful about it. But not on that last occasion.

I had walked back to my flat on autopilot. Pregnant. With Peter Owen's child. If I had the baby - and I knew in my heart of hearts that I would not be able to get rid of it - I would never be truly free of him. Every day for the rest of my life, the result of our relationship and worse, that awful last occasion when I had conceived. There, in front of me. Undeniable.

I had opened the door to my flat, dumped my bag, made myself a cup of tea and sat by my little window, staring out at the people in the street. Numb. What on Earth was I going to do? It is odd, but I never once considered contacting Peter and telling him. I had closed that chapter of my life and I didn't, for a second, imagine re-opening it. Instead, I thought about what I was going to tell Ted. How I was going to explain what had happened.

But how could I possibly explain that I'd had sex with another man? With Peter Owen. Ted didn't even know that Peter existed. It was too much to expect him to understand. Too much to expect him to understand why I had lied to him. It would have been too much for any man.

Ted was the best thing that had ever happened to me. So I didn't love him like I had loved Peter. Thank God. I didn't ever want to feel about a man, like I felt about Peter. I would never again allow myself to be compromised like I had allowed him to compromise me. Ted was kind, caring, devoted to me. He would have driven half the length of Britain to have been with me, thrown away his job and broken every speed limit that it was possible to break, just to be with me. If I had asked him to. Ted was everything that Peter Owen would never be. With Ted, I could have the things I wanted. A home. A life. *A family.* I laughed out loud at the irony of it. If I told Ted the truth, I would destroy any chance of building a new life with him. I would lose it all. I had believed that by ridding myself of Peter Owen, Smith and my secret world I was going to be able to take control of my life and to steer it in a new direction. But life had other ideas.

It was Rosemary who gave me the answer. She was the only friend I had. The one person who understood the scale of my anguish, in all its glory.

We had met on the Wednesday morning. Sitting on a park bench, watching a family of swans, picking their way along the bank of the lake, looking for scraps of bread left behind by the children who visited the park to feed the ducks, with their mothers. I had told her everything. Every appalling detail. Once I started I could not stop. Half way through it, she had taken hold of my hand and, when I had looked at her, there had been tears on her cheeks. When I had finished there was a long silence.

'Liz, my dear, you must not tell him.'

'I have to. I can't live with secrets and lies any more.'

There was another silence.

She squeezed my hand. 'I told you, when we first met, that secrets come at a cost and you, of all people, know that is the truth. But, sometimes, the truth comes at a cost also.'

I waited.

'Ted loves you. That shines through your story like a beacon of light. You have at last been able to rid yourself of Peter Owen, to say goodbye to Smith and to imagine a happier future.'

'How then can I repay him by lying to him?'

'Ted wants what you want. With Ted, you will have a chance to create the kind of life that you and he both desire. The life that you deserve. If you tell him, you risk dashing it all.'

'I don't know, Rosemary,' I said, staring out across the lake. I watched a group of seagulls, skimming the lake's surface. Occasionally one of them would dive into the water and emerge with a tiny fish.

'Do you love Ted?' Rosemary asked.

'I don't know. I don't think that I am capable of loving anyone right now. But I think I could grow to love him.'

She nodded.

'But the baby won't be his. It will never be his.'

'It will, if you make it so. You must put everything else out of your mind. Focus yourself on building a happy home and a happy life with Ted. I rather suspect that it will be somewhat easier than you fear. Make the child growing within you, his child. It can be. If you both want it to be.'

Ted got back into London late on Friday morning. He called me as soon as he arrived home. 'I have missed you so much, Liz. I can't tell you what a relief it is to be back.'

'You don't need to tell me. I know.'

'I thought you would be at work.'

'Yes, I should be, but I was so ill that I decided to take the week off. I feel a bit guilty about it now.'

'Are you alright? I would have come back, you know.'

'Yes, I know but I wasn't that bad and I'm fine now. I just needed the rest. But that's enough about me. How are you? When can I see you? I don't know that I can wait much longer.'

'I'm well. Tired, but well. Can I take a bath first?'

'Oh, I'm sorry. I suppose I could wait until tomorrow.'

'I don't think so. I'll get bathed, changed and I'll pick you up. Say in..' He paused.

I imagined him looking at this watch.

'An hour and a half?'

'Are you sure?'

'You are joking, right?'

'Good. There is something that I want to tell you.'

'What?'

'It will wait.'

'No, tell me now.'

I smiled. 'No. Later.'

Ted sighed. 'Well, at least tell me whether it is good or bad?'

I hesitated. 'That depends. You'll know when I tell you.'

I was already waiting by my window when I saw Ted's little Hillman Imp pull up outside. It was on odd choice of a car for such a tall man. He always seemed so completely uncomfortable in it. I'd decided what I was going to do. What I was going to say. But I was as nervous as hell.

I was wearing a little white mini dress with patterned tights and a pale blue cardigan. I'd had the dress hanging in my wardrobe for months. I don't know why I bought it. I was never very comfortable in mini dresses. But soon, I wouldn't be getting into anything mini, so it was now or never and, besides, I wanted to blow his socks off. I picked up my hand bag. I wouldn't be needing a coat. It was a beautifully sunny afternoon.

I saw Ted standing by the Imp as soon as I opened the door. I skipped across the pavement and threw myself into his arms. He lifted me off my feet and swung me in a circle. It was such a wonderful feeling to be with him that I couldn't let go. Suddenly, all the pain and worry seemed to evaporate and I found myself weeping.

'Here, what's with the tears?'

Still I would not let him go. I didn't want the moment to pass. He wrapped his big arms around me and held me, there in the street, in full view of the neighbours. He didn't care and neither did I.

'You smell so lovely,' I whispered in his ear. He smelt of soap.

'So do you.'

I was wearing Chanel Number Five. I was going to wear it every day from that day onwards. 'Where are you taking me?'

'Where would you like to go?'

I released him.

He looked at me a little oddly. Like he knew that I was up to something.

'Oh God, has my make up run?'

'You look beautiful.'

'Oh, no I look awful. I'm sorry,' I said.

'Liz, you do not look awful. You look bloody gorgeous.'

I kissed him. He tasted of toothpaste.

'So where do you want to go?'

'Take me home, Ted.'

'Er.. You are at home?'

'No, you idiot. Take me home.'

He looked at me blankly. I'm sure he was teasing.

'Your home.'

'Oh. Right.'

The journey to Muswell Hill took almost an hour. When we pulled into Wellfield Avenue, the sun was shining brightly but it could have been pouring. I didn't care. Nothing was going to dampen my spirits.

He'd inherited the house from his parents. Or, more accurately, from his mother. His father had been killed during the war. An only child, Ted and his mother had lived in Wellfield Avenue until, aged eighteen, Ted had joined the army. He had served for eight years and had left, a fully trained communications engineer.

She had passed away in 1965 and suddenly, the house had become Ted's. He had been reluctant at first, to return to the place where he had grown up but neither did he wish to sell it. So moving in had been the obvious solution.

It was a big house. Four bedrooms. As we walked up to the front door, I closed my eyes and tried to imagine myself living there. With Ted and a child. Maybe two. It was not so difficult to imagine.

'What are you doing?' Ted asked.

I opened my eyes and grinned at him. 'I'll tell you when we're inside.'

He shook his head. 'I don't know what's got into you, but it is good to see you so happy.'

'I'm happy because of you, Ted. Because you're home.' I took hold of his hand.

'Not half as happy as I am,' he said and he meant it. He inserted the key and we went inside. 'Shall I make a cup of tea?' he said. 'I'm gasping.'

'That would be nice,' I replied.

I'd been to the house several times but I'd never really noticed it before. Not properly. It was so big. There was a large open hall, with a red stone floor and rooms leading off to the left and right. I can't imagine what it must have been like for Ted in the house on his own, with nothing but the memories of his parents.

I followed him into the kitchen and stood by the door watching him while he filled the kettle. 'Do you like living here?' I asked suddenly.

'Sure I do. Why wouldn't I?'

'I don't know. Doesn't it seem strange without your mother?'

'Yes,' he said, thinking about it. 'It did at first, but I soon got to like the old place again. It's going to be a shame if I have to sell it.'

'What?'

'I can't really afford it. It costs an absolute fortune to heat and it needs a lot of work doing to it. My job pays well enough but it is a bit too much on my own.'

I stared at him.

He put the kettle on the stove and walked towards me.

I hugged him. 'Actually,' I said. 'That is what I wanted to talk to you about.'

'What?'

He looked so worried. My heart was in my mouth. 'How would you feel about me coming here?'

'Don't be daft. You can always come here. Anytime you like.'

God, he could be slow on the uptake. 'No, I mean. How would you feel about me really coming here?'

'What?'

I could see the cogs turning in his head. 'I mean, to stay.'

'What, like for a week or something?'

'Ted Stammers, are you teasing me?'

He wasn't. I could tell that from the look on his face. 'Alright. Let me try again,' I said. 'How would you feel about me coming here to live?'

'With me?'

I laughed. It must have been the tension and the look of bewilderment on his face. 'No, with the milkman. What do you think?'

'But what about your flat? Your job? Your friends?'

'Oh, for heaven's sake. My flat is rented. I can get a job in a school up here and excuse me but what friends?'

He looked at me and slowly, it began to dawn on him.

'I want to be with you Ted,' I said. 'Not just sometimes but always. You are the best thing that has ever happened to me. I think we could be happy here.' I hesitated. 'Providing, of course, that you feel the same.'

He actually cried. He stood in front of me with tears rolling down his cheeks. He wiped them away with his shirt sleeve. I don't think he could speak. He certainly didn't say very much. He just nodded.

'I'm ready Ted. I'm sorry that it has taken me so long. But I'm ready now.'

I held him while he sobbed and I found myself crying too. I didn't deserve such a gentle, sensitive man. I knew that. But I was going to take him. I was going to take the one chance for happiness that I'd been given.

We made love for the first time that afternoon. In the house that his parents had lived in and that we would live in, together, for some of the happiest years of my life. He took me with such tenderness, gently caressing my naked body, kissing my neck, stroking my breasts with his lips, opening me with his fingers so that, when he finally entered me, I was aroused, almost to the point of orgasm. When he was spent, I turned him onto his back and slowly lowered myself to his groin and, taking him in my mouth, made him hard again. When he was almost to the point of climax for a second time, I straddled him and took him again. Driving him deeper and deeper with the rhythm of my body, until I felt him jerk. I wanted every last drop. I wanted him to wash away the seed that had already been planted within me. I wanted him to have no doubts that the child, growing inside me, was his. I wanted him to take away every last vestige of the man who had, until that moment, blighted my life. When I collapsed on top of him, both us spent, I wanted his face and no other, to fill my dreams. I wanted it but it was never truly so.

I moved in with Ted almost immediately. I could not get out of my flat soon enough. It held memories for me that I wanted to forget.

Ted and I were married in St James's Church, Muswell Hill on Valentine's Day, the 14th February 1970 by which time I was already six months pregnant. Ted never suspected for a moment that the child wasn't his. When, a few weeks after our first time, I told him that I was pregnant, I'd never seen a man so proud.

I invited Rosemary Sellers to the wedding, but she would not come.

'Liz, my dear,' she had said one morning, sitting on the same bench where I'd told her everything only months before, 'I am a part of your life that has passed. I wish you every happiness in the world, but it is not a world that I should be a part of.'

'But, Rosemary you are my dearest friend. You know everything there is to know about me. It is because of you that I am about to begin a new life. How can I begin it without you?'

'Tush tush,' she had said. 'It is not because of me at all. You're your own woman. You don't need me poking my nose in, reminding you of the past.'

I took her hand. 'You won't disappear altogether, will you?'

'Darling, of course not. I will keep an...'

'You will spy on me,' I interrupted, grinning.

'I will keep on eye on you always and who knows, I might appear from time to time.'

I nodded. 'I would like that. I will think of you as my guardian angel.'

She smiled, but I saw a flash of sadness in her eyes. 'I am hardly that, dear.'

'Well, to me you are. Just so long as I can find you if I need you.'

'You know where I am.'

I thought for a moment.

'Actually, I don't, you know. I don't know anything about you. Not really. I don't know where you live. I have no way of contacting you.'

'Oh darling, of course you do. Just ask for me at Claridges.'

'At Claridges.' I said, shaking my head.

'Yes dear. I am always available for afternoon tea, should the need arise.'

Chapter Fifteen

Wednesday, 11th May 1977

It took some effort to keep myself together as I made my way up to the second floor at Excalibur House for my interview with Peter Owen. I'd left home that morning, determined to keep the voices in my head at bay, but with each step I took towards Peter, the louder I could hear their cries. One voice, panic stricken. Yelling at me to flee. Another telling me, with steely determination, that I had no choice but to proceed. And a third. A voice that I had told myself I had banished forever, but which now ran amok, urging me to abandon all caution and myself to fate, whether for good or ruination. By the time I reached the second floor office, I was was already exhausted with the effort of it.

'Please take a seat. Mr Owen should be ready for you shortly,' said the over-weight man with a crumpled suit who had met me at the door into the main office.

I sat down heavily, smoothing my skirt over my knees. The exhaustion had turned to nausea and for a moment I thought that I was going to throw up. 'Thank you…'

The man looked at me with concern. 'Are you alright? Can I get you a glass of water?'

'No… No, it's quite alright…' I stammered.

'Oh, I'm sorry, I should have introduced myself. Justin Hughes.'

I knew who he was from the briefing I'd been given by Smith.

He held out his hand. It was fat and sweaty and there was dirt under his finger nails. I shook it, reluctantly. 'Perhaps I will have that glass of water, after all.'

'Of course.'

I glanced around the open plan office. It was bigger than I had thought it would be. There were, perhaps, a dozen desks, three of them occupied. Two by women at typewriters. One of them looked up, caught my eye and smiled. She was pretty and it was a sympathetic enough smile. The kind of smile you give someone in a hospital waiting room. I did my best to return it.

The third was occupied by a tall man with his back to me. He had a telephone handset tucked under his chin. I didn't need to see his face. I recognised him instantly, despite the years that had passed since I had seen him last. After a few minutes, he put the phone down, got up and walked towards me.

I took a breath and smiled.

'Liz, how are you? It's good to see you,' said John Taggart, as he approached.

'Hello John. I'm very well,' I said, getting to my feet. I held out my hand and he shook it warmly.

'I was delighted when Peter told me about your application. I hope he has the good sense to appoint you. It would be great to have you back on the team, although things have moved on a little since then.'

'Thank you. Yes, I can see that.'

There was an awkward pause.

'So what have you been up to since we last saw you?' Taggart asked.

I took another breath and tried to calm the voices. I could do this. I had to do this. 'I'm teaching but, honestly John, you wouldn't believe the mess that they're making of our schools.'

'Aye, but it's not just schools, Liz. The country is sinking,' said Taggart, shaking his head, 'under a tide of communists and immigrants.'

I nodded. 'Do you know, we've got kids in the class I teach who can barely speak a word of English, let alone write it? What are they doing here John? Why do we keep taking more and more of them in?'

Taggart smiled. 'Still committed to the cause then?'

'More so,' I lied. 'Thirteen years of teaching in London schools has made certain of that.'

'Aye, I can imagine that it has.'

'There's only so much you can do from the inside. Especially when the system is so weighted against us.'

'Sounds like you've seen sense at last,' Taggart said.

I smiled. 'Yes, you could say that. If we're going to make a difference, it's the system we need to change. That's why I'm here.'

'Well said,' said a voice from behind me. It was a voice that I recognised. Hearing it brought my heart into my mouth.

Peter Owen.

He had aged. It was the first thing that I noticed about him. But, if anything, the grey flecks in his hair and the lines around his eyes had softened his appearance, somewhat. He had gained a little weight too. Not so much as all that, but enough to remind me that he was now a man in his middle years. As he showed me into the interview room, I couldn't help wondering whether middle age had served to moderate his appetite for young women as it had his appearance.

I had half expected an interview panel, but when he offered me a seat and sat opposite me, across a small coffee table, it became evident that there wasn't going to be any panel.

'Is this your office?' I said, which was a damn stupid thing to say. While it had a desk in one corner, it was perfectly obvious that the room served mainly as a meeting room.

'No, I have an office upstairs on the third floor.'

'Oh, I see,' I said, without meeting his eyes, 'It is bigger than I expected. I mean Excalibur House.' I was talking rubbish and I knew it. 'Well, not the whole building, but the part of it occupied by the Union…'

'Liz,' he interrupted.

'There must be space here for…'

'Liz.'

I stopped and looked into my lap.

He waited.

I looked up. 'I'm rambling, aren't I?'

'Yes, you are.'

'I'm sorry. I'm…'

'It's alright.'

'Yes. Right. I'm sorry,' I said, running my fingers through my hair.

'Shall we start at the beginning?' he said.

'Yes.'

'Your application. It was something of a surprise. To hear from you after all this time.'

I swallowed. It was as big a surprise to me as it was to him. 'I did think about calling you first,' I lied. 'But I wanted to begin as I mean to go on. I applied because I want the job, Peter. Because I want to work for the Union.'

He smiled.

'I wanted you to treat my application like any other. If I am successful, then I wanted it to be because I was the best person for the job. Not because of what happened between us.'

I waited for his response. It took a few moments to come.

'Liz, I have no doubt at all that you are the best person for the job. We worked together long enough for me to be absolutely confident about that.'

I looked at him and held his gaze. 'Thank you,' I said.

'Assuming, of course, that your political position has not changed.'

'Would I be here if it had?'

He laughed. 'I thought I was asking the questions.'

'I'm sorry. No, my political position has not changed. As I was saying to John, if anything my experience over these last few years has hardened it.'

'That's good. But the agenda has moved on Liz. The Union is already a force to be reckoned with, but we are no longer content to be on the fringes of British politics. The democratic system in this country has failed, utterly. The Opposition would see our manufacturing base destroyed in favour of the Jews that control our banking system, while the Government has already surrendered itself to the socialists and communists who are their trades union masters.'

'It is a disgrace, Peter. Something has to be be done and the Union is the only party capable of doing it. Of uniting the people of this country behind the nationalist flag and building a better future for Britain. That is why I am here.'

He held up his hand. 'But you must understand that we do not intend to share power. We intend to take it. You are right that we will unite the great majority of our people behind the banner of our cause, but there will be those who will oppose us. The Jewish establishment who, for generations, have been destroying our great empire. Who took us into a meaningless war that killed millions of brave British men. The blacks on our streets and the Asians in our corner shops. The communists in the trades unions. They will oppose us, Liz, and we must be prepared to deal with them when the time comes.'

I stared at him. The man I had known and loved was there behind the eyes. I could sense it. I could feel him, testing my resolve. Pulling me towards him. But there was also a hunger that had not been there before and a passion - not for me but for power. Its intensity frightened me, not simply for the havoc it might reek in my life and in the lives of those I held dear, but for the danger it might represent to anyone who stood in his way.

'I am ready, Peter.'

There was another pause.

'That is good to hear, Liz.'

I waited.

'It cannot have been easy to come here this morning.'

Smith had said that he would swallow it, that my return would blind his caution and that is precisely what was happening.

'Oh, it was not so difficult,' I lied.

He looked surprised.

'I can't pretend that it did not hurt at the time. Letting go of our relationship was the hardest thing I have ever done,' I said truthfully. 'But it was a long time ago and we have both moved on.'

He was watching me with an intensity that I could not interpret.

'You didn't marry, though,' he said, glancing at my application form, which he'd produced from his briefcase.

'No.' I glanced down into my lap.

He remained silent.

'I applied for the job, not because I want to rekindle what we had Peter,' I said, looking up at him. 'That is gone. I applied because I want to be a part of the Union's cause. If I am honest, I've been drifting since I severed my ties with the Right. For a time, I could not renew them, precisely because of what happened between us. But now I am ready. So, no, it was not so difficult to come here today.'

He nodded and then he held out his hand.

'Welcome to the Nationalist Union of Great Britain,' he said.

CHAPTER SIXTEEN

Wednesday, 25th May 1977

It was my third day at Excalibur House. I'd chosen a desk next to the pretty typist whose name turned out to be Grace Jones. She was fresh out of university, strikingly good looking and about as unlike her namesake as it was possible to be. The standard of her typing suggested that the written word had probably not been the subject of her studies.

I was supposed to be editing a piece that Peter had written for the Telegraph but, privately, I was debating whether Grace was really a few clowns short of a circus, or just playing the dumb blonde. If so, then she was pulling it off with considerable aplomb. The word around the office was that Justin Hughes kept her on for one reason and it wasn't her typographic skills.

And yet, there was something about Grace that led me to conclude that underneath the blond hair and endless typos, there might be a little more going on than people gave her credit for. She clearly had Hughes under her thumb and was well on her way with most of the other men in the office. I wondered what her end game was. Peter? And there it was, damn it. The tiniest pang of jealousy.

I stared at Peter's article. It was a powerful enough piece, but I was struggling to focus on it. My thoughts drifted from Grace to the events of the last week. God knows what Smith had said to Philpot but I'd been released from my position at the school with little more than a week's notice. Teresa had simply handed me a letter in a plain brown envelope on the Monday after my meeting with Smith. The letter confirmed my temporary secondment for the purpose of "career development". My job would be held open for a period of six months. Any extension beyond that would have to be separately agreed, in writing. And that was that. Philpot had spent the rest of the week avoiding me.

Then on my last day, my departure had been announced to the rest of the school at morning assembly. The ripple of voices that greeted the news had come mostly from the students in my form and there were several tearful hugs from them afterwards. The great majority of my colleagues, on the other hand, had remained tight lipped, limiting themselves to formal handshakes when they could no longer avoid them and whispered conversations when they thought that I was out of ear shot. According to a sixth former from my English class, the word around the school was that teachers didn't leave suddenly unless something needed covering up. Something pretty serious. The prevailing rumour was that I'd been caught shagging an as-yet unnamed student over the grand piano in the music room. So far as the kids seemed to be concerned, this had already given me a certain kudos which, according to my sixth form source, was well on the way to escalating me to legendary status.

Of course, for Simone, news of my departure had come as a complete surprise. I'd tried to talk to her. I'd been trying since the day after she'd seen me in the school car park with Smith, but the incident had already soured things between us. Or rather, my unwillingness to explain it to her with any semblance of honesty, had soured it.

She had seen through my explanation as soon as I had offered it. Don't ask me how. Explaining Smith away as the old flame I had mentioned seeing at the Tottenham meeting seemed obvious but Simone had known that it was not the truth. The confusion and hurt in her face had been plain. When I'd finally found the courage to tell her that I was leaving, she had stared at me with open-mouthed disbelief. Then she'd said 'You're not going to tell me what this is really all about are you?'

What could I have said that would have made it any better? For a moment, I had been lost for words. I had stood in front of her, desperately trying to tell her with my eyes that I had my reasons for saying nothing more and begging her to understand. Then, I had simply shaken my head. She had stared at me in silence, before stepping forward and embracing me. Then she had turned and walked away.

Ted took it better, which made me feel even worse about lying to him. When I told him that an opportunity had come up to do some development work at a Polytechnic in the City for six months, he'd been excited for me. Even when I told him that it would involve much longer hours and that he might have to get Harry and Kate off to school in the morning and pick them up from their childminder at night. He'd simply nodded and smiled. 'This might be your big chance, love. We'll manage.'

I'd lain awake next to him that night. Aching to tell him the truth. To tell him all of it. To unburden myself of the whole damned thing. It's strange how, at night, your perspectives shift, so completely. It is as though with the absence of daylight, the chains that confine you to reality are removed. If you're not careful, you can find yourself saying and doing all sorts of things that you wouldn't dare during daylight. Mostly the kind of things that you are quite likely to regret in the morning.

By the time I'd fallen asleep that night, I'd planned the whole thing. Exactly what I was going to tell him. Precisely what I was going to say. But, of course, when the alarm went off in the morning, I didn't tell him a thing. Not any of it.

But despite everything, what had worried me most during that final week at school - and it was still worrying me, sitting at my new desk at Excalibur House - wasn't how I was going to handle my feelings about Peter, or Smith or Ted or Simone. It was that I had been unable to contact Rosemary Sellers.

For a time, after Ted and I were married and true to her word, Rosemary had all but dropped out of my life. It had been a comforting thought, in the early days, that she was out there somewhere, keeping on eye on us, but when first Harry and then Kate were born life seemed to take on an altogether different focus and I thought about Rosemary less and less often. I suppose that she had been right: - I did need to forget about the past and build a new life.

If only it had been that simple. When Kate was about eighteen months old I had suffered from a bout of quite severe depression. I guess that I had been trying to atone for my dishonesty by being the perfect wife and mother, but the effort served only to bring my lies in to sharper focus. To highlight that, were the truth to come out, their world and mine would come crashing down.

With hindsight, I guess there comes a point for every new parent, when having children has so altered your life that you begin to wonder what happened to the person you once were. It is at that point, if you've any sense at all, that you put on your glad rags, head for a girls night out on the town and drink, dance or shag it out of your system and quite possibly all three. If I had thought that doing that could have helped I would have tried it. But alcohol only served to open the doors to my past and, whenever I did that, the only memories that came to meet me were of the ghosts that I had imprisoned there. As good as life with Ted and the children was - and it was very good - what depressed me most was the thought that my ghosts would never truly leave me.

So one afternoon, I had found myself at Claridges and, a day later, I was having afternoon tea with Rosemary Sellers. Since that day I'd taken to contacting Rosemary via the desk at Claridges, whenever I needed a lift or someone to confide in. Not often. No more than twice or maybe three times a year. But often enough to keep myself on an even keel.

Sometimes, after I left a message, there would be a telephone call to the house (she told Ted that she was a friend from my Ealing days) or occasionally, she would simply appear. Ted had learned to cope, quite well, with her sudden appearances. He would refer to her as 'loony tunes'. But others found her a little more challenging. Once, she had bowled into school in the middle of the afternoon, telling them that she was my Great Aunt Rosemary. She'd made quite an entrance and intimidated the hell out of Teresa by demanding that I be called out of class immediately on "important family business". It had been hilarious watching Teresa being outmanoeuvred by a greater force, for once. And, when she put her mind to it, Rosemary was a force to be reckoned with. She had never once let me down. Until now.

I'd gone to Claridges after the confrontation with Smith and had asked, as usual, for a message to be passed to Rosemary Sellers but, a day later, there had been no response. On the third day I had decided to try again and again found myself back at the Claridges desk. As usual, I handed Rosemary's card to the receptionist but, unusually, she had pressed a button beneath the counter and asked me to wait. Within moments, a man appeared from the office at the rear of the reception. I recognised him. I'd seen him at the hotel before and, once or twice, he had served tea to Rosemary and me. His name was Alphonse.

'Bonjour Mademoiselle. Would you accompany me, please?' he said, holding up a section of the reception desk and gesturing for me to follow.

He was impeccably well dressed. Along with a very expensive looking dark grey suit, he wore a pink tie and, in his breast pocket, a matching silk handkerchief, which he wore a little longer than the norm. This pink flourish enhanced his voice which was camp with a French accent. Indeed, it was so camp that I found myself wondering whether it was genuine.

'S'il vous plaît?'

I hesitated for a moment before stepping through the gap and following him into the office at the back of the reception.

I had rarely seen an office look so tidy and well organised. The place was spotless.

'Please, Mademoiselle, take a seat,' he said, closing the door and indicating a chair beside a truly vast mahogany desk.

'Is there something wrong?' I said, pulling out the seat.

He walked around the desk and sat down before he answered. 'I am afraid that it may be so.'

'Has something happened to Rosemary?'

He stared at me for a moment longer than was comfortable. 'We cannot be sure. We have not seen Madame Sellers for several weeks and she does not respond to our messages.'

'Several weeks? For how many, exactly?' I asked anxiously.

He hesitated. I guessed that he was trying to decide how much he could safely tell me. 'You will understand, Mademoiselle, the confidential nature of our service to Madame Sellers.'

I did understand it. I understood it very well. I thought for a moment. 'And yet, you asked to speak to me.'

Alphonse said nothing.

'Because you are concerned about what might have happened to her.'

'Oui.'

'Concerned enough to break her confidence?'

'Peut-être.'

'Then you are going to have to trust me.'

Alphonse stared at me. 'Perhaps we are going to have to trust each other.'

'Perhaps so.'

'Then tell me, Mademoiselle, how exactly did you meet Madame Sellers?'

He was asking me to put my cards on the table. It was not an unreasonable request, but neither was it wholly without risk. From what I knew, Rosemary had a long standing arrangement with the hotel staff, through which I, and possibly others, had been able to maintain contact with her. I could not be certain that the arrangement had been with Alphonse, but this seemed likely. In any event, right now, he was my only link to Rosemary. Either I took him into my confidence, or if something had happened to her, I might never find out or hear from her again. I took a breath. 'I was working undercover, monitoring a number of right wing groups, mostly in London.'

'Fascistes?' he asked, with apparent distaste.

'Yes. I had been doing so, I thought, with some success but in truth I had made a number of mistakes. The work had…' I hesitated, 'taken its toll.'

Alphonse nodded. 'Oui, je vous comprends.'

'I did not know it then, but I too was being watched.'

'You had been discovered?'

'Yes, but thankfully not by those who I was watching.'

He raised an eyebrow. 'By Madame Sellers, perhaps?'

I nodded. 'One evening she approached me. I had no idea who she was but there was something about her. Something that led me to trust her. And so we arranged to meet. Here at Claridges, actually.'

'Ah, oui, but of course.'

I sighed. 'It was a long time ago. Rosemary helped me at a time when I had nowhere else to go and we have been friends ever since. In fact, I count her as one of my dearest friends.'

Alphonse nodded.

There was a long silence.

'I owe Rosemary a very great deal, Alphonse. You should know that I would never betray her and, if she is in any kind of trouble, then I will leave no stone unturned in order to help her.'

Alphonse smiled. 'Merci, Mademoiselle. But it will not be easy. There is only a telephone number and she does not reply.'

'When did you last see her?'

'She had afternoon tea here…' He removed a small notebook from his pocket and leafed through its pages. 'It was on Friday, the twenty-second of April. We have not seen or heard from her since that day.'

'Which was what, four weeks ago?'

Alphonse nodded. 'Oui. Approximativement.'

'Has this ever happened before? She must go away sometimes.'

'Well, of course. But never without telling us.'

'You must have an address for her, surely?'

'Non. There is no address. Only a telephone number.'

I thought for a moment. 'Was she alone, when she was here on the twenty-second?'

'Oui,' Alphonse replied, nodding his head.

'Are you sure?' I asked.

'Oui. I remember it perfectly well. I served her myself.'

'But she must meet other people here. As well as me?'

Alphonse thought for a moment. 'Rarely, Mademoiselle. You are her only regular visitor here.'

This surprised me. 'But she did meet others here. Rarely, you said. Do you know who they were?'

'Non. The booking was always in Madame Sellers' name. As for the names of her guests, this we did not ask.'

This was hardly a surprise, given the nature of her work. 'When she is in London, does she stay here at Claridges?' I asked.

'When she is in London, oui.'

'And when she is not in London? Do you have any idea where she lives or stays?'

He shrugged. 'Madame Sellers and I have known each other for many years, but there is much, still, that I do not know.'

'Me too.'

'I'm afraid for her, Mademoiselle. Her...' he hesitated '*profession* exposes her to many risks.'

'Yes it does.' I thought for a moment. 'Do you know anything at all about what she was working on?'

Alphonse shook his head. 'Non. We never discussed this.'

'We don't have a lot to go on do we?'

'Non. Only the telephone number.'

'And when you dial it, there is no reply?'

He shook his head.

'Perhaps we could trace the number?'

He shook his head again. 'Non. It is, how do you say, ex-répertoire.'

I smiled. 'Ex-directory. Of course.'

I thought for a moment. 'But at least we could use the number to identify the town and then search for her by name.'

Alphonse stared at me. 'Then you know her real name?'

Her real name. Of course. I had not given it a great deal of thought. But it was obvious, now that I came to think about it. 'No. I don't.'

We sat in silence then.

'I think that there is much that we do not know about our friend.'

I nodded. 'There must be something. Some way to find her.'

Alphonse started to speak and then hesitated. I looked at him expectantly.

'What?'

'There was another contact. For use, only in an emergency.'

'A contact? Do you mean a name?'

'Oui.'

I laughed. 'So we use it. I think this qualifies as an emergency, don't you?'

'Unfortunately, we cannot.'

I looked at him in confusion.

'After her retirement, Madame Sellers was adamant that it was not to be used.'

After her retirement. 'What?'

'Madame Sellers asked me to destroy it. It was a promise.'

Seemingly, I knew even less about her than Alphonse did. 'And did you destroy it?'

He looked at me and shook his head. 'Non.'

'Do you have it with you?'

'Oui.'

'May I see it?'

He hesitated and then put his hand into his inside jacket pocket and removed a brown leather wallet, from which he took a small white card. He handed it to me.

On the card was printed a London telephone number and a man's name. That name was "Smith".

Chapter Seventeen

'Liz?'

I was staring at the article for The Telegraph, but my head was somewhere else. Several other places, in fact. I had been thinking hard about Alphonse's revelation, but I still hadn't managed to make any sense of it. Rosemary had repeatedly warned me about Smith. In fact, it had been her concern about Smith that had first prompted her to approach me, or so she had said. So why would she have had Alphonse call Smith in an emergency? Had Rosemary and Smith been working together? And why had Rosemary said nothing to me about her retirement?

'Liz?'

I looked up. 'Hmm?'

Smith. It was Smith who had forced me to join the NUGB. Smith who had threatened to reveal my secrets to Ted if I did not do as he wished. It was Smith who was already pressing me for intelligence about the Union's activities and it was Smith who Rosemary did not wish Alphonse to contact, now that she had retired. The bastard had been pulling the strings from the very beginning.

'Fancy a coffee?' Grace said.

'Sure. I'll come with you. I need to stretch my legs.'

I didn't need to stretch my legs. I needed to find Rosemary Sellers. I just didn't know how I was going to do it.

I followed Grace out into the kitchen. It was a fairly spartan room with grey-blue carpet squares on the floor, a sink, a fridge, a kettle and not much else. I stood by the window, looking down onto the hustle and bustle of Great Eastern Street. It was a beautiful morning. The good weather seemed to have encouraged people out of their offices. There were people of just about every shade and hue. I wondered how many of them knew that they passing the headquarters of the Nationalist Union of Great Britain.

'Here you go,' Grace said, handing me a hot cup. She stood beside me, watching the street scene outside. 'Roll on five o'clock,' she said.

I glanced sideways. It wasn't often that I felt old, but standing there next to Grace, I felt old alright. She didn't know how lucky she was. 'What are you up to tonight?' I asked, making conversation.

'Not much. Niall might come over and maybe we'll go for a drink or something.'

'Boyfriend?' I asked, trying to sound interested.

'What, Niall?' she laughed. 'You must be joking.'

I turned and looked at her. I wasn't joking, but neither was an explanation going to be forthcoming without a little prompting. 'No?' I said. *Come on Grace. Give me chance...*

She tilted her head towards me, glancing over her shoulder as she did so. 'Niall's as bent as a nine bob note,' she whispered into my ear.

'Oh.' I hadn't really been expecting that.

'He's such a sweetie. We were at school together. Best friends ever since. Keep it to yourself though. This lot can be a bit funny about things like that.'

'Don't tell me, he's black as well,' I said smiling. I couldn't help myself.

Grace looked horrified. 'No, of course not,' she said, looking about the room nervously.

Then she noticed the look on my face. I was grinning. 'Don't think I've ever met a black homo, have you?' she said conspiratorially.

'No, I don't think I ever have.' I was lying. I had. Several actually.

'They say,' she said, returning to a whisper, 'that they have the most enormous... you know...'

'Who have? Black men, homo's or both?' I said, trying to keep a straight face.

'Black men, idiot...'

As she said it, for once, Grace twigged that I was winding her up. 'Oh...' she said, slapping me gently on the arm and flushing. Then she lowered her voice again. 'Be a bit of waste though, wouldn't it? A queer with a big willy.'

'I'm not sure that Niall would see it that way,' I said, grinning and we both laughed.

'What's all the joviality about?' said a voice from the kitchen door. Grace was immediately silent.

I turned. It was John Taggart.

I mouthed *'It's alright'* at Grace and turned towards him. 'Just girls' stuff John.'

'Oh. Right. I've been looking for you Liz, I wanted to introduce you to Jimmy Dobson, our head of security.'

'Okay. Give me two minutes to swallow my coffee and I'll come over.'

'Sure.' Taggart turned and disappeared into the office.

Grace looked like a rabbit caught in headlights.

'Hey, it's alright,' I said, stroking her shoulder. 'It was just a joke and besides, John's alright.'

Grace looked at me doubtfully. 'He might be. But Jimmy Dobson isn't. That bloke gives me the bloody creeps.'

'Really?'

'Really. You haven't met him yet, have you?'

I shook my head.

'He's scary.'

Jimmy Dobson was a name that I recognised. I recognised it because Smith had told me about him. He had advised extreme caution and to stay away from him altogether if I possibly could. Which was a joke, because it wasn't going to be possible at all.

'Well, I guess I'm about to find out for myself.'

'Rather you than me,' Grace said and she meant it.

I drained my coffee and left Grace still standing at the window. 'Don't worry about me,' I said as I walked towards the kitchen door. 'I've had blokes like Dobson for breakfast.'

Grace looked doubtful and I was about to find out why.

I left the kitchen and strolled towards Taggart's desk. I could see Taggart and another man seated beside him. Presumably Dobson. He was a big man. Tall and wide.

Taggart saw me coming and got up. The other man remained seated.

'Ah, Liz, I wanted to introduce you. This is Jimmy Dobson, our head of security.'

Dobson didn't hold out his hand. He stared at me coldly. I tried to hold his gaze, but it wasn't easy. He looked even bigger up close. Long hair and a wide, square chin with sideburns that extended to his jaw line. Like Ray Dorset from *Mungo Jerry*.

'Mr Dobson,' I said.

Dobson nodded.

'I think Jimmy wants to have a word with you in private, Liz. So please take a seat and I'll leave you to it.'

He indicated that I should sit in his chair and, as I sat, walked away without further comment.

'So,' I said, swivelling my chair so that I was facing Dobson.

He remained silent.

'It's good to meet you Mr Dobson.'

Still nothing.

I smiled. 'What can I do for you?'

Dobson looked me up and down, lingering just a little too long on my legs.

I should have chosen trousers but all the trousers I possessed had been worn a hundred times. So I'd bought a couple of dress suits to keep at the safe house. I could change into them in the mornings and out of them again at night.

Besides, I have great legs. They're one of my best bits. And my arse looks pretty damn good in a skirt. I had wanted to give the right impression from the start. Sharp, well dressed and sexy as hell. I wanted to impress. Taggart, Hughes and the others. And one other in particular. I wanted to impress Peter Owen.

'You left the movement in 1969,' Dobson said, without expression.

Amen. The man actually spoke. 'Yes that's right,' I said as calmly as I could manage.

'Why?'

I didn't much like him.

'Personal reasons.' I wasn't going to give him any more than I had to.

'Which were?'

'Personal.'

He stared at me. I took a breath. I didn't much like him, but neither did I want to make an enemy of him, if I could avoid it. 'I'm sorry,' I smiled. 'What is it that you would like to know?'

'On your application form, you said that you are single.'

'That's right.'

'No children?'

'No.'

'How comes?'

'What?' I wasn't sure that I'd heard him correctly.

'How comes, that you are single with no children? Pretty girl. School teacher. No man. Why?'

I stared at him. If he was trying to make me feel uncomfortable, he was succeeding, but I was not about to let him think that I was intimidated by the hard man routine. 'Where did you get your management degree, Mr Dobson? I'd like to congratulate them on a job well done.'

'You think you are smart.'

I laughed uneasily. I hoped it didn't show. 'I think that I am here to do a job. How I conduct myself outside of work is my business.'

'No. You are working for the NUGB. That makes it my business.'

'Really. And what is that you do here, exactly?' I glanced over my shoulder. The desks around us were empty. I could see Grace in the distance. She was watching me but she was too far away to overhear our conversation.

Dobson ignored my question. 'Peter hired you before seeing any of the other candidates and without any checks. Why?'

'Did he? News to me. Perhaps you should ask him.'

'Oh, I intend to. But in the meantime, perhaps I will run the checks myself.'

'Fine by me.'

'And what do you suppose that I will find when I do?'

I thought for a moment. The answer to that depended on what checks he was going to run and how thorough they were. 'Look, Mr Dobson. I don't know what your problem is. If you want to waste your time checking me out, go ahead. Be my guest. But, if you intend to go poking your nose into my private life, don't expect any help from me. I am here to do a job and right now, I would quite like to be left to get on with it.'

I stared at him steadily. I might be shaking on the inside, but the bastard was sure as hell not going to see me shaking on the outside. 'If that is all?' I said and gave him my most condescending smile.

'For now.'

'Good,' I said, getting to my feet. 'I would like to be able to say that meeting you has been a pleasure but frankly, it hasn't.' I turned and walked away, in the rough direction of my desk. I had to stop myself from running.

Grace could see me coming. Audrey, the other typist was watching my approach too. I got the feeling that they'd been talking about me.

I slumped into my seat. Grace looked at me, worriedly.

'What a charmer,' I said.

'Told you so,' she whispered. 'Are you alright?' She glanced at Audrey.

'I'm fine. Like I said, I've had gorillas like that for my breakfast.'

It was then that the phone on my desk rang. *Saved by the bell.* I lifted the receiver.

'Liz? It's Peter.'

'Oh, hi,' I stammered, my heart in my mouth.

'Are you alright?'

'What? Me, oh yes, I'm fine.'

'Good. Have you had a chance to look at the piece for The Telegraph?'

'Yes. Yes it's good but I've made some amendments.'

'Excellent.'

'Right.'

There was a silence.

'Look, I'm aware that I haven't seen much of you since you started. I've been a little pre-occupied. But I've got some time now. Could you come up? We can go through your amendments together. I'd like to get the thing nailed and out by the end of the day.'

'Yes, sure.' It was turning into one hell of a morning.

'And then maybe we could have lunch? There's a couple of other things I'd like to chew over with you.'

Shit. I wasn't ready. Not for lunch with Peter Owen. Certainly not after the grilling I'd just had from the gorilla. 'Oh. Okay. Yes. Right. I'll come straight up.' I put down the phone and ran my hand through my hair.

Grace looked at me, like she had a question.

'Peter wants to see me,' I said by way of explanation.

'Mr Owen?' Grace whispered.

I nodded.

I gathered my papers together, picked up my handbag and stood up. Taggart had returned to his desk. I could see that he was engaged in an animated discussion with Jimmy Dobson. Dobson's eyes followed me as I made my way across the office.

Wanker. I ignored him.

I made it to the landing. The lift door was open but there was no lift car. A temporary steel gate had been installed across the shaft. I could hear the engineers working above. Or was it below? I couldn't tell.

Shit. I needed to get myself sorted. Peter had been right. We'd only seen each other in passing, since Monday, and while a part of me had been disappointed, it was the part of me that I knew I had to keep in check.

I pushed the Ladies' room door open and went inside.

I walked over to the sink and stood, staring at myself in the mirror. I looked a mess. I rummaged in my handbag for a comb and my lipstick. I could feel my heart beating fast. Too fast. And I could see the rose flush on my neck.

I forced myself to picture Ted and the children. They were my reality. Not this. I was here for a purpose. Smith's purpose. I could not change that. I was going to get the job done and then I was going to get the hell out. I took a deep breath and tried to relax. I tidied my hair, refreshed my lipstick, put the comb and the lippy back in my bag, turned and left.

My feet were still heavy, though, as I climbed the stairs.

Chapter Eighteen

Thursday, 26th May 1977

I parked, for the fourth consecutive day, on the road in front of the cafe, exactly as Smith had instructed. I took the keys from the ignition, opened the door and got out of the car. I looked at my watch. It was warm for 7.20am, even in the shade beneath the canopy of the horse chestnut trees.

I glanced over towards the cafe. It was closed, which was a shame. I could have done with a coffee.

I walked around to the back of the car and lifted the boot lid. As I did so, a man appeared in the door way at the side of the cafe. He stood and lit a cigarette. He was watching me. Obviously.

I took my bag out of the boot, slung it over my shoulder, closed the boot lid and turned the key in the lock. Then I walked towards him. He watched me approach, in between drags. As I neared him, he nodded. I returned the gesture. He was short and muscular, with a Mediterranean complexion. Probably Greek or Turkish. I could feel his eyes watching me, boring a hole in the back of my head, as I walked away.

I took the footpath toward the park's western boundary and crossed the railway by the footbridge, just as a train rumbled by below, rattling the steel panels that ran down both sides of the bridge. I guessed that they were there to stop kids dropping things down onto the trains. Or the mentally ill from throwing themselves onto the rails.

On the other side of the bridge, the pathway forked. Up ahead, the main path emerged onto Oxford Road. To the right, the pathway disappeared into a dense standing of trees. I peered along the main path and, satisfied that I had not been observed, turned to the right.

The way through the trees was empty and silent, save for a blackbird's sudden alarm call that sent a small flock of sparrows chattering up into the trees and my heart into my mouth. After a few minutes, I left the path and entered the back garden to the safe house, through a wooden gate.

The approach to the stairs at the back of the house was mostly hidden from the view of the surrounding houses by overhanging trees. I made my way up the metal stairs, my feet clanking noisily on the steps. At the top, I inserted a key and opened the door. I entered and immediately froze. The flat was silent but I could smell coffee. I stood, rooted to the spot and listened. I could hear nothing. The hairs on the back of my neck bristled. *Shit*. There was someone in the flat. I could feel it. I took two careful steps forward.

'Coffee?'

It was a male voice. In the two seconds it took my brain to recognise it, I almost died. *Smith*. He appeared in the doorway at the end of the hall.

'Jesus Christ. What the hell are you doing here?' I said.

'And, a very good morning to you too,' he replied, evidently enjoying my discomfort.

I brushed past him, into the kitchen and threw my bag onto the kitchen table. 'Jesus. Warn me next time, would you?'

He ignored me.

I poured myself some coffee from the cafetiere.

'So, how's it going?' he said, almost cheerily.

'Fine.'

'Did you see Christos at the cafe?'

'Yes, I saw him. He's a bit obvious isn't he?'

Smith shrugged.

I pulled out a chair and sat down at the table. 'What do you want, anyway?' I said, still irritated.

'I wanted to check that you're okay.'

'Fine. I said I'm fine.'

'Any problems?'

I hesitated. 'No.' *Damn it.* He'd picked up on the hesitation. 'No problems,' I said, returning his stare.

'Excellent. So are you ready to get to work?'

'What?'

'Liz, we don't have a lot of time. If you're settled in, then we've got work to do.'

'This is day four. Give me a bloody chance.'

Smith pulled out a chair and sat down opposite me. 'How is it going with Owen?'

'Fine. It's going fine.'

'You had lunch with him yesterday.'

It wasn't a question. He knew. Which meant that he'd been watching me. Or if not Smith, then he had an informant.

'Yes, we had lunch. It was his idea, not mine,' I added.

'That's good. It means he trusts you. The closer you can get to him, the easier this is going to be.'

For you, maybe. I thought it, but I said nothing.

'Support for the Union is growing and Owen already has some powerful friends, both in Parliament and elsewhere.'

'Not entirely unreasonable, for a political party.'

'Indeed. But we have good reason to believe that he has established a network of supporters within both the armed forces and the police, through which he already exerts considerable influence. This is already causing local… difficulties. It cannot continue unchecked.'

'Difficulties? What difficulties?'

'In London, at least, NUGB members seem to be able do more or less as they please. It is causing… tensions.' Smith leaned back in his chair. 'I want you to find out who these supporters are. I need names.'

I thought about it. 'If you're so worried about Peter Owen and the NUGB, why isn't the Service crawling all over them?'

Smith hesitated.

'And why me? I mean, I'm hardly your most committed or experienced operative am I? There must be any number of established agents who could have done a better job.'

'You were close to Owen. He trusts you. You've been there three days and he's already taken you to lunch. Think how long it would have taken us to get someone else in that close. Months. Years. Maybe never. Your relationship with him made you and makes you our first choice.'

I didn't believe him. Forcing me, under duress, was never going to make me the first choice. It didn't add up. 'I don't have a relationship with Owen. Not anymore. I have a husband and two children. Remember?'

I regretted saying it as soon as the words had left my mouth. I waited for the inevitable threat, but to his credit, Smith held back. 'I take it that you read the newspapers?' he said after a moment.

I ignored the question.

'The country is on the brink. Inflation is out of control, the Unions seems intent on destroying what is left of our industry, the IRA are trying to bomb their way out of Britain. The Government is one step away from paralysis. One more crisis, Liz. Just one. And the lights start going out.'

'A not unreasonable analysis. Your point is?'

Smith sighed. 'My point is that time is running out. The NUGB are preparing to make their move and, unfortunately, the mood in the country is beginning to swing their way.'

'Perhaps. But you still haven't answered my question. If they're such a threat, why isn't the Service crawling all over them?'

'We're doing what we can but, at present, there are a number of competing priorities.'

Interesting. 'Which presumably means that not everyone is agreed about the threat they pose. This is beginning to sound more like a personal crusade, than a campaign to save the nation.'

A flash of irritation played across Smith's face. 'We are all agreed about the threat. But in case you hadn't noticed, we're already engaged in a war with the republicans in Northern

Ireland and, while they continue to export their butchery to the mainland, they are seen as a more pressing and immediate priority.'

I was beginning to annoy him. I could see it in his face. There seemed little point in pressing him further. I knew where that would end up. 'So for now at least, we're on our own. Is that what you're saying?'

He ignored the question again. 'Right now, I need names Liz. Whatever Owen is up to, I need to know who is involved. I need to know who he is talking to. Who he is leaning on. What they're planning. And I need to know it quickly.'

I drained my coffee cup. 'Fine. I'm on to it. Now, if you don't mind, I need to get changed.'

Smith, gestured for me to continue.

I got up and took my bag into the little bedroom at the rear of the flat. I walked across to the wardrobe took one of the dresses from a hanger and threw it across the bed. I kicked off my shoes and stood in front of the dressing table, thinking about what Smith had said. Banking on my relationship with Peter was such a risk. Relationships always are. How could he have had any clear idea about how this one was going to turn out?

I undid my belt, wriggled out of my trousers and put them on a hanger in the wardrobe. So, what had led him to blackmail me back into service? Something had. Smith wasn't stupid but then neither was I.

I pulled my blouse off over my head, threw it over the back of a chair and adjusted my bra.

'You know, it would help us if you renewed your sexual relationship with Mr Owen.'

I whirled round. Smith was standing in the bedroom door way, watching me. 'What the fuck is wrong with you,?' I said, hurriedly reaching for the dress.

'Pillow talk, Liz. It works every time.' As he said it, his eyes dropped, just for a second.

I slipped the dress over my head and thought about the two hours and fifteen minutes I'd spent with Peter. Whether I was willing to admit it to Smith or not, the truth was it had taken

Peter no more than a few minutes to begin to loosen the bonds that I had spent so long tying and re-tying into place. That, as Peter had tugged at each knot, I had felt the old wounds again, opening with the same exquisite agony. And I had struggled to stop myself wanting more. Just as it had always been.

I walked across to Smith. I felt tiny, standing in front of him, without my shoes on. 'You're all heart,' I said and shut the bedroom door in his face.

He watched her from the shadows of the alleyway as she opened the gate, stepped out onto the pavement, turned and walked away. He was about to follow, when something caught his eye. He waited briefly and then crossed the road, opened the gate and approached the building's front door. Fumbling in his pocket, he produced a set of keys.

The postman opened the gate behind him. 'Morning, mate.'

'I'll take those,' he said, holding out his hand.

The postman looked at him doubtfully.

'I'm her brother. I'll make sure she gets them,' he said, taking the letters from the postman's hand.

The postman shrugged and walked away.

He waited a few moments and then examined each of the envelopes in turn. When he'd finished, he pushed all but one through the letter box.

From the window above, Smith watched the man walk off in the direction that she had taken only minutes before. He had recognised him, as soon as he had stepped out from the alley between the buildings opposite. Jimmy Dobson. The man with no background. Liz Muir was going to have to be careful. She might think that her heart belonged to Owen, but Smith knew that Dobson was more than capable of putting a knife between her ribs and claiming it for himself.

Chapter Nineteen

There was only so much that I was going to be able to discover through my day to day work at Excalibur House and with Dobson watching my every move, Smith had probably been right. My relationship with Peter was the key. But getting close to Peter, let alone into his bed, was the one thing I could not afford to do. I knew where that would lead. I'd already felt the pull of it. The only way I was going to survive was to get Smith the information he wanted and get the hell out. The longer it took and the closer I got to Peter, the greater the risk of sinking back into the mire.

It was a process that was already underway, with every day that began and ended with a lie and every knot that was untied through my contact with Peter Owen.

I needed results and I needed them fast. Which meant getting access to his office. The trouble was that I could not work out how I was going to do it and had almost given up, when the answer landed in my lap, or rather, on Grace Jones's desk.

I had just come back from lunch to find Justin Hughes perched on the corner of her desk, on the pretence of correcting her latest typographic effort. To be fair, it did sound like the resulting letter was going to end up more correcting fluid than ink. But, as I walked towards them, it was obvious that Hughes was at least as interested in ogling her cleavage than he was in creating a masterwork of the English language. When he saw me, he coughed nervously and hauled himself upright. 'Well I suppose that it will do, but will you please be more careful next time, Grace?'

'Yes, Mr Hughes,' she said in the girly voice that she reserved for him. 'I'm so sorry. I don't know what I was thinking.'

He smiled at her in the kind of patronising way that only middle aged men can, nodded at me and walked away.

It was then that I saw that he had left his keys behind on her desk. Hughes was the main key holder for the building and there was every possibility that the bunch included the key to Peter's office.

'What was that all about?' I said, taking off my jacket and dropping it over the keys.

'The usual,' said Grace.

'Tits or typing?' I whispered.

'Tits, definitely although, honestly, the typing was poor, even for me. So I gave him an extra good look.'

We both giggled.

I was thinking hard and then it came to me. 'Oh, did you send that fax?'

Grace looked at me blankly. 'Which fax?'

'You know, the one to the BBC. They've been after an interview with Peter for Nationwide. I said that we'd fax them with his availability.'

Grace flushed. 'No, I completely forgot. I'll do it now.'

'Would you? I haven't mastered the fax machine yet. The letter is in the out-tray.'

'Of course.' She got up and walked off in the direction of the facsimile machine.

I glanced over my shoulder, before scooping up my jacket, along with the keys and returned to my desk, dropping them into my handbag as I sat down.

After a few minutes, Grace returned. 'Done,' she said.

'Thanks.'

I needed to move quickly. It was only going to be a matter of time before Hughes noticed that his keys were missing. Certainly, he'd notice it when it came to locking up the building at the end of the day.

I gave myself a few minutes to formulate a plan and then got to my feet. Grace looked up. I mouthed 'girl's room' and headed for the door, clutching my handbag. I didn't look back.

Outside, I pressed the lift call button and prayed. I couldn't, for the life of me, think of an excuse for using the newly repaired lift, let alone for being on third floor.

Thankfully, the lift arrived after a few moments. I stepped into the car and pressed "3" on the control panel. The doors shut and the lift began to move.

There were four offices on the third floor, along with the board room and two smaller meeting rooms. One of the offices was vacant. I knew that, because Peter had offered it to me but I had declined it, choosing instead to sit in the open plan office on the second floor. The others belonged to Peter, John Taggart and to Jimmy Dobson. Peter and John were out all day at a meeting in Sheffield and I knew that nothing was scheduled for the meeting rooms. I had no idea where Dobson was. Nobody ever did. Which meant that getting into Peter's office was going to be a gamble.

As the lift came to a halt, I settled on a reason for being on the third floor and prayed that I was not going to need it.

The lift door opened. I tried to steady my nerves.

The third floor corridor was empty and silent. Dobson's door, the first on the left, was shut. I had no intention of opening it. As were the doors to the vacant office next to Dobson's, John Taggart's office and both meeting rooms. Peter's office was the last door on the right, opposite the boardroom.

The boardroom had double swing doors. There was no sign of any lock. I looked over my shoulder, nervously. The corridor was still empty. I tried the door to Peter's office. It was locked. I knelt and examined the barrel.

It occurred to me that it might be safer to check the bunch for the right key, from the seclusion of the board room. That way, I'd be less likely to disturb Dobson if, in fact, he was in his office. I eased open the double doors and stepped inside. The board room was massive, with a polished table running the room's entire length and seating for... I counted them... *twenty two*. Each seating position had a microphone with a push button.

I opened my bag and found the key with the matching number stamped on its bow. I was about to step back out into the corridor when I spotted another small door at the rear of the room. Curiosity got the better of me. I walked across to the door and tried the handle. It was unlocked.

It opened into a narrow hall, with small rooms to the left and right. The room to the right was a store room, containing mostly office supplies. The room to the left was a kitchenette, presumably used to service board meetings. At the end of the hallway was another door. I knelt down and examined the lock, stood up and smiled to myself. It had the same number that had been stamped on the barrel of the lock on Peter's door. I inserted the key, opened the door and stepped into Peter Owen's office.

The temptation was to begin the search, but that had not been my plan. Hughes would miss the keys. He might already be missing them. And when he did, all hell was going to be let loose, especially if Dobson was in the building. My plan had been to leave the door to Peter's office unlocked in the hope that Hughes wouldn't bother checking it. After all, he'd know that Peter had been out all day.

The back door was a godsend. Hughes would have even less reason to check the doors from the boardroom, so all being well, I'd be able to return by that route.

I glanced around the office. It smelt of books, pipe tobacco and Peter's after shave.

I left the room the way I had come. Two minutes later, I was stood by the boardroom doors, listening for any sound from the corridor outside. There was none. I inched one of the doors open, slowly. The way was clear. I stepped out into the corridor and let the door close behind me, praying that it wouldn't squeak on its hinges. I was sweating like a pig.

Miraculously, I made it back to my desk without incident.

'I found these outside, by the lift,' I said, pulling Hughes's keys from my bag and showing them to Grace. 'Somebody must have dropped them.'

She looked at me slightly oddly. 'Not mine,' she said. 'They look like office keys.'

'Hmm... I guess I should give them to Dobson.'

Grace looked worried. 'I wouldn't. They're probably Justin's. He's always losing them. He got a right bollocking from Dobson a couple of weeks back, for leaving them in the front door.'

I mouthed 'No!' and pulled a face.

Grace nodded. 'He's such an ass, but I'd still rather have him as my boss than Jimmy Dobson.'

'I can understand that. Any idea where he is?'

'I think I saw him go into the kitchen.'

I got to my feet. 'I'll see if they're his.'

I found Hughes standing by the kettle waiting for it to boil. To say that he was pleased that I'd returned his keys to him, rather than handing them to Dobson, would be something of an understatement. I thought he was going to kiss me. Thankfully he didn't.

I watched the office empty. By half past six, there was just me and Justin Hughes. I got up, and wandered over to his desk. 'Haven't you got a home to go to?' I said, conversationally.

'What, and miss out on this little pleasure,' he said, indicating the pile of papers in front of him.

He didn't look like he wanted to strike up a conversation.

'Well, I think I'll get off now.'

He looked up. 'Sure. Look, thanks again for rescuing my keys. I appreciate it.'

'No problem. To give her some credit, it was Grace who suggested that I should hand them to you, rather than to Mr Dobson.'

'Was it?' He looked surprised and pleased, all at the same time. It was not a pretty sight.

'Yup.' And then I added 'I know she's a bit ditzy but she's got her strengths.'

'I know that,' he said, smiling. 'It's just a shame that typing isn't one of them. It's a bit of problem, given the job we employ her to do.'

I laughed. 'I know, but she does try.' *And her tits are pretty good too.* I thought it, but I didn't say it.

'She does that,' he said, raising an eyebrow.

'It's a man's world Justin. Us girls have to stick together.'

'Sounds good to me,' he said, giving me a slightly scary wink.

Sleaze bag or idiot? I really couldn't decide which. 'See you in the morning?' I ventured

'Bright and early.'

I used the stairs, except that I wasn't leaving. Instead, I walked down two flights. The first floor was vacant. According to Grace, there had been talk of it being rented to a firm of solicitors, but that had never happened. I walked to the far end of the empty office and took the rear stairs back to the second floor. From the stair well landing I could see into the NUGB office through a narrow glass window in the fire door. Hughes was still seated at his desk. I looked at my watch. I had told Ted that I was going to be late. I wondered, how late I was going to be.

Shortly after seven o'clock, Hughes suddenly gathered his papers together, stuffed them in his briefcase, picked his nose and clambered to his feet. It was at that moment that a voice in my head said "Step away from the window" which was fortunate, because as I did, Hughes turned and started to walk towards me. I took two steps backwards and gambled that

Hughes was not about to check whether anyone was hiding on the stairway landing. Which, of course, they were. But Hughes wasn't to know that.

Nothing happened.

After a few minutes, I stepped forward again and peered through the little window, into the office. Hughes was checking the row of steel filing cabinets that were arranged down one side of the office. Satisfied that they were locked, he walked towards the exit, switched off the lights and was gone.

I breathed out. Then I returned to the first floor, found a window that overlooked Great Eastern Street and waited. I didn't have long to wait. Less than ten minutes later, Hughes emerged and strolled away towards the bus stop on the opposite side of the street.

Hughes hadn't checked the rear door into Peter's office. Or, if he had, he had been kind enough to leave it unlocked for me. As I stepped in through the doorway I couldn't help but congratulate myself on a plan well laid and executed.

What light there was filtered into the office from the large window overlooking Great Eastern Street. It was a relief that Hughes had left before sunset. Otherwise I'd have been searching in the dark.

I sat down at the desk. The first thing that I noticed was a framed picture of Peter with his wife, Emma. I felt the familiar stab of jealousy that I felt whenever I thought about her. It wasn't that she was on holiday with him, it was the look on their faces and on her face, in particular. She was happy. They were happy. I had spent years longing to be with him. Longing to have the life with him that Emma was evidently enjoying. It might be an uncomfortable thought but I thought it nonetheless. Part of me wanted it to be the woman in the picture. Part of me wanted to be Emma Owen.

And yet there they were. Mr and Mrs Owen. And here I was, about to rifle through his desk like some bloody stalker. I felt like the outsider I was. Peter had got on with his life and, to be fair, so had I. But, while I'd got on with it, I'd never been able to get over my relationship with him. Not truly. For me, it had been there, in the background. Underneath and behind everything that I did. Every time I looked at my son.

At that moment, I wanted to leave. I wanted to go home and stay home. But, whether I liked it or not, and I didn't, I was there for a reason and that reason was not going to disappear anytime soon.

I reached across the desk, pulled a tray of papers towards me and started to read. After five minutes or so I'd learned nothing of great consequence.

I tried the desk drawers. Both the pedestals were locked. The slim drawer between them wasn't. I searched its contents. Again nothing of any consequence.

I sat back and looked at the locked drawers. I wasn't going to find anything if I couldn't get into them. I closed my eyes and waited for inspiration. When I opened them, there it was. Peter's coat was hanging on the back of his office door.

I should have wondered what it was doing there, but I didn't. Instead, I got up, walked over to the jacket and went through the pockets, one at a time and in one of the pockets were his desk keys.

I unlocked both pedestals and slid open the largest drawer. It contained a rack of suspended files. I flicked through them until I found one marked "Confidential". It contained correspondence to and from the Union's solicitor, Neil Hardman. He had been been a busy man. The file contained papers relating to various public disorder and criminal damage cases involving NUGB members. Some of the names were familiar. Others were not. In every case, any charges appeared to have been dropped, usually on the basis that there was "insufficient evidence" or because the "witness no longer wishes to pursue a complaint". One, dated 28 April 1977, related to the arrest of James Dobson and his detention at Hackney Police Station. The charge wasn't stated, but two names and an address had been written by hand in the margin: - the names were "Broadbent" and "Jack Donaldson".

Broadbent. Something about the name was familiar but I couldn't quite place it. Jack Donaldson, on the other hand, was a complete blank.

But then it wasn't so much the names that held my attention as the handwriting. It was Peter's. Unmistakably. Whatever Dobson had done to get himself into trouble, Peter had been involved in getting him out of it. That Peter had appointed and continued to employ him was puzzling enough. Dobson exuded intimidation and violence like it flowed in his veins. Helpful, perhaps, if you needed a hired heavy, but the head of security of a political party with ambitions in Westminster? Dobson was a liability, surely. Why anyone, least of all Peter, would want to involve himself in digging Dobson out of trouble was a mystery to me.

The second file that caught my attention contained a number of financial records. They detailed sums of money paid into and out of various bank accounts, mostly in Switzerland. There were some large sums. I leafed through the pages and made a note of the payees. At last something I could give Smith to get him off my back.

I was about to close the file when I noticed that regular sums were being paid in from a single source, referred as "B.E.L.". I searched back through the records, looking for any hint of what or who the initials might be referring to, but there was none. Whoever, or whatever "BEL" were, they were depositing significant sums. I tried to total the amounts paid in over the preceding twelve months but lost count. I lost count because it was at that point that I heard voices. I froze.

Shit.

The voices were getting steadily louder. I had to move but my arms and legs were like lead.

Shit. Shit. I stuffed the papers back into the file, stuffed the files back in the drawers, closed them and locked them, all in the space of five seconds. By now the voices were outside Peter's office door. There was no time to put the keys back. I had to make a decision.

Shit. Shit. Shit. Leave them or take them?

I left them in the lock of the right hand pedestal and moved. Fast.

I made for the back door but I was going to be too late. I heard the handle on the main door turn. I slipped out of the back door and almost slammed it behind me in my haste. I caught it, just in time. When they entered the office, I still had my fingers between the door and the jamb.

'I'll be glad to get home tonight, John, I'll tell you that. It has been one hell of a day.'

Peter.

'Aye, you and me both.'

And John Taggart.

'Doing anything nice with Emma tonight?' Taggart asked.

I felt my stomach twist.

'That depends on what kind of mood she's in,' Peter joked.

I didn't want to see the look on his face. I felt sick.

'Fancy a drink before you go? I've got a particularly good Scotch in my bottom drawer,' he offered.

Shit. Shit. Shit.

'Do you know, I won't. As much as I am, as you well know, partial to a wee dram, it'll just send me to sleep on the train and I want to read the paper from… what was his name, Littleton, was it?' said Taggart.

'Littleheath.'

'Aye, that's the man. Seemed to know his stuff but I want to go over it again.'

'Good. Let me know what you think.'

'I will,' replied Taggart.

'I wasn't entirely convinced. I can't help wondering whether he has the stomach for it.'

'Still, he seems to getting the job done. It's a reasonably tight ship down there.'

I was trying to make a mental note of the names and failing. All I could think of was what kind of mood Emma was going to be when Peter got home. I'd have left my knickers in his jacket pocket if I'd known.

'True. But when we make our move John, people like him are going to have to be up for it. If he thinks they're going to hand us the keys to Downing Street on a plate, he's going to be sorely disappointed. There will be resistance, especially in the regions and we can't risk any weak links. When we move, we all move.'

'Aye. There'll be no second chances.'

I heard one of the men walk across the room toward my hiding place.

'Where are you tomorrow?' It was Taggart's voice.

'I'll be here in the morning and then I have a lunchtime meeting with our friend at the Treasury. I doubt that I'll be back after that.'

'Well put in a word for me, will you? My bloody tax bill last year was a disgrace.'

The sound of the two men's laughter, echoed around the room and I was, at last, able to slip my fingers out of the gap and close the door.

Shit. Shit. I closed my eyes and let some air into my lungs, backing away from the door as quietly as I could. I'd have to wait until they were gone, before risking the corridor, and hope to God that Peter didn't notice the keys hanging from his desk.

After a few minutes the sound of voices ceased and I heard the office door being closed. I waited a further ten minutes and then put my ear to the door. Silence. I figured that they'd left, but could I be sure? I walked around to the board room door and risked a glimpse into the corridor. It was in darkness which was surely a good sign.

The thought crossed my mind to go and retrieve the desk keys but, in the end, I decided to leave them where they were. What else was I going to do with them? I wasn't going to be able to return them to Peter's jacket pocket, that was for sure and it would be more likely to raise suspicion if Peter discovered them missing altogether.

I left the building via the fire escape, at the bottom of which was a door, with a push bar, to the rear yard at the back of the building. I stepped out into the evening and took a whole lung full of cool air.

Thank God for that.

Chapter Twenty

Friday, 27th May 1977

Broadbent let the car door close behind him, walked across the pavement and up the steps to Shoreditch Police Station and in through the blue doors.

'Good morning Sir,' said the Desk Sergeant. 'D.I. Banner is expecting you.'

'Thank you.'

The Sergeant buzzed the door.

Broadbent made his way up to the C.I.D. room on the first floor. It was the usual hive of inactivity. Michael Banner had a cup in his hand and his feet on the desk. When he saw Broadbent, he swiftly removed them and stood up. 'Morning, Sir.'

'Detective Inspector.'

'Are you and the Missus well?'

Banner always did that and it was bloody irritating. 'We're fine Banner. I see that I don't need to ask you whether you're busy,' Broadbent said caustically.

'Oh, we're busy alright. I just got back from Bart's. Nasty business,' Banner replied, ignoring the dig.

'So you said. Locals taking slices out of each other again?'

'Seems that way. But the reason I called you, was the woman they admitted a couple of weeks ago.'

Broadbent glanced towards the door. 'Not here Banner. Can we use the C.I.'s room?'

They walked across to the vacant office.

Broadbent closed the door behind them. 'So, what's the news? And it was more than three weeks ago, by the the way.'

Banner appeared to ignore that dig as well. 'Well, Sir, as you know, she was picked up late at night, around the back of Great Eastern Street. Face smashed to a pulp, ruptured spleen, wrist looked like it had been put through a mangle.'

'Yes, I do recall. Don't tell me that you've actually managed to identify her?'

'No, Sir.'

'Nothing?'

Banner shook his head. 'No identification on her at all and no matching records. Anywhere.'

'What about Missing Persons?'

'Nothing,' Banner replied.

'So either she hasn't been missed or, more likely, whoever is missing her is keeping schtum, for reasons known only to themselves.'

Banner said nothing.

'Which kind of makes you wonder doesn't it?'

Banner shrugged. 'I suppose so.'

Broadbent sighed and fell silent.

Banner said nothing.

'She is still alive, I take it?' Broadbent said, breaking the silence. 'Please don't tell me that she's croaked.'

'No, Sir. She's definitely still alive. But that's about as much as you can say for it. Her assailant did a pretty solid job.'

'She has still not regained consciousness?'

'Actually that's why I called you.'

Broadbent raised an eyebrow.

'Apparently, she opened her eyes for the first time last night.'

'She woke up?'

'Not exactly Sir, no. She was semi-conscious for seconds only. But they're running tests and they're hopeful'

'Hopeful.' Broadbent was losing patience.

'Yes, Sir.'

'Banner, surely you didn't call me over just to tell me that.'

'No, Sir. While she was awake, she became somewhat agitated and they had to sedate her.'

'Oh, great. She shows signs of waking up, so they knock her out. Thank God for the dear old NHS. What would we do without it?'

'That's what I thought but, according to the nurse I spoke to, it's standard procedure. They keep them under and wake them up slowly. It's better that way.' Banner hesitated. He could see the irritation in Broadbent's face. 'Anyhow, she opened her eyes. Just for a few seconds. And she spoke. It was very slurred but the nurse was sure that she was speaking German.'

Broadbent was interested now. 'German?'

Banner nodded. 'Yup.'

'Was she sure?'

'That's what the nurse said.'

'So, what did she say in German?'

'Not a clue. The nurse doesn't speak it.'

'Oh, for heaven's sake...' Broadbent put his head in his hands. 'How does she know that it was German, if she doesn't speak a word of it?'

Banner hesitated. 'Good question. However, at least it gives us something to work on. I've already lodged enquiries with both German embassies.'

'Good luck with the G.D.R.' Broadbent said tersely. 'If she's one of theirs, they'll have her on a plane back to East Berlin faster than you can say Erich Honecker.'

'Erik who?' said Banner, looking confused.

'Honecker. He's the... Oh, never mind.' Broadbent sighed. 'Is that it then?' he said, getting to his feet.

'Actually, Sir, there was something else.'

Broadbent waited.

'Amongst the German, the nurse did recognise a name and an English one at that.'

Broadbent raised an eyebrow. 'And?'

'Dobson.'

Broadbent stared and slowly sat back down on the edge of the table. 'Dobson?'

Banner nodded.

'Just "Dobson". Nothing else?'

'That's what she said.'

'Could she have misheard? Is there a German word that sounds like "Dobson"?'

Banner frowned. 'Buggered if I know, Sir. But she seemed pretty certain about it.'

Broadbent got up, walked across to the window and gazed out in silence.

'Luke Street is no more than five minutes from the Union's place in Great Eastern Street and Dobson's got plenty of form. It's pretty obvious when you think about it,' Banner said.

'He may have form, Banner, but is there anything linking him to the woman?'

'No, Sir. But then there's nothing linking anyone to her. In fact, until we can identify her, there's nothing, full stop.'

Banner had a point.

'If she's German, then that might at least explain why we've been unable to trace her,' Broadbent was thinking out loud. 'But why would Jimmy Dobson have an interest in a German national?'

'Not a clue, Sir. Yet.'

Broadbent did not reply.

'I could always bring him in,' said Banner, hopefully.

Broadbent turned abruptly. 'No. I don't want Dobson brought in again unless we have an absolutely cast iron case. And I do mean, cast iron. Otherwise, the slippery bastard will be out and we'd have tipped him off that we've linked him to the woman. Which might have unfortunate consequences, not least for her.'

D.I.Banner was thoughtful 'You don't think he'd try to finish the job, do you?'

'I wouldn't put it past him.' Broadbent paused. 'He had a pretty good shot at it the first time.'

Banner was silent.

'Who else knows about this?' Broadbent asked suddenly.

'Nobody, yet. I thought you should be the first to know, Sir.'

'Good. Let's keep it that way. Ask the C.I. to call me when he gets back would you?'

'Yes, Sir.'

'In the mean time, I want a guard at the hospital. Day and night.'

Banner looked like he was about to argue.

'I know you don't have the resources, Banner. I'll clear it with the C.I. In the meantime, pull a few strings.'

'Did you have any particular strings in mind?'

'I'll leave that to your fertile imagination, Banner. Somebody must owe you a favour. Oh and tell the hospital that if she regains consciousness again to keep it under their hats. They inform you and you inform me, day or night. I don't want anyone moving on this without my personal authorisation, is that clear?'

'Yes, Sir.'

Broadbent leant back in the police car's velour rear seat and closed his eyes. *Jimmy Dobson. The invisible fucking man*. Of all the scumbags in East London it had to be him. He had tried to nail him. Repeatedly. And with good reason. Dobson was more than a public menace. When it came to Jimmy Dobson, so far as Broadbent was concerned, it was personal.

It was personal because two years earlier, almost to the day, it had been Dobson who had followed him, Dobson who had taken the pictures and, when Paulo, hearing the camera clicks, had gone to confront him, it had been Dobson who had beaten him almost senseless. It was Dobson who had handed the pictures to Peter Owen and it was thanks to Dobson that Owen now had Broadbent in his pocket. And so Broadbent had set about discovering all that there was to know about James Dobson.

The trouble was that, try as he might, the man simply didn't have a history prior to the summer of 1975. Which meant that Dobson had a secret that he wanted to hide. People didn't re-invent themselves for no good reason. Broadbent understood that better than most. Still, until and unless he could discover it, the fact was that Dobson was practically bomb proof.

Broadbent didn't think of himself as a bent copper. He couldn't. True, he had played the politics game. It was either that or go nowhere fast and he had wanted a career. In the Met, playing politics meant choosing a side. It was as simple as that. You could sit on the fence and watch the promotion train trundle off into the distance or you could play the game.

So Broadbent had learned to play the game and to play it to the highest of standards. He'd built a career on it. Until Owen had unleashed Jimmy Dobson, Broadbent's uncanny knack for backing the right horse had worked for him every time. Owen had been the exception to the rule and for more reasons than one.

Owen's politics, to which Broadbent had not the slightest affinity, ought to have been a line in the sand. A line that he stayed well behind. But, even in the early days, Owen had been a man of influence and something else. He'd had an aura of power about him that Broadbent had found himself drawn to.

So, when one of the Union's thugs had got himself into a spot of bother, he had approached Owen and pulled a few strings. All fine and dandy. The trouble was that influence had not been enough. Owen had wanted control. And to gain it, he had let Dobson loose.

Broadbent had discovered his sexuality at college. Up to that point he had thought himself asexual. Girls had certainly never done it for him, like they had seemed to do it for the other boys at school and all that his fondness for male company had ever bought him was grief. At college, he'd had his first proper sexual relationship with a man. While the sex had been a revelation, the relationship had been ultimately short-lived and it's collapse had caused him yet more grief.

On top of that, it had been plain, given his chosen career path, that to appear anything other than heterosexual was always going to be a problem. And so he had ditched any thought that he would ever find himself a long term partner, male or female. Until, that is, Alison had come along.

He'd met her while travelling, before starting as a probationer with the Met. Alison had never been demanding between the sheets, thank God. She had always regarded sex as a slightly unpleasant but necessary evil if you wanted to start a family. In that regard, they had suited each other down to the ground and he'd soon found that sporting a woman on his arm had certain advantages. It allowed him to join the ranks of the normal for one thing and, to ascend the ranks of the Metropolitan Police Force, normality was a precondition.

Later, their marriage had provided the perfect cover when, having arrested a young man called Paulo Diomedi in the public toilets at Victoria Station, he'd been unable to resist the delights that Paulo had offered him in return for a swift release. The trouble was that having sampled them, it had proved impossible to return to a largely sexless life with a woman who, though she loved him, was incapable of satisfying his true desires.

So he had kept his occasional night time activities a secret from her and their relationship had continued to work, for both of them. Broadbent had taken the view that what she didn't know couldn't hurt her. She had given birth to Mark, his career had gone from strength to strength and it had all worked out.

Until Dobson had photographed him, one night, at the rear of a night club in South Kensington with his tongue down Paulo's throat and his hand down his trousers. From that point on, Owen had him where he wanted him and Broadbent had spent every day knowing that, unless he did Owen's bidding and even if he did, his career could come to an abrupt halt whenever Owen willed it. Not a position that he intended to remain in for any longer than was strictly necessary, but one which, for now, he had little choice but to endure.

Broadbent also fully intended to settle the score with Jimmy Dobson. First, he needed to retrieve the photographs. Then he'd find the evidence to bang him up so tight that not even Owen would come to his rescue. For one thing, Dobson was going to pay for what he had done to Paulo. But turning the tables on Owen was going to be a good deal more difficult and, in any case, while he was on the up and up, Owen's patronage still had its advantages. And so, for the time being at least, Chief Superintendent Simon Broadbent continued to play the game. Not because he was a bent copper, but because he was bent and Owen had the photographs to prove it.

Chapter Twenty-One

Thursday, 2nd June 1977

'Are you sure you're alright with this?' I said to Ted. He was hovering. I could see him in the mirror's reflection. 'I really don't mind, you know, if you'd rather I didn't?'

I really didn't mind. Peter had asked me to attend a dinner with him at the Friday Society at which he was giving an important speech. I was uneasy about it for several reasons, not least because when he'd asked, I had been excited at the prospect of spending an evening with him. An evening when he ought to have been accompanied by Emma. An evening that I ought to have been spending at home with my husband.

Suddenly, I wanted Ted to know. I wanted him to understand. To see all that had happened and the risk of it happening again. I wanted him to stop it. To stop me.

'Don't be daft. When have I ever stopped you going out?'

He hadn't. Not ever. He'd always trusted me.

I'd told him that one of my new colleagues at the college was celebrating a promotion and had invited a group of us to dinner. I told him that I didn't really want to go. That I would have preferred to stay at home with him and the children. But that it was important for me to meet people. In other words, I'd lied. Again.

'Well, no, I know that. I just meant, if you minded. I mean, you've done so much since I got the secondment. It feels like I'm hardly ever here. It's not very fair on you, is it?' I said, honestly. It wasn't very fair on him. It wasn't fair at all. None of it was. Somehow, his acceptance only made it worse.

Ted put his arms around my shoulders and kissed me on the top of my head.

I wanted to tell him. For a crazy moment, I wanted to turn around, look up into his eyes and tell him everything. To tell him that Peter had never been the man that he was. That Ted had been more of a father to Harry than Peter would and could ever be. That it had only ever been a madness. A terrible mistake that had blighted my life and that I was only involved with Peter now, to protect us - Ted, the children and me - from the havoc that Smith had threatened to wreak, had I refused.

'Daft bat,' he said.

I put my hairbrush down, and looked at Ted's reflection in the dressing table mirror. He was watching me with a grin on his face. I turned.

'Come here, you big oaf,' I said, grabbing his arm and pulling towards me. 'I love you,' I said, kissing him. 'You know that, don't you?'

'Of course I know it,' he said. 'Now you'd better put a move on. You said you wanted to be there by eight. It's already after seven.'

The conversation with Ted had put me in a strange frame of mind. I was angry with him. For being so bloody understanding. For never putting his foot down. For failing to stop me. He was too good to me. Too trusting. I didn't deserve it.

I was angry with Peter too. For asking me to accompany him. For failing to... Oh, I don't know. For making me feel the way I felt about him. And with Smith, the architect of everything, who was exploiting us all for his own purpose.

It was a juvenile way of thinking, of course. To blame everyone but myself. But it was the best that I could do. Ted's unquestioning trust served only to highlight the scale of my betrayal. To blame them was an act of self preservation. A refuge. For as long as I was angry with them, I wouldn't have to face the reality of what I was doing. I could lock it away, where it could fester with the rest of my lies.

I waited by the window. Angry. Hurting. Trying to avoid the truth.

And why had Peter insisted on coming to the safe house? I felt vulnerable there. Smith, or his minions, had gone to some effort to make the place look occupied and I had added what I could, but it seemed obvious to me that it wasn't anybody's home, let alone mine. It was the little things that were missing. The left over food in the fridge. The bin full of rubbish. The coins in the fruit bowl. The detritus of everyday life. Its absence stood out like a sore thumb. An idiot would have spotted it.

I took the little mirror out of my handbag and checked my face again. I'd done it at least five times. Why was I bothering? Did I care what Peter thought of me? Did I care whether he still found me attractive? Ted and the children were what mattered. I repeated it over and over, like a mantra. I was here for one reason and one reason only. Peter Owen was nothing more to me than a job. A job that I needed to do to be free of Smith and his threats. I made myself repeat it. I was still repeating it in when Peter's car pulled up outside. I didn't wait. I went straight down to meet him.

'You look stunning,' Peter said, as I slid onto the passenger seat beside him. It wasn't an easy thing to do in the evening dress I was wearing. I'd bought it, with Grace, the day before from a boutique in Shoreditch High Street, along with a pair of shoes. I couldn't remember the last time I'd worn high heels.

'Thanks.'

He released the handbrake.

'Thank you so much for agreeing to accompany me Liz. I really appreciate it.'

I caught his eye as he reversed the car. 'I would have thought that your wife would have been more appropriate.' I said it like an accusation and immediately regretted it.

Peter did not reply. The car accelerated.

'Won't most of the guests be accompanied by their wives?' I added in a more contrite tone.

'Yes, I expect so.'

It was my turn to remain silent. Why did I feel so utterly wretched?

We turned left, into Upper Tollington Park.

'Did you manage to put the finishing touches to the speech?' he said, breaking the silence.

'Of course.'

There was another, uncomfortable pause.

'I asked you to accompany me because…' he said suddenly.

I looked sideways at him.

He continued to stare at the road ahead. 'I wanted your support. We may have to adjust the speech at the last minute. You'll be able to help me with that. Nobody else could.'

Bullshit.

'Besides, I want to introduce you to a number of the guests. Partly for your benefit. They're good contacts to have. And partly for mine. There will be people there who will be impressed.'

It was a compliment of sorts and, of course, networking had been Smith's reason for insisting that I should attend. He'd been delighted that Peter had asked me. But there was another reason. We both knew it. I waited.

'And I wanted to spend some more time with you, Liz.'

I flushed. *Damn it.* 'I told you, I'm here to do a job Peter,' but the colour of my neck said otherwise.

'Which is fair enough,' he said, glancing sideways. 'Look, I'm not coming onto you. I wouldn't do that. But I enjoy being with you and you've got to admit,' he continued without a pause, 'that we do work well together.'

We did. We always had. Being together had never been the problem. The problem had only ever been the time we spent apart. The times when I had needed him and he had let me down. In favour of her. Always.

'I know that,' I said.

Peter's invitation to speak at the Society's annual dinner, had been a breakthrough of sorts, but his speech had turned out to be a triumph. True, he was speaking to the largely converted, but the Union had hitherto struggled to break into the mainstream, branded as it was as a one-issue party by the press. Peter had wanted to set out the Union's blueprint for government. To demonstrate that the Party had a comprehensive plan to address the shortcomings of the old parties. It was a radical agenda that would undoubtedly scare both the liberals and the socialists, but then it was not the liberals and socialists that he hoped to win over.

The problem with the first draft, was that it had been lack-lustre. Heavy on detail, but lacking vision. The speech needed to play to his strengths as an inspirational leader. It had taken me the best part of two days to correct it, but the finished article was a real barn-stormer. When Peter sat down, to thunderous applause, I knew that we had found the formula. When he turned towards me, his eyes seemed almost alight, burning with ambition and desire. It was hard not to be caught up in the passion of the moment.

'Congratulations, Peter. An excellent speech.' The voice came from behind us as were making our way out of the dining hall.

On arrival, our greeting had been lukewarm at best and the many whispered conversations and pointed looks, during dinner, had made socialising an uncomfortable experience, especially with the dragon of a woman seated beside me. She had blanked me to such an extent that by the fourth course, I'd have happily stuck my knife in her podgy little fingers as she reached for the cheese board. *Cow.*

Our departure, on the other hand, was another matter entirely. The great and the good were queuing up to speak to Peter and Mrs Podgy fingers was conspicuous by her absence.

'Thank you Sir John. I will share a secret with you,' Peter said conspiratorially to the overweight man before us. 'Can I introduce you to Miss Elizabeth Muir?' He dropped his voice. 'My wonderful speech writer.'

I held out my hand but, instead of shaking it, Sir John Kirkbride took it in his hand and kissed it. 'You are fortunate indeed to have such a wonderful speech writer Peter, and luckier still to be accompanied by such a beautiful woman.'

He had said it with panache, but it still made me squirm. 'Thank you, Sir John. Peter is exaggerating, of course. I can assure you that the speech needed very little input from me.'

Sir John smiled. 'And loyal too. You must tell me where you found such a treasure.' Sir John was struggling to keep his eyes from my cleavage which, though a good deal less spectacular than Grace's, was obviously tickling his fancy.

Peter laughed. 'I take it that we can count on your attendance at the conference in August?' he said, quietly.

Sir John nodded. 'Certainly. And after tonight, I suspect that there will be several others joining our cause.'

'Good news indeed. Your continued support means a great deal to me, John.'

Peter had glanced over Sir John's shoulder during his final exchange. 'Will you excuse us?'

Sir John nodded. 'Of course. A pleasure to meet you, Miss Muir.'

I smiled, as Peter took my arm. I suppose that I should have said that the pleasure had been all mine. But it hadn't and I'd had my fill of lies.

'Well done,' he whispered. 'He'd been wavering, but the old boy was completely smitten.'

'Yes, I did notice that. What's so special about his support? I thought that he retired from Scotland Yard last year.'

Peter looked at me as though surprised. 'He did, but his connections go all the way to the top.'

'Ah, Peter,' said a woman's voice to our left. I turned.

'Hilary, how wonderful to see you. You are a vision, as ever.'

I took an immediate dislike to the woman who had approached us. My guess was that she was in her late fifties. She was stick thin and had a narrow pointed face. Her steel grey hair had been sculpted into place with so much hair spray it looked almost metallic. But it was her narrow, piercing green eyes that put me on guard.

'A vision, indeed,' she said, without the trace of a smile or, in fact, any other emotion. 'And which of your women is this?' she said, looking at me with such distaste that she might have swallowed a pickled onion.

Peter didn't bat an eyelid. 'This, Hilary, is Elizabeth Muir. Liz, can I introduce you to Hilary Banks. Hilary is the C.E.O. of Banks Electrical.'

'Hello,' I said, blankly. I had no interest in Banks Electrical and even less in its chief executive.

'Charmed,' she said and immediately glanced away. 'And how is Mrs Owen?' she said, addressing Peter once more.

He smiled. 'Emma is very well, thank you. Liz has recently joined us and is already proving to be an invaluable addition to the Team.'

She turned and gave me another look of pure venom. 'I suppose that a little new blood doesn't hurt from time to time, providing of course, that it is of a suitable pedigree.'

I swallowed. Pudgy Fingers was one thing. But this old trout was quite another. I was about to speak, when Peter interrupted, putting his hand on my arm as though he thought that I might reach out and throttle her at any moment. Which wasn't far off the mark, as it happens. 'I understand that John has spoken to you about the conference?'

'Indeed he has.'

'And that we just need to agree a final date?'

She nodded.

'I will ask him to do that in the next few days if I may.'

'Then I will await Mr Taggart's call.' She turned as if to walk away.

'Oh and Hilary?'

She turned.

'My head of security will be in touch. We will require full access and complete secrecy. You do understand that, don't you?'

She sniffed. 'Mr Dobson and I have already discussed and agreed the security arrangements. I must say,' she said, glancing at me once again, 'that at least you have chosen your head of security well.'

And with that she was gone.

I turned to Peter with my mouth agape.

He held up his hand. 'I know. I know,' he whispered.

'Suitable pedigree?' I mouthed.

Peter held my indignant gaze for a moment, before we both laughed out loud.

'Congratulations,' he said. 'You have passed the test.'

We drove away, still laughing. After the pressure of the evening and the blackness of my mood, the absurdity of Hilary Banks's rudeness had, unexpectedly, served to raise my spirits.

'Where on Earth did you dig that old relic up from?'

'I'm sorry. I should have warned you.'

'Yes, you should have. Honestly, Peter, I could have strangled her.'

'Oh, Hilary has her uses. The Banks family has been funding us since the beginning, you know.'

I hesitated. So Banks Electrical was the "BEL" mentioned in the documents in Peter's office. 'You mean the Union?'

Peter nodded. 'Not just the Union, either. Stanley Banks, her father, put a lot of money into Mosley's New Party in the 1930's, until they were all interned.'

'Banks was interned?'

'Yes. Along with Mosley and most of the BUF leadership. After the war, Banks was a little more careful but he continued to fund several groups and, when he died, Hilary took up the mantle.'

I was silent.

'Didn't you ever wonder where all the money came from back at Ealing?'

I turned and stared at him. I certainly had wondered. 'Hang on. You're saying that the Bank's family pay-rolled the Ealing group too?'

Peter nodded. 'And not just Ealing. They were funding groups and initiatives across the country.'

There was a pause.

'The conference you mentioned,' I said after a few moments.

Peter said nothing. But his expression had changed the moment that I had mentioned it.

'They're backing that too?' I ventured.

'Hilary is providing the venue.'

I waited. My heart was in my mouth. Had I had asked one too many questions?

'What we're planning will change the landscape, Liz. Once and for all, but we must be careful.'

I said nothing.

'There are forces at work, that will attempt to counter us. They probably already are.' He fell silent.

'You needn't say any more. When the time comes, I will be ready,' I whispered.

He reached for my hand. His touch sent a tingle of electricity through my arm and into my chest. 'I don't doubt it. Not for a moment. But the Council has decided on the strictest secrecy,' he said solemnly. 'Mind you, those Council members present tonight will certainly have been impressed.'

'There were Council members present?' I had guessed as much.

'Several.'

'If you doubt me Peter, I would rather know.'

He lifted my hand up to his mouth and kissed it.

I closed my eyes and let the wave of longing break over me.

'I have never doubted you. You must know that. I was a fool to have ever let you go,' he said quietly.

'You didn't let me go. You made a choice and so did I. You chose your life…' I hesitated, 'with Emma,' I said in a small voice. 'And I chose to be without you, rather than to share you with another woman.' That was the truth of it.

'And I have regretted it many times,' he said.

Without warning the stop lights on the car in front of us suddenly flared red and Peter hit the brakes hard. The car came to a halt with a jerk. The moment had passed. He turned and smiled at me.

'Come on,' I said, evenly. 'Things have moved on and you, Mr Owen, have far greater things to concern you than wondering about what might have been. You are on the verge of power. I can feel it. Look at the reaction tonight. You had them eating out of your hands. Let's not try to turn the clocks back.'

I said it, but I did not mean it. Inside, my chest felt like ashes. I forced a vision of Ted's face into my mind and then the children, one after the other, and tried to hold them there.

'You're right,' he said, pulling away again slowly. 'Look, would you mind if we stopped off at the office on our way? I forgot some papers when I was there this afternoon. I need them for a meeting in the morning. It is not far out of our way.'

'No, of course not.'

We pulled into the car park at the rear of Excalibur House.

'You can wait here if you like. I'll only be a few minutes,' Peter offered.

I peered out through the windscreen, into the darkness and shivered. 'I'd rather come with you, if that's alright.'

Peter looked at me and smiled. 'I don't remember you being afraid of the dark.'

'I don't remember you being around enough to notice,' I said, exposing my bitterness again. I cursed myself silently.

Peter looked away.

'I'm sorry. That was unnecessary.'

Peter let us into the building through the rear door. We took the lift to the third floor, in silence, both of us deep in thought.

The only sound in the corridor to his office, was made by the tapping of our footsteps which seemed to echo in a way that I had never noticed during the day. Buildings seem so different when they are empty. When they're full, they take on the identity of the people and organisations that occupy them. But at night, when everyone has gone home, it is as though they rediscover themselves.

'What was this place, before it was an office?' I ventured. 'Do you know?' My voice sounded like an intrusion.

'Workshops, apparently, for the furniture trade,' Peter said, taking his keys from his pocket. 'There was a time when most of London's furniture was made in the East End.'

Inside, Peter's office the blinds were down and it was pitch black. Peter switched on the light and walked across to his desk.

I watched him unlock a desk drawer and remove a blue pocket file. I'd been wondering about the keys since I left them in the lock on the pedestal a week earlier. Evidently he'd found them and thought nothing of it. I pretended to explore the office with casual disinterest. I stopped in front of picture on the wall. 'Where was this taken?' I said, trying to make out the fuzzy faces in the photograph. Peter's was one of them.

Peter looked up. 'Don't you recognise it?' he said, watching me.

'Should I?' I said, looking more closely.

Peter got up.

'It was taken at Ealing,' he said.

'Was it?'

He had walked across the room and was standing beside me.

'In the refectory. That,' he said, pointing at one of the faces in the picture, 'is Michael Fitzsimons. He was Secretary of State for Education and Science at the time.'

'Fraternising with a Labour minister?' I said, mockingly.

'Actually, he crossed the floor shortly after that picture was taken. He's now a Conservative peer and one of our staunchest allies. Unofficially, of course.'

I turned and looked at Peter. We held each other's gaze.

'And surely, you recognise this one,' he said, looking back at the picture and pointing at another face.

I didn't. Until I looked more closely. 'God,' I said, laughing. 'Is that Sir John?'

Peter smiled. 'Yes, he was a little less portly in those days.'

'You're not kidding.'

Peter laughed. 'Do you mind, if I leave you for a few moments. I need to visit the bathroom.'

'No, of course not,' I said evenly.

'Make yourself at home.'

As soon as Peter had left the room, I went to his desk and the file that he'd taken from the drawer. It was risky. If Peter returned while I was looking through the file, I'd be done for. But it was too good an opportunity to miss. My hands were shaking as I pulled out the papers and flicked through them hurriedly.

I tried to scan them as quickly as I could. They included the minutes of the last NUGB Council meeting, along with a number of papers that had been tabled at the meeting. Followed by what looked like two papers assessing potential security arrangements at different meeting venues. The final paper was a list of names. The first half a dozen or so were NUGB Council members - I knew that. I didn't recognise most of the others. But I did notice their titles. It was an impressive array. Lords, Right Honourables and a smattering of military ranks, as well as Sirs, including John Kirkbride. I tried to memorise as many of them as I could. It was one hell of an attendance list, if that is what it was.

I had barely stuffed the papers back into the file, when the door swung open and Peter entered the room. As he came through the door I grabbed the picture of Peter and Emma that had been sitting on the desk in front of me.

Peter stood still, staring at me.

'I'm sorry,' I stammered, looking at the picture. 'I couldn't help myself. You both look so... so bloody happy.'

Peter didn't move. For a moment I was certain that he'd seen me with the file. I felt my knees begin to shake.

'We were,' he said quietly.

'Well, I'm glad,' I said. There was no bitterness in it. Just sadness.

'Liz...' He took a step towards me.

I dropped the picture onto his desk. 'At least one of us was happy,' I said, avoiding his eyes.

And then he was in front of me and I was in his arms. I stared up into his face and it was as though everything had narrowed. I could see nothing but him. I could feel only his hands.

'But there was not a day when I didn't think of you,' he said.

'Nor I, of you.'

'Not a day when I did not regret what I had lost.'

And then his lips were on mine and his hands were inside my dress.

Chapter Twenty-Two

It was in Peter's car, on our way back to the safe house, that I remembered where I'd heard the name "Broadbent". I'd been thinking about everything that had happened since that day, only weeks before, when I'd heard the news about Karl Dixon's murder. I'd been thinking that it had all started with that single, terrible event. An event that had ended one life and sent several others in a different direction, including mine. There, sitting next to Peter, it struck me for the first time that all of the events since might, in fact, be linked in some way that I had overlooked. Chief Superintendent Simon Broadbent. Sitting next to the Deputy Commissioner, on the stage at Tottenham Town Hall. Where Smith had reappeared after an absence of seven years. From the meeting with Smith on the tube train later that evening. To his ultimatum. My arrival at the NUGB. Into the arms of Peter Owen. The man who I could not resist. The man who I might never have been able to resist without Rosemary Muir. Who was absent and in whose absence, I had succumbed once again. Is was as though all of these events had conspired to put me back where I had been. Facing the same dilemma that I had always faced.

'Are you alright? You're very quiet,' Peter said, solemnly.

I turned and looked at him.

Destiny. I'd been kidding myself that I could escape it. By accepting Smith's proposition, in that empty interview room all those years before, I had chosen a path. And while I'd tried to jump sideways onto another, it had led me back to the same point. All that I had done was to delay the inevitable. All that I could do now was to walk the path that I had chosen. To the bitter end. And there, sitting beside Peter, I could see no end but a bitter one. At that moment it seemed to me that I was trapped. Not by Smith, but by destiny. A destiny that would condemn me to live and relive these agonies, until the journey was complete.

'I don't know, Peter. I thought that I had done with it. That I didn't feel the same. That we had both moved on. And yet here we are again. I need to time to think.'

There was a sadness in his eyes. Perhaps he was having similar thoughts to mine. He nodded but said nothing more. There was nothing more to be said.

Chief Superintendent Simon Broadbent, who had been at the meeting in Tottenham. And Jimmy Dobson's arrest. The day after the meeting and five days after Karl Dixon's murder. And in the margin of the document I'd read in Peter's office, Dobson's name and one other. Jack Donaldson. In Peter's handwriting. How had I missed the connection?

But Peter could not have had anything to do with Karl's murder. Not Peter. The man sitting next to me. The man who I had just made love to. Sprawled on his office desk, with my dress dragged up around my waist. I couldn't think that. I wouldn't think it.

'If it helps, please believe me when I say that I did not plan it. That I had no idea that anything like that was going to happen.'

'I know,' I said. 'It was me who didn't want to stay in the car. Remember?'

Peter said nothing.

I was suddenly struck by a sense of deja-vu. I smiled, ruefully.

He glanced at me. 'What?'

'Do you remember that day in Birmingham. The first time you ever kissed me?'

'Of course I do.'

'Do you remember the drive back to London?'

He nodded.

'You said that it was always going to happen. Sooner or later. And I said that I had known that it would. I just didn't know that it was going to happen that day?'

'I remember.'

'Like history repeating itself, Peter. Will we ever escape it?'

'You make it sound like a curse.'

'Well, isn't it? If it is love, then it is a funny kind of love that only ever brings such pain and heartache.'

He was silent for a moment. 'Do you really think that?' he said, as though such a thing was unthinkable.

I looked at him. Here was the man who I had longed for, endlessly, since that day back in the bar at Ealing. Who had been the cause of all my suffering. Whose ghost had haunted me through my marriage to Ted and the birth of our children. Who had caused me nothing but the most hideous pain. Back again to cause me some more. And worse. To destroy the lives of others - Ted, the children, even Emma Owen - innocents, who deserved none of it. And yet, he was the man who I loved.

I watched him, as he looked left and right at a junction. He was, at the moment, the most beautiful man that I had ever seen. 'I don't know. I need to think. Right now I can't think of anything that has brought me as much suffering. If this is love as God intended it, Peter, then our maker is a cruel God indeed.'

He reached out and took my hand. 'Don't say that.'

'Why not? It's the truth. Isn't it?'

He was silent. 'I don't want to lose you, Liz. Not again.'

He had no idea. How would he feel if he knew the truth? If he knew that I was married to another man. That I had betrayed him. Over and over again. That my betrayal had been the very reason for our meeting and for everything that had happened since. How would he feel if he knew that I had given birth to his child? That I had kept him from his son. That I had lied to Harry by calling Ted his father. That, apart from Rosemary who was, herself, a secret, I had lied to Ted and to every other person who had known me since. Would he love me then? Would any of them? This was the curse. The same curse that had always been. Revealed in all its terrible glory. Returned to tear our lives apart again.

The dawning of the next day day brought me no respite. I couldn't have them both. I had never been able to live with the lies and I would never be able to live with them. There were plenty of people who did. People who lived double lives, maintaining long lasting relationships and even secret families. Secrets that sometimes endured until their death, when weeping spouses, standing at the graveside, were suddenly confronted by the truth. But I'd never be able to survive such a life.

In the days that followed, I saw Peter secretly when I could and, though I tried to resist him, and could sometimes do so physically, I could never resist my feelings for him. Freed from the prison to which they had been consigned, they now ran out of control again.

It was madness. Pointless. There was no hope for our relationship, least of all while I was betraying him to Smith. But an attempt to cut my ties with Smith was out of the question. He would expose me and I would lose it all. Ted was the answer. As he'd been the answer seven years before. But my relationship with him was also flawed. Built, as it was, on a foundation of lies. If there was a choice to be made, I could not see it.

Peter's time was increasingly taken up with preparations. There were endless Council meetings at Excalibur House, and soon I was able to pass the names of the whole of the NUGB leadership group to Smith. He would appear at the safe house and take careful note of the details that I passed to him. Always without comment and always, he wanted more. Whenever I wavered, the threat was repeated. Never directly, but Smith never left me in any doubt about the consequences should I fail him.

In all this time, I could discover nothing of the whereabouts of Rosemary nor any news of what had happened to her. Whenever I saw Alphonse at Claridges, which I did whenever I could, it was always the same. Try has he might, Alphonse could discover nothing of what had befallen her. By the end of June, all of our attempts to find her, or to discover anything beyond the little that we knew of her, had failed.

At the beginning of July, I finally discovered the date and the venue for the conference that Peter and the NUGB Council had been planning, relentlessly for weeks. Smith was insistent that I must discover its purpose but Peter would not reveal it and there was only so far that I could go to draw the details out of him.

As the date approached, security at Excalibur House was progressively tightened so that any further search of Peter's office was out of the question. Jimmy Dobson made certain of that.

That Dobson knew something of my relationship with Peter and disliked it, was without doubt. He watched me like a hawk. It was Peter who kept him at bay, I was certain of it and thankful for it too. The more I learned of the way that Dobson operated the more intensely I disliked him and the more afraid of him I became. And I could not help but feel that Dobson's interest in me went deeper. I would notice him watching me and, whenever I caught his eye, he would stare at me and then slowly lower his eyes to my breasts or my legs. Then he would look at me and smile. If it was designed to intimidate, it worked.

As the days wore on, the old pressures began to build. The double life. At home with Ted and the children. At Excalibur House. With Peter. Dobson. Smith. Always Smith. Pressing me, relentlessly for more. Urging me on. No matter the cost. I could feel the strain mounting. I could feel myself beginning to slide, slowly towards crisis. The same crisis that had claimed me before. Then, it had been Rosemary who had saved me and Ted who had given me a future. Now I was on my own.

Isolated, completely, from everyone and anyone who could help.

Always in the back of my mind, were the questions about Karl Dixon's murder. If Dobson had been involved, and the more I learned about him the more I was inclined to believe that he had, I could not believe that Peter knew of it. And yet, it had been been Peter's handwriting on the document I had seen. It gnawed away at me. I found myself arguing, privately, with the voice in my head. Peter could not possibly be sheltering a murderer. He would not do that.

And so, as July drew to a close, I resolved to discover the truth about Karl Dixon's murder.

Chapter Twenty-Three

Wednesday, 27th July 1977

Jack Donaldson's name was in the phone book. When I called him, he was friendly enough but when I mentioned the name Karl Dixon, he fell silent.

'Mr Donaldson?'

'I don't know anything about that. Where did you get my name? Who are you?'

I couldn't give him my real name. I couldn't risk it. 'My name is Hannah Leeson. I'm a friend of Karl's family. I just want to ask you a few questions.'

'I don't know anything about him. I'm sorry.'

'Mr Donaldson, please, I...'

The phone went dead.

Pelham Road in Wood Green is on the Noel Park estate. Begun in the 1880's and added to subsequently, the houses are a mix of old, red bricked dwellings and more modern terraced council houses, built in the 1950's. As I turned into Pelham Road and found a place to park the car, I remembered visiting my Auntie Anne in nearby Morley Avenue when I was a child. I remembered it, mainly because the house had no inside toilet. We had to use an outhouse in the garden. It was so cold in the winter that if you didn't need to go when you went out, you certainly did within a few minutes of closing the toilet door.

Jack Donaldson's was one of the older houses at the end of a terrace. I opened the front gate and knocked on the blue front door. There was no answer but I could hear a dog barking inside, so I guessed that Mr Donaldson was at home. I knelt down and pushed open the letter box. 'Mr Donaldson, it's Hannah Leeson.'

Only the dog replied.

'Mr Donaldson, please. I need to speak to you.'

'Go away,' called out a voice. 'I'm not talking to the press. I've got nothing to say.'

'I'm not a reporter, Mr Donaldson. I'm just a friend. I'm sorry to trouble you like this. But I need to speak to you. Please, Mr Donaldson. I swear that I have nothing whatever to do with the newspapers.'

There was no reply. I stood up. It was no use. He was not going to talk to me. I turned and was about to make my way back to the car when I heard the door being unbolted. It was opened a few inches, held in place by a security chain.

'What do you want?'

'Just five minutes of your time, that's all.'

'Are you on your own?'

'Yes.'

The door closed and I heard the chain being released. After a few seconds the door opened again.

'Come inside. Quickly.'

I stepped into the house. It smelt of boiled cabbage. It was like stepping back in time and reminded me very much of my Aunt's house.

Jack Donaldson closed and locked the door behind me. 'Trudy. Be quiet,' he called out.

The dog continued to bark.

'I'll have to let her out or she'll not stop. You're not afraid of dogs are you?'

'No,' I said, a little nervously. 'As long as she doesn't bite.'

'Trudy wouldn't hurt a fly,' he said, walking towards a door at the end of the hallway. 'She'll check you out, mind.'

Jack Donaldson looked as though he was in his late seventies. He was a short, thin man, with fine grey hair. He walked with a slight stoop, but appeared agile enough. My guess was that taking Trudy for walks had helped to keep him reasonably fit.

He opened the door and Trudy emerged. It was quite comical really. For all the noise, she was the smallest Jack Russell I think I've ever seen and she looked almost as old as her owner.

'Trudy. Stop it now.'

Trudy approached me, growling.

'Hold out your hand.'

'What?' I said, looking at the little dog, dubiously.

'Hold out your hand and let her sniff you. She'll make up her mind soon enough.'

I bent down with my hand outstretched. Trudy sniffed, appeared to consider me for a moment and then licked my fingers. 'Have I passed?'

'Looks like it,' he said.

He showed me into the little living room.

It was tiny. Just enough room for a small sofa, a floral arm chair with a blanket it on it, a television on a stand, a short wooden stool and not much else.

'Sit down.'

I went to sit on the arm chair.

Trudy growled.

'No, not there. That's Trudy's. Here,' he said, indicating that I should sit on the sofa.

As if on cue, Trudy jumped up onto the floral chair, walked in a circle several times and sat down on the blanket.

The old man picked up the stool and positioned it beside Trudy's chair and sat down, with a groan. 'You said five minutes.'

I took a breath. 'Yes. I did.'

'So?'

'My name is Hannah Leeson,' I lied. 'I taught Karl Dixon. Before he was killed.'

'What's that got to do with me?'

I hesitated. 'I don't know.'

I didn't know. All I had was his and Broadbent's name on a letter I'd seen in a file in Peter's office. 'But I think that you might be involved in some way.'

'Involved? What do you mean involved?'

'I don't know.'

'You don't know much, do you?'

I looked at him. 'I saw your name and address. On a letter.'

There was a flash of concern in his eyes. 'What letter?'

'I can't tell you that. I'm sorry.'

He shook his head.

'Look, I'm not trying to cause trouble. I'm just trying to find out what happened to Karl.' I hesitated. 'I think I might know who did it.'

'Then go to the police.'

'I can't.'

'Why not?'

I looked into my lap. 'Because I'm afraid.'

'Afraid of what?'

'I think that the police already know but have chosen not to do anything about it.'

He was silent.

'Does the name Broadbent mean anything to you?'

'No.'

'He's a policeman. A senior policeman.'

'Well, I've never heard of him.'

It was my turn to be silent.

'This Broadbent. Does he know who did it?' the old man asked.

'Perhaps. His name was along side yours on the letter that I saw.'

He was silent again.

'Perhaps you saw something?' I said hopefully.

He ignored the question. 'You said that you were afraid.'

I nodded.

'Why would you be afraid of the police? Even if they do know who did it. If you go to them, what harm could come of it?'

I struggled to answer that. 'It's not the police that I'm afraid of, Mr Donaldson. It's the man who I think killed Karl and the people he works for.'

'Then forget about it. Why put yourself in the path of danger? You said that you didn't want any trouble. So don't go about stirring it up. Leave it alone.'

'I can't do that. I need to know. Karl was such a lovely boy. He was bright too, you know. He had a great future ahead of him. He had such a loving family...' I stopped.

'So what?'

I hesitated. How could I tell him that I was working for the same organisation that I suspected of sheltering Karl's murderer? I chose my words carefully. 'If I am right about the man I suspect and that the police are protecting him, then I think that I might be in danger.'

He stared at me. I couldn't begin to tell what he was thinking.

'I can't just walk away, Mr Donaldson. I can't explain to you why, other than to promise you that I am trying to do the right thing and that I care about what happened to Karl Dixon. I can't walk away, but I need to know how much danger I might be in. Can you help me, Mr Donaldson? Do you know anything about what happened to Karl? Anything at all?'

His face softened. 'Jack. My name's Jack.'

I smiled. 'Will you help me, Jack?'

He gave me a long stare. 'This stays between us. You're not the only one who is afraid.'

I nodded. 'I promise.'

'I was out walking Trudy. The night that the boy was killed. I take her for a walk most nights,' he said, glancing at the dog. 'Or I used to.' He shook his head. 'We were in Westbury Avenue. I heard voices. Harsh voices. Swearing. I looked down into the alley that runs through to Frome Road. There were three of them. One was holding the boy against the fence. People have been mugged in that alley before. I thought they were nicking his money or something. What could I do? I'm seventy four. I didn't want them to turn on Trudy and me, so I carried on walking. But the man who had the boy pushed up against the fence. I saw him in the light from the street lamp. Clear as daylight. I might not be as fit as I used to be, but my eyesight is still pretty damn good.'

'You saw Karl's murderer?'

'Yes. I didn't know then that he'd stabbed him. I just thought it was a mugging.'

'What did he look like?'

'He was tall and heavily built. Long hair. Dark sideburns. Big square chin. Looked like a boxer.'

I nodded.

'There'd been trouble in Wood Green that day. A big demonstration. NUGB. He looked to me like one of them.'

I swallowed hard. Dobson. It had to be. 'What about the other men? Did you see them too?'

'Not really. There was another big bloke. Long hair, I think and a smaller fella. But I couldn't really see them. They were standing back, in the shadows and I didn't hang about. I walked away as quickly as I could.' He paused. 'Anyway, when I heard it on the News on the Monday, I knew it was them.'

'And you called the police?'

He hesitated. 'A day or two later. I didn't want to get involved. A lot of people round here... Well you know...'

I did know.

'There are too many bloody immigrants,' he said defensively. 'I've lived round here all my life. Used to be that you could go out and never see a black face. Now, if you get on the bus, you're the only white one. Including the bloody conductor.'

It was sad that people like Jack Donaldson felt that way, but all too many did. That was why the NUGB's support was growing. 'And now there's one less,' I said, bitterly.

'I'm not saying that what they did was right. It wasn't that lad's fault, was it?'

'No it wasn't. He was a London boy too, you know. Born here, just like you and me.'

He nodded. 'So I called them. On the Tuesday, I think it was.' He thought for a moment. 'Yes, that's right. The Tuesday. They picked me up and took me to Wood Green Police Station to make a statement.'

'And did you?'

'Yes, I did and not only that, I agreed to do an identity parade. They took me to Hackney on the Wednesday morning, it was. Early. I was all geared up for it. Ethel next door, had Trudy. I didn't want to leave her alone for too long. She gets lonely and Ethel loves Trudy almost as much as I do.'

'What happened?'

'I was sat there in the canteen. Waiting. I waited half the damn morning. Then, all of a sudden they said that they couldn't find enough people who looked like him to run the parade and I was brought home again.'

'Have you spoken to them since.'

'Yes. To tell them that I was mistaken about what I saw.'

'Why?'

'Because about an hour after I got home that day, there was knock on the door. I forgot to put the chain on. There were two of them. They pushed their way into the house. Trudy did her best, but in the end I had to shut her in the kitchen for her own safety.'

He looked down into his lap. 'They said that I had been mistaken that night. That I had not seen anything and that's what I was going to tell the police. If I didn't they'd come back and start with Trudy.' The old man's hand strayed involuntarily to the little dog curled up on the arm chair.

We were both silent. I didn't quite know what to say. I could hardly blame him for withdrawing his statement. 'Who were they? Did you recognise them?'

'Not really. But one was big with long hair. He had a cross tattooed on his neck. The other was skinny. I mean really skinny. Pasty. Like he needed a good hot dinner down him.'

'Do you think they were the two other men you saw in the alley?'

'Maybe,' he said, shrugging. 'But I couldn't swear to it.'

'What did you do?' I asked.

'What do you think I did? I phoned the bloody police and told them that I was withdrawing my statement. That I'd been mistaken.'

'And you've heard nothing since?'

'Nope. Bloody good job too.'

I sighed.

'I'm sorry Miss…'

'Leeson,' I said. 'Hannah.'

'Hannah. Me and Trudy are on our own here. Maybe if it had been forty years ago. We had the Blackshirts then, you know. Just before the War. And I fought the Nazis, same as we all did. But now?' He smiled wryly. 'You can blame me if you like. For letting them get away with it. For being a coward. I don't care.'

'I don't blame you. I just don't know what I'm going to do, that's all.'

He looked at me. 'Walk away. What else are you going to do on your own? Do you want to end just like that boy?'

'Karl Dixon,' I said.

'Like Karl Dixon?'

'I know. The trouble is, I can't walk away, Jack. Not even if I wanted to.'

Not even if I wanted to. That's what I'd said. I was sitting in my car in Pelham Road, a short distance from Jack Donaldson's house, thinking about our conversation. I sagged back in the seat and closed my eyes. Peter had changed. There was nobody else in his life. He had stayed with Emma out of convenience. He didn't love her. Not really. He'd told me as much. He'd stayed with her because it was good for his public image. Good for the Union. There would be a time for us. He had said so.

I pictured Peter in my my mind. He could not possibly know that Jimmy Dobson had killed Karl Dixon. Peter might be driven by a burning ambition, but he wasn't an accomplice to murder. I couldn't think that of him.

Dobson was the problem. Why could Peter not see it? Why would he have used his connections to get Dobson out of trouble? There was little doubt in my mind that Dobson was the murderer. Had he managed to convince Peter that he was innocent? That he'd had nothing to do with the murder? The answer to that question lay with Chief Superintendent Simon Broadbent - the second name on the letter in Peter's office. But at that moment, I could not imagine how I was ever going to be able to check that out.

I turned the key in the car's ignition and started the engine. As I pulled away, I should have noticed the white Cortina that pulled out behind me. I should have noticed the man sitting behind the wheel, watching me. But I didn't.

I drove back to Finsbury Park, plagued by doubt. I parked the car in the space across from the cafe in the Park, walked the short distance to the house and let myself in by the front door. I glanced at my watch. It was almost seven. Ted would be wondering where I had got to. Again. I ran several excuses around my head. As I turned to close the door behind me, a foot appeared between the door and its frame and the door was pushed open. Jimmy Dobson stepped into the hallway.

I backed away. 'What are you doing here?' I stammered.

He closed the door. 'Good evening Liz.'

I tried to compose myself. 'I said, what are you doing here?'

'I thought that it was time.'

'Time? Time for what?'

'Time I took a look around your flat. Time that we got to know each other a little better, perhaps.'

'What are you talking about?'

He grinned again. 'Come now. Is this anyway to welcome a trusted colleague?'

'I'm sorry. It's not convenient. I'm going out tonight. He's picking me up in twenty minutes,' I lied.

'Is that so?'

I stared at him. 'Yes, it is.'

'Odd then that you had time to visit our friend in Wood Green.'

I felt my stomach twist. 'What friend? What are you talking about?' I turned and started to walk towards the stairs.

I felt a hand on my arm. He pulled me around and towards him so that his face was just a few inches from mine. 'You know exactly what I'm talking about. Let's cease the pretence shall we?'

I tried to pull my arm away. 'What pretence? Get off me.'

But his grip tightened. 'I don't think so,' he said, shoving me forwards. 'Upstairs.'

I went because I had little choice but to go. As I climbed the stairs, all I could think of was Ted and the children and what it would mean for them if I had been discovered.

'Open the door,' he said, when we had reached the landing.

I did as he asked.

He closed the door behind us and pushed me into the flat's living room.

'What do you want?' I said, trying to sound braver than I was feeling.

He hesitated. 'I want us to come to an understanding.'

'About what?'

He picked up a book from the bookshelf on the wall. 'Tell me something. This book. What is it?'

'What?'

'The author or the title. Either will do. Tell me.'

'I can't remember.'

He dropped it on the floor. 'Or this one,' he said, selecting another.

'I don't know. I read it months ago.'

He dropped the book onto the floor beside the first. 'Or this one.'

I remained silent.

'Or this.'

I stood staring at him. 'What is this?'

He ignored my question. 'Then let's try something else. Why is it that the post here is never addressed to you?'

'What are you talking about? Of course its addressed to me.'

He smiled as he removed an envelope from his pocket. "Mr R.Foxton," he read out. 'Richard, I believe. Never Miss E.Muir. Tell me, why is that?'

'I've not been here long. He was the tenant before me,' I said, thinking fast. 'Apparently. I never met him.'

He walked across the room and pulled open a drawer in a unit by the doorway into the kitchen. 'How long have you lived here, exactly?' he said, riffling through the drawer's contents.

I was beginning to sweat. 'And how is that any of your business?'

He hesitated. 'A third question, then. What were you doing in Pelham Road this afternoon?'

That he knew that I had been there was clear. It was pointless to deny it. 'I was visiting an old friend of my father's.'

He laughed out loud. 'Well, there's a coincidence.'

'Okay. I'm sorry but I've had enough of this...'

Without warning he strode towards me. I backed away instinctively, but not quickly enough. Quite suddenly, his right hand was around my throat. 'Owen might have fallen for your lies, for quite understandable reasons,' he said, leering into my face. 'But you would be wise to avoid treating me like an idiot, Liz Muir.'

His grasp was like a vice and I was immediately struggling for air.

'I wonder whether Owen would be quite so smitten with you if he knew what I know about you.'

I was becoming dizzy. I tried to pull his hand from my neck.

'If you wish to breath, remain still. Is that understood?'

I tried to nod.

His grasp loosened.

I took a gulp of air. If Dobson knew about my double life then all was lost. Worse, if he knew about Ted and the children then their safety was already compromised. But he had asked me how long I'd lived at the flat and had said *Miss Muir*. And, if he knew everything, he'd hardly have been asking questions about the books on my bookshelves.

'I want to know how you came to suspect me.'

'Suspect you?' He was fishing. 'Suspect you of what?'

He pushed me away with a sudden movement that made me stagger backwards.

'Don't fuck with me,' he said with a viscousness that I could almost taste.

I leant against the wall to steady myself. Suddenly I was furious. Furious with him. Furious with Smith. But most of all, with myself. For letting this happen. 'Get out, you bastard. Get the hell out of my flat,' I said icily.

He ignored me. 'I will ask you once more. How did you come to suspect me?'

I stared at him.

Then his mood seemed to change. 'No matter. It was our friend in Pelham Road, no doubt. This friend of your fathers.' He said it casually, as though only mildly interested in the answer.

The bastard was unhinged. I swallowed hard. If he had concluded that Jack Donaldson had been my source, then the old man would be in danger too.

I shook my head. 'No.'

'He told you that he saw me sticking the *nigger*?'

His words revolted me and I could not disguise it. 'No,' I said between gritted teeth. 'He was afraid. He told me nothing.'

'A wise man.'

I said nothing.

'Then the woman, perhaps?'

Woman? What woman?

He was watching my reaction.

'The watcher.'

What watcher?

'No matter. I have silenced her. For now at least.'

Silenced her. Was somebody else watching him? Watching the Union? Smith had made no mention of it. 'I have no idea what you're...'

'Which brings me back to the *nigger*,' he interrupted. 'A former pupil of yours, I understand.'

My heart felt like it had stopped. I looked at him. I was going to have to come up with some explanation. I nodded.

'Does Owen know this?'

I sighed. 'I have no idea.'

'Well I have. He doesn't. I wonder what else he doesn't know?'

'It is not how it seems.'

He walked across to the front window, drew the curtain aside and stood for several moments staring down into the street. 'What I struggle to understand,' he said after a few moments, 'is why someone who claims to be so committed to our cause and to the Union would be so bothered by the murder of a *nigger*. Were you fucking him?' He said it without turning.

'You sicken me,' I said.

'Then tell me,' he said, turning to face me.

'Fuck you.' I couldn't help myself.

He grinned. 'One last question. Does Owen know that you meet another man here?'

My mind reeled. 'What?' He had to be referring to Smith. 'He's a friend. An old friend. I have known him longer than I have known Peter,' which was the truth.

'Nevertheless you have not told Owen about him.'

'Why should I? He is just a friend.'

He shook his head. 'It is his flat, I think.'

I said nothing.

'Richard Foxton. The name on your gas bill and on just about every other bill that comes here.'

'No. Foxton was the last tenant here. I've told you that. I have never even met him.'

'Then who is this friend?'

'He is none of your fucking business, that's who he is. Now get out.'

He considered me in silence for several moments before speaking. 'It is obvious that you joined us to discover who killed Karl Dixon. So now you know. I killed him. I pushed a knife into his guts. I watched the pain in his eyes as I twisted the blade. I watched him slump to the ground at my feet. One less *nigger*.'

I felt a surge of hatred for him that was so intense that for a moment I considered taking a run at him.

'What will you do with this knowledge? Go to the police?' he smiled.

So Jimmy Dobson wasn't as clever as he thought himself to be. His assumption that he was the focus of my deception, revealed a weakness. A weakness that even now was preventing him from looking any further.

'Be my guest,' he said unexpectedly.

'What?'

'Go to the police. Call them now, if you wish. Ask for the Chief Superintendent who led the investigation.'

'Broadbent?' I said it without thinking.

For a moment, Dobson looked surprised. 'Yes, Broadbent. But you will find no ally there. Nor anywhere else. The forces of the law are already with us.'

'If you say so,' I said dismissively.

'But while it will do you no good to know that I killed the boy, knowing what I know about you is going to be of considerable assistance to me,' he said with a cold certainty.

'What do you mean?'

He walked across to me. I stood my ground.

'You and I are going to become more closely acquainted. Intimately, in fact,' he said, touching my cheek.

I turned my head away. 'I don't think so.'

'It will be the price of my silence.'

'No.'

'First you're going to show me your bedroom and then you're going to show me what's inside your knickers.'

I took a step backwards. He was deranged. But he was also convinced that I was only interested in exposing him. I knew, with a sinking feeling in my stomach, that it was going to be in my best interest to let him believe that he had won.

'You can struggle if you wish. In fact I would enjoy it if you did. But you will open your legs and your mouth to me and, in return, I will keep mine firmly closed the next time I speak to Peter Owen.'

'You're mad.'

'Oh, I don't think so. It will be our private arrangement.'

He pulled me towards him and, suddenly, his mouth was on mine and his hand was under my skirt.

I needed time. But sex with him was unthinkable.

He pushed his fingers between my legs.

'Not here,' I whispered. 'Please. My friend will be here at any moment.'

And at that precise moment, a car blared its horn from the street outside my flat. The timing of it could not have been more perfect had it been rehearsed a thousand times. I had absolutely no idea who it was but at that moment I wanted to rush out into the street and throw my arms around the hapless driver - male or female.

Dobson returned to the window and pulled the curtain aside by a few inches. 'A dark coloured Granada.'

Smith. Unbelievably.

'It's him. Please. I will come to you. I swear it. Please don't talk to Peter.'

He looked at me and slowly raised his fingers to his mouth. Then he smiled. 'I will have you Liz Muir.'

I pointed in the direction of the hall.

'The back door. It is through there.'

And he was gone.

Chapter Twenty-Four

'I want him out of this.'

'That is not an option.' Smith pulled out a seat at the kitchen table and sat down.

'No, not an option. A promise. And one that you made a long time ago. What was it that you said - that if I offered my loyalty, it would be returned? So return it. Or was that just bullshit?'

'Liz, calm down.'

'Calm down? Unless I convince him that he's got me where he wants me, he will go to Peter and the whole thing will unravel. Do you get that?'

Smith looked at me. 'Then convince him.'

I couldn't quite believe what I was hearing. 'Are you mad? He's a fucking murderer. He killed Karl Dixon. If you think…' A sudden thought stopped me in my tracks. *Of course.* 'You knew.'

Smith stayed silent.

'You knew, didn't you?'

Smith watched me. 'Yes. We knew.'

'And you didn't think to tell me.'

'Yes, I considered it. But what would telling you have achieved? Your job is to infiltrate the Union. Not to find Karl Dixon's killer, whatever Mr Dobson believes.'

'Because you didn't need me for that. You already knew who killed Karl.'

'Correct.'

'So what are you doing about it?'

'We will deal with Dobson in due course. But for now, it serves our purpose that he remains in place and still better if he believes that he has the upper hand.'

'So what? I'm supposed to open my legs to him? Would that serve your fucking purpose?'

'If you hold your nerve and do the job that you were placed to do, it will not come to that. The conference is a little over two weeks away. You must find out what they're planning. For now, Dobson will be kept busy with preparations. If he believes that he has you in his pocket, then he will be content to wait. Men like him are more interested in power than they are in sex."

'You think?'

'Yes, I think.'

'And then what?'

'And then we will see what we will see.'

Meanwhile, I'd have to live with the knowledge that Dobson might, at any moment, turn Peter against me. 'Not good enough. Dobson already suspects that this is not my flat. If he discovers that I live in Muswell Hill with two children and a husband, they will not be safe.'

'Then you must be more careful,' Smith said dismissively. 'You should not have allowed him to follow you to Wood Green. You should not have *been* in Wood Green.'

'I did not allow him to follow me. I am a school teacher, not James fucking Bond,' I hurled.

'You are an experienced field officer, Liz. I would have expected more of you.'

I had taken about as much as I was going to take from Smith. 'Fuck you.'

'And I suggest that you familiarise yourself with the contents of your bookshelves.'

He said it with the tiniest hint of irritation but, in saying it, had revealed something that perhaps he had intended should remain hidden.

'I didn't mention the books,' I said, slowly.

Smith remained silent.

'This place is bugged.'

Smith said nothing.

'I don't believe it. You've got the place bugged. Haven't you?'

'Liz, it's a safe house. What did you expect?'

'Are there cameras too? What, so you sit back at headquarters watching me in the fucking shower?'

'We monitor the house to ensure that you are safe. When Dobson turned up, a call was immediately placed to me and I was here in less than fifteen minutes. There's no need to thank me, Liz,' he said sarcastically. 'But you might want to remember that without our surveillance it would have been Dobson keeping you company right now, rather than me.'

Which was true, whether I chose to acknowledge it or not.

'I didn't tell you because I wanted you to act naturally when you are here. That's all. I can remove the surveillance if that is what you would prefer.'

I hesitated. 'I want Dobson out of it.'

'I'm sorry Liz, I can't do that.'

'You mean you won't do that.'

Smith said nothing.

'Then I want out. I'm not doing this anymore. I've had enough.'

It was a stupid thing to say. I knew what the reply was going to be. But perhaps I needed to hear it again.

'I'm sorry Liz. We're just two weeks away from the conference. A conference at which we have every reason to believe that the Union will finalise their plans. We must know what they are. You will find out. That is non-negotiable.'

'Or what? Come on, let's have it, you bastard. Let me hear the words.'

'Liz, there is no need for this. You know the position.'

'Alright, I'll say it for you. Or you will pay my husband a visit and tell him that he is not the father of our son. That his wife has lied to him all along and is still lying to him? You would do that? Destroy not just my life, but the lives of Ted and the children. Destroy a family.'

Smith had bowed his head. After a few moments he looked up. 'It is not as simple as that and you know it. We didn't force you into Peter Owen's bed back then, and we haven't forced you back into his bed now.'

I opened my mouth to speak, but nothing came out.

'If we're putting our cards on the table, let us at least be clear about that. These were your choices and, like all choices, there are consequences. One of which is that you will do what we ask of you. I'm sorry, but that is the way that it is.'

It was as though he had slapped me. I could feel my face burning. He was right. Of course. They had been my choices.

Smith got to his feet. 'I'm sorry Liz. Find out what the Union is planning. Infiltrate the conference. I don't care how. But do it. You know the consequences if you do not.' He did up the buttons on the front of his coat.

'One thing,' I said quietly as he walked towards the door.

He turned and looked at me.

'The woman Dobson mentioned.'

Smith looked at me blankly.

'Dobson said that he had silenced a woman who has been watching them. Who was he talking about?'

Smith did not answer.

'I want to know. You said that I was the only agent assigned to the Union. If there are others, I want to know.'

'Why?'

'That's my business.'

Smith hesitated. 'I don't know.'

'What do you mean, you don't know?'

'I mean, I don't know who he was referring to. We had no other agent assigned.'

'So she was not one of yours?'

'If someone was watching him, she was not working for us, no.'

'So who the hell was she working for?'

Smith looked at me for several moments. He chose his words carefully. 'Before you were assigned, there was an agent working on an associated matter. But her assignment was a failure and she was retired.'

Retired. The word echoed around my head. 'When?'

'Last year.'

'What was her name?'

Smith smiled.

I stared at him. 'Where is she now?'

'So far as I am concerned she is at home, enjoying her retirement.'

I started to speak.

Smith held up his hand. 'If Dobson was referring to her, then I had no idea that she was still working on the case and I don't know who she was working for. But it was not for us.'

I had already said too much. I could see it in Smith's eyes.

'If you know who Dobson was talking about, you need to tell me Liz.'

It was my turn to remain silent.

'Liz?'

I chose my words carefully. 'I don't. But if I did, I wouldn't tell you. Trust works both ways,' I said, bitterly.

'If he was referring to our retired operative then we will find her. Dobson said that he had silenced her *for now*. Which means that he hasn't yet silenced her permanently. If he gets to her again before we do, then this may well be a temporary state of affairs.'

'I told you, I have no idea who he was talking about.' But I did know and the more I thought about it, the more certain I was.

'Liz, do not involve yourself in this.'

I laughed. 'I'd say that I was about as involved as I could be, wouldn't you?'

'No, I wouldn't. This is much bigger than you could possibly imagine.'

He sounded almost desperate. Which was odd. If all the Service wanted to do was protect her, then why was he so keen that I should stay out of it?

'I'm warning you. Do not involve yourself in this…'

'Or you will do what, precisely?' I said defiantly. 'Go to Ted and reveal all?' I laughed. 'At which point, you will have lost your only source inside the Union. I don't think so.'

He stared at me for a long moment and then he turned and left.

I spent the next ten minutes pacing back and forth, occasionally, pulling the curtain aside to check the street below. When I was certain both that Smith had gone and that Dobson wasn't coming back, I put on my coat, picked up my bag and left. But I did not return to the car. I walked the short distance to the telephone box on the corner of Oxford Road and dialled a number.

'Alphonse? I think I might know what happened to Rosemary,' I said, breathlessly.

'Where have you been? It's half nine.'

After speaking to Alphonse, I'd returned to the car and driven back to Muswell Hill by the long route. I'd stopped several times to make sure that I wasn't being followed.

'I'm sorry, I got caught for a late meeting and then the bloody car wouldn't start.' I took my coat off, threw it over a chair and ran my fingers through my hair.

'You could at least have called. I've been worried sick. You should have been home hours ago.'

'I couldn't find a telephone box. In the end, somebody stopped and helped me jump start the bloody thing.'

I was lying and the way Ted was looking at me, I suspected that he knew it.

'The battery was flat?'

'As a bloody pancake.'

'But it was only fitted a couple of months ago.'

For once Ted was not letting it go and I could feel my face beginning to redden. 'I know it was only fitted a couple of months ago,' I snapped. 'I must have left the lights on or something.'

'Alright, there is no need to be so defensive. I was just worried, that's all.'

'I'm not being defensive. I just didn't expect the third degree.'

'Well, it's not the first time is it?'

He was right. It wasn't.

I sighed. 'I told you, when I was offered the job, that it would involve a lot of late working. We discussed it. You wanted me to take the job. Remember?'

He stared at me. 'Are you sure there isn't something you need to tell me?'

'Like what?'

He said nothing.

'I said, like what?'

He shook his head and turned away.

'No, hang on,' I said, grabbing him by the arm. 'What the hell do you mean?'

'Do I have to spell it out?'

'Well it might help,' I said angrily. 'I'm not a fucking mind reader.'

'There's no need to swear, Liz.'

'Oh really? I get home after a long day and my husband accuses me of…' I stopped myself.

He looked at me. He didn't say anything more. He didn't need to. Instead, he turned and walked away.

'Where are you going?' I said, shakily.

'I'm going to bed. I've got to be up at five. Your dinner's in the oven and, in case you were wondering, the kids are fine.'

And with that he was gone.

It was the first time that Ted and I had ever properly argued. We'd bickered sometimes like all married couples do. When Harry was four years old he'd picked up some bug and gone into convulsions. It had scared the living daylights out of Ted and he'd shouted at me in the car, on the way to hospital, that it was my fault for taking him to the playgroup when I'd known there been a bug going round. Then he had burst into tears. It was the closest I'd ever seen him to losing it.

Tonight was different. Behind the ill temper, there was hurt in his face and something else. Something I'd never seen in him before. He had known that I was lying, that much was obvious. What I saw in his face was bewilderment.

Chapter Twenty-Five

Thursday, 28th July 1977

'And you are certain that she was taken to Bart's?'

The telephone box smelt of cigarettes and something else. I tried not to think about it.

'Oui, Mademoiselle. After I spoke to you yesterday, I contacted a friend of mine who is a journalist at the Mirror. He remembered the story. The victim was taken to St Bartholomew's Hospital,' Alphonse replied.

I remembered the newspaper article. I had remembered it the moment Smith had said that she had been *retired*. Dobson had said *"I have silenced her, for now at least"*. The link was so obvious. It had been a vicious assault that had left the female victim in a coma. And it had happened just a few streets away from the office. 'Does he know where she is now?'

'Non. There was some interest in doing a follow up piece but, when they made enquiries, they were told that she had not spoken since the attack. Without an interview there was no story and the newspaper lost interest.'

It was lunchtime and I'd left Excalibur House on the pretext of getting something to eat, but had headed for the nearest telephone box.

'All he knew was that she was moved to a nursing home. The hospital would tell him nothing more. I am sorry Mademoiselle.'

'At least she is still alive. Or she was when they transferred her.'

'Oui. For this, we must thank the Almighty.'

I closed my eyes. Somewhere out there, Rosemary Sellers was very probably laying in a nursing home bed. I had no idea what she was thinking or whether she remembered anything of what had happened to her. But I did know that she was in trouble. 'We need to find her, Alphonse. Before Smith does.'

'This man Smith. You believe that he means to harm her?'

I thought about it. 'I don't know. But I do know that I don't trust him. And evidently neither did Rosemary. She warned me about him many times and why else would she have told you to destroy his card?'

'This is so.'

'So how are we going to find her? There must be hundreds of nursing homes in London.'

Alphonse did not reply.

'Alphonse?'

'I have an idea.'

'You do?'

'Oui, I...'

At that point the pips began to sound.

'Shit,' I muttered, fumbling for another ten pence. When I finally found it, the coin was rejected.

'Mademoiselle?'

Shit. 'Alphonse?'

More pip tones.

'I'll call you. On my way home.'

And then the line went dead.

The office had been a hive of activity all afternoon. Preparations for the conference were in full swing. Fortunately, Dobson was nowhere to be seen. Neither Grace nor Audrey had any idea where he was and I was not about to ask Peter, who I saw only briefly when he asked me to bring some documents up to his office. It was an excuse of course.

When I opened his office door Peter was standing at the window, puffing on his pipe and looking down into Great Eastern Street. For the first time it struck me how statesmanlike he looked. One floor below, the Union's staff were running around like headless chickens, but here, in his office, Peter exuded a calmness and, most of all, a sense of unshakeable confidence.

I stood in the doorway watching him. Truly, he looked like a prime minister in waiting. Waiting to be told that he had been called to the Palace. I couldn't help but feel a certain amount of pride for him and, perhaps, a little awe. There was something about him that I was seeing for the first time. I could not believe that he could possibly have had anything to do with covering up Karl Dixon's murder. He might use the likes of Dobson and the other Union thugs, but they were simply a means unto an end. Peter occupied a different plane. He would dispense with them once he had attained power. And, looking at him standing there, silhouetted against the sunlight that was streaming in through the window, I knew that he would attain it. 'You wanted to see me, Peter?'

He turned towards me and smiled. 'Of course.'

I returned his smile and closed the door. 'You look preoccupied,' I ventured.

'Yes, you could say that. The conference in two week's time is critical, Liz. Not just for us, but for the future of our country.'

The conference was going to be significant. Certainly the most significant right-wing gathering ever marshalled together by the Union, and very probably the most significant that had taken place in Britain since before the War. But beyond that I still knew nothing of the agenda, nor the plans that were to be discussed and, perhaps, finalised. As far as I knew, none of the other Union staff beyond the executive inner circle, did. 'I wish I could do more to help, Peter.'

Peter flashed me a smile. 'You have already done much Liz, both for the Union and for me. I have great plans for you…' He hesitated. 'For us.'

My pulse quickened. It always did in his presence. It was madness. It could never be. I knew it. I'd betray him. I had already betrayed him a hundred times over. 'I want to be there with you Peter. By your side.'

Peter smiled. 'You know that if it was up to me, that is precisely where you would be, and where you will be one day. But the committee has already agreed that only essential personnel should be allowed to be present.'

'And I am not essential,' I pouted. I actually pouted.

'Of course you are, but the committee also agreed that the judgement is Jimmy's, as our head of security, in the first instance and Jimmy will not countenance your presence.'

The mention of Dobson made me flinch. I couldn't hide it.

Peter held up his hand. 'And I can understand the committee's position. We must have absolute secrecy. Were our plans to be revealed to the forces that oppose us, our cause would almost certainly fail. The Right would be wiped out, perhaps for a generation.'

I dropped my eyes. 'And you cannot override him?' I said with the tiniest hint of ridicule.

Peter looked at me oddly. 'I could. Of course. But to override my own head of security? When we both know that he has suspicions about our relationship? He could cause us both difficulty at the worst possible time.'

'Jimmy Dobson seems to have made himself indispensable, doesn't he?'

I was pushing it too far.

Peter said nothing, but raised an eyebrow.

'I'm sorry, Peter. I just don't like Dobson. The man's intimidating. Especially towards women. I'm not the only one here who thinks so.'

I could say it, but in truth there was only so far I could go. If Peter moved against Dobson now he would certainly reveal what he regarded as my secret and, while he was a good deal wide of the mark, I could not risk the impact that a revelation at this point might have.

'Dobson is good at his job which, for now at least, makes him a necessity. But if he has bothered you in some way I will speak to him.'

Oh, he's bothered me alright. 'No, no. That will not be necessary. I can look after myself, Peter.'

Peter covered the distance between us in three strides and then his arm was around my waste and I was lifted off my feet.

'Of that. Liz Muir, I have no doubt at all.'

The Admiral Duncan in Old Compton Street was quiet, as Alphonse had anticipated that it would be on a Thursday afternoon. By eight o'clock, the old public house would be heaving with its mix of regulars, tourists and visitors to the London gay scene, but by day, to the uninitiated at least, it gave every impression of being just another London pub.

Alphonse, however, was hardly among the uninitiated. He was immediately recognised by the tall barman, who nodded towards him as he approached. 'Alphonse. How are you?' the barman said, holding out his hand across the bar.

'Niall. I am well,' Alphonse replied, shaking the barman's hand. It was always a pleasure to see Niall. He was in his thirties, blond and his biceps were easily the size of small tree trunks.

'Good. That's good. We haven't seen you in here in ages. You haven't gone and settled down have you? I'd be gutted.'

Alphonse smiled wryly. 'Non. I am still unattached.'

'Well, thank God for that.'

'You flatter an old man…'

Niall began to protest but Alphonse dismissed the protest with a wave of his hand. 'Did I say that I was complaining? Flattery is good for the soul.'

Both men laughed.

'What's your poison?' asked the barman.

Alphonse considered the question. 'Café s'il vous plaît.'

'Coffee? It must be serious.'

'Oui. All too serious, mon ami.'

Niall's smile faded. 'Trouble?'

'Non. Or perhaps I should say not yet. But when when my guest arrives, we must speak in private.'

'Sure. Use the table in the far corner. I'll make sure that you're not disturbed.'

'Merci.'

As Alphonse turned, the pub door opened and a tall man with short greying hair entered. He stood motionless for a moment, his eyes sweeping the room.

'Your guest?' whispered Niall.

'Oui.'

Having surveyed the pub, the man walked towards them. Alphonse held out his hand.

The man shook it without speaking.

'A drink perhaps?' said Alphonse.

'Scotch,' the man said, aiming the order at the barman. 'Straight. No ice. No water.'

Niall nodded. 'Over there,' he said, gesturing to the table in the corner. 'I will bring your drinks over.'

'Merci,' said Alphonse.

The two men walked across the pub and settled themselves around the table.

The man made no attempt at small talk. 'So. What's this all about?'

Alphonse hesitated. 'First, I must ask whether we can talk in confidence?'

The man considered the question. 'That depends.'

'On what?'

'On what it is that you are going to say.'

Alphonse remained silent.

The man sighed. 'Look, let's cut the amateur dramatics, shall we? We both know plenty about each other that we'd rather stayed between us, do we not?'

Alphonse nodded. 'Oui.'

'So you keep my secrets and I keep yours. That's how it works. You know that.'

'But this is a little different.'

'How different?'

Alphonse considered the question. 'I wish to ask a favour.'

The man smiled. 'Now where have I heard that one before? If I had a pound for every favour asked of me, Alphonse, I would be a wealthy man indeed.'

Their conversation paused while Niall delivered their drinks. When the barman was gone and Alphonse had poured his coffee, he broke the silence. 'Some weeks ago, on the fourth of May, I believe, a woman was attacked. It was in Shoreditch. In Luke Street.'

'Go on.'

'You know the case?'

The man's expression gave little away, but Alphonse thought that he saw a flicker of interest in his eyes. 'Perhaps.'

'She was taken to St Bartholomew's Hospital.' Alphonse waited but the man said nothing. 'I need to know where she is now.'

'Why?'

Alphonse sighed. 'I cannot tell you this.'

The man shrugged. 'Then I don't feel inclined to help you.'

Alphonse sipped his coffee. 'This woman,' he said 'I am told that she has not spoken.'

The man said nothing.

'And that the police have not been able to identify her.'

'Do you know who she is?'

Alphonse took another mouthful of coffee. 'Perhaps. But I must see her, to be certain.'

'And if she is who you think she is, what is this woman to you, Alphonse?'

Alphonse said nothing.

'Then we have something of an impasse. I might know where she is and you might know who she is.'

'Indeed,' said Alphonse, solemnly.

The two men were silent.

The man emptied his whisky glass. 'I'll cut you a deal. I will tell you where she is and if you recognise her, you will tell me her name. You will give me your word.'

Alphonse was silent for a moment. 'Very well. You have my word.'

'One other thing.'

Alphonse waited.

'You will also tell me who she was working for. You do know, I take it?'

Alphonse looked at the man and shrugged. 'Perhaps.'

'That's the deal then, Alphonse. I want her name and the identity of her employer.'

Alphonse nodded. 'Very well.'

The man smiled, reached into his jacket pocket and removed a notepad. He wrote an address on a page which he then tore from the pad and handed to the Frenchman.

'Your word, Alphonse. I will be expecting a call.'

'Merci.'

'And watch your back. You are not the only one who has an interest in this woman.'

Chapter Twenty-Six

Chief Superintendent Broadbent sat at his desk with a glass of Scotch in his hand. The call from Alphonse had been unexpected. They had known each other for long enough but he hardly counted Alphonse as a close friend. Come to think of it, he didn't count anyone as a particularly close friend. But Paulo Diomedi had adored Alphonse. He had introduced them one night in a bar in Camden Town. Alphonse had taken Paulo under his wing when he found him, beaten and bloody, in an alley in Kentish Town. Paulo had been fifteen then and living in a squat with a couple of heroine addicts. From what Paulo had said, Alphonse had, for apparently altruistic reasons, extricated him from the squat and set him up in a bedsit in Mornington Crescent. He'd even paid the rent for the first three months. Broadbent had been suspicious of his motives but Paulo had insisted that Alphonse had never once asked for, nor taken, anything in return.

If the call had been unexpected then the subject of their conversation had been a complete surprise. What could Alphonse possibly know about the woman from Luke Street? And if he knew who she was, did he also know what she had been doing there and why Dobson had attacked her?

Broadbent reached for the telephone on his desk. 'Get me D.I.Banner at Shoreditch would you?'

I leant heavily against the side of the telephone box. Otherwise, I think I would have fallen over.

'Mademoiselle?'

He couldn't be serious. The implications of Alphonse's last sentence were ricocheting around my head like angry bees in an upturned jam jar. 'Broadbent? You have got to be kidding me.'

'Non, I am not, as you say, kidding you.'

'Chief Superintendent Simon Broadbent?'

'Oui. Is there something that is wrong?'

Yes, there was something that was wrong. There was something that was very wrong. 'You're telling me that you went to see Chief Superintendent Simon Broadbent and that he gave you the address of Rosemary's nursing home?'

'Oui.'

'No. No. No. This can't be happening. What did you tell him?'

'Pardon?'

'What did you tell him? In order to get this information.'

'I told him nothing. I made an arrangement.'

'What arrangement?'

'I told him that I would give him Rosemary's name, once I had seen her.'

'You told him what? What the hell did you tell him that for?'

'I had no choice. Without this promise, he would not have given me the address. Mademoiselle, if there is something wrong, perhaps you will tell me?'

I ran my free hand through my hair. Why would Broadbent have revealed Rosemary's whereabouts? Unless it was some kind of trap. For all I knew he could be on the phone to Jimmy Dobson at that very moment. *Simon Broadbent. For fuck's sake.* 'Please tell me that you didn't give him my name.'

'Of course not.'

'Well thank God for that.'

'Mademoiselle, if I have done something wrong, perhaps you will tell me what it is.' There was more than a hint of upset in Alphonse's voice.

I took a deep breath. 'Look, I'm sorry Alphonse. But Broadbent is involved in this up to his neck.'

'Simon? How is Simon involved?'

'Dobson assaulted Rosemary, right?'

'Oui.'

'Dobson also killed Karl Dixon, the young man I used to teach.'

'Oui. You have told me this.'

'A murder for which he was arrested and then released suddenly, without charge.'

Alphonse said nothing.

'Why do you think that was?'

There was silence at the other end of the line.

'Because Dobson has friends inside the police force, that's why. And I have very good reason to think that he has one friend, in particular.'

'You cannot mean Simon.'

'Oh, yes I can.'

'Non, that cannot be,' Alphonse said firmly.

His certainty surprised me. 'Why do you say that?'

There was another hesitation.

'Alphonse?'

'This man Dobson. He is a fascist, yes? He works for the Union of fascists.'

'For the Nationalist Union of Great Britain, yes.'

'Simon is no friend of this Union. It is impossible.'

'Because?' I waited.

'Because he has the same reason that I have to hate fascism.'

It took a few moments for the penny to drop.

'You mean Broadbent is gay?'

Alphonse was momentarily silent. 'Oui.'

A sudden thought struck me. 'Don't tell me that you and him are…'

'Mademoiselle, please.' He sounded more exasperated than insulted.

'Then how do you know?'

'I have known Simon for some years. He may be many things, but he is not a supporter of fascism.'

Whether gay or not, Dobson had said that Broadbent was in the Union's pocket. So what was he doing giving Alphonse the address? It didn't add up.

'We have to get to Rosemary, Alphonse. Whatever his motives, I don't trust him. If Broadbent speaks to Dobson, he may very well decide to silence her permanently.'

Alphonse said nothing.

'We're going to have to get her out of there and, if we achieve that little miracle, then we're going to have to hide her. Somewhere neither Broadbent, Dobson or Smith will find her. And we going to have to do it right under Broadbent's nose.'

'You are right.'

'And we're going to have to do it now. You managed to find Rosemary. You can bet your life that Smith won't be far behind.'

'Oui. But how?'

'Right now, I don't have the slightest idea. But in the next few hours we are going to have to come up with something.'

Broadbent waited while the telephone line clicked. The connection between Alphonse and the woman from Luke Street was intriguing but it was what it might lead to that intrigued him more. Dobson hadn't attacked the woman for no reason and, from the lack of noise from the Union, it looked as though he had been acting alone. Who was she and why had Dobson gone to such trouble to silence her? What did she know about him?

'D.I.Banner,' said a voice on the end of the line.

'Banner, it's Broadbent.'

'Good afternoon, Sir. How are you and the…'

'Shut up Banner. The woman from Luke Street. Are you still watching her?'

It was evident from Banner's hesitation that he was not. 'Er… Not since she left Bart's Sir, no.'

'Why the hell not?'

'Sir, we have limited resources, besides…'

'I know what resources you've got Banner. I allocate them, remember?'

'Yes, but…'

'And if I say that I want someone guarded, then I want someone guarded.'

'Yes, Sir but…'

'Did I not say that I wanted someone watching her, day and night?'

'Not exactly, Sir, no.'

'What?'

'You said you wanted someone at the hospital, day and night, Sir. Which is what we had. But she is no longer at…'

'I know that she's no longer at the damn hospital, you idiot.'

Banner did not reply.

Broadbent sighed. 'In a moment, Banner, you will get off your lardy arse and get over there.'

'Sir, but I'm just going off…'

'No, you *were* just going off duty. You're not now. You're going to call the nursing home and tell them to expect a visitor. His name is Alphonse Richelieu. Under no circumstances is this man to be left alone with the woman from Luke Street. I want someone in the room with them and I want to know exactly what he says to her.'

'How do you spell that surname?'

'R-I-C-H-E-L-I-E-U. It's French.'

'French. Right.'

'In a moment I will fax you his picture. Once you've spoken to the nursing home, you're going to drive over there in an unmarked car. Then you're going to sit outside and, when, Mr Richelieu arrives, you're going to call it in. Do you understand? I want to know when he arrives and I want to know when he leaves. Once he's out, find out what he said to her. If she so much as farts in response, I want the whole thing, chapter and verse.'

Banner sniggered.

'Something funny Banner?'

'No, Sir.'

'Good. And don't screw this up.'

'Sir, what if he doesn't turn up?'

'Then you will sit there until he does. If you're still there in the morning then I might send someone to relieve you. If I can spare the resource.'

'But Sir…'

'That's an order Banner.'

'Yes, Sir.'

Chapter Twenty-Seven

I made another phone call before I left to meet Alphonse and it was not an easy conversation. I ran a host of excuses through my head as I dialled the number. The trouble was that I had already exhausted most of them. So when Ted answered the phone I decided to tell him the truth. Or something approaching it.

'Look, I'm really sorry but I'm going to be late home again tonight.'

There was a pause.

'Why?'

The irony was that the truth was going to sound so unlikely. I took a breath. 'Well, I haven't told you but I've been really worried about Rose.'

'Rose who?'

'Rosemary Sellers. From Ealing?'

'Why?'

'I haven't seen or heard anything from her since April. I've called her a few times, but she's never at home.'

'So maybe she's away on holiday or something.'

'Yes, that's what I thought. But it's really not like her to just go off. So I spoke to one of her friends and he said that he hadn't heard from her either and that he'd been worrying about it too.'

'I didn't think you knew any of her friends.'

'Well no, I don't really. But I remembered meeting her at Claridges once and her introducing me to a chap who works there who she has known for years. So I spoke to him. The thing is Ted, he reminded me about that woman who was assaulted in Shoreditch? Do you remember it? The one they were unable to identify?'

Ted did not reply.

'Back at the beginning of May? It was all over the papers.'

'Vaguely.'

'Well, this friend of hers read me out the description and it does sound awfully like her. Rose I mean.'

'Oh come on. Why would it be Rose?'

The skepticism in Ted's voice was understandable. 'It turns out that Rose was in London that night and he hasn't heard a word from her since and neither have I.'

'So why hasn't he done something about it?'

'He has. He reported her missing. But the police were not interested. If she'd been a child, it might have been a different matter. But a woman in her fifties? Well anyway, I phoned the police earlier this afternoon and they want me to go to see the woman. To see if I can identify her.'

'Tonight?'

'Yes.'

'Why can't this friend of hers do it?'

Shit. Good question. 'Well I suppose he could. But he's working, so I said that I would. I didn't think you'd mind.'

Ted ignored the comment.

'Where?'

He was testing me. I could tell. 'A nursing home. In Alexandra Park.'

'Which one?'

'Erm… hang on.' I'd written the name and address in my diary. I fumbled in my bag. 'Mistle Thrush House. It's in Vallance Road.'

Ted was silent.

'I know it's a long shot, Ted. It probably isn't her at all. But this woman's in a terribly bad way. If it's Rose, I'd feel awful if I didn't help to identify her.'

'Alright,' he said irritably.

'Look, I know that I haven't been around much lately and I'm sorry. I really am. It's been one thing after another. I promise that I'll make it up to you. Perhaps we could take a long weekend or something. All of us. Soon. Maybe rent that cottage down on the South Coast. You know, the one we stayed in just after Kate was born.'

'Maybe.'

His voice had softened. Ever so slightly.

'I just can't bear to think of Rose suffering in some bloody awful nursing home, with nobody looking out for her.'

'Fine.'

'Okay.'

There was a silence. I waited.

'I love you.' There was an edge of desperation in his voice that was uncomfortable to hear.

'I love you too, darling. I'll be home as soon as I can. Kiss the kids goodnight from me.'

'I will.'

I put the phone down and ran my hand through my hair. He had put up with a lot. More than many men would. But even Ted had his limits. It was not going to take much more to push him over the edge and then what? Telling him a half truth about Rose was one thing, but I was no more able to tell him the rest now than I had ever been.

I had intended to drive to meet Alphonse, but as I stepped out of the call box, I decided that it would be safer to take the train. It was no more than a ten minute walk to the station and then a short train ride up to Alexandra Palace. If Dobson was still watching me, he would expect me to take the car. I figured that I'd be more likely to spot him on foot. I looked at my watch. It was six twenty-five. If I was quick and there was a train, I could be at the station at Alexandra Palace shortly after seven.

I set off, glancing repeatedly over my shoulder as I walked. There was no obvious sign of Dobson. I walked at such a pace that my calves began to sting. All I could think about was what the hell we were going to do with Rosemary. Perhaps a hotel room at Claridges? *Too obvious.* I dismissed the idea. Broadbent would be bound to suspect Alphonse. Claridges would be the first place he'd look.

And there was another problem. We had no idea what sort of shape she was going to be in. She might still require care, if not medical treatment. How the hell were we going to manage that? As I walked into the station foyer I had absolutely no idea.

The biggest problem of all was that if Rosemary disappeared from the nursing home, Broadbent would assume that Alphonse was behind it. If Broadbent was in league with Dobson, then Alphonse would be in double jeopardy. And then, of course, there was Smith. If I got to Rosemary first he'd know it and while I'd bluffed him at the flat, did I really know how he would react? He had warned me against becoming involved. What had he said? *This is much bigger than you could imagine.* He was right. I didn't even know what Rosemary had been doing in Luke Street.

But there was one thing I did know with absolute certainty. I could not, after everything that Rosemary had done for me, leave her at the mercy of Dobson, Broadbent and Smith. It was the only thing I knew and it was this thought that drove me forward. I simply had to act. Whatever the consequences.

The station was packed with commuters. I stood in the queue for a ticket, glancing over my shoulders every few seconds, fully expecting to see Dobson come strolling towards me. Or Smith watching me from the shadows. But there was no sign of either man.

I was lucky. A northbound service was pulling into the station as I climbed the stairs to the platform. It was a slow train, stopping at all stations to Hertford North. I boarded the first carriage. It was mostly empty. I found a backwards facing seat, near the front so that I could see anyone who got onto the train.

Which is why, when the train stopped at Harringay, I spotted her immediately.

Simone saw me and, for a split second, held my gaze. Then she turned away. I couldn't blame her. I had walked away from our friendship without explanation and with scant regard for her feelings. I had not done so out of choice, but Simone didn't know that. She didn't know it because I hadn't told her. She was just another of the people in my life who I had let down.

I looked down into my lap and, quite suddenly, the insanity of it all struck me like a punch in the guts. *What the hell am I doing?*

It was seeing a face from my other life. The life in which I was a regular person with a regular job and a husband and two children. Yet, here I was, on my way to meet a man who I barely knew, to somehow kidnap a retired MI5 agent from a nursing home in Alexandra Park and to hide her, I knew not where, so that she could not be found by the combined resources of the British Security Service, the Metropolitan Police Force and a racist maniac from the Nationalist Union of Great Britain. It was insane. One, short glimpse of Simone Jackson was all I had needed to see the preposterousness of the thing. I wanted to stand up and shout "Stop the train. I want to get off." But I didn't. I closed my eyes. And when I opened them and looked up, Simone was standing in front of me.

'Alright if I sit down?' she said, nodding at the vacant seat next to mine.

I shrugged. 'If you want. There's plenty of empty seats if you'd rather sit elsewhere.'

Simone sucked her teeth and sat in the seat next to mine. 'You look like shit,' she said in a low voice.

'Thanks,' I said, without argument. I very probably did. 'How's school?'

'Same as. How's…'

I looked back into my lap.

'You never told me where you were going, did you?' she said. It was more a statement of fact than a question.

I shook my head.

We were both silent.

'Why not?' Simone said after a few moments.

'I couldn't. I didn't want to have to lie to you.'

Simone shook her head and sighed. 'You didn't need to lie to me, Liz. It was obvious that the whole thing was a crock of shit.'

'You don't understand,' I said weakly.

'You're damn right there.'

I turned towards her and held her gaze. 'I still can't. I'm sorry.'

'Why? We always trusted each other. What happened?'

'It was never a question of not trusting you Simone, believe me.'

But it was. Kind of.

'Then what?'

I wanted to tell her but I couldn't. It was no use. 'You have no idea, Simone.'

'I have no idea because you won't tell me.' She stared at me, her face full of concern. Despite everything. 'You're in trouble. I can see it.'

I nodded and suddenly my eyes were full of tears.

She took hold of my hand and was about to speak but stopped herself. Instead, we sat in silence. After a moment she reached into her bag, pulled out a tissue and handed it to me.

'Where are you going?' I said, wiping my eyes.

'Wood Green. C&A's. It's my mum's birthday tomorrow.'

'How is she?'

'She's fine.'

I smiled.

'I can help, Liz. Whatever trouble you're in. I can help.'

Maybe she could. But would she want to? If she knew the truth. Even half of it. 'It's not that simple.'

Simone sighed. 'Life never is. But it's a damn site simpler if you let people in.'

'You think so?' I'd been alone with my secrets for so long that I doubted that I knew how.

'Yes. I do. It is about trust, you know. The kind of trust that exists between family, friends, those who love each other.'

'Trust,' I said bitterly. 'I don't deserve it, least of all from the people who love me.'

Simone was silent for a moment. 'So you've done some shitty things. Who hasn't? But…'

'Not the same,' I interrupted. 'Not on my scale. Believe me.'

'Alright. So you've done some *really* shitty things. I don't know. I'm not even sure that I want to know. Because in the end, it doesn't really matter. You're my friend. Maybe you don't deserve my trust. I'll be judge of that, when and if the time comes. But I sure as hell deserve yours.'

I turned and looked at her. That she deserved it was beyond question.

'If you need help, Liz, maybe you should trust me enough to ask for it.'

If I needed help. There was no 'if' about it.

'I'm meeting someone. Will you come with me?' I said, holding her gaze.

She nodded.

Chapter Twenty-Eight

Banner parked the unmarked police car under a tree and checked the rear view mirror. It was an ideal spot. He could see almost the street's entire length in the mirror and, up ahead, the entrance to the nursing home. Vallance Road was a quiet, residential street with large semi-detached houses on either side. Mistle Thrush House looked the same as the other houses in the street, except for the concrete ramp, with its steel-grey handrails, leading from the pavement to establishment's the front door.

It would be impossible for anyone to approach the building, either by car or on foot, without him observing them, even after dusk, which was still an hour or so away. Providing, of course, that he could stay awake. It had been a long day and he had a feeling that it was going to get a good deal longer before he's be able to hit the sack.

He reached into his inside jacket pocket and withdrew a sheet of paper which he unfolded and rested on top of the dashboard. *Alphonse Richelieu.* The Chief Super had said nothing about who this man was and what interest he might have in the woman from Luke Street. Which had piqued Banner's curiosity. It had seemed odd, from the start, that nobody had reported the woman missing. If she was indeed a German national, as they now suspected, it was odder still that neither of the embassies had claimed her. In fact, to date, this Alphonse Richelieu had been the only person to have expressed the slightest interest in the woman. Other than the Chief Super, of course. There was a lot more going here, than he was letting on, Banner had little doubt about that. But what, exactly?

'Golf-Delta-Four-Seven from Golf-Delta.'

Banner had been waiting for the call. He fumbled for the volume control with one hand and reached for the microphone with the other. 'Golf-Delta-Four-Seven, go ahead.'

'Golf-Delta-Four-Seven, from Golf-Delta, we have the result of your subject enquiry.'

'Roger Golf-Delta, go ahead.'

'Subject is Alphonse Richelieu. I-C-1, born Montelimar, Southern France, 13-9-15. Address 57B Rudall Crescent, London, North-West-Three. Several convictions between 1942 and 51 for gross indecency with another male, for which he served a two-year custodial sentence in 1952. Nothing since.'

Well bugger me. A bloody shirt lifter. 'Roger Golf-Delta. Anything on his employment?'

'Standby.'

And a flat in Hampstead. Nice.

'Golf-Delta-Four-Seven, subject is employed at Claridges Hotel in Central London. It says here that he's their "Back of House Manager", whatever that means.'

'Roger Golf-Delta. With a flat in Hampstead, I'd say that it means he's paid a great deal more than you or me. Golf-Delta-Four-Seven out.'

Banner yawned. He wasn't sure where any of that had got him but at least it would give him something to think about while he waited.

'Oh and Four-Seven, Three-Two says that she forgot to put sugar in your coffee. Out.'

Oh for fuck's sake. Banner reached for the glove compartment and pulled out his Thermos.

I found Alphonse standing at the bar. His eye caught mine as we entered and I saw a flicker of alarm as he registered the fact that I was not alone.

'Alphonse, this is Simone Jackson,' I said as soon we had covered the space between the door and the bar. 'She is a friend.'

Alphonse nodded.

I could sense his ill ease. 'I think that she may be able to help us.'

There was an awkward silence.

'Look, I need to visit the ladies',' Simone said. 'So how about I leave you two to talk about me while I am gone?'

I turned towards her and mouthed 'Thank you,' silently.

I watched her walk away and turned to face Alphonse. 'I'm sorry. I had no idea that I was going to bump into Simone. But I got on the train and there she was. And, well, I found myself thinking that we could use some help.'

'Is this wise, Mademoiselle?' Alphonse said tensely. 'Can we trust her?'

There was that word again. I took a breath. 'Right now there are only three people in this world in whom I have complete trust. You Alphonse are one, Rosemary of course is another, and Simone is the third.'

'We must be certain. This may turn out to be a dangerous business,' he said, looking at me gravely.

I nodded. 'I know. Which is where I am hoping that Simone may come in. You and I, Alphonse, are compromised. Broadbent knows about your interest in Rosemary and Smith knows about mine. Let's hope that Smith is still several steps behind us, but Broadbent will be expecting you to turn up at the nursing home. If he's got any sense at all, he'll be watching the place. You are hardly going to be able to march in, in full view, and march back out again with Rosemary Sellers.'

'But you are right, of course.'

'And even if he isn't watching the place, when Rosemary goes missing, he will undoubtedly conclude that you are the culprit.'

'It is a chance that perhaps I must take.'

'I had reached much the same conclusion. But perhaps with Simone's help we can conjure a disappearing act that will leave you, at least, in the clear.'

'And you?'

'Smith will suspect me. Whether I go into Mistle Thrush House or not. There is no way to avoid that. But I will deny it and Smith... well let's just say that he has good reason not to want me exposed. For now, anyway.'

'But this Smith is dangerous, no?'

'Oh yes. You've no idea how dangerous he is to me right now. But it works both ways. I need him and he needs me. I think that for the next fortnight at least, he will not want to move against me.'

'Let us hope that you are right. About Smith... and your friend,' Alphonse said, glancing over my shoulder.

I turned. Simone had emerged from a door in the far corner of the bar. I waited for her to re-join us.

'Well? Are we on?' she said, grinning.

'Are you sure, Simone? What we are about to do is probably illegal, quite likely to fail and may very well land us all in a police cell or worse.'

'How much worse?'

'You have no idea,' I said, shaking my head.

'Then tell me. Both of you.'

I looked at Alphonse. He nodded.

'I think we had better all sit down,' I said.

Banner looked at his watch. It was eight-thirty five. He'd already watched two visitors come and go from the nursing home, but neither had been male. If Richelieu was going to make his move it would surely be soon. Otherwise the elderly residents would be in bed and the staff would be locking up for the night. He reached across for his Thermos, undid the cap and poured himself another cup of sugarless coffee. Up ahead, a car turned into Vallance Road, Just as he was screwing the cap back into place. He watched the car approach and pull up a short distance from the nursing home.

Banner noted the car's occupants as they got out. Two women. One black. One white. He returned the flask to the glove box and watched, with only minor interest, as the two women walked towards the nursing home. They were probably staff. Or visitors, perhaps. But either way they were of little interest to him.

Simone and I walked up the ramp to the nursing home's front door. I glanced at her nervously. 'Go for it,' she said with an encouraging nod.

I glanced back over my shoulder towards the car. 'Do you think he's alright?' I whispered, reaching for the doorbell.

'I'm sure he's fine.'

I heard the door being unbolted. It was opened by a nurse. She was wearing a pink uniform and looked about fourteen years old.

'Hello,' I said, smiling. 'We've come to see Dorothy Leeson.'

The nurse glanced from me to Simone and back again. 'Dorothy Leeson?' she said, doubtfully.

'Yes.' I tried to sound as though I expected her to recognise the name when, in truth, I knew perfectly well that she wouldn't.

'Um, I don't think we've got anyone here of that name.'

'Well I do hope you have. Because we've travelled an awfully long way if you haven't,' I said, glancing at Simone.

The nurse opened her mouth to speak but appeared to think better of it.

'Torquay,' said Simone. 'It's taken us four and a half hours to drive here to see our sister-in-God.'

'This is Sister Valerie,' I said, by way of an introduction. 'I'm Hannah Leeson.'

The nurse looked at me blankly.

'Dorothy Leeson is my mother?'

'Oh. Right.'

Simone sniffed, produced a handkerchief from her pocket, blew her nose loudly and began to weep. I put my arm around her shoulder and turned back to the nurse. 'She's been so worried about Dorothy,' I said. 'We all have.'

'All?' said the nurse, glancing over our shoulders as though she expected the congregation at any moment.

'At the church,' I said reassuringly.

'Oh. Right. Well, I... I honestly don't think we've got anyone here called Leeson.'

It was time to let a little irritation creep into my voice. 'You don't *think* that you've got anyone here called Leeson?' I said looking at the nurse.

The nurse blinked.

'Well, do you, or don't you?'

A flash of doubt crossed the young nurse's face. 'Well, I... um...' she stammered.

'You do, I take it, know who is here and who isn't?'

'Yes... of course... but I'm just a temp and I suppose that its possible that...'

'Four and a half hours,' Simone spluttered and blew her nose again.

'A temp?' I added. 'Look, I don't wish to appear rude but do you think we could see whoever's in charge?'

'Yes... yes of course,' said the nurse, who was now looking like a rabbit caught in headlights. 'I suppose you'd better come in.' She stepped backwards and ushered us inside.

I took a brief look over my shoulder, as I stepped over the threshold. There was no sign of Alphonse.

I hadn't been in a nursing home since my Great Aunt Dorothy was admitted to one when I was at school. I had forgotten the smell. A mixture of urine and stale clothes. In this case, mostly urine.

The building had what once would have been a very grand hallway and a fine wooden stair case. But the worn carpets and tired decor gave the impression of a building in decline.

'Would you mind waiting in the office?' the nurse said, apologetically. 'I'll go and find the senior.'

She led us across the hall, through a doorway into a corridor and unlocked a door to our left with a key from the bunch suspended on her belt.

The room into which we were shown would be more accurately described as a cupboard than an office. There was barely enough room for the desk and two chairs that filled it, let alone the large grey filing cabinet wedged into the corner by the window. Staff facilities were evidently not uppermost on the proprietor's list of priorities.

'This is the office?' I said, more to myself than to anyone else.

'Yes, I'm sorry. It is a bit... um... well, small, isn't it?'

Simone was still weeping.

'Do you think that you could get Sister Valerie something to drink? She's been distraught these last few days.'

The nurse glanced sideways at Simone. 'Oh. Yes, of course. Would you like a cup of tea?' she said to Simone, in the most patronising voice imaginable.

'Would you mind?' Simone said, looking like tragedy incarnate.

'Sugar?'

Simone shook her head. 'No. Thank you.'

'And, if you don't mind, I need to go to the bathroom,' I said, keeping a pretence of irritation in my voice.

'Right. Yes. The visitor's toilet is on the first floor. Turn left at the top of the stairs, through the fire doors. The toilet is on the right, at the end of the hallway. Next to the lift.'

'Is your friend going to be alright?' the nurse said, as we stepped out into the corridor.

'I do hope so,' I said, doing my best to sound concerned. 'Sister Valerie is a little highly strung at the best of times.'

The nurse turned and I followed her back along the corridor and into the hallway.

'Up there,' she said, gesturing towards the stairs.

I could hear the sound of a television coming from a room across the hallway and, as we passed its doorway, I caught sight of a number of elderly women sitting in what looked like plastic covered arm chairs.

I walked across to the stair case, watching the nurse from the corner of my eye as she disappeared through a door at the hallway's far end. As soon as she was out of sight I went back to the room with the television, put my head around the door and scanned the faces. None of them belonged to Rosemary, but I hadn't really expected to find her there.

All but one of the women was asleep. The woman who wasn't, glanced at me and smiled. She spoke, but I couldn't hear what she said, above the noise from the television. I glanced at the screen. Star Wars with the volume turned up. Nice. They looked like a Star Wars kind of audience. Was this what we all had waiting for us? I tried to dismiss the thought as I made my way up the stairs.

The smell of stale urine seemed to be getting worse as I ascended. It reached its peak as I passed through the fire door at the top. There was a complete lack of ventilation in the corridor beyond and, with precious little natural light and several radiators working overtime, it felt and smelt like the mouth of hell.

That anyone should be forced by circumstance to end their days in a place like this was depressing enough, but whoever had placed Rosemary here needed a bullet through the side of their head. Had I a gun and they'd been stood in front of me at that moment I might very well have obliged.

The fetid hallway ran the length of the building with rooms off to the left and right. I knocked on the first of the bedroom doors I came to. There was no reply. I pushed the handle and opened the door. Apart from the linoleum on the floor, the room was homely enough, furnished as it was with an assortment of old furniture which, presumably, had been admitted to the nursing home along with the occupant. He - the occupant was an elderly man - was asleep, in bed. At least I hoped he was sleeping. I closed the door as quietly as I could.

The second and third doors were locked. But the next one - room number seven, for some reason (the room numbers did not appear to run in any kind of sequence) - opened when I pushed down on the door handle.

Inside, the woman lying in the bed was a shadow of the person I had known. Her eyes were dull and sunken and her face so painfully thin, that it was as though there was nothing between her skin and the bone beneath.

I guess that I should have been more prepared for it. I'd been so focussed on finding her, that I hadn't given much thought to her likely appearance. But, in truth, no amount of thinking would have fully prepared me. Until that moment, I had only ever seen her looking like a million dollars. The woman lying on the bed in front of me looked a like a concentration camp victim. She was, however, Rosemary Sellers. I stared at her with a mixture of abject horror and overwhelming relief. 'Rosemary?' I said, when I had regained something of my composure.

She turned her head slowly. At first her face was entirely blank. It shook me to see her features so devoid of life and expression.

'Rosemary? It's Liz.'

She blinked several times and licked her lips.

'Are you thirsty?'

There was the slightest hint of a nod.

I could already feel my eyes beginning to well. *How could they have left you left like this?*

I walked across to the side of her bed and poured her some water from a jug on the bedside cabinet. I put the glass down and helped her up, propping a pillow behind her shoulders so that she could sit. She felt like she weighed nothing at all. I gave her the water which she took in her left hand. She appeared to have limited use of her right arm, which was strapped from the elbow to her wrist. She drained the glass.

I sat down on the side of the bed. 'Rosemary, do you recognise me?' I said, trying to keep my emotions in check.

She handed me the glass and leaned back against the pillows, staring at me in silence.

'I'm Liz Muir. We…'

The words died on my lips and for a moment I was overcome. Here was my dear friend. One of the most intelligent women I'd ever known. A woman of secrets, certainly. But also a woman of great wisdom, compassion, determination. Life. Reduced to this by circumstance and the brutality of one man. 'We're friends Rosemary. In fact you are my closest friend. You know things about me that nobody else in this world knows.' I felt a tear trickle down my cheek.

She reached across, took my hand and gave it the gentlest of squeezes.

I looked directly into her piercing blue eyes, searching for a trace of the Rosemary Sellers I knew. 'Rosemary,' I said, blinking, 'do you remember how you got here?'

She shook her head slowly.

'You were attacked and…' I didn't know how to say it. I didn't want to freak her out. But neither did I have the time to explain it at a pace she might be able to understand. 'We need to get you to somewhere safe, so that it doesn't happen again. Do you understand?'

She looked at me blankly.

'Can you walk?'

She pointed, weakly, to the corner of the room where a wheel chair was folded up against the wall.

'I've got to go back downstairs now. But I will be back in a few minutes…'

I stopped. She was staring at me intently. I couldn't tell whether she had understood. 'I'll be back. I promise.'

I let go of her hand, got up and walked towards the door.

'Liz?' It was a tiny, rasping voice. A voice that made the hairs on the back of my neck stand on end.

I stopped and turned.

'You're Liz,' she said again, weakly.

'Yes, I am,' I said, grinning through the anguish that I felt in my chest. 'I'm your friend. And I am going to get you out of here if it is the last thing I ever do.'

She stared at me for a moment and then nodded.

Chapter Twenty-Nine

Banner checked the car's rear view mirror for what must have been the hundredth time. The street was mostly still, with only the occasional passing car or pedestrian out walking their dog. There had been absolutely no sign of the Frenchman and it was beginning to get dark. Surely if he was going to show, it would be soon. What the point was of sitting here all night Banner didn't have the faintest idea. The Frenchman was hardly going to turn up at half past one in the morning. But Broadbent had been adamant. Which was all very well. He wasn't the poor sod who was going to have to sit here the whole bloody night.

I had just got to the bottom of the stairs, when the young nurse reappeared. She was accompanied by an older woman, wearing a blue uniform. Short, over-weight, and with her mousey coloured hair tied into a bun, she looked altogether more formidable.

'My name is Joan,' said the nurse with the bun, offering me her hand.

'Hannah Leeson,' I said shaking it as forcefully as I could.

'And you are here to see?'

'My mother, Dorothy Leeson.'

'There must be some kind of mistake. We don't have anyone here called Dorothy Leeson. Would you like to come into the office and we'll try to sort this out for you.'

Joan with the bun showed me to the office. The younger nurse followed us in and handed Simone her cup of tea before scuttling away, closing the office door behind her.

'My name is Joan.'

'I'm Sister Valerie,' said Simone.

'Valerie is from the Church that Dorothy used to attend before she…' I hesitated.

Simone glanced at me. 'Disappeared,' she said, bursting into tears.

I hoped to God that she wasn't over doing the amateur dramatics.

'Disappeared?' the nurse said, reaching across the desk to retrieve a box of tissues.

'My mother went missing. At the beginning of May,' I said. 'We've been searching for her ever since.'

The nurse looked at each of us in turn. 'And what makes you think that we have her here?' she said, turning her attention to me.

'Well, the hospital.' I said it as though it was obvious.

'The hospital?'

'Yes, we've phoned dozens of them. All over the country.'

'Hundreds,' said Simone, blowing her nose.

'Without any luck,' I added. 'Until yesterday.'

It was difficult to judge whether the nurse was buying it.

'Sister Valerie spoke to somebody at St Bartholomew's Hospital, didn't you Valerie?'

'Praise the Lord, yes.'

'And they told you that Mrs Leeson was here?'

Valerie nodded. 'They said that a woman matching her description was transferred here. It is Dorothy. Jesus has told me so,' Simone said, with conviction.

The nurse looked at her dubiously. 'Could you describe your mother to me, Miss Leeson,' the nurse said, turning towards me.

I described Rosemary as accurately as I could.

The nurse listened in silence. When I was finished she reached across to the filing cabinet, pulled open a drawer and removed a file, from which took a sheet of paper with a photograph clipped to it. 'Is this your mother?' she said, handing it to me.

I looked at the picture and smiled broadly. 'Thank God. Yes it is.'

'Praise be to Jesus Christ,' said Simone, clambering to her feet. She was hugging herself and swaying, her lips apparently moving in a silent prayer of thanks.

The nurse looked startled. 'Yes. But before you can see her,' she said, looking at Simone nervously. 'I need to warn you that she may not recognise you. She was…' She hesitated. 'I'm sorry to have to tell you that your mother was the victim of a very serious assault.'

'No! Not Sister Dorothy?' Simone said, covering her face with her hands.

'And I need to speak to the authorities before you see her.'

It was this that triggered a performance from Simone that had she been auditioning for an episode of Coronation Street would surely have landed her the part. 'We must see her,' she wailed. 'We must. The Lord has brought us to her.'

'I'm sure he has,' said the nurse, trying to assert her authority, 'but… Dorothy is very frail and…'

But Simone was having none of it. She made straight for the door and, as the nurse tried to get up, the two collided. Feigning hysteria, and doing it remarkably well, Simone stepped back, swayed from left to right and fainted. She went down like she had been struck by lightning.

'Valerie?' I said leaping to my feet. 'She needs water. Where is the kitchen?'

The nurse was already on the floor trying to arrange Simone's limp body into the recovery position.

'Out in the hallway. Second door on the left. But I don't…'

I didn't wait for her to finish. I went out through the office door and ran for the stairs.

When I opened her bedroom door Rosemary was seated on the side of her bed. Somehow she had managed to find a pair of pink, fluffy slippers. As I entered, she tried to stand.

'No, don't get up,' I said anxiously. 'Do you have a coat?'

She pointed at a cupboard in the corner of the room, from which I hurriedly retrieved a long tweed coat. I draped it around her shoulders.

'Don't move,' I said, as she tried again to stand. I ran across to the wheel chair, unfolded it in front of her and helped her into the chair. Then I knelt in front of her, and took hold of both her hands. 'Rosemary, do you know what is happening?'

Rosemary hesitated and then shook her head.

'Do you know who I am?'

'Liz.'

I smiled and squeezed her hands.

'Yes. Somebody hurt you.'

'Möller.'

I wasn't sure that I had heard her correctly.

'No, it was Jimmy Dobson.'

'Jimmy Dobson,' Rosemary repeated.

'Yes, that's right. And he might hurt you again unless we can find somewhere to hide you. Do you understand?'

She looked confused. It was too much for her to take in.

'Don't be afraid, Rosemary. I promise you that we will look after you. I promise.' I held her gaze for several seconds and smiled.

She returned my smile, without breaking eye contact.

I will never forget her face in that moment. It was though I could see through her eyes, into her soul. Rosemary Sellers, the woman who shared all my secrets, was still there. I knew it.

I got to my feet, opened the door and looked out into the hallway. The way was clear. I held the door open with my foot and manoeuvred the wheelchair out into the hall.

The commotion from downstairs was unbelievable. I could hear Simone wailing and voices calling out.

I pushed the wheelchair to the lift and pressed the call button. My heart was hammering in my chest. If we were caught now, I would end up in a police cell and that would be the end of it. The lift doors seemed to take an age to open. When, finally, they did, I wheeled Rosemary into the lift, pressed the button for the ground floor and stood, leaning against the wall of the lift car. We had made it this far. The trouble was that I was not entirely sure what I was going to do when the lift doors opened again.

Simone Jackson clambered to her feet and did the best impression of a mad woman that she could conjure. 'I must see Sister Dorothy,' she wailed. 'The Lord has willed it,' she said pushing past the nurse with the bun. She heaved open the office door and staggered out into the corridor.

The younger nurse appeared at the door to the hallway, looking completely terrified.

'Valerie you must calm down,' shouted the elder nurse from the office doorway.

But Simone's part of their plan was to create chaos and she had barely started. She opened her mouth and wailed whatever gibberish came into her head.

'Stay with her,' yelled the elder nurse above the commotion. 'Don't let her anywhere near the residents. I'm going to call for backup.'

Simone caught a glimpse of her over her shoulder as she disappeared back into the office.

The younger nurse stood her ground. 'Please calm down,' she said, looking as though she was about to burst into tears.

Simone screamed like a banshee and charged her. It was all that she could think to do. The young nurse took one look at the approaching mad woman and turned to flee. But it was too late. Simone crashed into her, knocking her off her feet. They both burst through the doorway and landed in a heap on the hallway floor. Simone tore the bunch of keys from the younger's nurses waist band and staggered to her feet. 'The Lord will smite you down,' she yelled.

'No. Please,' screamed the terrified nurse. She had clambered up onto all fours.

'Then flee child. Flee. Before the wrath of the Lord descendeth upon ye,' yelled Simone.

The warning was all that the young nurse needed. She leapt up and ran, disappearing into the television room, slamming the door behind her with a loud crash.

Simone turned and darted to the office door. She tried three keys before she found the correct one and turned the lock, leaving the key in the place so that Joan with the bun would be unable to get out. Then she ran back along the corridor which, at the its far end, opened into a foyer in front of the lift. As she entered the foyer the lift doors opened and out from the lift emerged a frail looking woman in a wheelchair.

Banner had closed his eyes momentarily when the radio spluttered back into life. 'Golf-Delta-Four-Seven this is Yankee-Delta.'

Yankee-Delta? What the hell do Wood Green want? Banner reached for the microphone. As he did so, he upset the coffee that he'd been balancing on his lap. 'Oh, for fuck sake,' he said out loud, trying to brush the coffee that was pooling in his lap. Fortunately it had already gone cold.

'Golf-Delta-Four-Seven this is Yankee-Delta.'

'Yankee-Delta, this is Golf-Delta-Four-Seven, go ahead.'

'Golf-Delta-Four-Seven, we've received a call from a Mistle Thrush nursing home, in Vallance Road, North Twenty-Two. The caller said that she had spoken to you earlier. What is your location?'

A disturbance? 'Yankee Delta, I'm outside the nursing home in Vallance Road, but there is no sign of any disturbance.'

'Four-Seven, report is of an I-C-3 female who has become hysterical. Could you assist?'

Bollocks. 'Roger Yankee-Delta. Show me assigned.' *An I-C-3.* He'd seen a black woman entering the place a little earlier.

'Roger Golf-Delta-Four-Seven, we're sending back up.'

Well thank Christ for that. 'I am so obliged, Yankee-Delta,' he said sarcastically. 'Four-Seven out.'

Banner clipped the microphone to its holder on the dashboard and let out an exasperated sigh. He got out out of the car and let the door wing closed behind him.

The street was completely quiet. There was no sign of any disturbance, but he supposed that anything could be happening inside. He crossed the road, walked up the ramp and rang the door bell. There was no reply. He knelt down, pushed open the letter box and peered inside. *Jesus, what is that smell?*

'Hello,' he called out. 'This is the Police.'

Still nothing.

He got to his feet and banged his fist on the door.

Then, to his left, he heard a sash window being hauled open. 'Over here,' called out a voice. 'I'm locked in the office.'

Locked in the office? What the f... He turned and walked along the front of the building until he drew level with the open window.

A middle aged woman with her hair in a bun was peering out. 'We have a maniac on the loose. She locked me in here.'

'Can somebody else let me in?'

'Yes. There's another nurse. Her name's Janine.'

Banner walked back to the door, knelt down and again called through the letter box. 'Janine? This is Detective Inspector Banner from Hackney Police. Are you alright? Can you let me in?'

He peered in as a nurse emerged from a doorway to the right. As she did so an alarm sounded from inside.

D.I.Banner got to his feet, shaking his head. *What the hell is going on?*

To say that I was relieved to find Simone waiting for me when the lift doors opened would be a understatement.

'Are you OK?' she said, her forehead covered in sweat.

'I'm better for seeing you, that's for sure. Rosemary, this is Simone.'

Simone knelt down in front of the wheelchair. 'Hello Rosemary. It is good to meet you.'

Rosemary looked at her blankly.

'Any idea what we do next?' I had absolutely no idea.

'Yes. Fire door over there,' Simone said pointing. 'Come on. Quickly. I scared the pink one shitless and locked the older one in the office, but I wouldn't put it past her to break her way out. She certainly has the build for it.'

Simone strode across to the fire door and pushed the bar. The door swung open, letting the cool evening air flood in. I took a lungful. It was as though I was breathing for the first time in hours.

As I pushed Rosemary's wheelchair out through the doorway I noticed a red light illuminate in a panel attached to the doorframe. 'Alarm?' I said looking up at the light and then at Simone.

'Let's not wait to find out.'

The fire door opened onto a pathway that ran around the side of the building toward the street. I manoeuvred the wheelchair carefully and followed Simone. She stopped suddenly at the building's corner, turned and put her finger to her mouth.

'What?' I mouthed silently.

'Somebody is at the door.'

I started to reply but Simone silenced me. 'Shh. I want to hear what he's saying.'

I waited.

'Shit,' she whispered after a few moments. 'Police.'

'I knew it,' I whispered back. 'I knew they'd be watching. What are we going to do now?'

But the possibility of hearing anything further was suddenly obliterated by the sound of an alarm going off inside the building.

Simone put her head gingerly around the corner.

'He's gone in. Pinky must have found some courage. Come on!' Simone said.

Simone stepped out and ran ahead of me, across the nursing home's front lawn and out onto the street toward the waiting car. She tore open the car's rear door and stood, waiting for me to catch up, glancing from left to right, nervously.

'Where the hell is he?' I said, as I approached, pushing Rosemary's wheelchair.

'I don't know. Look the keys are in the ignition. Quickly.'

I turned towards Rosemary. 'Can you get up?'

She tried. She really did. But in the end I had to lift her. Which was easy. She weighed little more than a child. I placed her on the back seat as carefully as I could. 'Don't worry. It's going to be fine,' I said and squeezed her hand.

She grinned back at me. This time and in the circumstances it was just, plain, unnerving.

I turned in time to see Alphonse approaching us. 'Where the hell were you?' I said, tensely.

'I was making, how do you say, "adaptations" to the policeman's car. So that he cannot follow you.'

I smiled. 'Now that, my friend, is just plain cunning.'

'Oui. Now you must go.'

'Are you sure that you will be alright?'

'But, of course.'

'Alphonse, I think I love you,' I said and I kissed him on the cheek.

'Merci, Mademoiselle. Now go.'

Simone had loaded the wheelchair into the boot and was already in the driver's seat. I got in beside her and closed the door.

'Where to madam?' said Simone.

'I don't care. Just get out us the hell out of here.'

Simone started the car, looked over her shoulder and pulled out into the middle of the road. I could already hear distant sirens.

The first thing that Banner did was free the senior nurse from the office. The junior nurse in the pink uniform was shaking like a leaf.

'Janine, pull yourself together and go and look after the residents. I'll deal with this.'

'I'm D.I.Banner. I spoke to you earlier. About Mr Richelieu?' Banner shouted above the wail of the alarm.

'Oh, yes.'

'We received reports of a disturbance?'

'A what?'

The nurse was evidently having difficulty hearing him above the sound of the alarm. 'A disturbance,' Banner shouted.

'Is that what you'd call it?' said the senior nurse. 'The woman's a bloody psychopath.'

'Woman? What woman?'

'There were two of them. One black. One white.'

'Look, do you think you could silence that bloody alarm?'

'Hang on a minute,' said the nurse, walking across to a panel on the wall.

Banner followed.

The nurse punched a combination into the keypad but the alarm continued to wail. 'Shit, the bloody thing's always doing this.'

'Where are they now?'

'How the hell should I know. I've been locked in the bloody office. I've called Mr Evangelou. The owner. He's got the master key,' the Nurse said trying the combination again.

'Do you have any idea what they wanted?'

'Yes. They came to see the woman you called about.'

Banner's heart felt like it had stopped. 'The woman from Bart's?'

'Yes. One of them said she was the woman's daughter. The white one.'

'Well it would hardly have been the black one, now would it?' Banner could feel his patience fraying.

'Don't you take that tone with me,' the nurse shouted back.

Banner held up his hand. 'Did they identify her? The woman from Bart's, I mean.'

'Yes. They said that her name is Dorothy Leeson.'

Banner considered this unexpected development. It was a breakthrough, of sorts. If he could apprehend them, then he might very well be able to take the credit for finally identifying the woman. Which would surely go down well with the Chief Super.

'Are they with her now?'

'I've told you. I don't know.'

At that moment the doorbell rang. Banner barely heard it above the noise.

'That'll be Mr Evangelou,' the nurse shouted.

'I'll get it,' said Banner.

He walked across to the front door and opened it, expecting to greet the nursing home's owner. But it wasn't the owner who was stood in front of him. It was the Frenchman. Alphonse Richelieu.

Chapter Thirty

'Bonsoir. My name is Alphonse Richelieu. I have come to see one of the ladies who live here.'

For once, Banner was lost for words. It was not a common phenomenon.

'You have not been able to identify her, I believe?' Alphonse peered around the dumbstruck policeman. 'Is there a problem of some kind?'

'What?' Banner managed.

'The siren. There is, perhaps, some sort of emergency? Can I be of any assistance?'

Banner took a step backwards.

'It's the door alarm,' shouted the nurse from across the hall. She was still attempting to neutralise it. 'Just a minute and I'll shut the bloody thing off.'

'Come in, close the door and stay there. Do you understand?' shouted the policeman.

'Certainly, Monsieur,' Alphonse said, stepping into the hall.

'Do not move from here. I mean it. Not an inch.'

Alphonse did his best to look confused but nodded in agreement.

Banner turned, just as the alarm was finally silenced. He raced across the hall. 'Door alarm. Which door. Where?' he yelled at the nurse.

She looked at the control panel on which a single red light was still flashing. 'Ground floor fire door, beside the lift.'

'Where?' Banner yelled.

'Um, ground floor. Beside the lift,' the nurse replied, looking at Banner like he was a complete idiot.

Banner grabbed her shoulder. 'Where, for God's sake? Where?'

The nurse gave him a look like daggers but pointed to the door leading to the office from which she had recently emerged. 'End of the corridor,' she said icily.

Banner didn't wait. He ran at the door, full pelt, and tore down the corridor like his life depended on it. If what he feared had come to pass, then he reflected as he ran that it very probably did.

At the bottom of the corridor he staggered to a halt. 'Oh fuck,' he said out loud.

He grabbed the already open door, dived out into the alley and ran to the front of the building. There was no sign of them. He turned, re-entered the building and ran back to the hallway where the nurse was talking to Alphonse, who had remained rooted to the spot, where Banner had left him.

'Which room? The woman from Bart's, which room?'

The nurse turned. 'Room seven on the first floor.'

Banner opened his mouth to speak but the nurse interrupted him. 'Up the stairs to the first floor. Main corridor. Room on the left.'

Banner ran up the stairs, through the fire door at the top and along the corridor until he found room seven. The door was ajar. He tore it open and stepped inside. The room was empty.

Banner reached for the tape recorder and pressed the record button.

'The date is Friday, 29th July 1977, the time is…' He looked at his watch. '23.15 and this interview is taking place at Wood Green Police Station. I am Detective Inspector Michael Banner. Also present in the room are Chief Superintendent Simon Broadbent. Your name please.'

'I am Alphonse Richelieu.'

'And your date of birth Mr Richelieu?'

'I was born on the thirteenth of September, Nineteen..' Alphonse hesitated. 'Fifteen.'

'And your address?'

'57B Rudall Crescent, London, North-West-Three.'

'Thank you. Mr Richelieu, I must caution you that you are not obliged to say anything unless you wish to do so but whatever you say will be taken down in writing and may be given in evidence. Do you understand?'

'Oui, Monsieur.'

'In English, if you don't mind,' Banner said, irritably.

'Yes.'

'You have been arrested in connection with the disappearance, earlier this evening, of a female resident of the Mistle Thrush Nursing Home, in Alexandra Park. Do you understand?'

'Yes, I do but ...'

'There'll be time for that in a moment,' he interrupted. 'You arrived at the Mistle Thrush Nursing Home at approximately eight forty?'

'Oui... Yes, that is correct.'

'Could you tell us, what was the purpose of your visit?'

'I was there to see one of the women who live... lived there,' Alphonse corrected himself.

'And the name of the resident who you wished to see was?'

Alphonse hesitated. 'That, I do not know, Officer Banner.'

'Detective Inspector. I am D.I.Banner.'

'Pardon.'

'What was her name Richelieu?'

'Since I was unable to see her, I cannot say.'

'Alright. If you do not know who she was, why did you want to see her?'

'I had reason to suspect that I might know.'

'What reason?'

Alphonse sighed. 'An acquaintance of mine went missing at the end of April this year. I later learned from the media that a woman had been assaulted and that the police had been unable to identify her. I thought that this woman and my acquaintance might have been one and the same.'

'Who is this acquaintance of yours?'

'I am not willing to say.'

'What? Why not?'

Alphonse pondered the question. 'I am not willing to say.'

Banner was already losing his patience. 'Don't play games with me Richelieu. Who was this woman?'

'I am not, as you say, playing games, D.I.Banner. I am simply not willing to name her unless I know that she was the woman at the nursing home.'

'Why not?'

'If it was her, then by naming her I might be of some assistance in aiding her recovery and putting her back in touch with her family. But if it was not her, then nothing would be gained by me naming my acquaintance. Is that not the case, Monsieur?'

'Alright. This acquaintance of yours. You say she went missing?'

'Oui.'

'In what circumstances?'

'If I knew that, Monsieur, I might have had more luck finding her.'

Broadbent chewed his bottom lip. 'Where? Where was she last seen?'

'In London. Beyond that I am not willing to say.'

'Look, Richelieu,' Banner snarled. 'Right now, you're in a great deal of trouble. Unless you cooperate with us, you're going to be in a whole lot more.'

'D.I.Banner, am I not cooperating? I am willing, perfectly, to answer your questions. But I am not willing to name a woman who may have nothing whatever to do with your enquiries. It is as simple as that. You may, as you English say, take it or leave it.'

'You cocky bloody fro…'

'D.I.Banner,' said a voice from the back of the room.

The intervention stopped Banner in his tracks.

'Is this going anywhere? Perhaps we should show Mr Richelieu the woman's photograph.'

'Yes, Sir.' Banner reached into a file on the table in front of him, removed a photograph and pushed it across the table.

'For the tape, I am passing a photograph of the woman from Mistle Thrush Nursing Home to Mr Richelieu.'

Alphonse looked at the photograph.

'Do you recognise the woman in the photograph, Mr Richelieu?'

'Non.'

Banner turned and looked at the Chief Superintendent. 'Are you sure about that?' he said, turning back to the Frenchman.

'Yes. I am positive.'

'Might I remind you that you are under caution?'

'Certainly. But I do not know this woman D.I.Banner.'

'You are telling us that this is not a photograph of your acquaintance?'

'That is correct. I have never, in my life, met this woman.'

'Oh come on. You are seriously trying to tell us that you attended Mistle Thrush House believing that the woman there might be your friend, but that you were mistaken?'

'Apparently so. This comes as a disappointment to me, Monsieur. But she is not my acquaintance and unfortunately I cannot therefore identify her.'

Banner chewed his lip some more. The Frenchman was lying. Banner was certain of it. 'Does the name Dorothy Leeson mean anything to you?' he asked.

Alphonse appeared to consider the question. 'I do not believe so, non Monsieur.'

'You don't believe so. Does it or doesn't it?'

'No it does not. I do not believe that I know anyone of that name.'

'Mr Richelieu, minutes before your arrival at the nursing home, the woman in the photograph was abducted by, we believe, two women. What do you know about that?'

'I know nothing of it, Monsieur.'

Banner laughed out loud. 'It is pure coincidence, is it, that your arrival in Vallance Road and the woman's abduction coincided almost exactly and yet the two are not connected?'

'D.I.Banner, if I was in some way involved in the abduction of this woman, why would I have knocked at the front door, only minutes later, asking to see her? Would I have walked in through the front door and waited patiently while you ran around like the chicken without a head?'

'Don't get smart with me,' yelled Banner, bringing his fist down on the desk.

'Banner. Get a grip,' said the second policeman from the back of the room. 'He does have a point.'

Banner took a deep breath. The interview was going rapidly down the pan, along with his career and the Frenchman appeared more than happy to pull the chain. 'How did you get to Vallance Road?'

'I took the bus from Turnpike Lane to Muswell Hill and then I walked. I enjoy walking.'

'Which bus route?'

'W2.'

'You are sure about that, are you?'

'Oui. Quite sure.'

'Which route did you take on foot?'

'Hmm.. Let me see,' Alphonse said, scratching his chin. 'I walked along Dukes Avenue I think it was, then I turned left and then I turned right. I do not know the name of the roads.'

'So you entered Vallance Road from the southern end?'

Alphonse shrugged. 'That I do not know, Monsieur. I did not have with me...' he hesitated. 'Une boussole... what is the English word?'

'Compass,' said the second policeman.

'Oui, as you say. Compass. I do not know whether it was from the south or the north.'

Banner looked at him icily. 'Did any vehicle pass you while you were walking along Vallance Road?' he said between gritted teeth.

The Frenchman thought carefully. 'Non. I do not believe so.'

'Describe what you saw as you approached the nursing home.'

'What is there to describe Monsieur? The street was empty.'

'Were there any vehicles parked outside the nursing home?'

'Yes, I believe your car was parked there, Monsieur.'

Banner looked over his shoulder at the second policeman. 'And how, exactly, did you know that it was my car?' he said triumphantly, turning back towards the Frenchman.

'But, at the time, I did not. It was only when we departed, that you identified the vehicle, Detective Inspector. Your precise words, if I remember them correctly, were "I don't fucking believe it. Somebody has slashed my fucking tyres.".' As he said it, Alphonse could not resist a smile.

Banner's face turned an unpleasant shade of purple. 'I don't suppose that you saw anyone tampering with the vehicle?' he said between clenched teeth.

'Non.'

'No, of course you didn't.'

Alphonse shrugged. 'I saw what I saw, Monsieur. And I did not see what I did not see.'

'And when you got closer to Mistle Thrush House, did you see anyone leaving the premises?' Banner persisted.

'Non.'

'Mr Richelieu, we know that two women left the building seconds before you arrived. They were pushing the woman in a wheelchair. Unless they were invisible, you must have seen them.'

'But I did not. I saw nothing and I know nothing about this missing woman D.I.Banner,' Alphonse said, tapping the photograph on the desk in front of him with his index finger.

Banner stared at him.

'I am sorry Monsieur. I wish that this woman was my acquaintance. At least then I would know that she is still alive. Now I must return to my search.'

'I don't buy it Richelieu. Not for one bloody minute. If you are searching for someone, tell me, why would you not wish to involve the police? Why would you be unwilling, even, to tell us her name?'

'There are many reasons why this might be so. Perhaps I do not wish to expose my acquaintance to the attention of the police until I am sure of her situation. Being missing, D.I.Banner, ce n'est pas un crime.'

Banner looked over his shoulder at the Chief Superintendent.

'It is not a crime,' said Broadbent.

'And neither is visiting an elderly woman in a nursing home. Now, if you have no other reason to keep me here, perhaps you might kindly restore me to my liberty. We French value our liberty above all else, Monsieur.'

Banner could sense Broadbent sharpening his knives.

Chapter Thirty-One

I spent the weekend itching to see Rosemary, but with things between Ted and me so strained, there was just no way I could get out.

Telling him the truth about my visit to Mistle Thrush House had not, in hindsight, been such a great idea. If the story attracted any media attention, I was going to struggle to come up with an explanation of my part in the evening's events. In the end, I had decided to play the whole thing down. I told him that the woman had been gone by the time that I'd arrived, following some fuss involving a visitor who had turned up, identified the woman as her mother, and promptly discharged her. If the story blew. I'd simply plead ignorance. In the event, her disappearance made neither the television nor local radio news, which surprised me. I wondered whether Smith had anything to do with that.

I did at least manage to call Simone while Ted was out. 'I haven't got long. How is she?' I'd said a little breathlessly when, finally, I'd been able to make the call.

'She's settling down well, actually' Simone had reported. 'Mum's doing a fantastic job. I knew she would.'

After our escape from Vallance Road, we'd driven to Tottenham, as sedately as we could. Had we been stopped by the police we'd have been stymied, but in fact the journey had gone without a hitch.

It had been Simone's suggestion that we hide Rosemary at her mother's flat on the Broadwater Farm estate. She'd come up with the idea while she, Alphonse and I had been sat in The Gate, trying to put together a workable rescue plan.

'Mum's a retired nurse. She even did a stint on the head injuries ward at the Prince of Wales. So she'll know exactly how to care for her.'

'Yes but what about the secrecy? Nobody can know that Rosemary is there. It won't be just the police who will be looking for her. Rosemary is a retired intelligence officer, Simone.'

'Yeah? Well spooks don't scare me and they won't scare Mum.'

'Well they should. Believe you me,' I'd said and I'd meant it.

'Look, unless what you've told me is a crock full of shit, we're not actually going to be breaking the law are we?'

'Um… yes. We're going to be kidnapping a resident from an old people's home.'

'No we're not. She's coming of her own volition, right?'

I'd thought about it.

'If Rosemary refuses to come, presumably we're not going to be able to take her?' Simone had said.

'Simone is right, perhaps, Mademoiselle,' Alphonse had added.

'With Leroy away for a couple of months, there's a spare room at mum's and I'm only a floor away. If we need to move her, there's always the back up of using my flat.'

'But how's your mum going to feel about harbouring a missing person?'

'We won't know that until I call her. I saw a phone box outside. But Mum's amazing. If I tell her the truth, that Rosemary is at risk from the police and from a racist thug, I can't see her turning her away. And the way that people on The Farm feel about the police and the NUGB right now, I can't see anyone wanting to turn her in. If we play our cards right, they won't even know she's there. Think about it Liz, what better place to hide her than in the middle of the Broadwater Farm Estate?'

I had to hand it to Simone. Hiding Rosemary at her mum's was a masterstroke and so it was agreed.

I sat down on the foot of the stairs.

'It's certainly a relief to know that, for now anyway, she is safe. Has she spoken at all?'

'Just the occasional word. But mostly she seems to use gestures. Mum thinks that there's a lot more going on in her head than manages to find its way to her mouth. She left a newspaper in her room this morning and found Rosemary with it, when she went in with a cup of tea.'

'Rosemary was reading?'

'It certainly looked that way, but its difficult to be sure.'

'And your mum is managing?'

'Liz, relax. Mum is in her element. She's been missing nursing since she packed it in. She's one of those people who loves caring for others. And watching them together this morning, it looks to me like they've already hit it off.'

'Really? I can't imagine Rosemary and your mum having much in common, to be honest.'

'Maybe not. But that doesn't seem to be getting in their way.'

I hesitated. 'What about you, Simone?'

'What about me?'

'I told you as much as I could yesterday.'

'I know you did.'

But there was more that I couldn't tell her. A lot more.

'Look Liz, I'm not stupid. I can see that you're mixed up in something far bigger than rescuing Rosemary. Maybe, one day, you'll be able to tell me. Maybe not. Whatever. Have you murdered anyone?'

'No.'

'Have you stolen somebody's child?'

I swallowed hard. *Yes.* 'No, of course not.'

'So whatever you've done, I can at least stop worrying that its on that scale.'

She was trying to reassure me, but it wasn't working.

'Whatever you're mixed up in, whatever you've done, you're my friend and I know you.'

Which was exactly the point. She didn't. Nobody did. I wasn't even sure that I did anymore.

'And I trust you. You're a good person.'

She was wrong. I was using her. That was the truth. Just like I had used Ted. Just like I was using Peter. I had been dishonest with them all. 'I've tried Simone. To do the right thing. But sometimes it feels like I've made the most terrible mess of it all.'

'We all make messes, Liz. Balls up our own lives and the lives of others, but it doesn't make us bad people. Evil people.'

'Maybe not.' I heard a key being inserted in the front door and could see Ted's outline through the glass. 'I'm going to have to go, Simone. Thanks.'

'There's no need.'

'Yes there is,' I insisted.

Chapter Thirty-Two

Monday, 1st August 1977

The inevitable confrontation with Smith came more quickly than I thought it would. He was waiting for me at the safe house when I arrived.

'Good weekend?'

'Not particularly, no,' I answered casually.

He was difficult to gauge at the best of times but, if I'd had any doubt about whether he knew of Rosemary's disappearance when I arrived, it was quickly dispelled.

'After Friday evening's excesses, I would have thought that a quiet weekend at home with Ted and the children would have been exactly what you needed.'

'What are you talking about?' I replied evasively

Smith laughed. 'What have you done with her, Liz?'

'Done with who?'

Smith was seated at the kitchen table. He picked up his coffee cup. 'You're playing a dangerous game, you know. I warned you that this was bigger than you could imagine. You still have no idea, do you?'

I threw my bag on to the table in front of him. 'So tell me. Tell me what this is all about. Because I thought I knew. I thought we were trying to thwart the NUGB's great master plan. But do you know what, I'm beginning to wonder whether it is about that at all. So tell me. Come on. I'm all ears.'

Smith ignored the outburst. 'Where is she?'

I laughed. 'If you are talking about the woman who Dobson mentioned, I've absolutely no idea.'

'Very well. But be warned. We will find her, Liz. And when we do, it is not just you who will live to regret it. Whoever you've fooled into hiding her is going to be in very deep water indeed.'

I swallowed hard.

'Because you have lied to them haven't you?'

Smith was clever. He knew exactly how to turn the screw.

'Just like you've lied to your husband, to Jimmy Dobson and to Peter Owen. As a matter of interest, is there anyone you haven't lied to?'

I ignored the question.

'Does anyone know the truth? Apart from me that is,' he continued.

'Don't you dare. You've manipulated this whole thing. Right from the start. If I've lied, I've lied for you or because of you. You've wrecked my life and, do you know what, you're still doing it. You don't give a shit about me or anybody else. I don't know what your agenda is Smith and do you know what? I don't give a horse's shit. All I want is you out of my life. Permanently.'

'Then where is she?'

'I've no idea what you're talking about.'

For a moment, there was a flash of anger but he masked it quickly. 'She's not what she appears to be, you know. She's not even *who* she appears to be,' he said, changing tack. 'Did you ever stop to consider that?'

I'd guessed that Rosemary used a false identity. Alphonse and I had discussed that very possibility.

'She's using you Liz. Just like you use people. Except that she's better at it than you are. A lot better. She had a long career as an intelligence officer in which to perfect the art.'

I ignored him.

'Do you know her real name? Her address? The town she grew up in? Whether she has a family? Anything at all?'

I carried on ignoring him.

'Has she told you anything about the things she has done? The people she's manipulated and betrayed? The people whose lives she has destroyed?'

He was right, of course. I knew nothing of these things and, as he sewed the seeds of doubt, so I could not avoid the whispering voices in my head. Suppose that Rosemary was using me? Suppose she always had? Perhaps Smith wasn't the villain at all. I'd told Simone that she didn't know the half of it. But how much more did I really know about Rosemary Sellers than I had been able to tell Simone?'

'Keep going Smith. It's an impressive performance. I'm taking notes.'

He leant back in his chair and observed me, coldly. 'You're a fool, Liz.'

I laughed, bitterly. 'You're damn right there. I'm a fucking idiot. So do yourself a favour and fire me.'

'Fire you? I don't think so. You're going to find out what Owen is up to and then you're going to betray him. Like you always do. If I needed any more leverage than I already have then, by kidnapping a retired agent, you've handed it to me on a plate.'

'What are you talking about?' I asked it, but I didn't particularly want to hear the answer.

'One word. That's all it would take. One word. Did you think that the Service would tolerate the kidnapping of one of their own, retired or not? They're already looking, Liz. One word from me and they're perfectly capable of removing you and whoever else you've fooled into hiding her.' He put his coffee cup down and stood up.

'You've got less than a fortnight. I suggest you divert your full attention to the task. Infiltrate that conference.'

I opened my mouth to speak.

'I don't care how,' he interrupted. 'I want to know exactly what they're planning, when they're going to make their move and who will be involved.' He picked up his coat. 'In the meantime, give my regards to your house guest,' and with that, he turned and left.

Time was running out. I had discovered all that I was going to discover about the conference without actually being there and try as I might I could not conceive of a way to apply any pressure on Dobson, either directly or via Peter, that would convince him to countenance my presence there. Peter could not afford to undermine his own head of security and I could not afford to encourage any kind of confrontation between the two men. Dobson had me exactly where he wanted me and he knew it.

If Dobson was half as good at his job as Peter seemed to think he was then I couldn't see how I was going to find a way to get into the conference venue, uninvited and, even if I had been able to do it, I'd have been none the wiser without access to the conference room itself. As each day passed, I became increasingly sure that the task given to me by Smith was not achievable.

And so the pressure began to build. If the conference passed without result and I could not otherwise discover the Union's plans, Smith would have little reason not to turn against me. Especially as he knew that I was hiding Rosemary. And that was not all. With Dobson preoccupied with conference preparations I had been able to hold him off. But once the conference was over, he would be expecting payment for his silence. The thought of sex with Jimmy Dobson, the man who had murdered Karl Dixon, was too sickening to contemplate. It was also unlikely to be one-off requirement. Knowing what he knew, though flawed, would leave me vulnerable to his advances whenever and wherever he cared to make them.

In the middle of it all were my feelings for Peter Owen. I knew where they were leading me and, while I railed against it in my head, I could not escape the feeling that I was destined, somehow, to see it through to the end. To repeat the same cycle of deception and despair. As it had been since the very beginning and as it would be until it was done with me.

Neither could I escape the feeling, as the week wore on, that the end was fast approaching. Though it terrified me, a part of me was eager for it. Like a lemming charging toward the cliff edge, part of me longed for an end to it, even if it meant crashing headlong into the sea. It was nothing more than I deserved.

I managed to see Rosemary when I could and the progress that she was making under the care of Mrs Jackson provided an all too brief respite from the darkness that was beginning to envelop me. In the days following the escape from Mistle Thrush House, Rosemary regained her physical health surprisingly quickly though the same could not be said for her memory. There were flashes of recognition. Visits when she greeted me by name and we would sit quietly, holding hands while I talked and she listened. Over the course of a week or so, I told her my whole story again. I left nothing out. Spared no detail. I told it all.

Sometimes a word, or a description of some event would trigger something in Rosemary's mind. Then she would rise to her her feet, suddenly, and pace up and down her little room, mumbling to herself. One such trigger proved to be Jimmy Dobson's name. Almost without exception, the mere mention of it was enough to send her pacing, usually in a state of some agitation. Once, when she had been pacing for several minutes, she had turned to me, suddenly and said 'You must get away. He has killed and he will keep killing until he has what he wants.' She had spoken with startling lucidity but the memory had clearly caused her great distress and she had begun to cry, her voice fading away into mumbled sobs.

I had stood up and walked across to her. 'It's alright.' I'd put my arm around her and steered her back to her armchair.

Once she was seated, I'd tried a gentle question. 'What does he want, Rosemary? What is it the Jimmy Dobson wants so badly that he is prepared to kill for it?' But Rosemary had simply stared at me blankly.

And so it went on. Each time I saw her, behind those piercing blue eyes, there was a little more of the Rosemary I knew. It was as though the assault had driven her spirit from her body up into the heavens and that, gradually, wisp by wisp, memory by memory, it was floating back to her. But it was obvious that it was going to take many months for it to wholly return, if indeed it ever would.

Alphonse was also a frequent visitor. In fact Mrs Jackson and Alphonse appeared to be forming something of a bond. It was the most unlikely of friendships - Alphonse the camp Frenchman from Highgate and Flora Jackson, the stereotypical Trinidadian mum, from Tottenham. But from the outset there had been something between them and with time, somewhat bizarrely, I could see the two of them making a very odd, but happy couple.

It was also Alphonse who, quite unexpectedly, provided me with a way into the conference.

Chapter Thirty-Three

Monday, 15th August 1977

I had left Excalibur House early on the pretext of having an appointment at the dentist. It was a pretty lame excuse but I had, by then, neither the imagination nor the energy to think of a better one. I'd driven from Finsbury Park to Tottenham, as I did whenever I could, to see Rosemary, being careful to ensure that I was not followed. I parked, as I usually did, in Walpole Road and set off in the direction of the recreation ground. It was a walk of about ten minutes, to get to Mrs Jackson's flat in the block called "Debden" on Gloucester Road.

No sooner had I stepped into the alleyway that led from Walpole Road when I heard a familiar voice behind me. 'Mademoiselle?'

There was only one person who called me that. I turned. 'So you're parking out this way too, are you Alphonse?'

'But of course. Was it not you, yourself who suggested it?'

I smiled. 'Well at least someone is listening to me. Will you walk with me, through the park Monsieur?'

'I would be honoured, Mademoiselle.'

I took his arm.

'Actually, Liz, I am glad that we have this opportunity to speak.'

'Oh yes?'

'I had a visitor, this morning.'

'At work?'

'No, I was at home today.'

'Who?'

'Simon Broadbent.'

I stopped. 'Broadbent?'

'Do not be concerned. Come, let us walk.'

I took a breath and then a step forward.

'That Simon did not believe me at the interview with Monsieur Banner, it was obvious, yes?'

'He was always going to suspect your involvement.'

'As you say. So it is hardly a surprise that he wished to speak with me.'

'I guess not. What did he want?'

'It was not, so much, what he wanted as what he revealed, Mademoiselle. And in the revelation, what he may have in mind.'

'You are talking in riddles Alphonse.'

'Pardon. Then I will try to speak more plainly. Simon wishes to meet you.'

I almost fell over. 'He what? He knows about me?'

'Non. Not directly.'

'Then what do you mean he wants to meet me?'

'Simon knows that I was involved with the incident at Mistle Thrush House, but he cannot prove it, yes.'

'Yes. Yes, we have already established that.'

'And yet, Rosemary was taken by two women. A fact that he knows also.'

I said nothing.

'Simon reasons that I must know and be in contact with these women.'

I stared at him as we walked.

'Perhaps we should sit down?'

'What?'

'The bench?' he said, pointing. 'I would not wish you to fall to the ground.'

'Oh. Yes, alright.'

We walked across to the bench and sat, looking out across the field that stretched out in front of us.

'Remember that Simon does not know Rosemary's identity.'

'Okay.'

'But he does, I think, know the identity of her attacker.'

'So why doesn't he arrest the bastard? No, forget that, we both know why he does't do that.'

'A minute, Mademoiselle. Simon reasons that since her attacker works for the Union National and that the woman was attacked in a street near to the office of the Union National…'

'Stop right there. Did he say how he knows that it was Dobson?'

'Non, but he does know it, I believe.'

'Alright, I'm sorry. Please go on.'

'He reasons that there is likely to be a link between Rosemary, her attacker and the women that took her. That they are likely to have something in common. He has, as you say, put together two and two.'

'And what does he think that something is?'

'The Union National.'

'You said not to worry, Alphonse. If Broadbent has linked this to the Union, then it is only a matter of time. There are not that many women with a direct link to the Union and fewer still who actually work there. Three to be precise.'

'That may be true.'

'So why does he want to meet me? He could pull each of us in turn, whenever he likes.'

Alphonse appeared to ponder the question. 'Whatever you think of Simon, I do not believe that he is an entirely bad man.'

I shook my head. 'Which I might be more inclined to believe if he hadn't already released Jimmy Dobson from a murder charge. And tell me, Alphonse, if Broadbent is not a bad man and he knows that Dobson attacked Rosemary, why has he not arrested him?'

'I have thought about this much.'
'And?'
'Perhaps, he cannot.'
I looked at him sceptically.
'Perhaps this Dobson has some hold over him. Perhaps this is why he released him and does not move against him. Perhaps he has little choice.'
'Or perhaps Broadbent is a bent copper…'
'Pardon?' Alphonse looked confused.
'Perhaps he is corrupt. Perhaps he has allied himself to the NUGB for his own purposes and now, suspecting a mole within the Union, is in league with Dobson to discover their identity.'
'Then as you say, Mademoiselle, why has he not "pulled" you already?'
'Because it is easier to lay a trap and have me walk straight into it? Alphonse, what other purpose could Simon Broadbent have?'
'I think that I have found an answer to that.'
I looked at him expectantly.
'Some years ago I befriended a young man called Paulo Diomedi. At the time, Paulo was living in a house of addicts and was working as a boy for rent. Une prostitute?'
I nodded.
'He told me that he was sixteen but I did not believe it. And he had already experimented with heroine. Had he stayed there, in a few years, he would have been dead. Of that I had little doubt. And so I helped him to get out. To find his own place.'
'Okay.'
'This is how I met Simon.'
It took a few moments for the penny to drop.
'Simon was one of his clients. But more than that, Simon became, how do you say, attached to him.'
'Broadbent and this Paulo were a couple?'
'Not exactly so. But Simon looked after him. They were close.'
'Okay.'

'Two years ago, Paulo was attacked and beaten. It was very serious. After this, he was not the same. His brain…'

'Like Rosemary,' I said under my breath.

'But that is not all. Later, when he had recovered, I asked Paulo what had happened. It was difficult for him to speak of it. His memory. His understanding. It was not good. But he managed to tell me that he had been with Simon and there had been a man with a camera. He had chased the man and it was this man who had attacked him.'

'A man with a camera? What did he mean?'

'I was never sure. But I have wondered. And so after Simon's visit this morning I visited Paulo. To ask him whether he had recalled anything more of his attacker.'

'And what did he say?'

'He said that Simon knows, that he has always known but that he has chosen to do nothing about this man. This has caused great bitterness between them.'

'Does Paulo know his attacker's name?'

'Non. He says that he does not.'

We were both silent for several minutes.

'Well I can guess. Jimmy Dobson,' I said out loud.

Alphonse said nothing.

'That Broadbent has been helping the NUGB is not in any doubt, Alphonse.'

Alphonse began a response, but I interrupted him. 'Alright. So we accept that his sexuality makes it an unlikely alliance. Why would a gay senior police officer ally himself with an organisation like the NUGB?'

'Because they have some hold over him,' said Alphonse.

'Blackmail,' I said under my breath.

'Exactement.'

'Well the timing certainly works. Dobson was hired by the NUGB in 1975. A man more suited to blackmail and extortion, you could not imagine.' I knew that as well as anyone.

Alphonse said nothing.

'And Paulo's beating has all of Dobson's trademark savagery.'

'So it would appear. Mademoiselle, I believe that Simon wishes to deal with Dobson and that this may be why he wishes to see you.'

We were both silent.

'But how does he imagine that I can help him with Dobson?'

'That, I do not know. He would not tell me. For that, he will speak only to you.'

This was all very well, but how could I possibly trust him? I would be revealing myself to a man who I had very good reason to believe was in the NUGB's pocket. One phone call would be all that it would take to bring the whole thing down and if that phone call was to Dobson… I shuddered. It wasn't worth thinking about. 'No. It's too risky. I don't think you understand just how risky it would be, Alphonse.'

'Perhaps I do not. But…' Alphonse's voice trailed away into silence.

Did I have a choice? That's what he was going to say.

'Perhaps Simon will be able to help you.'

I looked at Alphonse, but he did not meet my eyes. Instead he stared out, across the playing field, towards a group of children playing football.

'Help me?' I laughed, wryly. 'And how do you suppose that he will do that?'

Alphonse did not reply.

Chapter Thirty-Four

Tuesday, 16th August 1977

I left my car by the cafe in the Park. Parking there had a become a risk since Jimmy Dobson had followed me back from Pelham Road, but I felt safer knowing that Christos, who kept an eye on the safe house for Smith, would be watching.

It was a pleasant morning. Even beneath the shade of the trees, I could feel the sun's warmth on my skin. But the morning sunshine did little to thaw the cold that had taken hold of my insides. My guts felt like they were frozen solid.

I closed the car door and turned the key in the lock. This was suicide. After all that had happened. Everything I had done. I felt a wave of panic wash over me and, for a moment, I considered getting back in and driving away. Far away. From Broadbent, Dobson, Smith, even from Ted and the children. It was suicide.

I crossed the road that ran through the Park and found the footpath that led to the boating lake. Every step was an effort. It reminded me of my first day at school. It is funny the way that memory works. Something can have been out of your mind for half a lifetime. A feeling. A sound. A smell. And then boom, you're back there, just like it was yesterday. I'd felt so small. So alone. So afraid. Like I was walking to my doom.

He was sitting on a bench, beside the lake, throwing pieces of bread to the waiting ducks. He had already acquired quite a following.

I steeled myself and walked across to the bench. 'I see that you came prepared, Chief Superintendent,' I said, trying to sound like I was wasn't shrivelling inside.

'No, not really,' he replied, showing me a sandwich, part wrapped in silver foil. 'For some reason known only to herself, my wife insists on making me boiled egg and cress sandwiches. Can you think of anything worse? I think I'd rather eat charcoal.'

I sat down next to him.

For a moment, neither of us spoke.

'I don't suppose,' he said 'that you are willing to tell me who you're working for?'

It was a question that I should have anticipated. I swallowed hard. 'No, Chief Superintendent. I don't think so.'

Who did he think I was working for? I waited. And then I decided to fire one back. Except that it was not one, but several.

'I don't suppose that you are willing to tell me why, despite there being a perfectly good witness, Jimmy Dobson wasn't charged with Karl Dixon's murder.'

Broadbent didn't answer.

'Or why you haven't arrested Dobson for the attack in Luke Street, when no doubt you know full well that it was him.'

Broadbent remained silent.

'Or, come to think of it, why not a single instance of assault, burglary, arson or act of vandalism by Dobson's thugs at the NUGB over the last year or so, has resulted in charges being brought?'

It was an effort to stop myself.

'Touché Miss...' he turned and looked at me.

I kept my eyes fixed on a passing swan.

'Muir. It is Muir, isn't it?'

It wasn't a question. I could feel myself beginning to shake.

Get a bloody grip, 'Liz,' I said, trying for all the world to appear calm.

Broadbent was still looking at me. I could feel his eyes boring into the side of my head.

'Alphonse says that you are a good man, Chief Superintendent.'

'Does he indeed?'

'Yes, he does,' I said, turning towards him for the first time. It wasn't actually the truth. Alphonse had said that Broadbent wasn't a bad man which is not the same thing at all. 'But what I'm struggling to understand is why a good man, would be protecting a thug like Dobson.'

'Oh come on, Liz. I could say much the same about you.'

He was right. I was hardly a shining example of goodness and light. We had that much in common, at least. 'When I started doing what I do, Chief Superintendent, it was because I believed in it. I thought I was doing the right thing.'

'And now?'

'Now I have no choice. I do it because I have to.'

Broadbent smiled, but there was little joy in it. 'We all have our crosses to bear, Liz.'

I waited but Broadbent remained silent.

'And why do you bear yours Chief Superintendent?'

Broadbent sighed. 'For the same reason as you Liz, though I'm afraid my motives were never as noble.'

It was an interesting answer. 'Why did you ask to see me?' It was a straight question and this time it solicited a straight reply.

'Because I need your help.'

'My help?' I laughed. 'Why would I want to help you?'

Was he going to threaten me or offer some trade? I waited.

'I have been looking into your background Miss Muir. Or is it Mrs Stammers?'

I froze. 'If you are going to threaten me, Chief Superintendent, I'm afraid that you will have to join the queue.'

He smiled. 'I'm not going to threaten you, Liz. I'm going to make you an offer.'

'I'm listening.'

'Like I said, I have been looking into your background. It is a tangled web indeed. But my guess is that you are not at the

NUGB because you believe in their vision for a greater Britain.'

'I'm still listening.'

'I will not ask again for the identity of your employer but, presumably, you are working at the NUGB under cover.'

I said nothing.

'In which case, I must congratulate you, Liz. I know how difficult it must have been to get as close as you are to the NUGB leadership.'

If Broadbent was referring to my relationship with Peter, then he was far better informed than I had anticipated he would be. And that led me to wonder how.

'But then you have been at it for a very long time, I suppose…' His voice trailed off.

'You are remarkably well informed,' I said caustically.

'I am not without some resource, Liz. But no matter. If you are undercover, then I would imagine that you have an interest in the conference later this week.'

My head whipped around so that I was staring at him. 'How do you know about that?'

He smiled. 'I know about it, because I have been invited.'

I swallowed. Broadbent had been invited to the NUGB conference? I suppose it made sense.

'My guess is that you would value a set of ears at the conference table?'

'You are offering to tell me what is discussed at the conference?'

'Not exactly, no. Better than that. I am offering you these.' He put his hand into his inside pocket and pulled out a small, clear, plastic bag. Inside the bag was a tiny electronic device and some wires.

'What is it?'

'Ears, Liz.'

A bug. I laughed. 'If you attend the conference with that in your pocket, Chief Superintendent, you won't make it in through the door.'

'I do not intend to. There is only one person who could carry this into the conference without detection.'

'And that person is?'

'Jimmy Dobson.'

I tried to work out what he was suggesting. Broadbent saved me the trouble.

'Here's the deal. Jimmy Dobson has something that he should not have. A set of photographs in fact.'

So Alphonse had been right.

'I wish to have them.'

'These photographs. I take it that you feature in them?'

'Their subject is not a matter that need concern you.'

Which was fair enough.

'Suffice to say that, once they are safely back in my possession, Mr Dobson will find that I am not quite as willing to excuse his misdemeanours as I may have been in the past.'

I was silent for a moment. 'I'm sorry but how do you imagine that I could possibly help you with that,' I asked.

'Dobson keeps these photographs locked in a safe in his office, along with the negatives. The combination to the safe is in his notebook in his briefcase. The briefcase very rarely leaves his side. He is very likely to take the case with him, for example, to the conference later this week. Which makes it the perfect place in which to plant a device like this,' he said holding up the bag. 'I would like you to obtain the combination to Dobson's safe and to use it to recover the photographs. Having gained access to his case, you might want to plant this inside, I would suggest, beneath the lining. If, as I anticipate, Dobson takes the case into the conference then you will be able to hear what is said from a distance of up to three or four hundred yards.'

It was a possibility. 'But Dobson will have the whole place scanned for bugs,' I said doubtfully.

'Undoubtedly he will check both the venue and everyone who enters it. But will that extend to scanning his own brief case? Why would he do that when he knows that he's not carrying anything?'

I thought about it. 'I have two questions, Chief Superintendent. The first is how you imagine that I will be able to gain access to his briefcase. And the second is how you know all of this.'

Broadbent bowed his head. Then he looked up, put his hand into his pocket and removed a handheld radio. 'Jackie, would you join us please.'

A few seconds later, there were footsteps behind us.

'Liz Muir, meet D.I. Jackie James.'

I turned and looked straight into the rising sun. For a moment, I couldn't make out the woman's face. She stepped sideways and her face came into focus. It was fortunate that I was sitting down. Otherwise, I think I would have fallen over. 'Grace?'

'Good morning M'am.'

Chapter Thirty-Five

Wednesday 17th August 1977

D.I. James unlocked the door and stepped into the vacant room next to Dobson's office, being careful to close the door behind her as silently as she could. The room, a disused office, had a row of steel shelving units along one wall and an old office desk in the corner, opposite the door. The shelves were stacked with rows of box files. She had no idea what they contained. Nor did she care.

She checked her watch. It was 9.58am. She had two minutes to ready herself. This was not going to be a pleasant experience but she'd done something like it once before. It had worked then and it could work now. She took a deep breath to calm her nerves, re-arranged her skirt, straightened her hair and walked across to the the nearest shelving unit and checked her watch again. She watched the second hand as it crept toward ten o'clock. Then she reached up to the top shelf and pulled a row of box files down on top of herself. As the first file hit her on the shoulder she screamed, dramatically. The files spilled their contents across the floor.

James positioned herself carefully with her back to the door and bent down, on the pretext of trying to gather the files, pulling her short skirt up so that the tops of her legs and knickers were exposed. She heard the door of the office next door open and close, rapidly in succession. In the few seconds before the door into the room which she had arranged herself so invitingly, was flung violently open, she listened carefully. She could not tell whether he had locked his office door on exit. She prayed to God that he hadn't.

I had timed my lift journey almost to perfection. I stepped out into the foyer at thirty seconds before ten o'clock. I peered carefully through the glass panel into the third floor corridor to see Jimmy Dobson emerge from his office. He went straight into the adjacent room without turning to lock his office door.

I pulled open the door to the corridor and ran, as silently as I could to Dobson's office, being careful not to drop the small handbag that I was carrying. I opened the door and stepped inside. His brief case was on his desk, with the lid up. I went straight to the desk, put my handbag down and began rifling through the contents of the briefcase. My hands were shaking so violently that it was a challenge to turn the papers. I consoled myself with the thought that however stressful my part was in the liberation of Broadbent's photographs was going to be, it was as nothing compared to the trial that Grace - I couldn't think of her as D.I.James - would be experiencing in the room next door.

I found the note book and flipped through its contents. Surprisingly, most of the entries were in German. I had done a little a German at school but not enough to make sense of what was written. Towards the back, I found a list of names, addresses and telephone numbers. Did I have the time to copy them all? I looked at my watch. It was approaching three minutes past ten. I ignored the list and turned the page and there it was. "10R-25L-17R-32L". I pulled out a pen from my pocket and wrote the combination on the inside of my hand.

Now for the listening device.

I opened my handbag and removed the bag containing the bug, a small scalpel and a roll of double sided tape. I used the scalpel to open a small, two to three inch slit in the lining of the case's lid. I removed the bug and examined it. It was a little bulky, due to the battery inside, but I was sure that I'd made the hole large enough. I found the tiny dip switch and turned it on. Then I ran a strip of tape around the device and pushed it, along with its wire antenna, beneath the lining. I held the tip of the antenna and tipped the case up, so that the bug would drop into one corner of the lid. Then I manipulated the device, as tightly into the corner as was possible without emptying the case's contents entirely. I hoped that the tape would hold it in place. Finally, I taped the end of the antenna to the underside of the lid, beneath the lining, and then sealed the hole I had made in the lining with another piece of tape. I looked at my watch. Five minutes past. *Shit.*

I put the tape and scalpel back in my bag and walked across to the safe. It was on the floor in one corner. I knelt down and looked at the combination I'd written on my hand. I had precisely four minutes.

'What do you think you're doing?'

'Oh, I'm sorry, I...' stammered D.I. James, in the voice she normally reserved for Justin Hughes.

'How did you get in here? These are confidential files.'

James attempted to gather a pile of papers together. As she did so, she made a point of re-arranging herself on the floor for maximum affect. It was a bit obvious, but if there was one thing that was guaranteed to hold a man's attention it was the inside of a girl's thigh. Especially from behind.

She heard the door close.

'I asked you a question. How did you get in here.'

'I, er... I borrowed the keys from Mr Hughes.'

'Hughes gave you the keys?'

D.I. James sat up on her haunches and swivelled so that she was kneeling in front of him suggestively.

'Well, kind of. He asked me to leave some papers on Mr Taggart's desk.'

'Then what are you doing in here?'

'I, er...'

'Give those to me,' Dobson said, holding out his hand.

James handed him the papers.

Dobson looked at them. 'Get up.'

'I wasn't doing anything. I was just curious that's all.'

Dobson grabbed the top of her arm. 'I said get up,' he hissed, hauling her to her feet. 'I'll have Hughes's balls for this and as for you…'

James did her best to feign terror. It wasn't difficult. 'I'm sorry, Mr Dobson. It won't happen again.'

'No, it won't. I told Hughes that you were here on a trial basis. That trial has now come to an end.'

'Please, Mr Dobson, I'm sorry.'

'Hughes only hired you because of your tits anyway. He'll have to find someone else to dribble over.'

James looked at him and blinked. Then she ran her hand up the inside of his leg and onto the bulge between his legs. 'Please Mr Dobson. I wasn't doing anything. I didn't even get to read anything. I need this job. I've got my rent to pay.'

She squeezed him firmly.

He put a hand on her shoulder and pushed her down onto her knees.

Dear God, she thought, *I hope he had a bath this morning.*

I dialled the numbers into the lock but when I tried the handle, it wouldn't budge.

Shit. Shit. Shit.

My hands had been shaking so much that I must have mis-dialled the combination. I tried again.

I stopped. I was sure that I'd heard a low thud from the room next door.

I pictured Grace with Dobson. Had he hit her?

Ten minutes. He could kill her in that time.

I pulled the safe handle. The door swung open.

Inside was a pile of papers and several loose leaf cardboard box files. I lifted them out and sat back on my haunches. Lying at the bottom of the safe, where it had been hidden by the papers, was a grey/black revolver. I put the papers down, picked up the gun and held it out in front of me. For a moment I considered walking into the room next door and putting a bullet between Dobson's eyes. It was an appealing fantasy. The bastard more than deserved it. But it was a fantasy. I'd never handled a gun before, let alone fired one. I was, as I'd once said to Smith, a school teacher - not James fucking Bond.

I placed the gun back where I'd found it and rifled through the papers until I found an envelope marked "Broadbent". I opened the envelope and pulled out the contents. There were half a dozen photographs and a set of negatives. What struck more than anything else was what a handsome young man Paulo Diomedi had been. I wondered whether he still was.

I heard another thud from the next room.

I put the photographs and the negatives back in the envelope, stuffed the envelope in my bag and shut the safe door. Then I turned the combination wheel several times and got to my feet.

D.I. James sat back on her haunches.

'Get up, whore,' Dobson said flatly. He reached down and did up his zip.

She gagged. She couldn't help herself.

He grabbed her by the hair and hauled her to her feet. 'I said get up.'

'What are you doing?' she yelled.

Dobson grinned as he pulled her head backwards by the hair, so that she was looking straight up into his face. 'Not enough, bitch. Not if you want to save your job.'

'No, please.'

Dobson grinned and then spat in her face.

'You bastard.'

'That's better. You like it rough, huh?'

'Fuck off.'

Dobson grabbed hold of her shoulder with his free hand and attempted to spin her around, but unbeknown to Dobson, James had been trained in self defence and, as she came around, she bought her elbow back hard into the top of his chest.

The blow knocked the wind out of him and he staggered backwards, over turning a chair.

Within seconds he had recovered.

She backed away.

'So, you know how to handle yourself.'

He was still grinning. 'I'm beginning to like you.'

'The feeling isn't mutual.'

He took a step towards her.

James reached for a box file and threw it at him. He batted it away, effortlessly.

'Congratulations. I've decided to retain your services, after all.'

D.I. James knew that she was in trouble. She might have been trained but he was almost twice the size of her and, right now, he was blocking the way to the door. She braced herself for the inevitable onslaught.

I opened the door and risked a look out in the corridor. It was empty. I stepped out and let the door close silently behind me. I could hear raised voices from the room next door and then I heard a scream that sent shivers running down my spine. Grace was in trouble and I needed to act. For a moment I stood paralysed. If I burst into the room Dobson would know that it was more than a coincidence. But I couldn't just leave her there. I tore down the corridor, crashed through the doors and ran headlong into Justin Hughes. 'Justin. Thank God. It's Grace. I think Dobson's got her.'

'What?'

'In the room next to his. I heard screams.'

Justin Hughes paled. He hauled open the door and stepped into the corridor.

We both heard another scream and a crash.

'Jesus Christ,' Hughes said, turning to me. 'Go downstairs, Liz.'

'What?'

'Go. I don't want you hurt. Go. Now.'

I looked at him and ran for the stair well. I was no more than one flight down when the fire alarm sounded. Hughes might be a coward, but at least he was a clever one.

Inside the room, next to Dobson's, D.I. James was sprawled face down across a dusty wooden desk with an arm held behind her back. She could not move. Jimmy Dobson had wedged himself between her legs and was trying to undo his trouser belt with his free hand.

Suddenly a siren sounded. It was deafeningly loud.

The fire alarm, thought James. *Thank you Lord.*

Behind her, Dobson cursed and for a moment hesitated. He could still take her. She was powerless to resist him. He could smell her.

Outside the door, Hughes was also hesitating. He was afraid of Dobson. More afraid of him than he was of anyone. The man was a psychopath. But if Grace was in the room with him, he couldn't just abandon her. He knew what Dobson was capable of. He took a breath and banged his fist on the door. 'Fire alarm,' he yelled at the top of voice.

He put his ear to the door but could hear nothing above the siren.

He banged his fist on the door again. 'I said fire alarm. We've got to get out.'

Again nothing. His hand was hovering on the handle when suddenly the door burst open and Dobson emerged, doing up his trouser belt.

Hughes took several steps backwards but not before Dobson had grabbed him around the neck. 'One word of this to anyone, Hughes, and you're a dead man. Do you understand.'

Hughes simply gawped, unable to speak.

Dobson shook him by the throat until his eyes were bulging. 'One word. Do you understand?'

He tried to nod, choking with the effort.

Dobson released him and disappeared into his office.

Hughes stood retching.

Within moments, Dobson had re-emerged carrying his brief case. He turned and locked his office door before walking away briskly towards the stair well.

Hughes stepped forward and opened the door to the spare room. 'Grace?'

She was standing in the corner of the room with her arms around herself, sobbing.

'Oh, my God. What has he done?'

He rushed across to her and took her in his arms. 'What has he done to you?' He held at arms length and looked into her eyes. 'Did he…'

She shook her head. 'But he would have done, Mr Hughes. Had the fire alarm not sounded and you not come. Oh, Mr Hughes,' she said and she burst into tears.

Over Justin Hughes's shoulder she saw the door slowly open. A face appeared in the doorway. The face stared at her and mouthed "are you OK?".

D.I. James nodded slowly. 'I'm fine,' she mouthed over Hughes's shoulder.

'Dear God, the man's an animal,' said Justin Hughes.

Amen to that, thought D.I. James.

Chapter Thirty-Six

Thursday 18th August 1977

'I want the main room, the side rooms, the room upstairs, the hallways and the lift all swept again, thoroughly. Is that clear?'

The security specialist nodded. 'Of course.'

Dobson glanced upwards. 'Including that monstrosity.'

The man followed his eyes. 'The chandelier?'

'If you find anything, I want to know about it.'

'No problem.'

Dobson ran his eyes around the room. They lingered on the portrait above the fireplace. It was of a balding, elderly man in a dark suit. He was wearing a row of medals. Dobson walked across to the portrait.

'It's a Victoria Cross,' said the security specialist.

Dobson said nothing.

'First World War. Apparently, he took out half a dozen German machine gun posts at the Somme, single handedly.'

'How do you know this?' Dobson said, staring at the portrait.

'One of the cleaners.'

'The cleaners? Which one?'

'She was in here when we arrived, dusting the picture, actually.'

Dobson was silent for a moment. 'Take it down. Check behind it and check the frame.'

'But it's been up there for donkey's years. It will be a devil of a job to get it down.'

Dobson looked at the man. 'I said, take it down. When you've checked it, put it back up. And leave it unsecured. I will check it again myself.'

'Yes, Mr Dobson,' the man said with a sigh.

'When you've done in here, I want the room secured and one of your team left on the door until my men get here. Nobody is to enter from that point onwards. Under any circumstances.'

The security specialist nodded.

'And find the cleaner. I want to speak to her.'

'Yes, Sir.'

I had been walking for fifteen minutes and I was sweating like a pig. Even under the shade of the trees, out of the glare of the late summer sun, it was unusually hot. With little by way of any breeze, the canopy above seemed to be trapping the humidity so that my clothes were sticking to me uncomfortably.

The path through the woods wound its way steadily toward Ashridge House. Apart form the heat, the going was reasonably easy, while I stayed on the pathway. But I'd have to leave it eventually. Dobson would no doubt have arranged for the woods surrounding the conference venue to be searched and I needed to get close enough to receive the signal from the radio device I'd planted in his briefcase. Providing, of course, that he had taken the brief case into the venue with him. If he hadn't... I didn't even want to think about it.

As I topped a ridge, the house came into view in the distance. It was a sprawling building in grey stone in the gothic revival style. The house had been built between 1808 and 1825. I'd looked it up. It's builder, the Duke of Bridgewater had been known as the 'Canal Duke', because of his family's enthusiasm for canal building. But after the first World War, when it was used as a convalescent home, the house had been bought by the Broughton family who had used it as a training centre for the Conservative Party and latterly, through their links to the Party, by the Banks company.

The closer I got to the house, the more wary I became. Dobson's security people would be watching the woods around the house for any sign of incursion and I could not afford to be spotted.

I stopped, walked to the side of the pathway and removed my backpack. I sat down on a log, undid the strings holding the bag closed and pulled out the scanner which Broadbent had provided. I extended the antenna, plugged in an earphone, inserted the single ear piece into my ear and switched the radio on. I could hear nothing. I backed off the squelch, as I'd been shown and a very faint signal could be heard, intermittently. Nothing more than dull voices in the background, broken by loud hissing as the signal faded in and out.

Shit, I need to get closer.

I re-packed the bag, got to my feet and continued on the pathway as it meandered downwards towards the house. The closer I got, the more fearful I became and, when a break in the undergrowth appeared to my left, I decided that it was time to leave the path.

The going was tougher away from the path and by the time I had found a small clearing, I was scratched to hell, even through my jeans. But at least I was unlikely to be spotted from the house. If I stood up I could just about see the building over the top of the scrub. But more importantly while seated, I'd be completely invisible from both the house and the path through the woods.

I found a place to sit and tried the radio again. This time the signal was much clearer, although I could hear nothing but mumbled voices. My guess was that the briefcase had been left in a corner somewhere, or possibly in a separate room while the meeting was being set up. I prayed that it wasn't left there for the meeting itself or the whole exercise would have been for nought.

The black Jaguar XJ6 pulled up at the main gates. After a few moments the gates swung inwards and the Jaguar advanced. It stopped beside the gatehouse. The uniformed gateman emerged, straightening his peaked cap and approached the car. He waited patiently as the driver's tinted window was lowered. The driver handed him a small card. The gateman examined it. 'Very good. Follow the drive around to your right and pull up inside the marquee. When your passenger has alighted, you may park in the car park to the rear of the main building. You will be given further instruction there.'

He handed the card back to the driver who took it, without reply. The tinted window hummed back into position and the Jaguar pulled away.

The gateman wondered about the Jaguar's passenger, or passengers. He couldn't tell. He didn't much like letting people through the gate without knowing who they were. But the afternoon's meeting in the mansion was different. There'd been security people crawling all over the place for most of the morning. Poking their noses where they didn't belong. They had even checked the telephone in the gatehouse. In the ten years he'd staffed the gate, he'd never experienced the like of it.

He watched as the Jaguar's tail lights came on in the distance. Then he shook his head, returned to the gatehouse and picked up the phone. 'Car eleven is on the drive,' he said into the mouthpiece.

He listened to the response. 'Don't ask me. Couldn't see a bloody thing. Tinted windows.'

He listened again. 'I know. All very cloak and daggers, if you ask me. Better go. There's another car at the gate.'

The gateman put down the phone and pressed the gate release. He watched the gate swing open and the Daimler advanced towards him.

He stepped out of the gatehouse and approached the car. The rear passenger window was already down.

'Evening M'am.'

'Good afternoon Morris,' said a voice from inside. 'Has Mr Owen arrived yet? I want to have a private word with him before the conference begins in earnest.'

'I'm not sure M'am. But there has only been one car and I don't think it was his.'

'Well, call me in my room when he arrives, would you?'

Morris thought for a moment. 'Sorry M'am, but I've been told not to ask for any names.'

'What?'

'No names M'am. Mr Dobson's security people were adamant. I'm not altogether happy about it. If you don't mind me saying so M'am.'

There was silence from inside in the car.

'M'am?'

'Morris, are you ever going to stop calling me M'am? It makes me sound like the Queen Mother.'

'Sorry, Mrs Banks.'

'Apology accepted. Now you won't forget to call me when Mr Owen arrives, will you.'

'But, M'am…'

The Daimler pulled away.

From my concealment in the woods north of Ashridge House I was able to watch the arrival of each of the cars in turn. I had bought a small pair of binoculars with me, in the hope of being able to identify people as they disembarked. But Dobson had evidently thought of everything. Once they had been checked at the gate, each car drove along the drive towards the house but then swung to the right in a wide semi circle and disappeared into a marquee erected outside the building's main entrance. The cars then re-appeared at the opposite end of the marquee, presumably minus their passengers. They then vanished from view around the back of the building. I counted twenty five cars in all.

I had still been able to learn little through my earphone. The bug in Dobson's brief case seemed to be working well enough. The problem was that, wherever it had been left, had thus far been out of range of any discussion. I looked at my watch. It was 1.50pm. I reached into my bag and removed the cassette recorder and connected it to the record output on the scanner. *This has to work. It has to.*

I had been listening intently for about thirty minutes when I heard voices. Not through the ear piece, but in the woods. They were getting louder.

My instinct was to pack up my rucksack and run but, had I done so, anyone on the footpath would certainly have heard my movements through the undergrowth. While I had come as far from the footpath as I could, it was still possible that someone might catch a reflection or a flash of colour from my clothing and so I lay flat on the ground.

I don't know what made it so obvious that they were security guards, rather than walkers out for a stretch in the woods. But somehow I knew that they were. I held my breath and, eventually, they passed by. Once their voices had receded, I got up, dusted myself off, found my seating position and resumed listening.

Just before half past two I heard approaching foot steps through the ear piece, the locks on the brief case being released and the sound of papers being shuffled. I waited. A few minutes later I heard Peter's voice. As clearly as though he were standing next to me. Followed by another voice that I recognised only too well.

Chapter Thirty-Seven

Jimmy Dobson walked into the conference room. The tables and seating were arranged in a wide oval. Each seating position had a note pad, pen and a glass. Dobson walked to the front of the room and put down his briefcase. He released the lock. As he raised the lid of the case, the main doors opened and another man stepped into the room.

'Jimmy,' said Peter Owen. 'I understand that you wanted to see me?'

'Yes.'

'Will it take long? The delegates are assembling and I do not want to delay them.'

'It will not take long.'

'Well?'

'The incident on Wednesday.'

'The false alarm?'

'Yes. Hughes said that the system had malfunctioned but I do not believe that was the case.'

'We've discussed this Jimmy,' Owen said irritably. 'This is not the time or the place to discuss it again.'

'This morning, before I left the office to come here, I checked the contents of my safe.'

Owen sighed. 'The safe in your office?'

Dobson ignored the question. 'The photographs of Chief Superintendent Broadbent have been taken.'

'Are you sure?'

'I am certain. I believe that they were taken on Wednesday, during the incident.'

'How do you know that?'

'I last checked the safe on Tuesday, just before I left the office. The photographs were still there.'

'Was anything else missing?'

'No.'

Owen was silent.

'I was out of my office for no more than ten minutes. In that time I believe that somebody went in and opened the safe.'

'Have you any idea who?'

'I believe that whoever it was, was in league with the typist.'

'With Jones? You can't be serious. She hasn't got the intelligence to be involved in something like that.'

'Nevertheless, I believe that she deliberately lured me out of my office so that her accomplice could enter my room and take the photographs.'

'I find that very hard to believe. And do you have any candidates for this accomplice?'

'Yes, I have two. Hughes is the…'

'Oh come on. Justin? A safe cracker?' Owen laughed. 'What motive could he possibly have for taking the photographs?'

Dobson did not reply.

'And who is your second candidate?' Owen said still grinning.

'Liz Muir.'

Owen's smile died and he looked at Dobson coldly. 'No, I will not believe that of Liz. You have had an issue with Liz since the day we recruited her, but I cannot accept that she would be involved in anything like this. I have known her for years. She has always shown me the utmost loyalty.'

'Do you think so? I have discovered some interesting facts about…'

'Jimmy, stop,' Owen interrupted.

'Like the fact that she taught Karl Dixon.'

'Karl Dixon? She's never said anything about that to me.'

'I wonder why. Did she say anything about going to see the old man who told the police that he saw us?'

'The witness? Why would she want to go and see him?'

'Because she is conspiring with Broadbent to have the case re-opened. You will recall that Broadbent dropped the case against me only after he was reminded about the existence of the photographs.'

'Enough,' Owen interrupted. 'This is nothing but paranoia.'

'Do you know that she regularly meets a man at her flat in Finsbury Park?'

'A man? What man?'

'I don't know, yet. But I will find out. A lover perhaps? Did she tell you about him?'

A shadow of doubt passed across Owen's face. 'I'm sorry, I don't have time for this,' he said, getting to his feet.

'Need I remind you, Peter, that Broadbent is one of our guests today. We should remove him, now.'

Owen stopped and turned. 'No. The delegates are gathering outside. I won't have the meeting disrupted by this fishing exercise of yours.'

'Nevertheless, the photographs are missing.'

Owen hesitated.

'Broadbent is the only person with an interest in these photographs, is he not? If he has them, then we may no longer be able to guarantee his loyalty.'

Owen reflected on his head of security's words. 'Very well. Escort him upstairs and have a couple of your people hold him there. But do it with some subtlety would you? I do not want any kind of scene. And I want you back down here for the main session. Is that understood?'

'It will be my pleasure.'

'And call the office. Tell Justin that I want to see him and Grace in my office when we get back. Tell him that I don't care how late it is. Neither of them is to leave until I say so.'

'And Liz Muir?'

'I will talk to Liz,' Owen snapped.

'As you wish.'

I sat listening to the exchange with a growing sense of alarm. For the first time, Peter was doubting me. I could hear it in his voice. And who could blame him? Dobson had been correct. So far, it had not occurred to him that whoever had opened his safe had obtained the combination from the note book in his brief case. But it was surely only a matter of time. If Dobson found the bug, I would have no other means of discovering the Union's plans. Especially with Broadbent held in the room on the second floor.

My thoughts turned to Broadbent. What were they going to do with him? Peter would surely not allow Dobson to hurt him and even Dobson could hardly blame Broadbent for wanting to liberate the photographs. Broadbent's motives were troubling me, however. So far as I could tell, he had been working for Peter and the Union prior to the photographs being taken. Why? Why would a gay police officer ever have involved himself with the NUGB in the first place? At our meeting by the lake in Finsbury park, he'd said that his motives had not been as noble as mine. So what were they? Was he simply an opportunist? Did Peter and the NUGB really wield sufficient influence within the force to attract a man like Broadbent? Had Broadbent been so driven by ambition that he was willing to ally himself with an organisation that was famously homophobic?

I strained to make sense of the voices coming from my earpiece. Dobson had taken his briefcase with him but whatever was happening, the sounds were too muffled to tell.

And Grace/D.I.Jackson was now in danger. During the brief conversation I'd managed to have with her since the events of Wednesday she'd said little about what Dobson had done, or tried to do to her while they'd been in the room next door to his office. But it didn't take much imagination to guess. And Hughes had also been tight lipped when I'd asked him about what had happened. He'd looked completely terrified and mumbled something under his breath about Dobson being a maniac. That he was afraid of Dobson was all too evident and I could hardly blame him for that.

Dobson left the conference room and emerged into a wide lobby where a throng of delegates were standing about in small groups, drinking coffee and talking in hushed tones. He scanned the lobby and quickly identified his quarry. The policeman appeared to be in deep conversation with a young man who Dobson did not immediately recognise.

Dobson walked across to the lobby entrance where two suited guards were stood, with their arms folded across their chests, watching the proceedings dispassionately. 'You,' he said to the first of the guards.

'Sir?'

'In a moment, I'm going to ask one of the guests to join us in the hallway outside. He is to be escorted upstairs.'

'Yes, Sir.'

'If he declines to come with us, or makes any attempt to leave, you are to take him by force, but I do not wish there to be any disturbance, so far as the other guests are concerned. Is that clear?'

'Yes, Sir.'

'You,' Dobson said, turning to the second guard, 'Come with me.'

The guard nodded and unfolded his arms.

Dobson turned and strolled, purposefully toward Broadbent, the second guard following closely behind.

'Excuse me,' Dobson said when they had reached the two men. 'I need to speak to Chief Superintendent Broadbent in private. It is a matter of some urgency. Chief Superintendent,' he said turning to the policeman, 'would you come with me please.'

Broadbent made his excuses politely enough and followed Dobson out into the hall. 'What's this about, Dobson?' He said the name, like it tasted bad in his mouth.

'Mr Owen, would like to see you. Upstairs,' Dobson said without emotion.

'But I just saw Peter go into the conference room,' Broadbent said, glancing at the two guards, one after the other.

'That's right. You did. He will be joining us at his convenience.'

The policeman took a step backwards.

Dobson turned to the two guards. 'Escort the Chief Superintendent upstairs.'

The two guards stepped forwards.

'What is this?' said Broadbent, looking back towards the lobby in alarm.

'If you will, Sir,' one of the guards said, taking hold of his arm.

The two guards made short work of bundling him out of the hallway and up the building's main stair case.

Dobson followed them. He couldn't hide a sly smile.

Dobson closed the door, walked across the room and placed the briefcase on the table in front of Broadbent who was stood, sweating, between the two guards. He turned, pulled out a chair, and placed it behind the policeman. 'Sit down.'

'I'd rather stand.'

Dobson returned to the table, snapped open the two silver catches, opened the lid and reached into the briefcase.

Broadbent watched his movements with interest.

'I said, sit down,' Dobson repeated.

Broadbent recognised the object that Dobson had removed from the case. It was a Heckler & Koch P9S, semi-automatic pistol. The gun carried by several police forces in West Germany, a fact he had learned, two years earlier, from a German colleague who had visited the Met from the force in Düsseldorf. Broadbent glanced towards the door.

'That would be unwise,' Dobson said, reaching once again into his briefcase and removing a second, smaller object, which Broadbent also recognised.

'I'm going to ask you once more. Sit down Chief Superintendent.'

Broadbent watched as Dobson fitted the silencer to the barrel of the P9S. He sat down, slowly.

'You,' Dobson said to one of the guards. 'Go and find me some tape.'

'Tape? Where I am going to find tape?' said the guard.

'I don't care, you fuckwit,' Dobson barked. 'Just find it.'

The guard nodded and left the room.

'I hope you've got a firearms certificate for that,' Broadbent said, confidently.

Dobson turned towards him, weighing the gun in his hand.

'Look, cut the crap Dobson. What's this all about?'

'I think you know.'

Broadbent said nothing.

'You are going to tell me who took the photographs from my safe.'

Broadbent smiled. 'Getting careless, are we?'

'You misunderstand. You *are* going to tell me. The only issue here is how much blood you're going to lose in the process.'

Broadbent gazed at him, coldly. 'I took them,' he said after a few moments. 'I think I had the right, don't you?'

'You took them,' Dobson said flatly. 'And how did you manage that?'

Broadbent thought about it for a moment. 'Perhaps Excalibur House is not as secure as you seem to think it is.'

Dobson said nothing.

'Perhaps Peter Owen needs to think about replacing his head of security.'

Dobson positioned himself directly in front of the policeman. 'Who took the photographs from my safe?'

Broadbent looked up at Dobson. 'You don't scare me, you piece of shit. I'm a senior London police officer. I've been threatened by people who would have you shitting your pants.'

Broadbent had been expecting the blow before it landed, but that didn't make it hurt any less. Dobson struck him across the side of the face with the butt of the pistol. The blow was so hard that it almost knocked him off the chair. The remaining guard stepped forward and hauled him upright.

Broadbent opened an eye and braced himself but there was no second blow. Instead, the second guard reappeared.

'Tape him to the chair. Tape his hands, feet and mouth. And don't forget to leave his nostrils free. I'd quite like it if he was alive when I come back. Because I will be back,' he said, grabbing Broadbent's hair and hauling his head up so that he could stare into the policeman's face. 'Make no mistake about that.'

I had winced at the sound of the blow. It was an awful sound, like a hammer hitting wet clay. Whatever Broadbent's motives had been for involving himself with the NUGB, he didn't deserve the punishment that Dobson had just meted out. Peter surely wouldn't countenance it. Dobson was an animal. The vicious thug who had killed Karl Dixon and who had beaten Rosemary Sellers half to death. Peter would surely now see the man for what he was.

I listened through the ear piece, as Dobson collected his brief case and left the room. I heard a door close and the muffled sound of his foot steps. A few minutes later there were hollow voices and the the sound of the briefcase being opened again. And then one voice became suddenly clear. It was Peter's.

'And so Ladies and Gentleman, we come to the events of the next few days. Only those of you who need to know have been given the full details. Though I do not doubt the loyalty of everyone here, we cannot be too careful. I would ask you all to understand this, as we go through the presentation that follows. There will be time for questions afterwards. Jimmy, before you sit down, would you please dim the lights. John, would you do the honours please.'

'Aye.' It was John Taggart's voice.

There was a pause, I imagined for a projector to be switched on or something similar.

'At precisely 9 am on Monday morning there will be an explosion in Central London,' Peter began. 'We will be using Semtex of the type used by the Provisional I.R.A. Indeed, it was stolen from a shipment destined for the Republic.'

There was a pause.

'The target has been carefully selected to achieve our mission objective, which as you know is to disrupt national government to the point of collapse.'

There was another pause.

'Those of you who might otherwise have been at the target venue have been warned. Take the day off or find some reason not to be there. It shouldn't be too difficult.'

There was a ripple of laughter.

'Disruption will be extensive.'

Another pause.

'Approximately twenty minutes after the explosion, sources in Northern Ireland, claiming to represent the I.R.A. will admit responsibility. One hour after that admission has been made, the Anti-Terrorist branch at New Scotland Yard will release a statement acknowledging the authenticity of the claim. So far as the world is concerned, this will be the latest atrocity by the I.R.A.'

Another ripple of voices.

'Shortly after the explosion, the Army will, quite naturally, deploy forces to protect Government buildings. They will evacuate and then seal off the following area marked red on the map…'

A further pause.

'At one o'clock, we will release a statement condemning the I.R.A., re-iterating our intent to resist them at all costs and to use every means at our disposal to defeat them. We will simultaneously announce the formation of an interim Government of National Security along with a provisional cabinet. Those of you who will be taking provisional cabinet positions, have already been informed.'

A murmur ran around the room.

'We must act swiftly, with certainty and, if necessary by force both in London and elsewhere. Regional plans have already been approved and those in command will receive further briefing later today. We must be ready. We can expect to encounter significant resistance. The new Government will act swiftly and with all necessary means to uphold order. But along with regional command, we will be relying on you all to counter any dissent on the ground in the first instance.'

Another pause.

'We must expect and be prepared for casualties but if we act swiftly and with purpose, I am confident that they can be kept to a minimum. Remember, Ladies and Gentlemen, we act for the future of our great country and its proud people…'

But I had ceased to listen. The implications of the words I'd just heard were reverberating around my head.

Chapter Thirty-Eight

Broadbent sat, immobilised by the tape around his ankles and wrists, staring at the guard. He could feel the side of his face beginning to swell from Dobson's blow and a dull ache which had spread from his cheek bone down into his jaw and upper neck.

The bastard had enjoyed hitting him. Broadbent had seen it in his eyes. But if Dobson had thought that he was beaten, he was going to be disappointed. Broadbent was going to make sure that Dobson paid for that blow, as he would pay for what he had done to Paulo Diomedi and the others. And Liz Muir was the ace in his pocket, whether she knew it or not.

He tried to speak, but the tape across his mouth prevented it.

'Don't look at me mate,' said the guard. 'I'm just the hired help.'

He couldn't tell how long he'd been tied to the chair. He'd drifted in and out of consciousness after Dobson's departure. He looked toward the table where the briefcase had been and then across to the window. She would have heard and recorded the assault, along with Dobson's words. If he returned with his briefcase, she would hear whatever else they had in store for him. Broadbent gritted his teeth beneath the tape. *Bring it on, you bastard. Bring it on.*

He was still gritting them when the door opened and Dobson re-entered, followed by Peter Owen. 'Jesus, I told you to hold him here, not torture him.'

Owen looked shocked.

'It was necessary. We must know who took the photographs.' Dobson put his briefcase down on the table in front of them.

Broadbent tried not to stare at the case.

Owen sighed. 'Indeed we must. You,' he said addressing the nearest guard, 'remove the tape from his mouth.'

Broadbent flinched as the guard reached for the tape. The jolt, as he tore it from his face, made Broadbent's head spin. He allowed his chin to sag onto his chest.

'All of you, outside.'

Dobson looked at Owen but did not move.

'I said, outside. Now.'

The guards were already at the door. Dobson hesitated and then followed. When the three men had closed the door, Owen sat on the table in front of Broadbent. 'I cannot blame you for wishing to have the photographs in your possession, Simon. But you will understand that, if there are traitors in our midst, we must know who they are. We cannot and will not allow them to disrupt our plans, or worse, to betray us.'

Broadbent looked up. 'There was no need for the photographs, Peter. No need.'

Owen smiled, weakly. 'They were not my idea.'

Had there been a hint of regret in his voice?

'But you were happy enough to use them.'

Owen sighed. 'Yes,' he said, 'I was. I have done many things that do not sit easily with me. That I would not have chosen to do. But, what I have done, I have done out of necessity.'

Broadbent, snorted in derision.

'This is a battle for the future of our country,' Owen continued. 'Not some tale of chivalry from Arthurian legend. The forces arrayed against us are considerable and engaging them can be been a nasty business. I am sorry if we upset your sensitivities, Simon, but when Jimmy told me that certain pictures had come into his possession, pictures that would guarantee the future loyalty of our first tame Chief

Superintendent, forgive me, but my first thought was not to put him in chains and cast him into the nearest dungeon.'

'Was it also Dobson's idea to beat the young man I was with so badly that, to do this day, he can remember little of the assault.'

Owen said nothing.

'Paulo Diomedi. Did you even know his name? A young man who, aged fourteen, was thrown onto the streets by his mother because he'd finally found the courage to tell her that his father had been abusing him since shortly after his ninth birthday.'

'Oh, please,' Owen said dismissively. 'Spare me the sob story.'

'Was Paulo part of this force arrayed against you? Was Dobson fighting the good fight, when he kicked him so hard in the head that he fractured his skull?'

'Jimmy went too far,' Owen snapped. 'It was unfortunate.'

'Unfortunate? Dobson is an animal and you know it. You soil your cause by employing him.'

'My cause?' Owen said, angrily. 'Have you had a change of heart then Chief Superintendent?'

Broadbent stared back at him defiantly.

'Enough. That the photographs are missing is beyond doubt and, since you are the only person who would have any interest in them, it is also beyond doubt that you arranged for them to be taken. Taking them yourself could, perhaps, have been forgiven. But planting someone inside the NUGB was a serious mistake and one that we are not about to overlook.'

Broadbent said nothing.

'It will not take us long to find them, Simon. Jimmy has already drawn up a shortlist. You could save yourself, to say nothing of the people whose names appear on that list, a great deal of trouble by telling us.'

For a few moments the two men stared at each other in silence.

'Against my better judgement, I will offer you a deal,' Owen said. 'You will give me their name and I will give you my word that they will come to no harm. We will simply hold them until Monday's events have played out. They will then be released.'

'Your word,' Broadbent snorted, 'I used to think that you were an honourable man Peter. It was I who approached you, offering my support. Remember?'

Anger flashed in Owen's eyes. 'Oh, I remember, alright. I remember the power hungry junior officer, with the dirty little secret, who fancied his chances at the big time. I remember the strings I pulled to nurture your ascent through the ranks…' Owen hesitated and, with some effort, regained his composure. 'I don't have time for this,' he said calmly. 'If I walk out of this room without the names of whoever took the pictures from Jimmy's safe, and anyone else who aided them, it will be Jimmy who returns and Jimmy will not leave again until you have revealed them. We mean to discover their identity, Simon, and you *are* going to tell us.'

Broadbent swallowed the bile that he could taste in his mouth. 'This shortlist of Dobson's. Does it include the name of Liz Muir?'

It had not been his intention to play his ace so early. But now that he had, he wanted to savour the doubt in Owen's eyes. To enjoy his suffering. He watched as Owen climbed, woodenly, to his feet.

'What are you talking about?' Owen said, icily.

'Did you know that she is an undercover agent, Peter?'

Owen laughed. 'Really. Is that the best you can do?'

'Did you know that she has been working against you? That she has always worked against you?' Broadbent persisted.

'I don't believe you.'

Broadbent smiled. 'Of course you don't. You have my deepest sympathy. Betrayal is an ugly bed fellow, is it not?'

The blow came with little warning. Owen had covered the space between them in an instant. The pain was indescribable. Broadbent spat the mouthful of blood from the puncture in his lip onto the floor.

'The oldest trick in the book, Peter. And that you should have fallen for it. Proof, if we needed it, that even a man of your calibre, ultimately thinks with his cock.'

The second blow, sent blood, spraying onto the wall behind him. 'You're lying.'

'Am I? Are you sure?' Broadbent said, spitting blood. 'I wonder what else you don't know about Liz Muir. Did you know, for example, that three weeks ago, she was involved in the abduction of a woman from a nursing home in Muswell Hill? A woman who was found, beaten half to death, in a street behind Excalibur House. Which, as you are no doubt aware, was another of Jimmy Dobson's little misdemeanours. Or was that also nothing to do with you?'

Owen, waved his hand dismissively. 'What are you talking about. Why would Liz have abducted a woman from a nursing home in Muswell Hill?'

'Why indeed? But it is interesting, is it not, that she didn't see fit to tell you.'

'I'm not listening to any more of this rubbish,' said Owen, turning away.

Broadbent smiled through the blood. 'You ought to, Peter. Because it wasn't I who placed the real traitor in your midst. For that you might want to look a little closer to home.'

Owen turned. In his his eyes Broadbent could see a mixture of fury and doubt.

'Bring Dobson back in. I have something to show you both,' Broadbent said, watching the other man's eyes. 'I think that it will interest you.'

Owen stared at him. 'Why? So that you can spout more of your rubbish?'

'Bring him in,' Broadbent insisted.

Owen hesitated and then he walked across to the door and opened it. 'Jimmy?'

Dobson followed him back into the room.

Broadbent waited until they were standing in front of him.

'Well?' Owen said, 'Make it quick.'

Broadbent addressed Dobson. 'Peter seems to be having difficulty with the notion that it wasn't me who installed your traitor but that he installed her himself. In more ways than one, if the rumours are to be believed.'

'You said you had something to show us', Owen hissed, clenching his fists.

'I'd blame my head of security, personally,' Broadbent continued. 'And you're not the only one with designs on Liz Muir. Is he, Jimmy?'

Dobson took a step forwards.

Owen held him by the arm.

'This morning, Jimmy, I sent a file to the Director of Public Prosecutions by internal, Home Office, delivery. It contains evidence concerning the murder of one Karl Dixon, the assaults of the woman in Luke Street and of Paulo Diomedi, along with one or two other matters which, to be perfectly honest, I included purely out of spite. It will arrive at the DPP's office tomorrow morning. Assuming that I am still here to give the command, I may decide to have the file intercepted. If I am not, then I anticipate that a warrant will immediately be issued for your arrest.' Broadbent paused, savouring the moment.

'As for you, Peter, I would't make too many plans if I were you.'

'What are you talking about?'

'Jimmy, perhaps you would like to do the honours?'

Owen and Dobson exchanged glances.

'Liz Muir is a most intriguing and resourceful woman. While she was liberating my photographs from Jimmy's safe, she also went to the trouble of installing a listening device into the lid of that briefcase. Somewhere out there,' he said, gesturing towards the window with his head, 'she has no doubt been taking careful note of everything she has heard.' He paused, enjoying the effect that his words were having on the two men's faces.

'As well as recording it on cassette recorder that I supplied her with for that purpose.'

Within seconds Dobson had ripped open the lining of his briefcase. He turned with the listening device in his hand.

Owen stood in stony silence.

'I am a senior London police officer, Peter. If any harm comes to me, Dobson here will not be the only one to have his collar felt. In fact, I rather suspect that the contents of that tape will bring those forces arrayed against you, baying, to your door.'

Owen held out his hand. Dobson handed him the device. Owen let it fall to the floor. The he stamped on it. 'You're a minor irritation, Simon. A minor player. Nothing more. We count several more senior policemen than you among our supporters. You over-estimate your significance.'

Broadbent felt his confidence waver.

Owen turned to Dobson. 'Find her and retrieve the tape. I don't care how. The tape is the priority. Is that understood?'

'Yes,' Dobson said simply.

'And when you've done that, make arrangements for the Chief Superintendent's suicide, would you? I hear that bent coppers usually prefer to throw themselves from the tops of tall buildings, rather than face the humiliation of a long prison sentence. And Chief Superintendent Broadbent is bent in more than ways than one.'

'It will be my pleasure.'

Owen paused. He turned to Broadbent. 'Incidentally, our support already extends to some particularly senior contacts at the office of the DPP. By Monday afternoon, it will extend to the new DPP himself.' And with that, Owen marched from the room.

I had been betrayed. The irony of it took my breath away. I had deceived just about everyone who had ever trusted me and now the tables had been turned. By Simon Broadbent. I had listened to his words with disbelief. That Broadbent was driven by his own agenda had been plain, but his betrayal had been as unexpected as it was complete. It changed everything and as I listened to Peter's response, my disbelief turned to fear. A gut wrenching fear, that Peter would hate me and with good reason. He would be putting the pieces together in his mind. It would take him no time at all to realise that I had deceived him from the very start.

As I sat and began to shake, I knew that all hope was lost. He would never believe that my feelings for him had ever been genuine. As the signal from the bug was lost, I knew both that he would set Jimmy Dobson the task of finding me and that even if I managed to escape him, it would only be a matter of time before Dobson would discover the existence of Ted and the children.

My only hope was to get the tape to Smith. I had to get away. I tore off the earphone, bundled the recording equipment into my bag and began to clamber back through the undergrowth, trying desperately to hold down the tidal wave of panic that was spreading from my guts into my legs and arms. As I stumbled out on to the pathway, I could already hear voices in the distance. Abandoning any hope of stealth, I fled back through the woods, heedless of the risk that I would trip on some root or catch my foot in some trough in the dirt.

I ran so hard, that I began to feel light headed. For a while it was as though the woods had fallen silent, save for the thudding of my boots on the path and the rasping sounds of my breathing. Soon, even those sounds subsided, replaced by a buzzing in my ears, that became more intense, as I ploughed on. As the pathway veered to the right, I was suddenly afraid that I had lost my way.

I ran on, glancing left and right for some landmark that I might recognise. I had left my car about a mile away, in small lay-by, beside an open field on the main road that ran along the ridge above the woods. So long as I stuck to the main path, I told myself, I was running in the right direction. I ran on, sweating and stumbling, mindless of all else but the need to escape.

Just when my legs felt like they would carry me no further, I staggered out onto the road, sweating and breathless, my calf muscles stinging with the exertion. I stood, with my hands on my thighs, sucking great bucketfuls of air into my aching lungs.

Which way? WHICH FUCKING WAY?

But there was no time. As I straightened, I heard the sound of an approaching car.

I ran back into the woods, found the largest tree that I could and sank down on to my knees behind it, numb with fear and exhaustion.

It was Dobson. I could hear his voice shouting commands. I got up and ran again, back into the woods, but this time I took a path to the right which, I guessed, was in the rough direction of my car.

I don't know how far or for how long I ran, but quite suddenly the trees began to thin and then they were gone. I ran out into the sunshine and found myself at the edge of a shimmering wheat field. I stumbled along the field edge which I guessed - and it was only a guess - ran parallel to the road to my right. My only hope was to make it back to the car before Dobson caught me. And then I fell.

I let out a cry as a I went down. I couldn't help myself. My ankle felt like my foot had been torn off. My boot had caught in what looked like a rabbit hole. I freed it, biting back the pain which was lancing up the back of my left leg. As I got to my knees, crying in pain and fear, I saw Dobson. He exploded from the edge of the woods and out into the wheat field, perhaps sixty yards behind me. I clambered to my feet and ran again, heedless of the agony in my ankle. But it was slowing me. No matter how hard I drove myself forward.

Gunshot.

It wasn't the shot itself that registered with me - I'd never heard a gun being fired before, so I had no real idea what they sounded like. It was the bullet. I felt it fizz through the air, no more than a few feet from the side of my face. Dobson was going to kill me. I had absolutely no doubt about it.

I ran through the pain and terror, thinking of nothing but the need to escape and to protect Harry and Kate. I held their faces in my mind.

Another shot. And another. I fell again. And then I was on my feet once more, running, mindlessly. I could think of nothing. For no reason that I was aware of, I dived to my right, crashing through a hedgerow, which tore through my jeans and cut stinging slashes into the side of my face. And then I was on the road. No more than twenty yards ahead of me, was my car.

As I ran for the car I was vaguely aware that Dobson was no longer pursuing me or, if he was, he was doing so silently. I found the car and stood, frantically searching my pockets for my car keys. I found them, tore open the door, got in and drove away, the wheels spinning on the gravel of the lay-by.

I tore along the ridge, down, over the bridge across the Grand Union Canal, and at the bottom of the road, turned left, towards Berkhamsted and the A41 into London. It was as I pulled up at the lights beside the town's police station that I realised that I had lost the one thing that might have saved me. I felt the loss like a bereavement. And that is what it was. The death of all hope. I had lost my backpack, with the listening device and the cassette recorder inside.

Chapter Thirty-Nine

After my escape from Ashridge, I drove home. Numb. Exhausted. Empty. It was the beginning of the end and all that I wanted was to be with the children. To see that they were safe.

I had arrived, still limping, my clothes torn and dirty. Ted had looked at me like he didn't know me. It was the truth. He didn't.

I had expected a scene. Questions. Accusations. Bitterness. But Ted had said nothing. Nothing at all. Instead he waited. Waited for me to offer something by way of an explanation. Anything. But I could think of nothing to say.

I went upstairs to the bathroom, as much to escape his accusing stare as anything else. I closed and bolted the door, turned on the shower and began to remove my clothes, bending stiffly to slip the leg of my jeans over my swollen ankle. As I stood upright, hopping painfully from one foot to the other, the room suddenly tilted. For a moment, dizziness overcame me and I stumbled, throwing a hand out to prevent myself from falling. When I lifted my head, it was not my body that I saw reflected in the mirror, but the bodies of each of the women I had been. Drifting in and out of focus through the steam.

I got into the shower and let the steaming water run over my stinging face. My worlds were colliding. After all that I had done to keep them apart. Broadbent's words had sewn the seeds of my destruction. Peter was seeing me, for the first time, for what I was. It was only a matter of time before Ted and the others would learn the truth. And I could think of no way to stop it. No way at all.

After my shower, I got dressed and went downstairs, still numb and with no idea what to do. Ted and Kate were in the kitchen. She was sitting at the kitchen table, filling in pictures in her colouring book. I stood watching them.

When he saw me, he stood up and reached for his jacket. 'I'm going out,' he said, pushing past me.

'Where are you going?'

'I don't know.'

'When will you be back?'

'I don't know,' he barked.

I followed him down the hallway. 'Ted, I'm sorry. I…'

He turned and our eyes met. But I couldn't hold his stare. And then he was gone, the front door slamming behind him.

'Where is Daddy going?'

Kate was pulling at my hand.

'What?'

'Where's Daddy going?'

I looked down at her. I couldn't stay. We couldn't stay. Dobson might have the tape recording but it wouldn't be enough. I had heard what I heard. I couldn't un-hear it. And that knowledge would condemn me. But I couldn't leave the children.

I bent down, lifted Kate into my arms and hugged her. So tightly that she began to wriggle. I carried her to the foot of the stairs. 'Harry?' I called out.

I heard his muffled voice.

'Harry?'

I heard his footsteps.

'We're going on a little holiday,' I said to Kate. 'Just you, me and Harry.'

'Not Daddy?' she said in a small voice. 'I want Daddy to come.'

'Daddy has to go to work sweetheart.'

'Don't be silly Mummy. It's Saturday tomorrow. Daddy doesn't have to work until Monday.'

I drove towards the sea. I had no particular destination in mind. I just wanted to be by the sea. I have loved it since I was a child. My parents used to take me, every year, to a holiday park near Bembridge, on the Isle of Wight. I'd spend the whole holiday on the beach, exploring the rock pools and making sand castles, or fishing with my father from the sea wall. That is how I remember it, anyway. Ice cream and grey mullet.

As we turned onto the A13, I wondered what he would have thought of me and the mess I had made of my life. What he would have said, had I been able to go to him for advice. He'd been a kind man and, in many ways, a good father. We'd spent hours and hours together, waiting for the little bell on the end of one of our fishing rods to ring. But, I can't remember us ever having had a conversation of any personal consequence and, least of all, one that involved emotions - his or mine. I can't say that it had particularly bothered me at the time. You don't really become aware of these things until adulthood but, for me, that was too late. He had died when I was nineteen.

So, in my father's absence, I drove towards the sea to look for an answer in the waves.

We stayed in a bed and breakfast on Canvey Island that night. I'd called Ted from a telephone box on the sea front, while the children waited in the car, and told him that I was taking a break with the children. That I needed time to think. He'd accepted it, without question but I could tell from the emotion in his voice that he was heartbroken. It made me feel sick to think of what I had done to him. What I was doing. That it had come to this.

We spent the Saturday on the beach. The children had loved it and spent hours playing in the water in the warm summer sun. It felt like the first time for as long as I could remember that I'd been able to think. The trouble was that the more I thought about it, the more impossible my situation became. It went round and around in my head, always coming to the same point.

Smith was my only hope. If I went to him then, even without the tape, he'd be able to move against the NUGB. Surely.

In the middle of it was Peter. What he was planning was insane. A bomb detonated in Central London, could kill dozens of innocent people. Maybe more. Nothing could justify that. I had no choice but to betray him, even though I loved him above all else. Even if, by exposing him, I would end any hope of being with him.

And so I determined to return to London and to make my final move. But there was something that I needed to do first. I don't know what made me so sure. A voice in my head. A woman's voice. One that I had trusted and would always trust, no matter what Smith had said.

Sunday 21st August 1977

Rosemary Sellers sat by the window in her room, gazing down onto the little patch of green below the flat which she occupied with Flora Jackson. Muddled memories had slowly been returning to her. They came in random batches, with little connecting one to the other. Sometimes they would remain and sometimes they would flutter away again, like the sparrows that occasionally appeared on her window ledge to feed on the crusts that she left for them there.

She tried to read the newspapers that Flora bought her each morning and to watch the news on the little television set that she had put in her room. But it was all such a jumble and more often, she would do as she was doing now. Gaze from her window, her mind wandering from one scattered memory to the next.

She had no idea what the time was when she heard the door bell. But she had a thought for who it might be. There was something that she needed to say. Something important. It had been forming in her mind. She needed, only, to piece it all together.

She recognised the tell tale knock on her door. This visitor had a way of knocking that nobody else did.

'Enter.' The sound of her own voice startled her still.

'Rosemary,' said the visitor.

And then Rosemary Sellers remembered.

I crossed the room, bent down and kissed her on the cheek.

She reached up and held the side of my face. 'Liz. You're safe.'

Not exactly. I thought it, but I did not say it.

'Sit down,' she said when the moment had passed. 'There is something I need to tell you.'

I sat on the edge of her bed, beside her. 'You have remembered something?'

Rosemary nodded. 'The day I was attacked.'

I studied her face. There was an urgency in her eyes. Perhaps, to tell me while the memory persisted.

'I broke into the NUGB's office.'

I had already guessed as much. 'Why?'

'Dobson.'

'Jimmy Dobson?'

She nodded again. 'I needed to confirm certain facts about him.'

Why had she still been investigating Jimmy Dobson when she'd been retired from the Service? I wanted to ask the question but I didn't want to break her train of thought. 'Go on,' I said gently.

'I had been assigned to monitoring him in...' She paused, her mind appearing to wander.

I waited.

'Damn it. I can't remember. Does it matter?'

I shook my head. It really didn't.

'He'd been identified as a potential risk to national security. Shortly after his arrival in Britain.'

His arrival in Britain. Where had he come from? And then I remembered something.

'I needed to be sure about the date of his appointment by the Union. I needed to know whether it coincided with the disappearance of a man in Germany.'

'Möller,' I said.

Rosemary looked at me and beamed. 'Yes, that's right. How did you know?'

'You used the name. In the nursing home. I wondered about it. You were very confused.'

'Did I?'

'You did,' I said, smiling. 'Rosemary, who is this Möller?'

'He is wanted in Germany. For murder, among other things. I had reason to suspect that Dobson and Möller were one and the same.'

'And are they?'

'Yes, I believe so. But there were those within the Service who did not believe it or, more likely, who believed it but did not want me to follow this line of enquiry.' She paused again.

'When we met, all those years ago…' She smiled and reached out for my hand.

I took it.

'I told you that I knew Smith.'

'I remember,' I said. 'You said, rather cryptically, that you shared a common employer.'

'Yes…' she said, appearing to lose focus. She turned and gazed out of the window.

I waited.

'I was always suspicious of him,' she said, suddenly, turning back to face me. 'I seem to remember warning you.'

'You did. Many times.'

'Smith was among those who were most insistent that I should focus on Dobson's activities in Britain, rather than on his past. Möller's past.'

'And did you?' I ventured.

'No, I did not. But they delayed me.'

'They?'

'It was a mistake,' she continued, avoiding the question. Or perhaps she hadn't heard it. 'I should have moved more quickly to protect him...'

Rosemary was beginning to lose me.

'By the time that I got to him, it was too late.'

'By the time you got to who, Rosemary? Who were you trying to protect?'

Rosemary's face appeared to lose focus. 'I... have been trying to piece it together. I... I just can't seem to...'

I watched her struggling with her shattered memory. It was beginning to distress her.

'It's alright. It will come to you.' I said squeezing her hand gently.

She looked up and stared into my eyes. 'I should have acted. I should have...' She paused, searching my eyes as though willing me to tell her the rest.

But I couldn't.

'I was too late. He was dead. Because of me. An innocent man. My fault. I rather think that it has all been my fault.' A tear trickled from the corner of her eye and rolled down her cheek.

'Is that why you accepted retirement?' I asked quietly.

'Accepted it?' she laughed, bitterly. 'I handed it to them on a plate. I was thrown out.'

'So what were you doing at Excalibur House?'

Rosemary looked at me blankly.

'I mean, if you had been thrown out. Why were you still investigating Dobson?'

'Because...' she hesitated. 'There is something that I must find. To put it right. I must...' She looked around the room in confusion. 'I've...' Her eyes had filled with tears.

'Rosemary, it's alright. Slow down.'

I got up from the bed, knelt down in front of her and took hold of both her hands.

'Take your time. We can talk about it again. There's no rush.'

She stared at me. 'Yes. Yes there is, dear. Don't you see?'

But I didn't see. Not in the slightest.

'You mustn't trust him. You mustn't,' she said gripping my hands tightly.

I didn't trust Dobson. I never had.

'He was waiting for me.'

She'd lost me again.

'Who was waiting for you?'

'Möller. When I stepped out onto Great Eastern Street.'

I tried to follow her train of thought. Dobson had been waiting for her… 'Are you sure?'

She nodded.

'Had he been watching you?'

'No, no.' She shook her head in frustration. 'He knew. He told me.'

'What did he tell you?'

I thought about it. Dobson had known that she would be there. Because he had been told. 'Are you saying that he was tipped off?'

She nodded. 'Yes.'

'By who? Who knew that you were there?'

She stared at me.

Smith?

She nodded as though she had heard my thought.

'Smith? You're saying that Smith knew that you were there and that he tipped Dobson off?'

'Yes.'

I was struggling. *Smith?* Certainly, Smith had repeatedly refused to do anything about Dobson. Even when Dobson had threatened me. But why would Smith have tipped him off that Rosemary was at Excalibur House? 'How do you know that it was Smith?'

'I saw him, following me, earlier that evening. I thought I'd lost him.'

Had Smith wanted her removed? For what reason? To stop her discovering the truth about Möller/Dobson? I recalled Smith's reaction when I had revealed my interest in Rosemary. He had seemed almost desperate that I should stay out of it. He'd said that it was bigger than I could possibly imagine. The truth was that I still didn't know how big. 'Are you saying that Smith was trying to silence you, permanently?'

'Yes, I believe so.'

'Then why did he not finish the job while you were in hospital?'

'He should have. His failure to do so was an error.'

'But why?'

'I don't know. Perhaps he believed that I would not recover. That I was no longer a risk.'

'Alright. But why then allow us to take you from the nursing home? As soon as he realised that I intended to find you - and I as good as told him that I would - he could have moved against you then.'

'Yes, he could. And perhaps he would have done, given a little more time.'

I must have looked doubtful.

'Murder might be an easy crime to commit, Liz. But it is not so easy to get away with it. Even for someone like Smith. I think that he underestimated you and Alphonse. It was thanks to Alphonse, that you found me more quickly than he anticipated. I think that the speed with which you acted, may very well have saved my life.'

'What are you going to do?' Simone said, her voice full of concern. 'You know that you and the kids can stay here as long as you like, don't you?'

'I know, Simone. Thank you.' I could hear them playing in the bedroom along the hall.

I still couldn't tell her. Not everything. I told myself that the less she knew the less danger she'd be in. It was nonsense of course. The game was up. She'd find out sooner or later. But I just couldn't tell her.

My discussion with Rosemary had provided the final answer. If I could not trust Smith, and I had never really trusted him, then there was nothing further to be done. Running from Dobson would only lead him to Ted and, eventually, to the children. He'd use them to lure me out of whatever hole I decided to hide in. There was only one way to protect them. Peter Owen.

Our destinies had been intertwined since our first meeting. My agonies had started with him and it seemed fitting that, for better or worse, they should end with him. My life, or what was left of it, was over. Or at very least these were it's final moments.

I would tell him everything. Beg his forgiveness. Plead with him not to proceed with his plans. If he refused, then I would stand by his side until one end or another. If it was suicide, then it was a suicide that I deserved and for which an increasingly large part of me yearned. It was too much. It had always been too much. 'Will you look after the children for me?'

'Of course I will, Liz.'

'If I'm not back by tomorrow evening, call Ted. He'll come and get them.'

'Where are you going? Liz you're not going to do anything stupid are you?'

I smiled. 'Stupid is my middle name, Simone. Didn't you you know?'

'You're scaring me.'

I sighed. 'Seventeen years ago I made a decision. I'd been trained as a police officer. Remember, I told you that?'

Simone nodded.

'Well, when I told them that I was leaving, I was offered a job. In secret. And my life has been nothing but secrets and lies since.'

Simone stared at me, blinking.

'I told you when we met on the train that you didn't know the half of it. And it is better that you don't.'

'Better for who?'

'Better for you. Better for everyone. You'll find out soon enough. When you do, please know that I never intended it to happen as it has. I never intended the lies to take over my life as they have.'

Simone shook her head. 'Whatever it is Liz, you don't have to do it on your own. That's always been your problem. Secrets. Too many fucking secrets.'

She was damn right about that. I smiled. 'I know. But it is too late. If I could turn the clock back I would. But I can't. When I accepted that job, a train of events was set in motion. That train has been chasing me for seventeen years now and it is time to let it catch me.'

'What the hell does that mean?'

'It means that I'm going to do what I should have done right from the start. I'm going to tell the truth.'

Chapter Forty

Alphonse arrived as I was preparing to leave. I was glad that he had come. I wanted to tell him about Simon Broadbent's betrayal. I took no pleasure in it, but he needed to know.

'I am sorry Liz. It grieves me much that I was wrong about Simon. I do not understand him.'

'Power, Alphonse. It corrupts us all.'

'Perhaps it is so,' he said, averting his eyes.

'It wasn't your fault. Meeting Broadbent was always going to be a gamble and it almost paid off.'

'What do you think has become of him?'

'I really don't know. The last thing I heard before the bug went dead, he was threatening Dobson with arrest, which given his predicament, was probably not such a good idea.'

'And what about you? What is it that you are planning to do?'

'I am going to bring this whole thing, or my part in it anyway, to a close, one way or the other.'

Alphonse looked at me gravely. 'And you are sure that it is the right thing that you do.'

I smiled. 'It is the only thing I can do.'

Alphonse disappeared while I said my goodbye's to Simone, to Mrs Jackson and to the Harry and Kate. 'Simone will look after you until tomorrow and then Daddy will come and get you,' I said to Harry.

'Does he know where we are?' Harry said, very solemnly.

'Of course he does,' I lied. I doubted whether Ted had ever been to the Broadwater Farm Estate. 'Be a good boy for Simone and look after your sister.'

'I will.'

'Promise?'

'Yes, of course.' He sounded suddenly grown up.

'I'll see you in a couple of days.'

Harry nodded. 'Yes, Mummy.'

'And never forget how much I love you. Both of you. Always.'

I was determined not to cry. For their sake and for mine.

I decided to leave without speaking again to Rosemary. She was asleep in her chair by the window when I put my head around the door. Mrs Jackson had vowed to look after her until she was able to return home, wherever that was. I was still no closer to knowing Rosemary's true identity or anything about the wrong she felt so determined to put right. I'd probably never know.

Alphonse reappeared as I was stepping out of Mrs Jackson's front door. 'I will come down with you, if I may.'

I smiled at him. 'Of course.'

We walked along the passage way to the lift. When we were inside, Alphonse turned to me. 'I wish to give you this,' he said. He reached into his inside pocket and held out a small pistol.

'Where, in God's name, did you get that?' I gasped.

'Rosemary gave it to me for safe keeping many months ago. She referred to it as her insurance policy.'

'I don't want it. I've never used a gun and I do not intend to start now.'

'Mademoiselle, I know enough about what you and Rosemary do to know that it is a dangerous business.'

I looked at the gun dubiously.

'Having it is not the same thing as using it. But what you are going to do, it is not without risk?'

'No, it is not without risk.'

'Then let it be your insurance policy, as it was for Rosemary.'

He glanced towards the floor indicator. My eyes followed his. We were almost to the ground.

'Take it, Mademoiselle. And if you find yourself using it against Monsieur Dobson, make an extra hole in his head for me.'

I took it as the lift doors began to open.

We stepped out of the lift together.

'It's alright. I left my car across the recreation ground, in Walpole Road. I can take it from here.'

We embraced each other.

'Take care Alphonse and thank you. For trusting me.'

His eyes filled with tears. He said nothing. He simply nodded, turned and stepped back into the lift car.

Hadley Green Road, where Peter lived with his wife, was far grander than I had imagined it. The houses, arrayed along the street's south western side, overlook the Green, an expanse of acid grassland, ditches and ponds, which in 1471 played host to the soldiers of the Lancastrian and Yorkist armies at the Battle of Barnet. Legend has it that somewhere, buried beneath the grass, are the bodies of the men who lost their lives during the battle. As I turned off the main road, I wondered whether a young couple, sitting on a blanket beside a wide pond, enjoying the evening sunshine, had any idea at all that below them lay the bones of a thousand soldiers, looking up at them from their undiscovered graves. It was a sombre thought, reflecting my sombre mood.

I drove slowly. I had never been to Peter's house but I had memorised the address years before, fantasising that one day I would turn up and reveal our relationship to Emma. Now that I had arrived, it seemed as though I had crossed a threshold. As I passed the first of the street's impossibly elegant houses, with its wide front lawn and gravel path, I felt like an interloper. As though I had left my world and passed into another. A place in which I did not exist. A space I had no right to occupy. Like a ghost, rising from out of the grass. And, quite suddenly, I felt completely alone.

I slowed almost to a halt. *I should turn around and drive away, back to…*

To where? There was nowhere to go. I told myself that I had already made my choice.

I passed an enormous house, with a wide red-bricked wall, behind which I could see an orange wind-sock fluttering in the breeze. And then I saw it. Jimmy Dobson's white Ford Cortina.

It was parked opposite a large detached house, in white stone, with an oval balcony and a black front door. Peter's house. There was no doubt that the car was Dobson's. I recognised the number plate.

Shit. Shit. Shit.

It was too late to stop and reverse and so I accelerated gently away, passing both the house and the empty Cortina.

Dobson's presence complicated matters. What I had to say to Peter, I had to say to him alone. I was not going to give Dobson the pleasure of hearing it. If I had to, I'd find a place on the Green, where I could sit and wait for him to leave, before I made my move.

I turned right at the bottom of the road and drew up in the car park of the local church. St Mary, The Virgin. I said a prayer to her as I walked back towards the house.

I had decided not to stray too close to the house on my first pass. But as I approached it, curiosity got the better of me. Casting caution to the wind, I walked straight towards it, doing my best to avert my eyes as I passed by. Had Peter or Dobson been looking out into the street at that moment, they would certainly have spotted me but fortunately neither man were. What I saw, though, gave me an idea. At the side of the building was a gate and an alley, presumably through to the grounds at the rear. The gate was open.

I carried on walking and then, satisfied that nobody was watching, turned around and headed back towards the house.

This time, instead of passing by, I looked over my shoulder and stepped off the road, through the gate and into the alley.

I crept along the alley, as stealthily as I could, until I came to the building's corner. And then I stopped.

This is madness.

I knew that it was. But I'd come this far. I told myself that there was no going back. I felt for the bulge in my jacket pocket. I ought, probably, to have been holding the gun in my hand. But I was afraid of it. And so I left it there. Rosemary's insurance policy and now mine.

I put my back to the wall and took a breath to calm my nerves. And then I heard voices. Mens' voices. I strained to identify them. Peter, certainly. John Taggart - his accent unmistakable. Jimmy Dobson. And then a woman's voice. *Emma Owen?* It had to be.

I inched my head around the building's corner. She was wearing a pretty, white summer dress and had nothing on her feet. My mind took a snapshot of her. As I ducked back behind the wall, I was already examining it. Small feet. Pretty ankles. Exposed as she walked across the grass to the garden table. She'd been carrying a tray of drinks, laughing. My snapshot had sound. She was strikingly beautiful. Much more so than she had seemed in the photograph in Peter's office. She looked and sounded as though she didn't have a care in the world. A world that I had every intention of shattering. I shrank back behind the wall, feeling worse than an interloper.

'Thank you darling. Now, if you don't mind, we have business to discuss.'

It was Peter's voice.

'See you all later,' she said, breezily.

Silence. Presumably while she went back into the house.

'Before we move on to more pressing matters, there is something that has been niggling me about the woman from the nursing home.'

It was Peter's voice again.

'How did you know?' he asked.

'Know?' Dobson replied.

'That she would be there.'

'I didn't know.' It was Dobson's voice and he was lying. 'I had gone to the office, with the intention of working late. On the security arrangements for the conference. It was a coincidence.'

'She just so happened to emerge at that precise moment, did she?' Peter said sceptically. He evidently didn't believe him, any more than I did.

'No. I happened to look up. From the car park at the rear. I saw several flashes. Like those from a camera.'

'And yet you say that when you caught up with her, she had nothing on her. No identification.'

'No.'

'No camera?'

'No.'

There was a silence.

'We need to discover her identity, or at least the identity of her employer. You will run it past our connection at Millbank, won't you John?'

'Of course.' It was Taggart's voice.

'Along with the other matter.'

The three men were silent.

'Has there been any sign of her?' Peter said it quietly. So quietly that I could barely hear his voice.

'Nothing. But I will find her. You can be assured of that.' It was Dobson's voice.

'Without the tape,' said Taggart, 'she has no evidence and very few options. I have warned all our contacts to report any word of her. The moment she moves, we will have her. And in fourteen hour's time we will be unstoppable.'

'My only concern is who, exactly, she was working for. If it was someone at Millbank, I want to know about it,' Owen said calmly.

'It won't be. They're too busy with the Irish and the Campaign For Nuclear bloody Disarmament,' said Taggart.

I heard Peter and Dobson both laugh.

'Maybe not. But if not, then who would be interested enough in our activities to go to such lengths?'

'Given what Broadbent said, we should not exclude the possibility that she and the woman from the nursing home were working together.' It was Taggart again.

'Possibly.'

There was a pause.

'Find them, Dobson. Especially her.'

'Oh I intend to. I have plans for Muir.'

'Be my guest.' The bitterness in his voice was almost palpable. 'Just make sure that when you've finished with her, she's unrecognisable. A burning car perhaps.'

I slumped against the wall, heavily. My guts felt like they'd been ripped out. That he should hate me was understandable. It was no more than I deserved. But the words that he had used, were burning me already. From the inside out. He couldn't mean it. He'd been betrayed. They were the words of an injured man.

'Now to more important matters. Jimmy is the van ready?'

'It is. I went over it this afternoon. It is an exact replica of the Post Office van. Down to the smallest detail. Even the rubbish in the cab.'

'We must be absolutely certain. It may be a fleet vehicle, but something out of place and the engineer may become suspicious.'

Post Office. I heard it but it took a few moments to register.

'I told you, they've copied the interior down to the last detail.'

'And we are absolutely certain that it is the van that the engineer will use.'

Engineer.

'There are only two that have clearance to enter the Palace of Westminster. We have taken care of the other. Rest assured. Nothing has been left to chance.'

'Good.'

Palace of Westminster.

'All I need is the keys to the depot and I will make the switch later this evening.'

But I was no longer listening. There were several Post Office engineering depots in London. At times, Ted had worked from them all. He'd be working early on Monday morning and I knew that he had the high level clearance necessary to work at secure government and diplomatic locations. Only a select group of engineers did. A sudden fear stabbed at my chest.

I put my head around the wall and saw John Taggart hand Jimmy Dobson a set of keys.

'And the guard has been taken care of?'

'Yes. He will let me in and he will let me out again.'

'You are certain of his loyalty?'

'His wife and children were all the certainty he needs,' said Dobson.

'All set then,' Taggart said.

'And no mistakes Jimmy. We have a lot riding on this.'

The Palace of Westminster. It was unthinkable. They were going to bomb Parliament. What was it that Peter had said at the conference - to disrupt national government to the point of collapse? Disrupting it was one thing. But Peter wasn't going to disrupt government. He was going to destroy it. To commit the murder of countless Members of Parliament, their staff and anyone else who happened to be in the House at the time. Blown to pieces by a bomb placed in a Post Office van.

A Post Office van. I felt a wave of panic wash over me. *Ted's Post Office van.*

I had to stop it. My legs felt suddenly heavy. What Peter was planning was mass murder. He was deranged. Peter. My Peter. The man who I had loved, like no other. A killer. He couldn't… There was no time to think. *Ted's Post Office van.* Ted. I had to warn him.

The gun. If I stepped out from the alley. If I begged him. Pleaded with him to abandon their plan. Would he listen? I knew in my heart that he would not. His words echoed around my head. *"Just make sure that when you've finished with her, she's unrecognisable. A burning car perhaps."*

And if he did not, would I be able to use the gun? To shoot him where he stood? I knew that I was incapable of it. Despite the horror of what he was planning.

Ted's Post Office van.

I needed to move but my legs were like stone. If Dobson decided to leave by the alley, then he would be upon me.

Dobson. I had to stop him. At that moment, I hadn't the slightest idea how I was going to do it. But I knew, with a cold certainty, that he had to be stopped. And that meant getting to my car before Dobson got to his. Otherwise, I'd lose him.

And so I moved. Slowly, at first, back down the alley way and out onto the street. Then I ran. I ran as hard and as fast as I could.

Dobson's car was pointing northwards. If I could get back to my car, I could wait at the bottom of the road and pull out behind him.

Faster. Faster. Or I would be too late and Jimmy Dobson would be gone.

I turned a corner and almost ran into a telephone box.

Ted.

I could try to stop Dobson or I could warn Ted. There might not be another opportunity. I stood, rooted to the spot. *Dobson or Ted? DOBSON OR TED?* I screamed the question to myself in my head.

I tore open the heavy metal door and fumbled in my pocket for change. *Warn Ted. Warn Ted.* I ripped the handset from its cradle, dialled the number and waited for the pips. He answered.

Thank Christ.

I pushed the coin into the slot.

'Ted?'

Silence.

'Monday, where are you working?'

'Where are you?'

'It doesn't matter. Monday where are you working?'

'Where are the children?'

'They're safe. They're safe. Monday. Please. Where are you working?'

There was a silence.

I started to cry.

'You're ill Liz. Come home.'

'Ted please. I don't have any time. Where will you be on Monday?'

'Westminster.'

Westminster. Westminster. Westminster.

'Don't go. Take the day off. Don't go.'

'What are you talking about? I can't. It's an important job.'

'Ted, please don't go,' I sobbed. 'The van. Your van. There's a bomb.'

'What?'

'No time. I've got no time,' I screamed, tears of frustration tumbling down my cheeks.

'Jesus Christ, Liz.'

'Please. Don't go in. They're planting a bomb. In your fucking van. You've got to believe me.'

'What are you talking about. You're ill. Get to a hospital, Liz. You need help.'

'No. No. No. NO!' I was screaming. Sobbing.

'Where are the children? What have you done with the children?'

I could hear the fear in his voice.

'If you've hurt them…'

That he could even think it.

'Ted,' I sobbed. 'Please. Trust me.'

Trust me. It was useless. I slammed down the receiver and ran. As I hurtled towards the car, several people were emerging from the church. A young woman with a pram. I almost knocked her over.

I leapt into the car and pulled out, narrowly avoiding the woman.

Get out of the bloody way. Get out of…

She waved at me furiously.

Calm down. Calm down. Slow down.

I needed to drive normally. Otherwise, if I hadn't already missed him, Dobson would spot me immediately. I pulled over and stopped, a half a dozen yards short of the junction.

I've missed him. Calm down. He's gone. Calm down. It's too late.

I looked in my wing mirror. I could see the woman with the pram and a small group of onlookers, pointing at me. Two men started to walk towards me.

Fuck. Fuck. Fuck.

And then there he was. The Cortina pulled out a few yards ahead of me, turned left and then left again into the high street. I pulled away slowly and let two cars pass before I pulled out behind them.

Slow down. Stay calm. Don't lose him.

I wiped my eyes on my jacket sleeve and repeated it. Over and over.

I followed Dobson into London, repeating it like a mantra. *Calm down. Slow down. Don't lose him.*

After a while, the mantra subsided and I started to think. But thinking only made it worse.

Ted was going to be driving the van. To Westminster. He had security clearance. I knew that. They'd let him in. He'd drive into the palace at Westminster and then the bomb would explode. I began to cry. As I followed Dobson into London, several cars behind, I sobbed. Through fear and hopelessness and loss. I sobbed, so that I at times I was barely able to see though the windscreen to the white Cortina ahead.

Finally, as the light began to fade, Dobson pulled onto a small industrial park. I pulled up, some distance from the Cortina. I peered ahead and watched Dobson park the car, get out and walk across to a large garage. He knocked on a side door and two men came out. They stood, had a brief conversation and then all three men went inside.

I looked at my watch. It was just after nine o'clock.

I had to stop him from switching the vans. I had no idea how I was going to do it. But it was the only way to save Ted.

I considered bursting into the garage with the gun in my hand, but there were at least three of them and Dobson would undoubtedly be armed. I'd seen the gun in his safe. I'd never even held a gun until that day. I would be no match for them.

And so I waited. Without hope. Fearful. Heartbroken. Raging at my weakness and at my hopelessness. Praying for inspiration. Banging my hands on the steering wheel in fury when none came.

And then, when the raging was done, my resolve began to stiffen. Maybe it was the realisation that what was done was done. That I could not change what was in the past. And perhaps it was acceptance. Of the hand that I had been dealt. Of the game I had played, whether through choice or fate. This was the endgame. The final move. I could either play it or fold. And to fold now, when I was all that there was, standing between Ted and oblivion, was unthinkable. It would have been an act of supreme betrayal. Beyond everything that I had done. I knew that I could not do it.

I had to stop it and I was going to stop it. If I had to shoot Jimmy fucking Dobson/Möller in cold blood. If I died in the process. I was going to stop him. Ted had never once let me down. My mind flitted back to the first time that I'd met him. He'd been there for me through all of my agonies. Never once had he complained. Until now. And who could blame him? Maybe I was ill. Maybe Ted had been right. But I was going to stop Jimmy Dobson, come hell or high water. And slowly the crippling fear that had covered me like a lead shroud began to lift.

At ten-thirty, the garage doors rolled open and out from the garage came a Post Office van. I stared at it. It was hard to believe that onboard was a payload of explosive, the detonation of which would be sufficient to rock the country to its very core. To alter the course of the nation's history. I sat transfixed as the van approached.

At the very last moment I dived, flat across the passenger seat. I waited until the sound of the van's engine had receded and then I sat up. When I was satisfied that I would not be observed, I started the car and followed.

My resolve had been to stop him. I had cast it in concrete. But now that the task was ahead of me, I could see little opportunity. Had I been on a country road, with no other traffic around me, I might have attempted it. I could have swerved out from behind, overtaken the van, forced it off the road, and then leapt from my car, brandishing Rosemary's gun like Clint Eastwood. But North London Streets are rarely if ever completely devoid of traffic, even at ten thirty on a Sunday evening. Forcing a Semtex laden van from a North London street, risking a collision and the explosion that might very well follow, was out of the question, even if I could have managed it.

Instead, I followed. Through the streets of Wood Green and into Turnpike Lane. Less than a quarter of a mile from the place where Karl Dixon had been stabbed and murdered.

A picture of him came into my mind. He'd been here. Dancing with Sonia Smithson, just yards away on the common to my left. Happy and in love. And alive. I gritted my teeth. I was going to stop the bastard. Somehow.

The van continued along Turnpike Lane, over the New River and into Tottenham Lane. This was almost home territory. And then I knew where he was headed. Ted had mentioned it many times. The depot on Crouch Hill. Ted's team was based there. Though he sometimes worked from other depots. My blood turned to ice in my veins.

As I knew he would, Dobson turned into the depot.

I had failed.

There had been nothing that I could have done to prevent the switch but my failure still filled me with fury. I continued past the depot, turned left, followed the road around and re-emerged onto Crouch Hill. I pulled up, perhaps twenty yards from the depot entrance.

Shit. Shit. Fucking shit. I banged my hands on the steering wheel in frustration. But there was no time to think. In less than five minutes, the switched van re-emerged, baring the same number plates and looking, to all intents and purposes like the same van.

I followed it back to the lock up in Bounds Green, working the possibilities through in my mind. But, in the end, the next move was Dobson's and not mine.

Dobson had re-emerged in his Cortina within minutes of delivering the van back to the lock up garage. He drove away smoothly and, once again, I followed him. With no idea at all of how to stop the bombing but with every intention of putting a bullet between his eyes.

We didn't travel far. Home for Jimmy Dobson was a maisonette in quiet cul-de-sac in Woodside Park. It was leafy enough but the buildings looked run down. I pulled into a tiny car park, a short distance from where Dobson had parked the Cortina, watched him get out and walk across to his front door and disappear inside.

I sat in complete darkness for several minutes trying to decide what to do. I was still sitting in my car moments later when the driver's side window exploded and a fist dealt me a jarring blow to the side of my head. Jimmy Dobson tore open the door and dragged me from the car by the hair.

Chapter Forty-One

He shoved the car door shut with his foot and dragged me, semi conscious down the street. I don't remember whether lights came on in any of the houses that we passed. I don't know whether anyone looked out to see a man dragging me to his front door. But if anyone saw it, nobody came to my rescue.

I came to my senses, lying face down on his living room carpet.

'Good evening Liz. I am so pleased that you were able to join me.'

I opened my eyes. His boots were no more than a yard from my face. I tried to move but it hurt too much. I felt for the gun in my pocket.

Dobson laughed. 'I don't think so.'

I turned towards him. He was pointing the gun directly at me.

He grinned. 'It is a nice weapon. Walther PPK. Made in West Germany. Where all the best guns are. Strange that you should have a German gun.'

'It was given to me,' I said between gritted teeth. 'By a friend.'

'I wish that I had friends like yours,' he said, still grinning. He walked across to a table in the corner of the room still holding the gun in one hand, picked up a bottle and took a long swig. 'I am celebrating,' he said. 'How about you?'

I ignored him and tried to sit up but as I attempted to lever myself onto all fours, my head rolled like I was on a boat.

'Oh, before we go any further. All the windows and doors are locked. So trying to escape would be pointless.'

He was enjoying himself.

'Oh, and, of course, I'd shoot you.'

I tried to think but the more I thought about it, the more trouble I knew that I was in. Dobson was going to kill me. After he had finished with me. There was no hope. I could scream. Cry. I could beg for mercy. I could fight and give him the pleasure of overpowering me. Or I could hold my nerve and take it bravely. It didn't really matter which. That I was going to die was without question and only he would ever know how I had chosen to do it.

I managed to turn myself over and sit up. I watched him take another swig. It looked like whiskey.

'I'm going to enjoy this,' he said grinning. 'Unfortunately, I doubt that the same can be said for you.'

'Oh, you never know Möller. That is your real name isn't it?'

For a split second, I saw a shadow of doubt play across his face and his eye flick to a set of drawers against the wall by the window. I wondered why.

He hesitated. 'Very good. It is only fair to give you some credit. But sadly for you and fortunately for me, that knowledge is going to die with you.'

'Do you think so?' I said, bravely. Though I wasn't feeling it. I was feeling like I was going to throw up at any moment.

'Meaning?'

'Meaning that I'm not the only one who knows.'

It was one step too far and I quickly regretted it. He took several steps across the room and pointed the gun at my face. 'Open your mouth.'

I looked up at him. He hit me across the face with the side of the gun. Pain exploded in my head but I managed to stay upright.

'I said, open your mouth.'

I did it.

He pushed the gun barrel into my mouth so that I thought that I was going to choke. But I knew that he wasn't going to kill me there and then. To do so would have spoiled his fun.

'Who are you working for?'

He removed the gun from my mouth.

'His name is Smith. He works for the Security Service.'

'You're telling me that you work for MI5?'

I considered the question. 'I'm telling you that I work for Smith.'

If I was going to die, I might just as well set Dobson onto Smith. If he had tipped Dobson off about Rosemary's whereabouts, then the two of them were made for each other.

'He supplied the listening device?'

'No. The listening device was supplied by Chief Superintendent Broadbent.' He knew that already.

'Oh yes, I had forgotten about Broadbent. This Smith. How do you contact him? Where do you meet him?'

'Actually, you narrowly missed meeting him yourself, at the safe house in Finsbury Park. He was the man who arrived in the Granada, just as you were leaving.'

Dobson was thoughtful.

'And I believe that you, yourself have spoken to him at least once. He was the man who told you about the woman you assaulted in Luke Street.'

Dobson looked genuinely surprised, but he didn't deny it. He took another swig from his bottle. 'Is there anything else you would like to tell me?'

I thought about it. 'Yes. One more thing.' I waited.

'I'm listening.'

'Peter detests you, almost as much as I do. In fact, everyone detests you. I can't actually think of anyone who doesn't. But Peter most especially.'

'Is that so?' He took another swig.

And for the first time, I felt the tiniest glimmer of hope. That he might get drunk and make a mistake.

'Yes. It is. Remember, Möller, he has enough evidence of your misdemeanours to have you sent down for a very long time. If he chooses. And he told me that he has every intention of doing so, once you have outlived your usefulness, which I'd say was about now. Wouldn't you?'

Dobson/Möller's smile faded. 'If I go down, then I will take them all with me. I know as much about them, as they know about me. Rather more, in fact.'

I decided to press him. Perhaps foolishly. 'Ah yes, but then you are not going to be Prime Minister by tomorrow evening are you?'

And there it was again, a flash of doubt. He took another swig. And then he walked across to the drawers I had seem him look at, and exchanged the gun in his hand with another from the drawer, along with what looked like a silencer. He walked across the room and sat down on an arm chair, screwing the silencer into place. 'If I am going to shoot you It doesn't do to make too much noise,' he said.

I looked at the gun and began to shake. A picture of Harry and Kate came into my mind. They were playing in the garden. I shoved it back down.

'I think I'm finished with the small talk, as entertaining as it is. Time for the main event.'

I swallowed hard.

'Take off your clothes. All of them. Slowly.'

'Fuck you.'

He grinned. It was a pig ugly sight. 'Yes you will, but lets not rush things. A little foreplay perhaps.'

I said nothing.

'Either you do as you are told, or I am going to start putting holes in you. Feet and hands first. Then maybe nose, ears, breasts perhaps. None of them fatal of course.'

He meant it. Or if he didn't, he was doing a bloody good job at convincing me otherwise.

Harry and Kate would miss me most of all. Ted. Rosemary. Simone, Alphonse. Peter...

I took off my jacket and threw it on the floor. Then my shoes. Then my jeans. And then I hesitated. I was beginning to lose my nerve. I don't know how I'd managed to keep it. I could barely control the shaking.

He pointed the gun at my feet. 'What are you waiting for?'

I undid my shirt. Or tried to.

He watched me fumbling with the buttons. The bastard was getting off on it.

'And the rest. Now.'

I did as he wanted. And naked in front of him I sank to my knees and began to sob. I had been determined not to. But the sickening fear and loathing overcame me.

He dragged me, screaming and sobbing across the floor by the hair, into his bed room. And then he lifted me onto the bed. If I'd had my wits about me, it was then that I might have retaliated. He must have put the gun down to do it. But by then I was incapable of anything. I was lying face down. I felt something around my wrists. His belt. And then his hands were around my throat. Squeezing. So that I could not breath. I could not think. But I could feel. I felt the searing pain of him enter me from behind. And when he was done, I felt him turn me over, haul my legs above my head and I felt him enter me. Again and again. I felt him bite me while he did it. And then, thankfully, I passed out.

If I dreamt I don't remember it. But I do remember opening my eyes and the awful pain. I was lying face down on his bedroom floor. Bound by the feet and by the hands and with a neck tie between my teeth. Presumably so that I could not scream or call out. My whole body ached.

I lay still, listening and trying to push down the nausea. If I threw up now I stood every chance of choking. It was an effort to banish, from my mind, the knowledge of what he had done to me. But I'd had years of practice. That was one benefit of having lived a secret life.

I don't know how long I stayed like that. Silent. Still. Listening to the sound of him breathing.

When I turned my head to the side I saw the reason for his slumber. An empty whiskey bottle, lying on the floor on the opposite side of his bed. And there it was again. A flutter of hope.

Slowly, slowly I tried to move my hands. I could see over my shoulder that they were tied together by a leather belt. A poor choice. Still, it took me many minutes of painful wriggling to free them. Once they were free, however, the bonds on my legs and around my face were easier.

It was not so easy to stand. The stinging from between my legs was so intense that, after the first attempt, I had to lay back down again. Panting. It was then that I noticed the blood. I felt it cold against my skin. I slowly put my hand between my legs and winced as the stinging overcame me. When I brought my hand up to my face, it was covered in more blood.

You bastard. You evil fucking bastard. What have you done to me?

But it was pointless to rant, least of all to myself. Ranting was not going to get me away. I made it to my feet at the third attempt and stood, beside his bed, swaying. He was laying on his back, his pink belly rising and falling with his breath. His flaccid penis covered in blood. My blood. I wanted to wretch.

I steadied myself. And there it was. His gun. On the little cabinet beside his bed. Silencer still in place. I reached for it and he stirred. I froze and then picked it up. I pointed it, first at his groin and then at his head. I wanted to kill him. I wanted it, so badly. To make him pay for what he had done to me. To Rosemary. To Paulo Diomedi. To Simon Broadbent. To Karl Dixon. Most of all to Karl Dixon. I wanted him to wake up and to experience his own death. I wanted to watch him bleed slowly in front of me. I wanted it so badly that it made me sweat. But I couldn't do it. My hand shook. I had my teeth clamped so tightly together that my jaw ached. I could not pull the trigger.

I am perfectly willing to accept that it was cowardice. Standing there, naked and sweating and bleeding and hurting, I cannot say now what it was that stopped me. But it did. And so I choose the alternative. I chose escape. I inched from the room, gun in hand, praying that he would not stir.

Oddly, the first thing that I did was to quietly put on my clothes and shoes. It was odd, because until I found the keys I was not going to be able to escape. And if he awoke, would I have been any more able to pull the trigger? I didn't know. Maybe.

Once I was dressed, I found his jacket and in his pocket, two sets of keys. His house and car keys were on one bunch. On the other, I guessed, were the keys to the Post Office depot. I put them in my pocket. Carefully, so that they would not make a sound. Then I walked across to the room, found the key and opened the front door.

Then, whether stupidly or with courage, I cannot in all honesty say which, I returned to the set of drawers in which he had stashed Rosemary's gun. I opened the draw, removed the gun and put it in my inside pocket.

Under the weapon was a passport. I removed it and put that in my pocket too. And under that, was a pile of papers. I glanced at the uppermost. It was hand written in German. I pulled the papers out, rolled them up and slid them into the rear pocket of my jeans. And then I left, leaving the latch up so that the door did not click when I let it close.

I couldn't run, though the desire to do so was almost overwhelming. Instead I limped the short distance to my car. I could have taken his. But I didn't want to sit in his space. I wanted to be as far away from him as it was possible to be. I opened the driver's door with its absent window and, using a paperback that I found in the glove box, bent down to brush away the little beads of broken glass from the seat. The pain in my groin was intense and I knew that I was still bleeding. I tried not to think about what he had done. I leant against the side of the car, trying to swallow the bile in my throat.

My feet crunched on the mat as I got in. I started the engine. My hands were shaking on the cold steering wheel.

There was never any question in my mind about what I was going to do. I knew it, without thinking. I drove straight there. Ten minutes later, I was sitting outside the Post Office depot on Crouch Hill. I looked down at the clock on the dashboard.

Five-thirty in the morning. A little under three and a half hours until the bomb was due to detonate. Assuming that it was set to detonate by timer.

From what I could see from the outside, the depot was in darkness. Peter had mentioned a security guard. I felt for the gun in my pocket. If I had to confront him, I knew that I would. I got out of the car and walked the short distance to the gates. They were steel plated and locked with a heavy chain and padlock. The padlock was on the inside, reachable through a square hand hole in the right hand gate. Which confirmed the presence of the guard, who had evidently locked the gates following Dobson's departure.

I bent down and peered through the hole, into the yard beyond. Or tried to. I could see little but a few vague shapes in the inky darkness. I put my hand through and slowly worked the chain around so that the padlock was on the outside. Then I removed Dobson's keys from my pocket and undid the lock. Despite my best efforts the chain still rattled and clanked as I slid it free. I was certain that the guard would hear it.

When the chain was finally clear, I stood absolutely still and listened. All that I could hear was the sound of my heart hammering in my ears. I slowly inched the gate open, just wide enough to allow me to step through the gap, praying that it wouldn't squeal on its hinges.

The yard was silent and dark, save for a light which shone faintly from a window in a building to my left. Illuminated by the light, was the shape of the depot's night guard. He was sitting with his head down. Presumably at a desk. I couldn't tell whether he was awake or asleep. But I knew, with certainty, that had he looked up at that moment, he would have seen me, even in the darkness. I shrank away from the gate and dropped into a crouch beside an old steel oil drum.

The depot was full of vehicles. Once my eyes had adjusted to the light, or the lack of it, I counted seven in all. Two were of a type I recognised, but it was impossible to tell at a distance, which of them had been the van that Dobson had driven into the yard.

I tried to remember the van's number plate. I'd followed it from the garage all the way to the yard and, after the switch, its double all the way back to Bounds Green. But it would not come to me. I cursed silently and inched my way toward the vehicles, taking my eye from the guard only long enough to check the number plates of the two vans, as soon as I was near enough to make them out. And there it was. "KTS850S". The registration number sprang back into my head as soon as I saw it.

Fortunately, the van was facing the gate, obscuring the driver's door from the oblivious guard. I crept around the side of the van and reached, slowly for the door handle, hope swelling in my chest. And then it died. As I took hold of the door handle, I realised that I didn't have the keys. I had been so focussed on getting away from Dobson/Möller and into the yard, that I hadn't even considered them. He would have left them at the garage with the van's double. Without the keys, I was going nowhere.

Shit. Shit. Shit. How could I have been so stupid?

I tried the handle. The door opened with a clack that echoed around the yard. Dobson had failed to lock it. I stood stock still and felt for the gun. But still there was no sound from the guard. I eased myself up into the cab, my eyes fixed on the guard as he came into view through the passenger side window. It was fortunate that I was still watching him when he looked up. As he did so, I slid from the seat, pushing myself down into the footwell. Searing pain shot from my groin into my stomach like a lightning bolt. It left me gasping for air. I don't know how I avoided crying out.

You bastard. You bastard. It hurt. It hurt so much that it bought tears into my eyes. But I didn't cry out. I clamped my teeth and my eyes together and whimpered quietly, like an injured dog.

When the pain had finally eased, I opened my eyes and tried to focus. There, in the half light, hanging from beneath the steering column, was a bunch of cables. Which gave me an idea.

I'd never tried to hot wire a vehicle in my life before. But I'd seen it done. In some television drama or other. Was it an episode of *Softly, Softly?* I couldn't remember. But It was my only chance. I took the wires in my hand. Three bunches of four or five wires. What were the chances of randomly selecting the correct two? I tried to do the arithmetic in my head. It was simple. There was no chance.

Still, I had to try and so I selected two and was about to pull them when the back of my hand brushed against something taped to the underside of the steering column. I shifted my hand and pulled the tape away and with the tape was a key.

What was it that Peter had said to Dobson? *"No mistakes"?* It was a mistake alright, though presumably not Dobson's. But somebody had left it there. Whoever it was had given me a chance, where before there had been none.

I eased myself slowly back into the seat, my eyes fixed on the guard. I felt for the ignition and slid the key into place. It fitted. The moment I turned it, however, the guard was going to look up. It would take him no more than a few seconds to get to his feet. In a few more, he'd be running towards me.

I looked ahead at the gates. They were closed, exactly as I had left them. But at least they were unlocked.

I'd never driven anything as big as a van before. I didn't doubt that it was big enough to make it through the gates and out onto the street beyond. But what I did doubt was the effect that the impact might have on the van's hidden payload.

I closed my eyes and conjured the children's faces. They were in the back of the car, giggling. That day I'd threatened to box their ears. Harry, with his shock of thick, unruly, light brown hair and Kate with her elven features, their eyes twinkling back at me in the rear view mirror. I wasn't ready to leave them. If the van exploded, I'd be erased from their lives altogether. There wouldn't even be a body to bury.

I love you. I told them in my head. And then I gritted my teeth and turned the key. The engine spluttered into life. I revved it hard, engaged first gear, put my foot to the floor, took my foot off the clutch and said a silent prayer. The van surged forward and careered into the gate.

The sound of the impact was deafening. It was so loud that, in that moment, I was sure that the van had exploded. But a second later, the van had burst out onto the street. And ploughed, headlong, into the side of a white Ford Cortina.

Chapter Forty-Two

The force of the impact sent the Cortina spinning across the road and cracked the van's windscreen. The van juddered to a halt and stalled. For a moment, there was complete silence. It took me a few more to register what had happened. I stared at the ruined Cortina, hoping beyond hope that Dobson had at least been disabled by the crash. But my hope was short-lived. The Cortina's door flew open and out staggered Jimmy Dobson.

I could see the smouldering hatred in his face. But whatever the scale of his hatred, it would never match my own. Not after what he had done to me.

Not even close.

He stared at me. I turned the ignition key. The engine groaned but would not start. He grinned and raised his arm, a flash of silver-grey in his hand. I tried again. The engine roared into life. I pointed the van at him and took my foot off the clutch.

The gun shot still caught me by surprise, even though I'd registered the gun in his hand. It blew out the passenger window. He'd fired at me. In the middle of Crouch Hill.

But I have your gun in my pocket, you bastard.

At the last moment Dobson dived to his right. The van struck the Cortina another glancing blow. A further shot rang out. The bullet hit the side padding of my seat. I felt the thud.

He was firing at a van laden with explosive. If it ignited he would blow us both to Hell.

'Come on then!' I screamed. 'Come on!'

I jammed the gear stick into reverse and hit the accelerator. One of the Cortina's wings came away with the van.

A third shot. I heard it hit the side of the van. I jammed the gear stick into first, revved the engine insanely and roared away, the van's tyres squealing on the tar mac.

Where do you go with a van full of Semtex? I'd had a vague idea. That I would drive it out into the countryside and abandon it in field, or a lay-by somewhere. As far away as possible from anyone who might be harmed by the explosion. As I roared through Crouch End, red faced and still shaking from the confrontation with Dobson/Möller, I started to plan the route in my head.

I looked at the clock on the dashboard.

Ten to six.

A little over three hours.

I reached the foot of Muswell Hill. I was going to pass within spitting distance of home. If the bomb went off now, it would probably break our windows. The crazy thought struck me that perhaps I should drop in to see Ted. For a cup of tea. It was surreal and I laughed out loud with the madness of it.

I dropped down a gear, made it to the top of the hill and headed for the North Circular Road.

It had a been a madness. The whole if it. Everything that had happened since that day, in 1960, when I'd rejected the police force and joined… What had I joined? Who had I really been working for? The Security Service? Or Smith? The man in the grey suit. The man who had been pulling my strings from the very beginning.

Who are you?

'Who the hell are you?' I said it out loud and then screamed it. 'What the fuck is this all about?' I hurled it from the broken van window, out into the night. But there was no answer. There never would be. I'd been a pawn. Nothing more. A pawn in somebody else's game. And I'd lost. Everything. I gritted my teeth and pushed the accelerator to the floor. And then, as I joined the North Circular Road, I saw it.

Chapter Forty-Three

The Cortina or rather, what was left of it, came slowly into view. How he was managing to steer the car, given the damage that I had inflicted to the vehicle's front end was a mystery. But that is precisely what he was doing and more. In no time at all, Dobson was on my tail, veering the Cortina to the left and right as he attempted to come alongside.

I fought to prevent him and to control the van. But I was going to fail. Even in its damaged state the Cortina was more than a match for a Post Office van, loaded with heavy engineering equipment and God knew how many pounds of high explosive. We hurtled out of London. Horns blaring, as we passed the few cars that were on the road at such an early hour.

I don't know what made me reach for the rear view mirror and to adjust it so that I could see myself. But I did. The face that I saw for a few, fleeting seconds, was bruised and swollen beyond recognition. It was not my face, but the face of another woman. Crazed and staring. And then he was along side.

I saw the window come down and the steel grey gun in his hand. I pulled the steering wheel, hard to the right and rammed him. The Cortina veered away into the fast lane, sparks flaring from the front bumper as first it buckled, detached itself, and then disappeared beneath the car and clattered away into the distance. But still he persisted. I watched him regain control of the car, in my wing mirror. I saw a hand re-appear from the driver's window. And the flash of a shot. And another.

I tore my eyes from the mirror and scanned the road up ahead for an exit but I could see only fields.

In the last few minutes, before I lost control, I thought of my little elf and of Harry Stammers and what their lives were going to be like without a mother. I wondered what they would think about what I had done. About the choices I'd made. About the lies I'd told. I wondered what they would look like when they were older. What careers they would choose. Harry had always been such a clever child. Thoughtful. Intuitive. Methodical. And Kate. Free thinking. Creative. Without a care in the world. Where were their lives going to take them? Would they have children of their own? What, if anything, would they tell them about their grandmother? About me.

I felt the tyre blow out. There was a thud and the van lurched heavily. I fought to hold onto the wheel but I knew that it was no use. In the far distance I could hear wailing sirens. Too late. I saw an exit, surrounded by trees. The van veered, hard to the left and, as it mounted the verge, I felt myself letting go. Of the van. Of everything that had happened. Of those I had used and who had used me. What was it that I'd said to Simone? "When I accepted that job, a train of events was set in motion. That train has been chasing me for seventeen years now and it is time to let it catch me."?

Well here we are at last, at the final destination.

I smiled and thought of Ted. He was a good man. Loving and loyal to his very core. I'd never intended to hurt him. Never wanted to lie to him. I'd only ever wanted a normal life with him. A family. And in those half seconds, as the van began to roll, I knew that I loved him. Not the crazy, uncontrollable, destructive force that had afflicted me since I had first met Peter Owen. That had blighted me at every turn. That had twisted my life and the lives of others, driving me to the edge of despair. To this terrible, wasteful, empty, single moment in time. But in that moment. That split second. When my world seemed to stop. Completely still. Silent. Clear. I saw the nature of love. For the first time in my life.

And then time resumed in a fireball of light and sound.

Epilogue

Ted Stammers watched the car pull up outside and the two plain clothed police officers get out. He saw the glances that they exchanged. The look on their faces as they opened the front gate and walked up the garden path, towards the front door. One woman and one man. At least he assumed that they were police officers. He knew what they had come to tell him. He'd been expecting them.

She'd lied. Lied to him. To the children. To their friends. To everyone who she had ever known. It had all been nothing but lies and deceit. From the moment that he'd met her. Through the months before she'd married him, when he had waited so patiently for her. At their wedding and in the vows that she had taken. To the birth of the children. Through the happy years. Or so he had thought. Even that - their happiness together - had been a falsehood. That is all that she had ever been about. Secrets and lies.

He waited for the door bell to ring. He had no wish to welcome them into the house. His house. The house where he had grown up. Where they had lived and his mother had died. The closest he'd ever known to a family. Would ever know.

The door bell chimed.

'Dad, it's the door,' Harry called out from the top of the stairs.

He stepped into the hall. Kate had followed, clutching her teddy bear. 'Has Mummy come home?'

He closed his eyes and opened them again slowly. 'No, sweetheart.'

He bent down and kissed her. She and Harry were all that mattered now. All that ever would.

As he opened the door to them, Harry came tumbling down the stairs.

'Mr Stammers?'

'Come in.'

They stepped into the hall.

'This way.'

He turned towards the children. 'Wait outside both of you.'

'Yes, Dad,' Harry said solemnly, taking hold of Kate's hand.

Ted Stammers showed the two visitors into the living room and closed the door.

***

Postscript

In writing this, the second book in my *Harry Stammers Trilogy*, I have borrowed, a number of events and one or two character references from history. In the latter case, most particularly, I have referred to Sir Oswald Mosley. Mosley is referred to several times but especially in Chapter 3, in which he takes part in a debate at the fictitious *Ealing University* on Tuesday, 31 January 1961. On this day in history, Mosley took part in a debate at University College London and I have tried to reflect, reasonably accurately, some of the events at UCL that day, including the comment about cows! For this, I relied on contemporary newspaper reports and, in particular, on the report in UCL's fortnightly newspaper, published on 2 February 1961.[6]

Otherwise, Harry Stammers, who appears in *The Battle of Wood Green* only occasionally and as an eight year old child, Liz Muir and Ted Stammers, Peter Owen, Rosemary Sellers and all of the other characters who appear in the book are entirely fictitious. Any resemblance to real persons, living or dead, is coincidental and unintended.

While the story is also entirely fictitious, most of the places in the book are real and some of the plot is based on historic events. One or two of these places and events are worthy of a little further exploration, as this will hopefully be of interest to anyone who has read the book.

The Battle of Wood Green

On 23 April 1977 a rally took place on Ducketts Common, a small expanse of grass on the corner of Green Lanes and Turnpike Lane in North London, to oppose a march by the National Front. According to reports, there were twelve hundred National Front supporters and three thousand anti-racist rally goers, though to a lad of thirteen and a half (as I was at the time), it felt like there were considerably more than that, on both sides. It was, as far as I recall, my first political rally. Many more were to follow.

I was born in Hackney and, for the first sixteen years of my life, lived in Harringay at one end of Green Lanes, the place from which the London Borough of Haringey took its name. My father was a staunch trades unionist (he was a member of the General and Municipal Workers Union - now the General, Municipal, Boilermakers and Allied Trade Union or GMB) and considered himself to be a socialist. Which makes it all the more surprising to me that, at around the time of the Battle of Wood Green, he had considered voting for the National Front (I don't know whether he actually did, but I like to think not). That he was even considering it is indicative of the progress that the Front had made, during the 1970's, in garnering support from white, working class people in places like Harringay.

In the first chapter of *The Battle of Wood Green*, mention is made of the "uneasy coalition of Greek and Turkish Cypriots from Green Lanes" who had attended the rally on Ducketts Common, at which Karl Dixon throws a red and white striped traffic cone through a shop window. In reality, Harringay had, like much of London, experienced repeated waves of immigration over the years and tensions between the white and immigrant populations occasionally ran high. While in nearby Tottenham the predominant immigrant population was Black, Afro-Caribbean, it was Greek immigrants from Cyprus who made parts of Camden, Stoke Newington and Harringay their home. Particularly at the southern end and along the east side of Green Lanes from the junction with St Anne's Road to the heights of Manor House.

Though generally well received by the local population, this initial wave of Greek Cypriot immigrants had a significant impact on the character of the area. I remember, as a small boy, our local hairdresser's being taken over by a Greek Cypriot family from which point going to the hairdresser became known as *"Going up the Greeko's"*.

The hairdresser's wasn't the only shop to take on new owners. Many of the shops which had been run by local families, sometimes for generations, changed hands in favour of Greek Cypriot owners. Gradually, the area around the Harringay Stadium and Arena, at which my father had seen the boxer Henry Cooper fight, became a predominantly Greek Cypriot area, or that is how it seemed to me as a young man living there. In *"Bloody Foreigners: The Story of Immigration to Britain"* Robert Widner reports that "Haringey became the second biggest Cypriot town in the world" [1].

Some Turkish Cypriot immigration to Britain took place during the fifties and sixties but, after the Turkish invasion of Cyprus and partition in 1974, a further wave of Turkish Cypriot immigrants arrived in Britain, many of whom settled along the west side of Green Lanes and to the north, in the Turnpike Lane and Wood Green areas.

Whereas the Greek Cypriots were Christian and, for the most part, integrated with the indigenous population (if there is such a thing in London), the Turkish Cypriots were Muslims. Cultural and religious differences lead to greater segregation and eventually, to tensions with both the local white and immigrant Greek Cypriot populations. By the time that I left Harringay (in 1979), Green Lanes had, at times, resembled a battle zone, between the Greeks on the east side of the high street, the Turks on the west side, the Afro-Caribbean's in Tottenham a few miles further to the east (where, in the book, the Jackson's lived and gave shelter to Rosemary Sellers) and the local white kids, many of whom had unfortunately turned to the likes of the National Front to represent their interests.

Ducketts Common and the area around Turnpike Lane was thus an obvious flashpoint and so it became on that day in April 1977.

The Battle of Wood Green begins with Karl Dixon throwing a traffic cone through the window of *Freeman, Hardy and Willis,* a chain of shoe retailers which has since ceased to trade. This event never took place. In reality, while socialist and religious speakers addressed the crowd assembled on the Common, a contingent broke away to confront the National Front demonstrators making their way northwards, along Green Lanes. I was carried along with a group of hard-liners and kids, who were intent on throwing anything they could lay their hands on at the demonstrators. Outside Freeman, Hardy and Willis, which, as I remember it, was on the corner of Green Lanes and Westbury Avenue, we began throwing shoes from the racks outside the shoe shop, both at the demonstrators and at the police who, in those days, were rather less well equipped and prepared than they would be were such circumstances to arise today.

While the atmosphere was aggressive and highly charged, I must admit that it had something of a carnival atmosphere from my point of view. After the speeches that had filled me with the same sense of righteous indignation that prompted Karl Dixon to unleash his traffic cone, it felt tremendously exciting to be taking on the combined forces of the law and the far-right. Nowadays, I suppose, it would be guns and petrol bombs. That in those days it was platform heels and wooden clogs, was, I suppose a sign of gentler times.

Karl Dixon's excesses were brought to an end by a mounted policeman, as indeed were mine. I have been trodden on by a police horse twice in my life. Once, while queueing for tickets to Tottenham Hotspur's FA Cup Final replay against Manchester City in 1981 (which, thankfully, Spurs won), and once, in 1977, outside Freeman, Hardy and Willis during the Battle of Wood Green. It is not an experience I would particularly like to repeat.

Excalibur House & The National Front

In *The Battle of Wood Green* Peter Owen and his *Nationalist Union of Great Britain* are based at Excalibur House, located at 73 Great Eastern Street, Hackney in North East London. While the events in the book concerning the wholly fictitious NUGB take place in 1977, so far as I have been able to establish the National Front did not, in reality, move into the real Excalibur House until 1978. They remained there until the mid 1980's. [2]

The National Front enjoyed a thankfully brief period of popular support and limited electoral success during the late 1970's. In the May local elections in 1976, the party enjoyed its best result in Leicester, where the party's candidates won 14,566 votes, almost 20% of the total. In the Greater London County Council election in May 1977, they won 119,060 votes, beating the Liberal Party in 33 out of 92 constituencies.

By 1980, however, the Front's fortunes had reversed, due in large part to the success of the Conservative Party in the 1979 general election under Margaret Thatcher, whose right wing policies attracted many former National Front voters. Following the election in 1979, the National Front went into rapid decline, eventually fracturing into two separate organisations. In the 1990's it was effectively replaced by the far-right British National Party, which continues to exist, though thankfully on the margins of British politics.

The Front's residency at Excalibur House, like the general fortunes of the party, came to an inglorious and chaotic end sometime in the early 1980's. Determined to prevent a fascist organisation establishing a national headquarters on its turf, infamously left-wing Hackney Council, refused to grant planning permission, while the Front argued that it wasn't their HQ at all, but only a base for storage and printing. Eventually, control of the building became mired in the internal feuding that followed the Party's disastrous showing in the 1979 election.

For anyone who is interested, the building still stands today and is called *"Citfin House"*. It is used by the College of Central London. Many of the college's students are, with glorious irony, from overseas. The building's façade is unusual and certainly stands out, due to the arched styling of the main doorway and the windows to the stair well above it.

MI5

Founded in 1909, MI5, the Security Service, has its headquarters at Thames House on Millbank in London. It deals with counter-espionage and subversion within the United Kingdom. MI5, the structure of which is broadly unchanged since the ending of the Cold War, is organised into a number of branches. It is to the Service's F-branch, which covers counter-subversion and to F7, the wing responsible for the surveillance of political and campaigning groups, that the character 'Smith', in the book, would be most likely to have belonged.

The internal workings of MI5 are, of course, shrouded in secrecy, although much has been written on the subject. These sources suggest that the Service's efforts, during the 1960's and 70's, focussed mainly on infiltrating left wing groups and organisations and, in particular, on the Communist Party of Great Britain. Between 1974 and 1976, however, this extended to efforts by a coalition of Conservative politicians and elements of the armed forces and the intelligence services to subvert Harold Wilson's elected Labour Government.[5]

There are several references in *The Battle of Wood Green* to surveillance, by the Service, of the Campaign for Nuclear Disarmament. It is known that in 1977, MI5 opened a temporary file on CND's Bruce Kent who was seen as a possible anarchist. This became a permanent file when, in 1979, he became CND's Secretary General [3]. F-Branch also opened a file on Joan Ruddock in 1982 when she became CND Chair.[3]

Less has been written on the subversion of far-right groups by MI5. Arguably, the most well known case is that of Andy Carmichael, from the West Midlands, who was allegedly recruited by MI5 to infiltrate the National Front. He was allegedly approached by MI5 at a party in Cannock in the West Midlands, held in honour of the former conservative

Prime Minister, Margaret Thatcher. Carmichael, a former Conservative Party activist, became the Front's West Midlands chairman and sat on the party's national executive. He stood as a parliamentary candidate for the Birmingham Ladywood constituency in the 1997 general election and polled 685 votes. [4]

In *The Battle of Wood Green*, the characters Smith and Rosemary Sellers both have an interest in the fictitious *Nationalist Union of Great Britain*. Having worked for Smith during the 1960's to spy on a right wing group at 'Ealing University', the main character, Liz Muir, is forced by Smith to infiltrate the NUGB in order to discover the party's plans. It becomes evident that Rosemary Sellers is more interested in the character Jimmy Dobson and Smith's motives are never entirely revealed.

The Battle of Wood Green goes some way to explaining the disappearance of Liz Muir and her abandonment of Harry and his sister Kate, referred to in *The Shelter*, which is the first book in the trilogy. In an attempt to foil Peter Owen and the NUGB's plot to bomb the palace of Westminster and to seize control of the country, Muir hi-jacks a Semtex-laden Post Office van, which otherwise would have been driven to its destruction, unwittingly, by her husband Ted Stammers.

The third book in the series, entitled *Building 41*, sees the return of Bletchley Park curator Harry Stammers, as he sets out, once again, to discover the truth. A truth that links the wartime events in a pub near Bletchley, to his search for Martha Watts and the identities of Smith, Jimmy Dobson, Rosemary Sellers and, of course, the truth about his mother, Liz Stammers (nee Muir).

MI5's Barnard Road Garage

In Chapter 4 of *The Battle of Wood Green* mention is made of Barnard Road, from which Liz Muir obtains a dark brown Rover 2000TC, which she uses for a trip to Durham University. This is a reference to MI5's garage, at which vehicles were prepared for members of its staff by a specialist team of mechanics.[7] In the 1970's, this was located in

Barnard Road in Clapham, London. Barnard Road was located off St John's Road behind the present Marks and Spencers building. The existence of the garage was a closely guarded secret but it is known that it was discovered by the Russian KGB[8]. It was subsequently moved to Streatham High Street. Both these garages have since been demolished.

References

[1] Winder, Robert (2004). *Bloody Foreigners: The Story of Immigration to Britain*. London: Abacus. pp. 360–62. ISBN 0-349-11566-4.

[2] *The National Front's Hackney HQ* (2012), http://hackneyhistory.wordpress.com/2012/05/11/the-national-fronts-hackney-hq/

[3] Christopher Andrew, The Defence of the Realm: The Authorised History of MI5, Allen Lane, 2009.

[4] Civil Liberty (2011), http://www.civilliberty.org.uk/newsdetail.php?newsid=1164

[5] Spartacus Educational (Undated), http://www.spartacus.schoolnet.co.uk/FWWm5.htm

[6] The Fortnightly Newspaper of University College London (February 2nd 1961), Edition number 170 (front page).

[7] Civil Defence Today (undated), http://www.civildefence.co.uk/secret-bases.php

[8] Londonist (2011), http://londonist.com/2011/11/top-10-spy-sites-in-london.php

THE SHELTER
THE HARRY STAMMERS TRILOGY, BOOK ONE
ANDY MELLETT BROWN

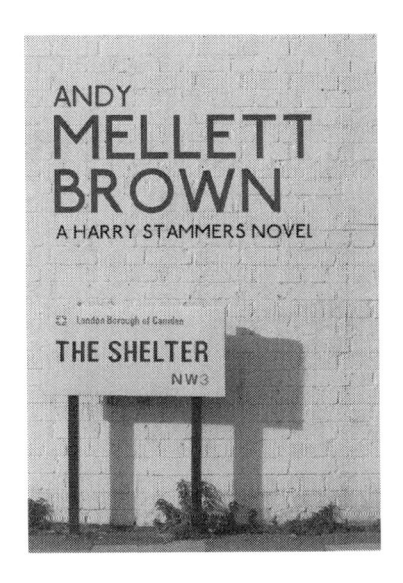

It is 10 November 1944 and a young woman in a woollen coat steps off a trolley bus into the darkness of wartime London and vanishes. Sixty years later, museum curator Harry Stammers receives an intriguing invitation from Bletchley Park veteran Elsie Sidthorpe. Aided by Ellen Carmichael Elsie's great niece, Stammers sets out to discover the truth about what happened to Martha Watts.

ANDY MELLETT BROWN was born in Harringay, North London and lived there until he was sixteen. He joined Haringey Social Services Department in 1982 and presently works, full-time, for the Care Quality Commission. He is President of The Milton Keynes Amateur Radio Society, whose members campaigned to save Bletchley Park before MKARS took up residency at the Park in 1994.

Published in June 2014, Andy's first novel, *The Shelter*, has earned him an ever growing and enthusiastic following. *The Battle of Wood Green* is the second in his *Harry Stammers Trilogy*. The third, entitled *The Battle of Wood Green* is due out in 2015.

Andy has lived in Leighton Buzzard, Bedfordshire with his wife, Patricia, since 2004.

* Photography by Janice Issitt

Made in the USA
Charleston, SC
15 November 2014